AnothER 4.0

dENiSE LEORa mADRE

Dedication

Howard University,
Thank you for three of the best years of my life.
This one's for you.

Table of Contents

Acknowledgments

To my Dude, Horace Lee Madre, Jr., my husband, protector, and favorite chef: You are the best gift God has ever given me. I can be who I am because you are who you are. I love you with all my chicken and owe you a piece of gum.

To my children: The seven of you have taught me so much about life, love, and myself. Thank you for those lessons and for being patient while I learned. You each own a piece of my heart.

To my parents, brother, and sister: You are the foundation on which my beautiful childhood was built, and your love stayed steady through the drifts and detours of my latter years. Thank you for being my anchors.

To Jess Molly Brown: Thank you for being my sanity and sounding board, my pre-reader and encourager-in-chief as I groused my way through the rewriting process and every other aspect of my life. You are the best part of Canada and my favorite souvenir from my *Twilight* years.

To Lissa Bryan and Kathie Spitz: Thank you for getting me through that very long night when I feared this book would never see the light of day. Your insights made me a better writer.

To T.M. Franklin: Thank you for bringing my cover idea to life, for all the pic teases and advice along the publishing trail. I have learned a ton from you and am so grateful for your patience with my many many questions.

To Dr. Lettie Austin of Howard University: Thank you for challenging me and teaching me more about English than I could possibly use in one lifetime. I know you're smiling down from Heaven with those trademark eyebrows, correcting my grammar.

To Mrs. Mitzi Brown of Masterman High School: Thank you for forcing "Tuesday Writing" upon me in 11th grade. Those mandated assignments provided the first opportunity to stretch my literary legs, and I haven't been the same since.

To my family and friends: You believed in my creativity from childhood and beyond, and I love and thank God for each and every one of you.

And to Jesus Christ, the One whose death freed me to live: Your ferocious love leaves me constantly breathless. I remain in awe of who You are, grateful and unashamed.

ANOTHER 4.0

OnE

August 1999

I scowled at the bug on my windshield.

The fat, ugly, freeloading bug on an otherwise pristine windshield.

It was a hair's breadth outside the arc of my left wiper, artfully dodging the blue mist and squeaky blade. I knew that after trying and failing six times to dislodge it.

Stupid, fat, ugly, freeloading, useless…

"Ignore the bug," came the soft nudge from the passenger seat. "Focus on the road."

"I am."

"You're drifting." Corina Nelson gazed out the

window, eyeballing the distance between our dusty rental and the dotted white line. "Not much, but you're drifting."

"I am not. I'm right behind this Lexus."

"Then the Lexus is drifting, too. I just want you to be safe."

"I know, Mom."

"I also reiterate my offer to drive. You've had your license only a month…."

"Five weeks and three days, thank you very much."

"…and you have nothing to prove to me."

I ignored the subtle emphasis on the last two words. The person to whom I felt obligated to prove myself lately wasn't here, citing an unmissable meeting at work. I snorted under my breath, refusing to let him ruin a trip he hadn't bothered to take.

Corina mistook my snort for an allergic reaction. "Where's your medicine?"

"In my bag, and I don't need it. That was a snort of derision."

"Is there a pill for that?" I cut my eyes at her, and she laughed. "You have to admit that was good."

"You should have been a comedienne."

"Nah, I like being a craftswoman." She checked her watch. "But I hate being late."

"It doesn't matter." I changed lanes to escape the octogenarian in the Lexus. "Only upperclassmen move in today, and most of them defected to the Towers."

"Why didn't you and Cherrie do that? Private suite with a real kitchen and bathroom instead of those broom closets Meridian calls showers."

"Because she's an RA, and I didn't want to risk

getting some wacky roommate."

"Pity. I send delightful care packages."

The sleek black cell phone in the center console rang, its cheery ringtone identifying the caller. "Great. Now I'm going to get in trouble."

"I'll handle Cherrie. You watch that classic pickup on your left. The driver is too busy singing to pay attention."

"Because that song rocks." I snapped my fingers. "Gotta love Trisha Yearwood."

"Never change, Daria." Corina smiled and answered my phone. "Hi, Cherrie! Yes, we're finally on our way.... Well, we got a late start because someone pulled a fast one last night." My cheeks flamed as she glanced at me. "She'll tell you all about it.... We'll be there as soon as I-95 lets us.... Oh, I'll ask her." She pulled the phone from her ear. "Cherrie can hold an '80s room' for you, whatever that means."

"The rooms numbered 79-92 are huge, big enough for Bernie to do a cartwheel."

"Fabulous," Corina said. "Fourth or fifth floor?"

"Where is she?"

She waited a beat. "Seventh."

Cherrie was beside the kitchen, so I needed dibs on laundry. "Fourth."

I crossed "proper room assignment" off my mental to-do list. Sophomore year needed to be seamless, and securing the right room was an encouraging first step.

"Do you need to use the bathroom?" Corina asked after ending the call. "We could stop in the Maryland House."

"What am I, a toddler? Besides, don't be using me

3

to feed your habit."

"Habit?" She batted her ridiculously long lashes. "Whatever do you mean?"

I honked at the bumper sticker-laden SUV in front of us. "Anytime you spend more than an hour in the car, you need a Cinnabon. And we left Philly two hours ago."

"That means I'm due for two."

"No time." I glanced at the clock on the dashboard, one of few working items in the car. "At this pace, we can get to Meridian by three o'clock."

"Just because you came into six months of Peanut Chews last night doesn't mean the rest of us don't need snacks." I smothered another smile, and she pouted. "I cannot believe you won't make a quick stop so your poor mother can have a treat. I gave you life, nursed you through chickenpox, and let you sleep in our bed for a week after *A Thief in the Night* gave you nightmares."

"First, there is nothing poor about Corina Davenport Nelson. Second, I didn't ask to be born. Third, it wasn't my fault I got sick, and fourth..." I shuddered. "That movie gave me nightmares and kept me from youth group forever."

"And now you're a heathen who deprives her mother of sustenance." She crossed her arms, and I deducted fifteen minutes from our travel time. "Fine."

Then my phone rang again, this ringtone of a decidedly different flavor.

"Too bad." Corina tsked. "You can't drive and talk at the same time, so you can't answer his call until we arrive in DC ... in another hour at the earliest." Her sigh was full of romantic regret. "If only there were a place to stop for a few minutes without detouring completely…"

I wanted to stick to my guns and try to salvage my fading timeline. But each ring of the phone chipped away at my resolve, and I switched to the left lane after passing the second sign for the Maryland House.

"Should I tell him you'll call him back?" She gave full voice to her laughter, sobering at my glare. "I mean, uh, watch the road."

As soon as Corina disappeared into the Maryland House, I pulled out my phone, giddiness bubbling to the surface. He answered on the second ring. "There she is."

I closed my eyes, envisioning Maurice's dark, handsome face, and my happy cheeks pressed against the buttons on my phone, creating a discordant song in our ears. "Sorry!"

He chuckled. "Is that our special greeting now?"

"It could be, if you like."

"I was thinking more like *Fortunate*."

I covered my mouth to stifle another phone-attacking grin. Though country music was the soundtrack to my life, Maxwell always hovered near the top of my charts. "Good choice."

"How's Corina?" he asked. "Is she angry?"

"She isn't."

He caught my drift. "Guess I didn't make things better with him, did I?"

"Not in the least." Not that I minded. "I still can't believe you showed up like that."

"There's little I wouldn't do for you, Duchess. You

know that."

"I know."

"How's the trip so far?"

"Corina's a blast, but the A/C is busted, so the windows are down."

"Guess crossing state lines isn't all it's cracked up to be."

My smile turned upside-down. "Do we have to do this today?"

"Do what?"

"You know what."

"Aw, Duch." He went full Barry White, dropping his voice a seductive octave. "I don't mean anything by it. But a ten-minute commute from my place to University City beats a sweaty trek down 95, that's all I'm saying."

I scraped the pad of my ring finger with my thumbnail.

"You're not mad, are you?" he asked.

"How could I be?"

"I only get this way because I love you." His words curled in my ear like so many ribbons of smoke. "I proved that last night, didn't I?"

"Yes."

"So can I get a giggle?"

I chuckled at the question, unable to resist its silly will. "You can get a giggle."

"How much for two?"

"A moogle and a boo." I shook my head. "I still don't know what that means."

"It means I love you. You and only you."

Our private rhyme always calmed the choppy

waters between us, and I finished the couplet. "That goes for me, too. You and only you."

"So when's your first major break?"

"Umm ..." I struggled to change my mental channel. "Thanksgiving, I think?"

"You can't come home before then?"

"I don't want to promise something I can't deliver, so I'll let you know."

There was an influx of raucous voices over the line. "Fellas, say hi to Daria."

"Hi, Daria!" filled my ears in unison.

"Tell them I said hi. Has the back-to-school rush started?"

"Yeah. I need to get somebody in here who can braid. 'Seem can do a lil' something, but he ain't fancy."

"I miss him."

"You miss him?" I heard a low laugh. "This bushy-bearded Negro?"

"Daria!" he shouted into the phone.

"Naseem!" Maurice's cousin kept me laughing when Maurice's moroseness got the best of him. "Hey, baby!"

"I'm breaking up this lovefest right now." The background noise faded, and I assumed Maurice had closed the door to his office. "I need to find him a woman so he can back off mine. It's bad enough I gotta worry about a bunch of smarty-art college buls."

"No, you don't. I'm yours, remember?"

"With 300 miles between us?"

"Howard is 150 miles from Philly."

"It might as well be a thousand."

"I miss you too, you know."

"Then why did you leave?"

"Because Howard couldn't pack up and move to Philly."

He didn't see the humor. "I miss you, Duch. Having you home this summer was like…it was butter, baby. And just when it got good, you up and left."

I saw Corina coming down the walk. Although she would speak to every person and pooch she passed, I had but two minutes. "Corina returns."

Maurice sighed. "And I got clients."

Corina's rich laughter floated toward me on the breeze, and I determined to stay cheerful. "Call me after your last head. Naseem can close up."

"But he opened today. You know, because I was out late last night."

"Yes, I know."

The silence dragged with despondency. "I love you, Duchess."

"I know."

"And I'm sorry for being a butthead."

"And I appreciate your effort not to use stronger language."

"And I appreciate your appreciation."

"I love you, too, Maurice. And we'll see each other before Thanksgiving, I promise."

"Call me from your room once you hook up your phone. And tell Corina I said 'thanks'."

"For what?"

"For bringing an angel into the world."

The uber-cheesy line lit up my face as my mother reached the car.

"Oh, geez." She rolled her eyes. "What did he say?"

He laughed. "Don't tell her."

"I wouldn't dare."

"Stay tight, Duch."

"Always."

I closed the phone and looked up at my mother. "So how's Maurice?" my mother asked.

I shrugged, trying to remain casual. "He's fine."

She chuckled. "You are so full of it. Here."

I accepted the Cinnabon bag through the window, and she opened my door. "What are you doing?" I asked.

"Taking over." She inclined her head toward the passenger seat. "Tell everyone you logged some highway miles. Exaggerate if you must. But your leg of this journey is over. Scoot."

Arguing with Corina was like arguing with Claire Huxtable, so I moved to the other seat.

"Besides." She took an inelegant bite from her bun and dropped it in the bag. "When you start daydreaming about Maurice in four and a half minutes, you won't have to worry about drifting into the adjacent lane."

I set down my Cinnabon bag and grabbed my Peanut Chews. "You've got frosting on your chin."

TWO

Three quarter-bags of candy and two traffic jams later, we arrived at Meridian Hill Hall. As Corina pulled into the long queue of cars waiting to enter the semi-circled driveway, I surveyed the surrounding chaos. Congested rolling carts and frustrated students peppered the front walk, but I refused to let them ruin this moment. I was here, where I belonged, and I took a deep breath to appreciate it.

Corina cut the engine and wiped her brow. "Do you see Cherrie?"

With all the activity in front of the eight-story building, my best friend should have been difficult to find. But even without her navy Campus Pal T-shirt and clipboard, her boundless energy would have drawn my attention. A hair above five feet tall, she had the presence of someone twice her size.

And the boldness to match.

"It's 94 degrees. Why are the windows down?" was her opening statement as she approached our van. "Is the A/C broken? Do you need me to send a nastygram to Budget? Because they're already on my list for last year's winter break fiasco."

Corina fanned herself with the rental receipt. "Would you like a job? I could use you when I deal with lazy vendors."

"A job at CoCo Davenport Designs?" She closed her eyes, a dreamy look about her face. "If only that fit into my life plan."

Corina laughed. "You and your life plan."

"I can't become the first black female rheumatologist elected to the World Health Organization Executive Board without it." She turned to me. "You're in 485. If you get in line now, you might get a cart by tomorrow."

"Where did all these people come from?" I asked as we wove our way through the crowd.

"Admissions." She spoke their name like a curse. "They assigned 1,200 freshmen to Meridian which can only house 900. Half these people are gonna end up sleeping in their rental cars." An irate parent burst through the front door, and Cherrie caught it before it slammed into us. "Or going back home."

The Meridian lobby teemed with apprehension and activity. Behind the reception desk to the right, a beleaguered staff person juggled three ringing lines as another worker filled the mailboxes with yellow flyers.

Frantic students sat in the seating area to the left, rummaging through overstuffed bookbags for room assignment forms. The dorm director emerged from the meeting room in the corner, waving Cherrie over.

"Take my ID," she said. "If there are two carts, you can get them both."

I took my place at the back of the line outside the main office, wishing I had brought my Discman. Students around me griped about missing validation stickers and contradictory letters from Financial Aid, and I sent up a little prayer on their frustrated behalfs.

Behalfs? Behalves?

English and its irregular plurals. Now there was a subject that could frustrate a person.

By the time Cherrie emerged from the meeting room, I had my key and Room Inspection Form. She took our IDs and secured two carts, pushing one toward a forlorn girl.

"You've been waiting a long time," Cherrie said. "Take it to 485 when you're done."

The girl threw her arms around Cherrie. "Thank you so much!"

"What if she doesn't bring it back?" I asked as the girl headed outside.

Cherrie shrugged. "I'm not worried about it."

"You're a saint."

"At least one of us is." Her eyes narrowed as we made our way back to the van. "Don't think I missed Corina's little allusion on the phone earlier. What happened last night?"

"I'll tell you when we get to The Diner, assuming we can still make it."

"We can, if you dump your stuff and organize it later."

"Are you serious?"

"Only for two hours, and we'll sort the boxes into zones."

I gripped the handlebar of the cart with clammy hands. I couldn't leave for work without cleaning my bathroom mirror, and she wanted me to abandon my precious things in an unclean space without assigning locations first?

"I'll dust and polish your floor tonight, as soon as I'm finished on campus." She held up two joined fingers. "Scout's honor."

I pushed the cart toward Corina with greater urgency. "Then let's get moving!"

Two busy hours later, Corina drove to Budget to return the van and promised to call upon arrival at Union Station. Before leaving, she notarized Cherrie's Letter of Promise regarding the thorough cleaning of my entire dorm room floor. "Inside the closet too," I added.

With the original on my desk and a copy in my back pocket, I linked arms with Cherrie and headed to The Diner on Eighteenth Street in Adams Morgan. The Diner was our favorite spot for its affordable cuisine, relaxed atmosphere, and 'round-the-clock service. There was no breakfast, lunch, or dinner for us. We grazed until the food or money ran out.

Cherrie ordered a cheeseburger platter with mozzarella sticks, and I kept it simple with soup and a sandwich. As soon as the waitress left the table, Cherrie rubbed her hands together.

"All right, Miss Thang. What happened last night?"

"In a minute. Tell me about Bernie first."

"Right." Her voice sobered. "They lost her paperwork."

I set down my iced tea. "Financial Aid?"

"Residence Life. She had everything in before the deadline, but when she didn't receive a Room Assignment Confirmation Letter, she went to the A Building. No record of her. And her room in the Towers for Summer Session II was only good through mid-August. She's been home since then."

The server brought our first courses, and we remembered Bernie as we prayed over our food. Our fearless trio wouldn't survive without her leadership and wit, and Detroit was too far away for commuting.

With a sigh, Cherrie reached for the pepper. "So hit me with the happy."

I pressed the back of my spoon into the French onion soup. "What's the last thing I told you?"

"That Maurice walks on water and his kisses are like being touched by an angel."

"Why do I keep you around?"

"Because I understand your 'Dear Daria' ways and *Never Ever After* references."

"Best Public Access Channel soap opera ever. Did you see Canyon confront Caprelle at the cookout yesterday?"

"Yes, girl! And I'm sure your English-majoring self got a real kick out of all that alliteration just now."

I couldn't deny it. "I was so mad when she lied

about why she was arguing with Rasool. Cuz you know that brotha got ideas."

"Mmm-hmm." Cherrie pursed her lips. "I don't trust him as far as I can throw him, but you're changing the subject."

"Am I?"

"Daria!"

"Okay, okay. But I hope this story is as good as you want it to be."

Things at home between Maurice and me were nothing short of amazing. We slipped back into each other's lives as if we never spent my freshman year in different states. I worked the coveted Monday-through-Friday day shift at Borders Books in Chestnut Hill, giving us plenty of daylight to burn. Not that we used it. Every chance we got, we were together, laughing and loving from one place to the other.

"Hold up," she said. "Define 'loving.' "

"That was strictly metaphorical. I couldn't even tell you what second base looks like."

"Just making sure."

"You think I'd leave you holding the V-card all by yourself?"

"With Maurice's lips nibbling your ear on the daily?" She pointed at me with a mozzarella stick. "In a heartbeat."

I sipped more tea to cool my warming cheeks. "It wasn't daily. Adrian wasn't trying to hear that, summer break or not."

"How are things there?"

"Don't ask."

" 'Kay. So last night…"

"Maurice worked late again. Back-to-school time is his peak season, so I couldn't be mad. But it was my last night in Philly, you know? He was going to try to see me in the morning, but Corina likes to get on the road early, and...."

"And you couldn't have a good goodbye with your parents there."

"Right. So we packed the minivan, and because Corina wakes the roosters and Adrian had a headache, the house was quiet by ten o'clock. I took a long soak in the tub, already missing the privilege."

Cherrie sighed. "I'm so glad I'm an RA. I couldn't live without a tub another year."

"Maurice called while I was getting dressed. He had a client with a jacked up hairline who came in two minutes before closing and asked for some complex design in his fade, and I told him Corina was letting me drive down, and..."

"You drove?" Her voice climbed two octaves. "Really?"

"From Philly to the Maryland House. With no accidents and minimal drifting."

She raised her hand across the table for a high-five. "That's what's up, young one."

"I'm three months older than you."

"But I've been driving longer."

"Anyway, he told me every single detail about this haircut, but the drivel couldn't distract me from missing him. He asked why I was quiet, and I said, 'I wish I could see you tonight.' He said, 'Stop wishing and put something on your feet.' I looked out the window, and he was parked across the street."

Cherrie's eyes were soft and dreamy. "Please keep going."

"He stepped out of the car with the phone to his ear. 'As much as I like the view from here,' he said, 'I want you closer.' Then it hit me: I'd have to sneak out to see him."

"Dun-dun-dunnnn," Cherrie sang.

"I slipped into my blue flip-flops and tiptoed downstairs. He promised I'd be back before anyone missed me, but the fact that he came was enough, you know?"

"Yeah. Well, not really. My only steady boyfriend was imaginary, and I'm pretty sure he was creeping with the Tooth Fairy."

Our food came, and the server smiled at our mushy expressions. "Whatever you're talking about must be good."

"It is!" we said together.

She laid a hand on her heart. "To be young and in love again."

Cherrie poured ketchup on her burger after the server went to refill someone's coffee. "Are we young?"

"Not anymore. We're sophomores."

"Quite right. Continue."

"I get in the car, and he pulls out a large mango from Rita's."

She gasped. "And did he also get a ..."

"Obviously."

"Water ice and a pretzel? If he took you to the Plateau, that would be the ultimate late-night Philly date."

"I know, but we couldn't get there and back in

17

time."

"So he took you to…"

"Borders." At her disappointment, I continued. "Because that's where we met. We pulled into the tiny parking lot, and he said, 'Four years ago, I walked into this store looking for a hot cup of coffee. And what I found was sweeter than the cinnamon rolls."

I took a bite of my turkey club, and Cherrie rolled an impatient index finger in a small circle. "Don't stop now!"

"He said he saw me fixing a display beside the info desk and that he lost his breath when I looked over and smiled. 'I don't remember anything about that moment except this.' He clicked a button on the stereo and sultry strings filled the car's cabin. 'This was the song playing on the PA,' he said, 'and I promised myself we'd dance together someday.' Next thing I knew, he opened my door and extended a hand."

Cherrie fanned herself with a dry napkin. "This is better than *Never Ever After*."

"It really was." Maurice wasn't sentimental, and with my departure date looming, he had been moody. But to think he'd planned this surprise based on a memory we both treasured? All the tension had been worthwhile.

"He pulled me close, and we danced right there in the parking lot. The building could have burned to the ground, and I wouldn't have noticed. The moment was so perfect it was as if tomorrow would never come.

"The song ended, and he lifted his head and kissed me like…" My eyes drifted shut, and I cleared my throat. "Well, the kiss was nice."

" 'Nice.' " Cherrie rolled her eyes. "You're hilarious."

"By the time we returned to my house, I was floating. Maurice calmed my every anxiety about starting sophomore year, and I knew we'd be fine. Until he asked why the living room light was on."

Cherrie's eyes widened. "Was it…"

"Of course. The best night of my life, and Adrian has to ruin it." I shook my head, trying to forget my father's words: *A man who loves you respects the rules of your father's house.*

"Maurice walked me inside, tried to apologize and explain, but Adrian would not be moved. He frowned at Maurice like gum on the bottom of his shoe and said, 'Hope you enjoyed your goodbye.' "

"Wow."

"Corina swept into the room, looking at Maurice with equal parts disapproval and delight. She accepted his apology and ushered my father upstairs, admonishing me to follow in five minutes. Maurice and I shared a last kiss, but the mood was ruined."

Cherrie finished her lemonade. "The good news is you got a swoon-worthy send-off, and your father is too far away to punish you for it."

"Always looking for the bright side." I signaled our server for a take-home container, ordering a piece of chocolate cake to go. "I hope you find it when you clean my floor."

"I'd find it much sooner if you came to the Ice Cream Social with me."

"That's what you're doing tonight? No wonder you wouldn't tell me."

"You had fun last year!"

"One, everything was fun when we were freshmen. Two, that's because I thought it was about ice cream."

"It is!" I held her gaze, and she laughed. "Okay, it turned into Club Haagen Daas with freaky freshman sprinkles. But the ice cream was good."

"This is better than good." I lifted my container of cake. "It's warm, chocolatey, and freaky freshman-free."

ThREE

Journal – Wednesday, September 20, 1999.
8:37 a.m.

These first weeks of school have flown by. Seems like yesterday I wandered the aisles at Safeway, taking my time to stock my makeshift pantry. Now I'm steeped in syllabi and lengthy reading assignments, praying for a reprieve.
As long as I keep my 4.0, it'll all be worth it. This year is a bigger challenge because I took a job at Borders in Pentagon City Mall. The commute is easy and the pay adequate, but working Tuesday and Thursday nights

means going straight from class and not getting home until midnight, plus my all-day Saturday shift.

Corina admired my ambition but thought it unnecessary.

"Your father opened that account specifically to avoid you working. That's how you earned that 4.0 freshman year: focusing all your energy on school. That doesn't have to change."

See? Even she couldn't pretend my relationship with Daddy hadn't changed since last year. Things deteriorated this summer to the point of silence for reasons I didn't understand and he didn't explain, and I couldn't pretend otherwise for the sake of using his money to live on.

But I didn't say any of that.

"Working builds character, Mom. Isn't that why you opened CoCo Davenport Designs when you were twenty-four?"

"I hate when you use my life against me."

With that, I won the round.

"How are things with you and Maurice?"

Or so I thought. "Fine. Why?"

"Wouldn't want you to think I don't understand how difficult it can be to maintain a long-distance relationship on top of everything else."

And once again I wondered if Corina were clairvoyant.

Or had bugged my cell phone.

Maurice and I are anything but fine, and I have no idea what to do about it. We do have our good moments: I call him when I leave Borders and again when I reach Columbus Heights station so he can "walk me" to Meridian. He calls me to referee arguments between him and Naseem—the other day they wondered which of them would make a better cartoon character.

But with six little words, he derails all the fun:

"When are you coming home again?"

I'm trying to be patient because I know why he's upset. During our very first conversation in the Borders Café, I told Maurice I was going to the University of Pennsylvania for undergrad. He spent the next two years banking on us living ten minutes apart and spending as much time together as our schedules allowed.

Until one last-minute decision changed my plan.

He can't seem to get over that I

A knock on the door snapped my writing reverie, and I dropped my pen.

"Daria!" Cherrie yelled. "Don't forget the 9:45 shuttle broke down yesterday, so the 9:30 will be crowded. And I need cocobread!" She banged a few more times and scurried away.

How she could be so chipper before breakfast was a question for the ages.

I marked the entry "to be continued," slid the thin satin bookmark between the pages, and returned the journal to its place of prominence in my desktop bookshelf. After stretching myself fully awake, I clicked on the radio while I ate breakfast at my quaint side table. WHUR FM confirmed yesterday's sunshine would continue today, so I'd be fine in a t-shirt. I'd packed my bookbag last night but felt the need to double-check it. Yesterday I was one pen short in Literary Criticism, and the lack of options drove me to distraction.

The back elevators were working for once, and I joined the small crowd waiting for them. As I got on, someone in the hallway yelled "Hold the elevator!" and I stuck out my foot to keep the doors from shutting. And the person who boarded was not only grateful but familiar.

"Mordecai Hill, as I live and breathe." I smiled as he bumped my shoulder. "I was starting to think you were commuting this year."

"Says the girl practically living in Founders Library. I heard they kicked you out last night."

"I was at Borders last night."

"Cleaning out their reference section, I'm sure." He lifted my bookbag. "I bet there are three dictionaries in here."

"For your information, there's only one. And a thesaurus. And a glossary of literary terms."

He laughed, his shoulder-length locs falling away from his face. "That's what I thought."

The doors opened on the second floor, and the few boarders earned a round of derisive applause. "You'll never work off the Freshman Fifteen that way!"

someone crowed behind me.

"So how was your summer?" Mordecai asked me when we reached the bottom floor.

"Good but too short. I didn't get to half my to-do list."

"Of course you had a summertime to-do list."

"Don't knock it till you've tried it. How was yours?"

"Eventful. Mel went to a week-long overnight camp for the first time."

"Oh, wow." His kid sister Melody was the apple of his dutiful eye. "Were there tears?"

"Only the first night. But I slept on her bedroom floor and felt much better."

We exited the building as the shuttle inched forward with the doors open. When we climbed on, Cherrie met my eyes, mouthing an apology for not saving me a seat. I held on to the back of the seat beside me, and Mordecai did the same as the bus pulled off.

Howard University had four off-campus housing units and provided shuttle service to and from campus. The Meridian Shuttle serviced Meridian Hill Hall and the East and West Towers. Another shuttle handled the Slowe and Carver dormitories, and a third shuttle went to the Shaw/Howard University Metrorail station. The shuttles were convenient when punctual and a nuisance when not. HU professors were unsympathetic when you blamed your tardiness on the shuttle and marked you late anyway. More than a few students missed more than a few tests because of the shuttle's inconsistency, yet every morning we lined up at stops across campus to press our luck again.

The Meridian shuttle pulled in front of Cramton Auditorium, where fashion shows, lectures, and other special events were held, and Cherrie and I disembarked. I waved goodbye to Mordecai who turned toward the Fine Arts building, and we headed across the street to the food trucks for Cherrie's cocoa and cocobread.

And ran smack into Bernie.

"My girl!" She leapt onto my back—quite a feat with my bookbag there—and spun me around. "What's good?"

"Your grip!" I laughed. "When did you get here?"

"Last week. I laid low until I got everything straightened out." She turned to Cherrie where she stood in line. "You treating?"

"Maybe." Her gaze darted between Bernie and me. "If you can help me…"

"Oh, yeah." Bernie put her arm around my shoulders. "We need a favor."

"What kind of favor?"

Bernie beamed. "The kind guaranteed to raise your GPA and academic standing."

Cherrie didn't look too sure, so I turned to her. "Spill it."

"Would you be willing to take another class this semester?"

I looked at her, back at Bernie, and extended my hand to Cherrie. "Hi, I don't think we've met. I'm Daria, your best friend who plans her schedule down to how long she'll brush her teeth."

"You'd love this class. A weekly literature seminar with no tests or essays, only discussion."

"Is it taught by a unicorn-riding leprechaun?"

26

Bernie laughed despite Cherrie's eye-rolling, and they placed their orders while I checked for a text message from Maurice. They were rare, but after last night's argument, it would be a nice way to start my day.

Nothing.

"Could you consider it?" Cherrie asked. "People keep dropping the class, and if we don't add another person, they'll cancel it. You know I'm stacking credits early…"

"Are you offering to polish my floors again?" I asked.

"And clean your windows and sharpen your pencils and fluff your pillows and…"

"And I'll massage your scalp." Bernie frowned at my straight hair. "Though I can't understand why you just won't go natural."

"Because I can't be a gorgeous blonde like you." I twirled one of her elbow-length locs. "They're like a long, silky dream."

"Hello?" Cherrie grabbed their bags and ushered us across the street. "What about this class?"

"Do it." Bernie bit into her cocobread, strawberry jam lining her bottom lip. "We've never taken a class together. It'll be a gas."

"Fine." That earned me an immediate squeal and hug from Cherrie. "But if this doesn't lead to rainbows and pots of gold, I'm never gonna forgive either of you."

Somehow during her impassioned plea to get me to add another class, Cherrie neglected to mention the class met tonight, and they'd already finished *Jazz*. But Morrison's masterpiece was on my laminated list of favorite novels, so I owned a dog-eared copy. After altering my evening plans to accommodate the schedule change, I grabbed a granola bar and banana from home and returned to campus to review the novel in my favorite non-Philly place in the world.

The lush green plaza of Howard's main campus, The Yard was bordered by classroom and administrative buildings, the Chapel, and Founders Library, and was the chosen venue for everything from graduation exercises to Homecoming festivities. A system of concrete pathways provided easy walking access, and the flagpole served as focal point and center. During warmer months, students were hard-pressed to attend class because The Yard offered many enjoyable distractions. Frisbee games, freestyle cyphers, and flirting opportunities lured many a scholar away during their four-plus years at the mecca, and even the most studious were not immune to their spell.

By some miracle, I found an empty bench in front of Frederick Douglass Hall. A group of freshmen jumped double-dutch to my right, and I pulled out my novel, singing along.

"Hey constellation, where have you been? All around the corner and back again..."

I was taking notes on Section 10 of Morrison's masterpiece when my phone buzzed in my bag. I unzipped the back compartment, my heart hitching when I saw the caller's name. "Hey."

"Hey, Duchess. Is this a good time?"

"Yeah. My next class is in an hour."

"Since when do you have a night class?"

"Since Cherrie brodied me this morning. But it only meets once a week and is nothing but reading. So it's right up my alley."

"Hasn't Cherrie brodied you enough at that place?" Before I could reply, he sighed. "I promised myself I'd stop doing that."

I turned sideways on the bench, tucking my foot beneath me. "Doing what?"

"Being an ass. Excuse my language, but there's no other way to say it. I've been a first-class ass, and I'm sorry."

My mind raced with replies, but nothing came out.

"Duch? You there?"

"Yeah. I just…I don't want to argue for the next three years, Maurice. I know I promised Penn." I looked out across The Yard, my heart swelling. "But being here…."

"I know. Things have changed."

"But change doesn't have to be bad. Being close to you would have been amazing, but this experience could be too, if we let it."

"I'm trying, Duchess. I really am. I just want us to be okay."

"We are. I promise."

After the initial awkwardness, our conversation flowed without argument or interruption until the Rankin Chapel bells rang at 5:30. "I almost forgot," he said. "Columbus Day."

I put my novel in my bag. "What about it?"

"Come home."

"That's what, two weeks away?"

"Three. And I think you could…"

"Hold on a second." My other line beeped, and I was surprised to see Cherrie's number. "What's up, girl?"

"Where are you?"

"By the benches talking to Maurice. I'll be up in a minute."

"Oh, I'm glad! Did you guys…wait, what benches?"

"The ones in front of Douglass."

"Crapenstein! You're on The Yard?"

"Yes." I came to my feet. "Why?"

"The class is in Just."

"What?" Just Hall was across The Yard at the back edge of the Lower Quad with a long, steep staircase between us. "Why didn't you tell me?"

"I was supposed to call between classes, but I had to run to the bookstore and there was a line, and…"

"Here I come." I clicked over to Maurice. "I gotta go."

"Is something wrong?"

"Not really. I just hate being late."

"It's cool. I'll check you later."

I stuffed the phone into my pocket and wove through the crowd toward the stairs beside the chapel. I had eight minutes before class started but liked to be first through the doors to pick my seat. The right seat was as important as the right class, and at this rate, I might be stuck in the back row with the slackers and chatters.

If that happened, I would drop this class. And possibly Cherrie's friendship.

When I huffed and puffed my way into Just Hall, I

heard the echo of doors closing up and down the hallway. I ran and reached Room 113 as the professor put her hand on the doorknob.

Her sharp gray eyes appraised me from hair to heel. "Who do we have here?"

Over her shoulder, Cherrie mouthed another apology, and I stared at my former best friend, fussing her out in my mind.

"Pardon me for boring you." My now-annoyed professor folded her arms across her chest. "But could you answer my question today?"

Cherrie was gonna do much more than clean my windows for this one.

FOUR

"I said I was sorry." Cherrie appeared on my left side as Bernie and I headed to lunch the next day. "You can't just stop talking to me."

"Bernadette, please tell Ms. Cummings to refrain from all conversation until she has completed her task list."

Bernie turned around. "Daria said…"

"Shut it, B. Daria, I messed up, okay? But it's not like Dr. Treble hates you or…"

"Really?" I turned to face her. " 'Ms. Nelson, promptness is your friend. I hope you two acquaint yourselves before next week. Your GPA will thank you.' Or let's talk about how she slid her designer cat-eye frames to the tip of her nose before answering any question I asked. Or how she read the answers on my first day questionnaire with a snide little 'hmm' afterwards."

Bernie snickered again then pointed at Cherrie. "She did it."

"It's bad enough I'm three weeks behind." This was why I never called academic audibles. "I made up with Maurice and planned to skip upstairs with time to spare. But because somebody forgot to tell me the class was in East Ja-Blip, I was late."

"Technically you weren't late because…" My glare made Cherrie look down at her shoes. "Never mind."

"I don't want a reputation for being careless. That's a label you can spend your entire academic career trying to shake. And it's bad enough I don't know what I'm doing yet."

"None of us do," Bernie said. "That's why we're in college. You don't see me crabbing about being a 24-year-old junior with two sophomores for best friends."

"That's because we're da bomb!" Cherrie said, and we looked at her. "I still can't pull that off, can I?"

"Nope." Bernie linked arms with her. "But I love you anyway because that's what friends do."

"Friends don't let friends be late!" I said as they charged ahead to enter Blackburn, leaving me and my moodiness behind.

The Armour J. Blackburn University Center was the cornerstone of student activity. In addition to the Art Gallery and Game Room, Blackburn housed offices for organizations like Student Government and Campus Pals. The first floor was also home to the Faculty Lounge & Restaurant where staff and students could enjoy a real lunch. In the basement were fundraising tables and social club sign-ups, the cafeteria where I never ate, and our beloved PunchOut.

The PunchOut was a raucous dungeon of a place with dark wood paneling, rectangular pillars, and inconsistent lighting. Four rows of six-person booths lined its walls, and square tables and chairs filled the middle. Its casual ambiance was perfect for everything from poetry slams to cramming sessions. The menu boasted basic fare: chicken wings and fingers, hamburgers, grilled cheese sandwiches, and fries. Other items were listed, but if you were foolish enough to order them, you would wait until everyone else got their wings and fries.

Laughing, bussin', and fussin' greeted me as I entered, reminding me why I loved Howard so much. You could dress your way and speak your slang without judgment or ridicule. But watch your mouth in the classroom. Some professors abhorred colloquial language whereas others celebrated their students' verbal dexterity. Loyalists in either sect possessed palpable racial pride and brandished their preferred diction as proof. Another paradox unique to those who are young, gifted, and black.

I ordered my usual—fingers, fries, and a Dr. Pepper with no ice—and joined Bernie in the waiting crowd with my fingers crossed. Being first in line guaranteed nothing as numbered tickets were meaningless down here. Everyone was equally subject to the whims of the PunchOut staff, and woe unto those who angered one of the overtired, underpaid workers.

Bernie watched Cherrie make the rounds, talking to

everyone with a pulse. "She should run for president."

"Provided she remembers to tell folks she's on the ballot."

Bernie chuckled. "Let it go, D."

"After I get my keyboard de-goop-a-fied."

"Okay: 51, 52, 76, 77, 78, 19!" came the bellow from behind the counter. A gaggle of students rushed forward, waving tickets like children at Willy Wonka's gate. Bernie and I looked at our numbers—79 and 86—and sighed.

"Did you set everything straight in the A-building?" I asked her.

"I set it off in the A-building. They betta be glad I found a place to stay."

"You got a room in the Towers?"

"Negative. My dad helped me get a spot off Georgia Ave."

"How'd he do that?"

"Because daddies can do anything."

I kept my derision to myself. My daddy was spending quality time with my voicemail as I refused to answer his calls.

"It's smaller than a breadbox," Bernie was saying, "but I have a private bath, a kitchenette with a perfect hair-washing sink, and no roommates. This is the best mistake Howard has ever made."

"Next up: 53, 54, 55, 21, 79!"

"I won!" Bernie spared a sympathetic pat for my shoulder. "See you in twenty."

Not quite so many minutes later, I joined Bernie at our table where she and her boyfriend Tone fought over her fries.

"I told you to get your own." She swatted his fingers as he bare-handed her order. "See? Now I'm'a be carb-deficient."

"Nothing wrong with that." He swirled a few fries in her container of mayonnaise. "Too many carbs aren't good for the body."

"You saying there's something wrong with my body?"

He wiped his mouth with an elaborate sweep of the napkin. "You know I love your body, girl. Did you forget about last night when..."

"Cherrie, thank God!" I grabbed her arm, plunking her beside me in the booth. "It was about to get all *Showtime After Dark* in here."

"I'm offended." Tone gave me his puppy dog look. "What Bernie and I share is tender and respectful. Our love can make doves cry."

I threw a french fry which he caught in his mouth. "Again!"

"Ms. Nelson," Cherrie said. "I know I promised to wash your windows and sharpen your pencils..."

"And fluff my pillows," I said.

"And I planned to do all of those things tomorrow night. But ..." She reached in her back pocket. "These might let me off the hook."

"Unless it's a Christ-signed pardon, forget it."

"What about free passes to the sneak preview of *To Have & to Hold* at Union Station?"

"What?" Bernie and I cried.

"What's that?" Tone asked.

"Only the most-anticipated black romantic comedy of the fall film season," I said.

"No wonder I didn't know. I'm only half black."

"But totally *perfecto*," Bernie said with a kiss to his cheek.

"I've got four passes," Cherrie said. "If we're all free tomorrow night…"

Bernie slapped me five across the table. "Book it."

I smiled as Cherrie handed me my ticket. "Now you're forgiven."

We left the theatre entertained and enthralled. *To Have & to Hold* was a must-see-again at Cramton Auditorium in three weeks and when it hit theaters in eight. The tale of a cruise ship vow-renewal gone wrong was so hilarious and heartwarming the characters felt like long-lost friends. It was the kind of African-American fare that allowed you to pardon the likes of *Puff & Pass* and *Anaconda's Afterparty*. Almost.

"Ah, black love," Cherrie gushed at our table in the food court. "That final scene made me wanna get married right now."

Bernie shook red pepper flakes on her supreme slice. "So you can honeymoon with the cocoalicious lead actor."

"And I called him," I said. "Don't tell Maurice."

"You also called the limp waiter," Bernie said.

Tone nearly spit out his soda. "Limp?"

Bernie shrugged as I defended my choice. "He was not limp. He worked a difficult service job with class and humility."

"He catered to that girl for three days, and when

they were finally alone, he didn't have the guts to ask her out." Bernie bit her pizza. "Limp."

"I enjoyed the movie," Cherrie said. "But had some problems with it."

"Surprise, surprise," Bernie muttered.

"Such as?" Tone asked.

"Sawyer the lawyer spends all weekend flirting with the event planner, then gives his wife a rose bouquet when she meets him at the dock? What was that?"

"A garden of guilt," I said. "Because he would have slept with ol' girl if the best man hadn't knocked on the door because he lost the rings."

"But did you hear what the bride said to her brother-in-law during karaoke?" Cherrie asked. "She whispered they could make beautiful music together."

"And her husband was three feet away!" I said. "That was foul."

"That was a joke," Tone said. "They have a bilingual duet on the soundtrack. It played during the end credits."

Bernie looked at Tone. "Of course you defend your *morenita*, right?"

"Hey, we *hispanohablantes* gotta stick together, *comprende*?" Tone laid his accent on thick, and Bernie giggled to her own chagrin.

"I loved the groom's vows though," Cherrie said.

"Yes, Lawd!" I said. "What was that last part?"

"I see you with my heart. I honor you with my life. I worship you with my body, and I offer you my all." Cherrie laid a hand on her heart. "I'm in love."

Tone scribbled on a napkin. " 'I honor you with

my' what?"

"No, no, no," Bernie said. "I've found the biggest flaw in the movie."

"Is this about that gorgeous, blue-eyed groomsman ending up alone?" Cherrie asked.

"I know, right?" Bernie noticed Tone watching her. "I mean, uh, was there someone like that in this movie?"

"Yeah," Tone said. "He played the role of 'Topless Travis,' like he was allergic to anything with sleeves."

Cherrie's lashes fluttered. "I forgot about that."

Tone set down his pen. "See? There's that female double-standard."

"What?" Bernie asked.

"Y'all can sit there and pee your panties if a…"

"Ewww!" Bernie, Cherrie, and I covered our ears.

"Please don't use that word," I said.

"What word?" he asked.

Cherrie shivered. "The one that started with 'p.' "

Tone frowned. "Panties?"

"Oh, God!" We protested in unison.

"I'm begging you to stop," Bernie said.

Tone scratched his head. "That's the p-word you don't want me to say?"

Bernie fixed her sternest glare on him. "You betta not say the other one, but we're asking you nicely not to say that one."

"Why not?"

"Girls hate that word," we said.

"Really?" Our expressions must have convinced him, and he picked up his pen. "Duly noted. But back to my point, why is it okay for you to scream and cream when Six-Pack Jenkins takes off his shirt, but she covered my eyes during that graphic love scene?"

"Which one?" Cherrie asked.

"All of them," Bernie said.

"See?" Tone shook his head. "Double-standard."

"It's different," we said together, causing Tone to look at each of us. "It creeps me out when you do that," he said.

"It's different," Bernie said, "because women's bodies are always objectified for the pleasure of the male ego."

"Women's bodies are the crown of creation," he said. "How is it objectification if we appreciate their beauty?"

"Because one doesn't ogle a Botticelli," Cherrie said.

"And because beauties also have brains," I said. "And the ogling doesn't involve appreciation of that."

"Fair enough," Tone said. "But do you do that to Maurice?"

"Do what?"

Tone stole a mushroom from Bernie's pizza. "Cover his eyes during the love scenes?"

I focused on my sesame chicken. "We don't have those kinds of problems."

"Why not?"

"Because we don't watch movies like that."

"But he took you to see *Café Latte*," Cherrie said.

"The exception proving the rule," I said.

"Is that because you're a...." Tone cleared his throat. "You know..."

"A virgin. It's not a dirty word." Bernie slapped his fingers. "And stop brodying my 'shrooms."

"But don't forget," I said to Tone, "Maurice is four years older than me, and Adrian wasn't changing his 'no underage dating' policy for nobody."

"It was crazy," Cherrie said. "I mean, technically they weren't even dating when Maurice went on her senior prom."

"Word?" Tone asked.

I nodded. "Other than chaperoned school dances, our so-called dates involved my lunch breaks at Borders or my parents' living room until I turned eighteen. By then, we only had five weeks before I came down here freshman year."

"He went through all that to be with you?" Tone picked up his taco. "He must love you."

"Yeah." I sipped my Snapple. "I believe he does."

Five

"Quiet down!" came an exasperated female voice. "The sooner we get started, the sooner we can get done."

This week, Meridian held its first dorm meetings of the year, and the fourth through sixth floors were up. I rushed off the shuttle to get a seat, hoping things would move quickly so I could get to my homework. We were halfway through our second book in Dr. Treble's class, not to mention the dozen-plus Latin roots to memorize for Vocabulary Building. I knew Mordecai would keep things moving tonight, and his female counterpart was no-nonsense. But once I stepped into the lounge, I knew the meeting would be a mess.

First, there weren't enough seats. Meridian had no space large enough to hold three floors of students, so no matter how they configured the long benches and armed chairs, half of us stood or copped a squat on the floor.

Second, east-side residents getting off the shuttle were cutting through the lounge to access the back elevators. Their trek was neither silent nor swift, and their conversations cared nothing for our need to get this meeting started and ended.

Third, someone burned a bag of popcorn in the back kitchen microwave and used cheap incense to poorly mask the stench. Add to this the apparent lateness of a fifth floor RA, and we were off to a banging start.

I leaned against a pole, dropping my bag beside me. Cherrie told me about her floor meeting last night, so I could have skipped this one as dorm policies affected us all the same. But it wasn't in my nature to miss a meeting held by a friend. And with this crowd showing no sign of calming, Mordecai needed all the rational attendees he could get.

My phone buzzed, and I smiled at Maurice's number. The room was too noisy for conversation, so I'd call him back after I reached my room. We hadn't spoken since yesterday morning, and with things going so well, it felt like an eternity. Maurice hadn't badmouthed Howard or mentioned Penn since our call on The Yard, and I promised to see him before Thanksgiving. It wouldn't be easy with his work schedule and my now eighteen credits, but I would figure something out.

When the fifth floor RA arrived, the room gradually came to order. From her clipped tone and agitated movements, she was in a bigger hurry than I was. She breezed through the obligatory welcome and the staff's

43

commitment to making this a successful, trouble-free year. She breathed long enough to let Mordecai talk about on-site amenities and the shuttle, and I gave him a thumbs-up from my perch in the back. Though I zoned out during the repetitive information, my ears perked up when his partner explained the nuances of visitation.

"Non-university students of either gender are permitted to stay overnight." She paused for whoops and whistles. "Guests must be approved at least three days before their arrival by completing the appropriate form available at the front desk. In addition to your name and room number, you must provide their name, address, and the range of dates for their stay. This is especially important for Homecoming when many will wish to have out-of-town visitors. Any questions?"

Students raised eager hands around me, but I latched on to her last statement.

Why didn't I think of this before?

I could almost see Maurice stroking his chin in thought. "Homecoming?"

"It's perfect. Come down Friday night and stay until Monday afternoon."

"They suspend classes?"

"No, but most professors love Homecoming, so the workload is light. They make up for it the following weeks, but I can catch up. What do you think?"

"I think one good turn deserves another."

"Meaning?"

"I'll come down for Homecoming if you come

home for Columbus Day."

"You and this Columbus Day thing." I glanced at my Women of the Bible wall calendar. "They're two weeks apart."

"Even better."

I paced my room. "I don't know."

"Come on, Duch. You invited me to spend the weekend in DC. How is that different than spending a weekend at my place?"

"Your place?"

"Yes. I want you to come home, here, to spend the weekend, here, with me."

He said "here" twice. And were that not clear enough, his emphasis on the last two words certainly were.

He wanted me to stay with him.

At his house.

In West Philly.

All weekend.

My mouth worked to form a response, but my vocal chords were stunned into silence.

Because Maurice and I couldn't officially date until last July, I'd only visited Maurice's place a handful of times. Only twice after dark and never overnight. Now he wanted me to stay there—sleep there—an entire weekend.

Two nights.

Three if I stayed until Monday.

Four if I arrived Thursday evening and stayed until Monday morning.

"Duchess?"

"Yes?" My voice was too high. "Did you say

45

something? Else, I mean?"

"Yeah, I did." He spoke as if approaching a skittish kitten. Or a scaredy cat.

If the paw print fits.

"Oh, um…what?"

"What do you think of my idea?"

"Your idea about me staying with you at your house for an entire weekend unsupervised?"

"You could say that."

"Right."

"Daria?"

"Yes?"

"Breathe."

"I am breathing."

"Your hands are clenched in little fists, and your eyes are shut so tight they're tearing up."

I relaxed my hands, my gaze darting around the room. "Did you sneak a Nanny Cam in here?"

"I just know my girl. Listen." He blew out a long breath. "I'm going through withdrawal up here. I thought last year was hard, but after this summer, being without you is torture. The only reason I haven't driven down there is I don't think I'd be able to leave."

"Maurice…"

"So let's test it out. You come up here first, and if I can stand to let you go, I'll come down for Homecoming." His voice deepened. "I just… I miss you, Duch. I feel like a scrub for saying so, but there it is."

"Don't feel like a scrub with me. When you say you miss me, it makes me feel loved."

"You are loved. You are loved and wanted and will you please come home for Columbus Day?"

I scanned my HU desk calendar, standing on the edge of yes. "I'll think about it. Not because I don't want to come, but I'm still adjusting to my classes, and I don't want to be there with my nose in the books all weekend."

"So that's not a 'no'?"

His enthusiasm touched my heart. "That is definitely not a 'no.' "

"Then I'll take it."

We ended our call shortly thereafter, and as I microwaved my late dinner of baked turkey wings and rice pilaf, I thought about his proposal.

It wasn't all that different than my Homecoming invitation and would be easier to navigate. Philly was my town too, so if things became too close for comfort, I knew dozens of outside distractions. He had an entire house for our amusement, not a larger-than-average dorm room. We might not even sleep in the same room.

Yeah, right.

The microwave beeped, and I set my food at the table, fanning the steam. With the direction my thoughts were taking, I needed to turn that hand around and fan myself.

In full disclosure, the sleeping arrangements were my biggest concern. It was stupid, as Maurice never pressured me or gave me reasons not to trust him. He wasn't luring me to West Philly to have his wicked way with me, and if we shared a bed, he would remain within my established boundaries. But the idea of sleeping in his bed...the place where he sometimes talked to me at night...his rumbling tenor curled around me like so much of his body would be...

47

My dorm phone rang, snapping me out of my flush-inducing thoughts. I reached for the receiver and was about to press 'Talk' when I noticed the phone number. Uncertain of the caller, I let the voicemail pick up, adjusting the volume to high.

"Daria, hey. Your mother said you didn't work Friday nights, so I thought you'd be home. Guess you're out having fun. And that's good. That's what I want. Um, listen, I wanted to say that I …"

I turned the volume all the way down and returned the receiver to the cradle. Stuffing down the guilt, I grabbed the VCR remote to catch up on *Never Ever After*. Hopefully Caprelle was having better luck with her father than I was with mine.

Six

Saturday afternoons at Borders were the best. When I wasn't ringing up customers at the register, I hid in Fiction doing some much-needed shelving. I cleared one utility cart before filling another, and before I knew it, I was getting off the Metro at Columbia Heights around the corner from Meridian. The forecast spelled rain in the next few days, so I crossed Sixteenth Street and headed to The Safeway.

All my neighbors seemed to have the same idea, so that should-have-been-short trip took an hour. By the time I made it back to Meridian, I was ready to hole up in my room until Monday morning. I hadn't found a church home in DC, and though the Rankin Chapel boasted anointed guest ministers, its services were too quiet for my Pentecostal self. I liked my praise loud and long, and Room 485 made a nice sanctuary every day of the week.

It also made for a den of disorder, and after putting away my groceries, I made a weekend chore list. While contemplating an emotion-based rearranging of my CDs, someone knocked on my door. As my ceiling light wasn't visible from outside, I pretended I wasn't home.

"Daria, if you don't open this door, I'm going to start singing!"

So much for that.

I opened the door, and my visitor sauntered in. "How are you always here when you don't live here?" I asked.

"Many reasons." Bernie flopped on my bed, sending a pillow to the floor. "I'm cool with Cherrie, and everybody loves Cherrie. I'm Antonio's girlfriend, and everybody respects the one legit athlete on Howard's basketball team. And I don't take no mess, and don't nobody want no mess."

I picked up my pillow, patting it to dislodge the dust. "Now you have to help me make my bed."

"Later." She crossed her feet at the ankles. "Get dressed."

I revised my chores list, moving "launder my comforter" closer to the top. "Why?"

"We're going out tonight."

I didn't bother turning around. "I went to work and braved The Safeway. I even went across the street during lunch for silly postcards to send Corina. I've done all the going out I'm going to do."

Bernie tilted her head, squinting at me. "Pants."

"What?"

She leapt off the bed, beelining for my closet. "You should wear pants."

"Bernie, I'm not..." Another knock at the door interrupted me.

"That's Cherrie. And yes, you are."

"Why aren't you dressed yet?" Cherrie asked as she entered.

"Because I'm not going." I admired her black wrap dress. "You look nice."

"Nice?" She rolled her eyes and joined Bernie. "For an English major, you have issues with adjectives."

"Pants, tank top, fitted vest." Bernie handed me the all-black items. "You can choose your own shoes."

Cherrie clapped her hands. "Yay!"

I rehung the clothes, closing my closet door as Bernie twirled out of the way. "What part of 'I'm not going' do you heffas not understand?"

"Come on." Cherrie opened my toiletry drawer, selecting my pink-tinted nail hardener. "You never come out with us."

"With good reason." I was not about the smoky smell and hard-up guys looking for a little bump and grind. "I'd rather stay here, clean up, and..."

"Watch *Café Latte* again." Bernie was in front of my DVD rack, holding the movie in question. "This one is out of sequence, which means it's next in your viewing queue."

I hated how well she knew me. "I haven't seen it in two weeks."

Cherrie gasped. "That might be a record."

I snatched the case from Bernie. "It's the only

romantic movie Maurice and I saw together. Why can't I watch it again?"

"Because the cast needs a night off," Cherrie said. "Besides, aren't you tired of it yet?"

"Never." Watching the twitterpated leads balance romance and ratings in front of their live morning show audience was my favorite pastime. "Every time I see it, I notice something new. Last time, I caught a look between Stephon and Alicia during her audition. The way his mouth quirked when she read the copy...."

Cherrie and Bernie stared at me then looked at each other. "She's definitely going."

"No, I'm not."

Two hours later, we piled in a cab, and I wondered why I bothered arguing with them.

I caught the driver's curious stares in the rearview mirror and laughed to myself. The combination of Bernie's six-foot stature, dark skin, and long blonde locs warranted a double-take on its own. But when posted beside the diminutive, curvy, and mocha-skinned Cherrie, the differences were almost comical. I was the literal middle ground: average height, brown skin, and neither thin nor thick. High school cross-country gave me a runner's build, but Corina's genes padded my hips and thighs. All in all, I couldn't complain.

"See?" Bernie said after we showed our IDs. "Isn't this better than romantic reruns?"

I mock-rolled my eyes, but my spirits lifted inside the club. Decadence was a popular club in Northeast DC with a trendy restaurant and bar on the street level and three floors of music above. It hosted concert after-parties where hip-hop celebs put in appearances, but the key to the club's popularity was its divide-and-conquer approach. Different genres—hip-hop & rap, old-school, go-go, reggae—were housed in different rooms so every hardcore fan had a place to call home.

The three of us headed straight for the old-school room on the second floor. The lighthearted lyrics with a dash of braggadocio echoed a simpler, more conscious time. Back then, male rappers settled scores with a mic not a Magnum, and female MCs flaunted skills instead of skin. We carved out a spot near the center of the floor and jumped in with both feet.

"This is my song!" I cried.

"I ain't heard this in years," Cherrie said as Bernie twirled her around.

Cherrie spun out from Bernie and did the Tootsie Roll. We laughed and copied her moves. As a larger crowd joined in, I followed up with the Roger Rabbit. Bernie and Cherrie did an elaborate Kid n' Play with a 720-degree turn. But Bernie stumped us all with an obscure Detroit dance called the Wacky Jackie.

We stayed in the Old-School Room for another extended set, and Cherrie got a hankering for reggae. I wasn't a huge fan, so I volunteered to go for bottled water. Bernie took my phone as insurance that I wouldn't bail, and I borrowed her wallet in exchange.

"Meet us by the far wall," she yelled. "And don't let nobody touch your booty."

She slapped me there for emphasis and sent me away. I weaved through the dancing crowd, stopping occasionally to contribute a head nod or shoulder shake when forward progress wasn't possible. The place was packed, but I saw dozens of HU faces in the crowd.

Looked like I picked the right night to venture out.

I crept down the crowded stairwell, keeping my eyes alert. Male passersby smiled—after looking me up and down—and I was oddly flattered and cautious. Cherrie often regaled us with horror stories about some uber-friendly dude at the club, so after the fourth "What the deal, shorty?" I kept my gaze focused on the floor.

Making my way to the second-floor bar, I plopped on the first empty stool I could find. I bought four bottles of water and opened one immediately. Cherrie could wind and wiggle until they ran out of soca, and with no need to rush, I took my sweet time finishing my water. The cranky bartender gave me the death stare when I asked for extra napkins, but her smiling partner slipped me some with a wink.

Dabbing my brow with the damp napkin, I turned to the dance floor. The music was off the hook, and people danced wherever they stood. With the crowd continuing to swell, I hoped no gunfire broke out, lest half of us get trampled in the stampede toward the exits. Such wasn't the norm at this club, but whenever alcohol, egos, and pheromones combined, a worst-case scenario was always possible.

I noticed everyone watching a couple in the middle of the floor. And as the crowd parted, I saw why. The girl's leopard-print legs were wrapped around the guy's waist as she was bent backwards with her palms on the floor, gyrating for all she was worth. I was about to add her name to the prayer list when I saw her partner's face.

Mordecai.

I hopped off the stool to get a closer look.

Sure enough, Mordecai was being assaulted by a set

of swirling hips, and from the look on his face, he wasn't sure how he felt about it. Before we could make eye contact, he leaned over to help ol' girl return to an upright position. With her feet on the ground and no trace of shame, she pressed her back into him, rolling her body to the thumping bass. She grabbed his hands and wrapped them around her waist to his evident surprise. He was torn between enjoyment and embarrassment, and I chuckled at his confusion.

But my laughter ended when his partner flipped her hair and revealed her face.

The Chesty Cheetah.

Of course.

The bane of my collegiate existence, The Chesty Cheetah was an effective nuisance in each class we shared. Whatever seat I chose on Tuesday in Freshman English, she occupied on Thursday. During my final presentation in Intro to Sociology, she blew an obnoxious bubble that popped when I reached my most important point. She seemed embarrassed and apologized, but the class laughed anyway, ruining the moment. This year, she and her lazy self lived in the Towers and insisted on taking the shuttle the whole block and a half to campus, like those cheetah-print heels were too good to walk in. Now she was assaulting poor Mordecai?

Her depravity knew no bounds.

The song changed, and Mordecai made a grateful escape. I tried to get his attention, but he disappeared into the crowd. And hopefully to a bathroom to wash his hands.

I made it upstairs to the Reggae Room and found

Bernie and Cherrie leaned against the wall as promised. Cherrie swayed from side-to-side, but Bernie rubbed her heel-free left foot. "Remind me never to wear those again."

"Rookie," Cherrie said.

Bernie and I exchanged wallet and phone. "You-know-who called," she said.

"He did?" I flipped the phone open, checking the time. "Did you answer?"

"Nah. Didn't know if you being here was a secret."

I handed out the water. "Why would I lie?"

"Maybe he'd get upset if he knew where you were."

"Why?" Cherrie asked. "It's not like she's backing that thang up on every guy she sees."

"Like The Chesty Cheetah was."

Bernie almost spit out her water. "You saw The Chesty Cheetah? Where?"

I told them about Mordecai getting freaked against his will, and Bernie snorted. "I wish I'd've seen that."

"She has a name," Cherrie said.

"What is it?" I asked, having blocked it from memory.

Cherrie gave us a blank stare, and Bernie laughed. "Chesty Cheetah it is."

She and Cherrie bickered over my animal print-loving nemesis while I texted Maurice. In an instant, my phone rang.

"Reese, I can't talk now." I could barely hear myself. "That's why I texted you."

"You didn't answer your dorm phone," he said. "Where are you?"

"At Decadence."

"Dunkin Donuts?"

"Club Decadence," I yelled. "With Bernie and Cherrie."

Despite the surrounding noise, there was no mistaking the silence on the other end. "You're at a club?"

"I was going to clean and watch a movie, but they overruled me." He didn't answer, and I thought about Bernie's words. "Are you upset?"

"Naw. I just…wow, I think I'd like to see that."

"See what?"

"You all decked out at the club. Maybe we can hit up Club Smokes when you come home for Columbus Day."

"Slow your roll, homie. I haven't agreed to Columbus Day."

He chuckled. "You will."

After sweating to the oldies for another two hours, we bagged it around one in the morning. Cherrie and I got out at Meridian, and Bernie directed the cab to her place, wanting to wash her locs. Maurice insisted I call when I got home, but he was so groggy I doubted he would remember our brief chat in the morning. Grabbing my toiletry caddy and supplies, I headed to my favorite stall, disinfecting the shower before disrobing. I hung up my clothes to wash tomorrow and collapsed in a sleepy heap as soon as my head hit the pillow.

The sound of the phone roused me before I was ready, and I muttered Shakespearean curses under my breath. "Yes?"

"Sorry. Didn't mean to wake you up."

The voice was familiar, but I couldn't place it. "Who is this?"

"Mordecai."

"Hey." I rolled over, rubbing sleep crud from my eyes. "What time is it?"

"Too early for me to be calling."

"It's cool." I glanced at the clock, surprised to find it was nigh noon. "So what's up?"

"You got a Fed Ex."

"Really?" No one sent packages like Corina Nelson, and I was overdue for one. "I'll be right down."

After brushing my teeth and washing my face, I shuffled downstairs in sweats and slippers to retrieve Corina's first love basket of the year. Mordecai met me in the back office to sign for it, and I smiled. "Did you enjoy yourself?"

"When?"

"Last night on the dance floor when The Chesty Cheetah wrapped herself around you like a python."

"You saw that?"

"I was getting water at the bar for the girls and me. Didn't realize I was in for drinks and a show."

"That was crazy." He handed me the pen. "I was minding my business, and all of a sudden, she…wait, what did you call her?"

"The Chesty Cheetah." I signed and dated the Package Receipt Form. "Because she's blessed up top and wears too-tight animal prints."

Mordecai's face blanked then he threw his head back and laughed. "Wow, that is…"

"Rude and wrong and all Bernie's fault. Where's my goodie box?"

"No box." He handed me a thin envelope. "Just this."

Without checking the return address, I turned the package over and opened it. And what fell into my hands caused my mouth to fall open.

Two round-trip Amtrak tickets to Philadelphia.

SEVEN

After chastising Maurice for such a bold move—and smiling at his rather insincere apology—I accepted his gift and promised to meet him at 30th Street Station in two weeks.

Despite my protests, we both knew I wouldn't miss a chance to see him. School was important, but spending time with Maurice was as important to me as retaining my 4.0, for I refused to renege on another promise to him.

Though my senior year of high school had been full of excitement, one lingering source of pain remained. Cherrie and I had spent seven years together at our progressive middle-slash-high school and were loath to go our separate ways. So when she asked me to take an

HBCU tour with her, I jumped at the chance.

"We can squeeze four years of college into one weekend," she said sadly.

Cherrie had already visited Spelman and leaned strongly toward its scholastic sisterhood, but Howard ran a close second, and she was excited for me to see it. I knew little about the school beyond its legendary Homecomings but tried to be enthusiastic as we pulled into DC.

We got off the bus, and I followed her onto The Yard. I don't know what happened next, couldn't explain if I wanted to, but as I stood there, something in my soul shifted into place, birthing a self-awareness that rendered me speechless and UPenn a non-option. Cherrie darn near choked with glee when I chose Howard, seconding my emotions with a choice of her own.

I savored Cherrie's enthusiasm but wasn't foolish enough to expect the same from my father or boyfriend. Despite their dissimilarities, they each expected me to realize my post-secondary dreams in West Philadelphia as planned, and I feared disappointing them both.

And what I feared soon came upon me.

Adrian's disapproval was deep and pervasive, poisoning our every interaction thereafter. I couldn't handle that from Maurice too, so I practically begged him to accept my decision. It was a long shot, as he'd spent two years looking forward to having me close by at Penn, but Maurice surprised me. He was compassionate and optimistic, assuring me Adrian would come around and we would be fine. After all that worrying, I couldn't believe I would get to have Howard and Maurice's support too.

Well, I shouldn't have believed it. Because I didn't have it.

If our relationship had been official for the whole summer, maybe my departure would have seemed less jolting to Maurice. But those five weeks of fleeting freedom were of little effect once I started at Howard. And from Labor Day freshman year until our recent phone conversation on The Yard, Maurice resented my collegiate choice. I stayed in constant touch last year with phone calls, emails, and the occasional greeting card, but after our sweet reunion this summer, we both needed more face-to-face time sophomore year.

Hence, this train ride to Philly.

Legal adult or not, I could never get the Parents Nelson to sanction a weekend at Maurice's place. So Corina thought I was busy with a Brit Lit project, helping Cherrie feng shui her room, and washing my linens. And by asking her to give Daddy a hug for me, I could have disappeared for a month without objection. But I didn't need a month. Just four days and three nights with my boyfriend.

I glanced out the window where the Schuylkill River ran alongside our track, and my heart sped up. Though we spoke every day this week, I couldn't wait to see Maurice, to hold his hand, kiss his lips. I shivered at the thought.

Slower than I preferred, the Metroliner pulled into 30th Street Station. Maurice had to meet me upstairs as non-ticket holders were not allowed on the platform, but I could survive the twelve-second escalator ride to the street level. I reached the top, and as if on instinct, I glanced to the left and looked right at Maurice.

"Let them pass!" an Amtrak worker shouted, his keen green eye on the baggage-laden passengers anxious to head downstairs. Maurice was far enough back not to warrant the warning but close enough that I could almost taste his smile.

My heart fluttered in my chest, and I nearly abandoned my rolling suitcase as I rushed to greet him. He met me halfway and scooped me up, his trimmed mustache tickling my neck as he buried his face there.

"Hey, Duchess."

The words warmed me from the inside out. "Hey, yourself."

"I missed you." His lips were chaste against my skin, but that didn't dull their impact. "So much."

"Ditto that."

"Let's take this outside, yeah?"

"Yeah."

He kissed my cheek before slipping one hand in mine, taking the bag from my shoulder with the other. At the taxi stand, a station worker steered us toward an unoccupied car. Maurice put my luggage in the trunk and joined me in the backseat, his hand around my waist.

"You might want to handle that." I glanced at the open door behind him. "Wouldn't want you falling out on Market Street."

"If I do." He shut the door with authority. "Just tuck and roll, baby."

I laughed. "I am not tucking and rolling out of anything."

"You say that now."

He put his arm around me, and I relaxed against

63

him as the cab pulled off. He threaded our fingers together, a quizzical tilt to his brow. "What?" I asked.

"I missed holding your hand. I thought seeing you would be enough, but…"

"But?"

He lifted my hand to his lips. "I'm glad I have you for an entire weekend."

I closed my eyes to savor the sensation, sighing when he turned my wrist and planted a second kiss there. "I missed you," he said.

I laid my free hand against his cheek. "I'm right here."

Center City yielded to University City, and I marveled at how much I missed my hometown. Maurice was my main reason to visit West Philly, but Adrian had childhood friends there and often brought me along for Bible study or other activities. I loved those trips, watching my dad in his element. He was the Recruitment Director in the UPenn Office of Minority Affairs, but his personal calling involved helping people meet Christ and discover the purpose for their lives.

Unless you were his daughter. Then his purpose became one of judgment, misunderstanding, and rejection.

"Duch?" Maurice's voice seemed to come out of nowhere. "You still here?"

"Sorry, lost in thought. What's up?"

"I need to pop in The Shop." I hadn't noticed we'd turned onto the block. "You mind?"

"Of course not. I'd love to visit the infamous Shop."

"Infamous?"

I startled him with a kiss to the cheek. "I mean that as a compliment."

Maurice asked the driver to wait and came around to take my hand. The Shop, as it was grandly named, occupied a popular corner on the razor's edge between University City and West Powelton. Maurice lived a few blocks away in a small row home, but his life was bisected by his time in The Shop.

An overhead bell announced our entry, but with the ceiling-to-ledge windows, those inside were already prepared.

"So this is why he ran outta here so fast," a gray-haired barber said. "I thought his Underroos were on fire."

"You know how he is about his lady." This speaker had a subtle accent, Jamaican perhaps. "You betta ask permission before smiling at her or he'll jack up your shape-up!"

More comments and laughter rang out as Maurice waved his hand. "This is why we don't get respectable clients," he said. "Because you Negroes don't know how to act."

"Whoa!" cried one customer. "I ain't respectable?"

"Brother, you got three bench warrants," the first speaker crowed. "And you owe so much child support, you gonna have to start paying in Sugar Babies."

He shook his head. "Y'all drawin."

"Nice to see you all again." I fought a laugh as I scanned the room. "Where's Naseem?"

"He's off today, but he'll be around this weekend." Maurice walked backward to his office, eyeing everyone in the room. "Behave."

"You say that like we don't know how to act," the first man snorted.

"You don't," came a husky female voice.

I turned around and saw a short, thin woman with a high black ponytail. Her dark fingers made quick work of the final braid, and she patted the young man's shoulder, prompting him to leap out of the chair and head to the marked bathroom.

"What's up?" Swiping her hands on navy blue apron, she then extended one with a smile. "I'm Suzika. Good to meet you, Daria."

"You too. His hair looks nice."

"Thanks. It's easy when they don't cry the whole time." She wiped down her chair. "You here all weekend?"

"Until Monday afternoon." An outburst of laughter startled me. "You must be some kind of woman to work with all these ..."

"Fools? Hooligans?" She rolled her eyes. "Yeah, they needed some estrogen up in here, and I've got the ovaries to dish it out."

"Ovaries?" someone shouted behind me. "Wait a minute! Zeke is a woman?"

"Shut it, Limpin' Larry!" she called back. "Or I'll give the story behind that name!"

I could see why people could hang here all day. "I'm glad you're keeping these boys in line."

"Somebody's got to. And I'm glad Maurice has you back. He's been a real grouch."

I cocked an eyebrow as he approached. "Is that so?"

"Don't believe a word she says." Maurice glanced at the Legends of Boxing calendar at her station.

"Especially at this time of the month."

I looked at Suzika. "Did he say that?"

"In front of two women who could dropkick him into next week?" She made a show of cracking her knuckles. "Naw, he couldn't be that stupid."

"Well, it's about that time, so...." Maurice steered me toward the front door as Suzika danced around like Laila Ali. "Say goodbye, Daria."

"Goodbye, Daria!" the crowd replied.

I laughed my way outside. "That was fun."

Maurice shut the shop door behind him. "I'm glad you enjoyed yourself."

Eight

Outside his house, Maurice paid the driver and retrieved my bags. He pulled out an Eagles keychain sporting two silver keys. Turning one in the lock, he pushed open the door with a smile. "Welcome home."

I avoided his eyes and crossed the threshold. "Don't you mean 'your' home?"

"This weekend." He closed the door behind us. "What's mine is yours, Duchess."

My thumbnail scratched the pad of my ring finger, and he chuckled. "So skittish. I hope to change that by Monday."

I couldn't reply, and he didn't expect me to. I leaned against the black leather sectional and slipped off my shoes, noting the beige rug had been upgraded to a blue and black showpiece that highlighted the abstract prints on the walls. The front bay window boasted coordinating floor-to-ceiling curtains, and there was an assortment of matching pillows on the couch. And the universal remote that controlled his stereo, widescreen television, and cable box sat on an oblong coffee table beside a tight arrangement of red roses in a blue vase.

"Since when do you keep flowers on the table?"

"Since yesterday." He came to stand behind me. "I wanted them same-day fresh but was afraid I'd run out of time."

"Out of time? Did you work today?"

"No." His arms encircled me as he rested his chin on my shoulder. "But I wanted everything perfect for your first weekend here."

I turned in his arms as sleeping butterflies stirred in my belly. "Being with you is perfect enough."

Maurice's gaze dropped to my lips. "May I kiss you now?"

And the butterflies flapped like crazy. "Please."

He slid his hands up my arms, leaned in, and gently pressed his lips against mine. Liquid heat seeped into my soul, and I needed his steadying hold to keep me upright. He retreated and advanced, tilting his head. I leaned the other way, parting my lips as he sighed. I clasped my hands behind his neck as he pressed us closer, my heart hammering in my chest.

This was where I normally tensed up and closed my mouth, fearing the sultry sensations such intimacy unleashed. My body tingled with anticipation for things I hadn't discovered and was too shy to investigate. So I stayed on the virginal side of the line with several feet to spare.

But that distance meant little with Maurice's lips moving as if he had forever to enjoy mine. Not with his heartbeat against my thin sweater, cadencing a song I longed to sing. And not without anyone to interrupt, no parents to avoid, or curfews to obey.

Just him and me and right now.

The doorbell rang, startling us both, and we jumped apart.

"There's dinner," he said. "I called Allegro's while we were at The Shop."

"Oh." I willed my heart to stop racing. "Good call."

"This should cover it." He handed me some money and grabbed my bags. "I'll put these upstairs."

"And I'll set the table." I kissed his cheek. "Thank you in advance."

"You're welcome in advance."

The doorbell rang again, and we went our separate ways. I appeased the delivery guy with a generous tip, and I went into the kitchen to set the table. The aroma of steak and fried onions was a hometown embrace, and my mouth watered as I placed the plates.

"Onion rings and vanilla cream soda?" I smiled as Maurice entered the kitchen. "You thought of everything."

"I aim to please."

After he said grace—which was shocking enough—I caught him up on my classes and reiterated how safe I was in DC. He pretended to believe the latter and reacquainted me with the folks from The Shop.

"Is it unusual to have a woman in The Shop?" I asked.

"With all your talk about equality between the sexes, I'm surprised you're asking that."

"I didn't think there were many female barbers."

"There ain't. But Zeke also does braids, cornrows, and locs. She's the real deal."

"I can see that." I dipped an onion ring in ketchup. "Girls who can do boys' hair are in high demand at Howard."

"And what other kinds of girls are in high demand down there?"

I snorted. "Whoever they are, I'm certainly not one of them."

"I doubt that."

"I'm serious. You should see some of these girls: full-makeup and stilettos first thing in the morning, and every day a fashion show. No, thank you."

"This is why I love you."

"Because I live in tees and jeans?"

"No. Because you're comfortable in your skin and not trying to be anyone else." He looked me up and down. "Then again…"

"What?"

"I would love to see you in some stilettos. And a tight red dress with cutouts on the side."

"Ain't gonna happen, cap'n. At least, not this weekend."

"There's always Homecoming."

"There definitely is." A yawn overtook my answer. "I'm sorry."

"You must be running on vapor by now."

"Happy vapor. That makes all the difference."

"Why don't you head upstairs?"

That woke me up. "Upstairs?"

"Were you going to sleep on the counter?"

"Uh, no." I ignored the heat traveling up my neck. "I just…um, I hadn't thought about…"

"Listen." He took my hands. "I put your bags in the hallway. You get ready for bed up there, and I'll do the same in the powder room then come find you. If you're in the guest room, I'll tuck you in, cut out the light, and sleep happy that you're in my house at all. If you're in my room, then we'll sleep in a way you're comfortable with. Okay?"

Relief flooded my body. "Okay."

"With that settled." He kissed my forehead. "I'll see you upstairs."

Maurice took our plates to the sink, and I took my first trip to his second floor.

At the top of the stairs was a small bedroom-turned-closet. I spotted the suits he wore to my proms and smiled at the memories. My luggage was outside the next room, which turned out to be the bathroom. I took a bird bath at the sink and donned my HU lounge pants and a baby tee with a blue and white scarf to protect my freshly pressed hair.

I cut out the light and grabbed my suitcase handle. For all my apprehension about the subject, I could never forsake the chance to sleep beside Maurice. I sped by the guest room as if it didn't exist and reached the threshold of the master bedroom. I stopped short of folding my hands in reverence, but the moment was no less sacred.

Stepping into the room, I set my bags beside the navy recliner, admiring the mahogany built-ins housing his music collection. Atop the double-sided chest of drawers were a grouping of photos, and I was touched to feature in all but the one of his parents. Then my gaze landed on the king-sized showpiece with its tufted leather headboard, and I gulped down my nerves.

"It's just furniture." I reminded myself. "It won't bite."

Choosing the side closest to the window, I took off my slippers and sat on the bed. The mattress yielded beneath my weight, encouraging my eagerness for sleep. Adjusting the pillows behind me, I scooted back and folded my hands atop the covers.

Like a moron.

"You're going to sleep not the dentist," I muttered. "Relax."

But I couldn't. Whether I lay on my side or my back, with pillows or without, I felt weird. Something was missing, and I didn't mean my hypoallergenic pillows with the customized density. It was something more important, something essential for my comfort. Something like...

"Here you are," he said.

Something like Maurice. Standing in the doorway.

"Are you surprised?" I asked.

"Yes." A lazy smile spread across his face. "In the best way."

He closed the door, and I chuckled at his expression. "I'm not going to freak out."

"I know. I just like watching you."

I pulled back the covers on his side. "Just get in before I change my mind." As he approached the bed, I noted his sweatpants and tank top. "I'm disappointed."

He paused, one knee on the bed. "Why?"

"I expected a smoking jacket and silk pajamas."

He laughed as he climbed in. "The best part is you're serious."

As he pulled up the covers, I slid underneath them and curled on my side. We lay facing each other, our eyes illuminated by lamp light and other precious things.

He cupped my cheek. "I can't believe you're here."

"Me either."

"I'm so happy."

"Me too." Another yawn overtook me. "I've got to stop doing that."

"You will in a minute." He sat up to turn out the light, and I rolled onto my stomach. Smiling at my fluttering eyelids, he kissed my forehead.

"Good night, Duchess."

I sighed in contentment. "Good night, Maurice."

NinE

"I left three messages yesterday," Bernie said when I answered the phone Sunday morning.

"Hello to you, too." I pulled on my socks. "I was busy."

"Mmm-hmm. Doing what?"

"Enjoying a luxurious soak in his clawfoot tub, checking my HU email for a Cultural Anthropology assignment, and trudging through *Of Scarlet and Sage*."

Bernie groaned. "Did you get to the funeral yet?"

"That was torture." Dr. Treble had us reading an obscure novel about a female amnesiac. "I read it three times and have no idea what happened."

"And there are no Cliffsnotes anywhere. Did you...what, Cherrie?"

"Give me the phone!" came a muffled voice. "It's important."

"Quickly." Bernie's voice faded into the background. "Don't be wasting my minutes."

"Did you see *Never Ever After* on Friday?" Cherrie asked.

"That's what you needed to ask?" Bernie's annoyance rang out. "Gimme my phone."

"Stop, Bernie! Did you?" Cherrie asked me.

"Haven't watched since Tuesday." I heard the doorbell downstairs. "I planned to marathon next weekend."

"We can watch together. I have to see your reaction to something."

"What happened?"

"Can't tell you." Her giddiness made me smile. "But I'll come over on….Bernie, no! I wasn't done!"

"Please insert 25 cents for an additional minute." Bernie's automated voice was impressive. "Or better yet, do not use my phone to discuss that pitiful excuse for a soap opera."

"I'll have you know it was nominated for a Daytime Emmy last year," Cherrie said.

"For what?" Bernie asked.

"A Creative Arts Emmy for Main Title Design."

"I rest my case."

"Duchess?" Maurice called from the bottom of the stairs. "You coming?"

"Be right there!" I yelled back. "Gotta go, girls."

"So you jump whenever he calls?" Bernie asked.

"When there's French toast involved? Yep."

"Good idea. Come on, Cherrie," Bernie said. "Let's

do brunch."

"I thought you were giving me a touch up."

There was a beat of silence. "Can't you wear a hat?"

Oh, how I missed their bickering. "See you Tuesday."

After a once-over in Maurice's mirror, I headed downstairs, a booming voice echoing in the room.

"There she is!" Naseem swept me in a hug. "I missed you."

"You saw me yesterday."

"But I couldn't hug you cuz Reese would've killed me."

Maurice watched him from the stove. "I'm two seconds off you now, for real for real."

"I'm sorry if the fellas were too rowdy yesterday." Suzika emerged from the powder room. "Children like to show off in front of company."

"It's cool." My ears still burned with the insults and innuendo from my two-hour visit to The Shop, but nothing could mar the memory of Maurice in his element. "It was the highlight of my weekend."

Maurice brought over a tray of French toast. "Really?"

"The outside-of-this-house highlight."

He kissed the top of my head. "Good answer."

Naseem made a gagging sound, and Suzika flicked his shoulder. "Don't hate."

"Ow, man!" He rubbed the tender spot. "If you weren't doing my hair, I'd tell you to leave."

"I would love to see you try."

I joined Maurice in the kitchen. "Are they always

77

like this?"

"I think they're in love and don't know it," he stage-whispered.

"I heard that," Suzika said. "Ain't no way."

Naseem put up a righteous fist. "Preach, sister."

We assembled around the table and feasted on the bounty Maurice made. I'd never seen him so domestic and relaxed. He sat beside me, his free hand resting on my knee whenever he got the chance. I laid my hand atop his, touched by the gesture.

I convinced Maurice to let me clean the kitchen while they settled in the living room. Naseem needed his hair braided but wanted to hang out, so Suzika agreed to come to Maurice's. I didn't mind the company; it'd be nice to balance out the female energy for once and not focus on how sad I'd be tomorrow afternoon when my little vacation ended.

Thank God Homecoming was two weeks away.

Suzika finished Naseem's hair as he and Maurice finished their second game of NBA Live, and she stretched. "What are we playing now?"

"Monopoly?" Naseem asked.

"Too long," I said.

"Spades?" Suzika asked.

"No," Maurice said. "You Negroes ain't breaking my coffee table."

"Why you lookin' at me?" Naseem asked. "I'm civilized."

"Like a wildebeest," Suzika said.

"Whatever. You probably renege."

She whipped her head to him. "Whatchu say?"

He licked his teeth. "Bet you cut your partners too."

She grabbed the metal afro pick. "I'll show you how I cut, partner…"

"Whoa!" I stepped between them. "How about Crazy Eights?"

They looked at each other, and Suzika nodded. "Bet."

"I'll get the cards," Maurice said. "And the sedatives."

"I'll get some snacks." Naseem looked at Suzika. "If you act like you got some home training, I might give you a yellow Skittle."

"You're a yellow Skittle."

Laughing as the boys left the room, Suzika and I cleared the coffee table. She picked up *Of Scarlet and Sage*, reading the back copy. "Is this good?"

"No, but it's required reading."

"You gonna be a teacher?"

"I don't know." I grabbed the other side of the table, and we moved it away from the couch. "I majored in English for the fun of the language, but beyond that, I have no clue what I'm doing."

"I'm going to cosmetology school once I get my money together, but me and college? High school was bad enough."

"I hear you. No sense going somewhere you don't want to be."

"Exactly."

"All right, worms and germs." Naseem tossed a bag of Skittles to Suzika. "Let's get this started."

Maurice sat beside me and dealt eight cards each. "What are we playing to?"

"World peace!" Naseem said with a mouthful of

candy.

"Three hundred," Suzika said. "And some common sense for him."

Laughter and bickering continued through the game as Naseem and Suzika disagreed on everything. When Suzika tried to stack a seven, eight, and nine of diamonds on a seven of hearts, Naseem removed the last two cards from the pile. "Get them weak jawns outta here."

"What?"

"We don't play like that."

"Yes, we do." She put them back. "It's stacksies."

"Stacksies is with the same card," he said. "That right there is some other-side-of-Locust-Street crap."

"He's right." As dealer, Maurice made the final decision. "About the stacksies, not the other thing."

Suzika took back her cards. "I'm'a remember that."

And she did when Naseem tried to block her Ace with an Ace of his own.

"Nope." She plucked his card and set it face-down in front of him. "You can't block a Skip."

"That ain't stacksies?"

"Not with a Skip," Maurice said. "How you gonna play a card if you got skipped?"

Naseem shook his head. "That's weak, man."

"I'm having a great time," Suzika said.

Naseem held out his hand. "Gimme back my Skittles."

"It's your turn, babe," I said to Maurice.

"What's that, an ace of diamonds?" he asked.

"You know it," Suzika said. "And if you ain't got none, you gotta eat the deck."

"And on that, we agree," Naseem said.

Maurice frowned at his hand. "I'm kinda stuck."

"Take your time," I said.

Maurice took my words literally, long enough for Naseem to nudge me with an elbow, angling his head toward his cousin.

"Um, Maurice?"

"Yeah, Duch?"

"Do you have any diamonds?"

"Yeah, I have a diamond."

Naseem threw up his hands. "Then what the…"

I silenced him with a look. "Good. Why don't you play it?"

"I would never play this diamond, Duchess." He reached into his pocket. "It's too precious."

I started to reply and noticed the small black velvet box in his hand.

"Yooo…" Naseem said, but I paid him no attention as Maurice dropped to his knees beside me.

"Look at you." He smiled. "So adorably nervous."

"Maurice, what are you…"

"You're all freaked out." He paused, but I couldn't deny it. "Would it help if I said this isn't what it looks like?"

"Yes," I said aloud.

At least, I thought I did.

"Okay. This isn't what it looks like. And this isn't me trying to keep you from going back to Howard tomorrow. But because I can't keep you with me, I'm hoping you'd keep this part of me with you."

He opened the box to reveal a princess-cut diamond solitaire on a white gold band. I gasped with the rest of the room, and he liberated the ring from its cushy nest.

"Daria Corinne Nelson, will you accept my promise ring?" I covered my mouth as my eyes widened, and he tsked. "I'll never hear your answer that way, Duchess."

"Maurice..." I laid my hand against his cheek. "This is...I don't even...you are..."

"She can't even talk!" Naseem crowed.

"Shut up," Suzika whispered. "He puttin' his thing down."

Maurice chuckled, but his gaze never left mine. Looking into his eyes, the fog cleared, and I smiled. "I love you, Maurice McClain. And I would be honored to wear your ring."

"That's my girl." He kissed me soundly, ignoring the cheers from our audience, and I held out my left hand. The ring slid on my finger with ease, and I stared at it in silent wonder.

"Guess he did have a diamond," Naseem said.

Ten

"Let me see it again!" Cherrie cried.

Not wanting to share the news over the phone, I asked the girls to meet me on The Yard Tuesday morning. Bernie took one look at the ring and demanded I call out of work and come to her apartment that night to dish. So far, the dishing was mostly Cherrie squealing.

"I cannot believe…" She trailed off, shaking her hand as she turned my hand this way and that. "This is better than when Canyon called Caprelle and…"

"Cherrie." Bernie poured the frosty chocolate chip mixture from the blender. "Can we have one moment without a side of *Never Ever After*?"

"One episode, B. I guarantee you'd be hooked."

Bernie turned to me. "That's some major hardware,

Sparky."

"Ain't it? The most beautiful ring anyone has ever given anyone ever."

"Although when Rasool proposed to…" Bernie glared at her, and Cherrie closed her mouth. "Never mind."

"But that was different." I said. "This isn't an engagement ring."

"Yeah, I know." Cherrie released my hand. "But how do you feel?"

"I can't describe it. Every time I see it there, I just…"

"I feel the same way, and I'm not even wearing it." Cherrie shivered with delight. "Were you surprised?"

"Completely. One minute we were playing Crazy Eights, and the next I was wearing a diamond."

"Why didn't y'all play Spades?" she asked.

"Be serious." Bernie bobbed a straw in her milkshake. "Can you see Daria playing Spades?"

Cherrie squinted at me. "Good point."

"I resent that," I said.

"But you can't deny it." Cherrie drained her milkshake and glanced at her watch. "Crap. I've got a Philly Club meeting about the pretzel drive. Sure you don't wanna come?"

"I just left Philly. I'm good for a while."

"It wouldn't kill you to get involved with something."

I raised my left hand. "I am involved with something."

"Whatever." She grabbed her bag and blew kisses at Bernie. "Later, B."

"See ya, Squirt." When the door closed behind Cherrie, Bernie came to the couch, placing a bowl of BBQ chips between us. "Now tell me what you haven't shared yet."

I plucked a chip from the bowl. "It was magical, Bernie. Everything he said, everything he did was perfect. And except for Naseem and Suzika visiting Sunday, we were alone in the house the entire time."

"And what was that like?"

"I don't know what you mean."

Bernie slapped my leg. "Don't be coy, heffa!"

My cheeks warmed. "That was nice too."

"You and these adjectives."

"What?" At Bernie's arm folding, I caved. "Okay. Sleeping with Maurice was the…"

"Hold up! You slept with him?"

"Well, I wasn't going to sleep in the guest room, even though he offered."

Bernie laid a hand on her chest. "Good lawd, you scared me."

"You thought we…"

"That's what 'sleeping with Maurice' means. You know, maybe English isn't your best subject. Or that ring kills brain cells." I smiled at my hand again. "Clearly the latter," she said.

"Fine. Sleeping beside Maurice was the most sensual experience of my life. Being cocooned in that huge, soft bed with him right next to me? Bliss."

"And you did that for three straight nights without jumping his bones? Tone and I failed on the second date."

"You and Tone spent the first date—if you can call

it that—grinding at 2K9 for three hours. I'm surprised you didn't do it on the dance floor."

"Yeah, but a whole weekend alone? Your chastity belt must be made of holy titanium."

"It wasn't that difficult. He stayed on his side of the bed Friday night, and Saturday we fell asleep on the couch watching movies."

"And Sunday night, after he gave you that ring?"

I looked away. "That was different. Chaste but so different. We kissed more that night than the first two years of our relationship. Homecoming cannot come fast enough."

Bernie took our empty glasses to the kitchen. "When does he get here?"

"He's meeting me at Meridian that Friday afternoon." I turned to see her putting the dishes in the sink. "What are you doing?"

"What does it look like?"

"Why are you doing that now?"

"I can't tidy up?"

"You use Lysol spray on your mirrors."

She set the clean glasses in the dish drain. "It cleans and deodorizes in one step."

"Lysol is a surface disinfectant that leaves streaks on glass, and you only clean when you're uncomfortable."

Bernie dried her hands and hung the dishtowel on the bar by the sink. "The timing."

"What do you mean?"

"It's not your birthday, not Valentine's Day or Christmas. But he gives you an extravagant gift before Homecoming, and I hope he doesn't expect something in return."

"Something like what?"

Bernie pursed her lips. "Do I need to draw you a picture?"

My mouth dropped open. "That is… wow."

"You asked."

"Maurice gave me this ring so I could keep him with me while we're apart, not as a down payment on future services rendered."

"Okay."

I folded my arms. "I don't like your tone."

"I'm not trying to have a tone. I'm trying to make a point." Bernie retrieved her jewelry box from the chestnut hutch against the far wall, removing a thin, gold necklace with a double-hearted pendant. "Tone gave me this last year before school let out. He was gonna be busy with basketball all summer and couldn't visit, and he wanted me to have a reminder of his feelings."

"I know."

"This is not a diamond ring in a velvet box presented on one knee."

"He was on both knees because we were on the floor playing cards. And velvet and diamonds aside, he said it's a promise ring."

"A promise of what? And who's promising who?"

"It's whom."

"She's correcting my grammar. She must be upset." Bernie returned to the couch. "Sweetie, do you remember how we met? You were on the phone in the trash chute closet arguing with Maurice. Said you were too angry to notice the stench."

"You and Tone don't argue?"

"Not as much as you and Maurice did."

"I admit last year was rough, but we're past it. Doesn't this ring prove that?"

"I hope so." She patted my hands. "I would hate to think he did something so sweet for selfish reasons."

On the walk back to Meridian, Bernie's assessment warred with Maurice's words when he offered me the ring.

Because I can't keep you with me, I was hoping you'd keep this part of me with you.

That didn't sound like bartering. Just a romantic gesture to send me back to Howard right.

Maurice kept asking if I liked the ring, thought it suited me or was too much. Why would he care unless his intentions were pure? He didn't mention Homecoming until our train station farewell. And only after kissing me senseless one last time.

"Two weeks," he said. "I'm already counting the days."

I understood Bernie's concerns. Being a few years older and street-wiser, she fancied herself my big sister and wanted to protect me. Last year's Maurice was insensitive and petty about Howard, so she thought I only agreed to Homecoming to appease him.

But she was wrong. Maurice and I were fine. Though diamond and my new best friend, this ring was a sparkling symbol of love and nothing more. If anything had been promised, Maurice promised to love me better and I promised to let him.

Starting with Homecoming next weekend.

Eleven

The morning of Yardfest, I popped up in bed before six. My heart raced, my fingers tingled, and a goofy smile kissed my face.

Maurice was coming today.

I smothered a scream so as not to wake my neighbors, but my feelings could not be suppressed. Maurice would be here, in my favorite non-Philly place on earth, for three whole days. Giddiness bubbled in my belly, and I shook it off with my covers. My first class was four hours away, but I had no time to waste.

I read my morning devotion during breakfast, adding prayers that Maurice would arrive safely and on time. Washing my bowl and spoon led to cleaning my sink and mirrors and polishing my floors. As they dried to a shine, I reviewed my notes for the Cultural Anthropology exam my killjoy professor insisted on giving today. What sort of treasonous heathen gives a test worth 20% of the final grade during Yardfest?

With my floors done, I stripped my bed and tossed everything into the washing machine. Selecting gray and white pinstripes, I changed my linen and debuted my guest pillow. As I set it on the bed, I envisioned Maurice lying against it, his face inches from mine as we talked or kissed or more.

I paused as memories of Columbus Day filled my mind. Though our activities remained modest, Maurice and I reached a new level of intimacy that weekend. The trust required to sleep beside someone is monumental, and though I never thought Maurice and I would have such a chance, I hoped to replicate it while he was here. But in light of my virginity, how would that work? Did we need rules? Hand signals? Chaperones?

I twisted my ring out of habit, the thought of physical intimacy reminding me of Bernie's concerns. They weren't hers alone, as they underscored my every conversation with Maurice since I left Philly. I wanted to discuss them but feared insulting him and his lovely gift, so I kept my mouth shut and focused on the positive parameters. This weekend was about overcoming our interstate dynamic by including him in my HU life, and the ring was the symbol of that sentiment. I refused to let anything mar it, including lack of a proper name. "Promise ring" invited too many questions, and "love gift" sounded like a folded five in a Baptist offering basket.

For now, I just called it beautiful.

Smiling at its glimmering location on my left hand, I grabbed my bath caddy and headed to my favorite stall, doing so now to avoid the coming chaos. After morning classes ended, everyone and her grandma would flock to the hallway showers before emerging in their official Yardfest attire. No self-respecting Bison attended morning classes all decked out, and though usually above the fracas, I donned my favorite baseball cap and sweats and boarded the 9:30 shuttle. Literary Criticism was tolerable, but Vocabulary Building was downright yawn-inducing. I respected Greek and Latin as much as the next scholar, but not even my charismatic professor could overcome their tedium.

Once I returned to my room, I opened my closet and drawers to finalize this weekend's outfits. With Cherrie's assistance, I chose two options for every possible occasion, including sleepwear qualifying as Victoria's most modest Secret. Today's ensemble came courtesy of Up Against the Wall in Adams Morgan. Though smaller than the Georgia Avenue location, it was close to Meridian and ideal for a last-minute, late-night run. The salesgirl insisted on some ultra-skinny Parasucos, but I declined, selecting fitted patchwork jeans with subtle tears in the thighs and knee. Pairing them with a red Baby Phat half shirt and black ankle boots, I was ready for Yardfest and my afternoon appointment with my boyfriend at five o'clock.

I hopped on the shuttle, self-conscious about my exposed midriff, and met my girls at Freedman's Totem in front of Cramton Auditorium. Cherrie seemed naked without a business-minded clipboard but was otherwise covered as usual. Her black pantsuit and semi-sheer blouse were as chic as her heels were sharp.

"You've never met a stiletto you didn't like, have you?" I asked.

"No, and I see my fashion sense is finally rubbing off on you." She looked at my wedge boots. "How high?"

"Two inches."

"This is a real Kodak moment." She pulled out a camera from her purse. "You'll be doubling that height by next May."

"In your dreams."

"You know Cherrie only dreams about that low-budget soap opera y'all watch," came the reply from behind me.

Cherrie whistled, snapping pictures. "That's how you do it, Miss B!"

With curly blonde locs flowing around her shoulders, Bernie sported a vibrant halter-necked, ankle-length dress with a thigh-high, left-of-center slit. Accenting this heavily-hyphenated ensemble were a faux ruby cocktail ring, an assortment of metallic bangles, and gold thong sandals.

"I think she locked up 'Most Likely to Appear on the Cover of *The Hilltop*,' " Cherrie said. "What say you?"

"I concur." I gave Bernie a hearty round of applause. "Well done."

"That makes you 'Most Likely to Run for Public Office,' " Bernie said to Cherrie.

Cherrie nodded her thanks. "Which leaves…"

Bernie turned to me. " 'Most Likely to be Ravished at Sunset.' "

I turned away with their snickers behind me and headed toward The Yard.

By now it had morphed into party central. A "Homecoming 1999" banner in HU blue and white was draped off Blackburn's balcony as the Fine Arts building advertised an Antebellum Art Collection with its own banner. One noticed the Fine Arts banner as it was behind the stage where this afternoon, the invited celebrity emcee would introduce the first musical acts, mostly new talent hoping to create positive buzz. A semi-famous performer would draw the crowd to the stage before the headlining artist touched down on HU soil.

Until then, Yardfesters found plenty in the way of self-entertainment. Along with admiring or mocking other people's outfits, we clicked flicks with old friends we hadn't seen since Freshman Orientation or made new friends among the hundreds of non-Bison who never missed our Homecoming. Vendors sold everything from handmade jewelry to organic facial cream, and patrons with independent means or their parents' money were eager to purchase quality black-owned products. Nothing happened at Howard without music, so the latest Destiny's Child video played on the Jumbotron near Locke Hall. All in all, Yardfest offered everything a person could want.

"I'm hungry," Bernie said, and with good reason. The offerings were delicious and diverse, and it wasn't unusual for one to scarf curry goat, jambalaya, and collard greens in a few hours and wash it down with a papaya mango smoothie.

Or some Pepto.

To prevent Bernie from gnawing her bracelets, we let her lead us through the labyrinth of savory smells, questionable fashion, and happy reunions. People who never ironed their clothes looked like *Vogue* centerfolds, and professors who never smiled were stepping with their frat brothers. Still others who never wore enough fabric stayed true to themselves.

"She know she wrong," Bernie whispered as we spotted The Chesty Cheetah. Today's ensemble was a zebra-print bustier atop painted-on leather pants. The cute top was two sizes too small, and as she bounced through the crowd, I feared she might put someone's eye out.

"Jiggly Puuuuff," I said, doubling us over in laughter.

Cherrie shook her head. "Y'all need to repent."

After getting three fried seafood platters with all the trimmings, we copped a squat on the Douglass steps and dug in. Cherrie had disposable placemats in her magic bag, and we were the envy of all present when she pulled them out.

"I'm surprised you didn't bring condiments," Bernie said.

Cherrie tossed her some salt and pepper packets. "Nothing worse than under-seasoned food."

We munched in silence, appreciating the mild weather and good vibrations. As I looked over The Yard, I thought about Maurice. He wouldn't see this display today, but that was for the best. Because my being at Howard wasn't about parties and preening. It was about the intangible power released when I arrived at the right place at the right time to do the right thing with the right people.

And if I had my way, Maurice would feel that power this weekend.

After realizing there was no escaping my Cultural Anthropology exam, I made it my business to spend less than a half hour on it. I walked into class at 2:06 and sauntered out at 2:33, resisting the urge to slam the paper on my professor's desk. Before meeting Thing One and Thing Two at the Flagpole, I wanted to check my minimal makeup in the *baño*. But as I walked down the hallway, Mordecai approached with an adorable girl sporting two righteous afro puffs.

"You must be Miss Melody," I said.

She beamed at Mordecai then me. "How did you know?"

"Because your big brother talks about you all the time. He's very proud of you."

"He is?" She stuck out her hand. "Then it's nice to meet you."

"I'm Daria."

"Hi, Daria. I'm…whoa!" She gaped at my ring. "Are you getting married?"

"No." I noticed Mordecai's querulous expression. "It's not that kind of ring. It's a promise ring."

"A promise of what?"

I smiled through my shock. "Love."

"Oh. Your nail polish matches my sweater."

"Thank you. And I have a purple one like that at home."

"Cool!" She turned to her brother. "Can I get some water?"

"Hurry up because we've gotta catch the shuttle."

She ran down the hallway, and Mordecai turned to me. "I hope she didn't embarrass you."

"It's okay. She's not the first to think this ring means more than it does."

Mordecai lifted my hand. "This is serious stonery not to mean anything."

"It means something, just not everything. People give promise rings, and I think it was a nice gesture."

"What's the opposite of hyperbole? Because you have a terrible case of it."

"Shut up." I punched his arm. "Where are you guys heading?"

"Nifty Fifties then *Tarzan* at Pentagon City Mall."

"She doesn't have school today?"

"Her private school is closed every Yardfest Friday. I bet her principal is out there right now."

When Melody returned, the three of us walked toward the Douglass front exit. But my phone buzzed in my pocket, and I wished Mordecai and Melody farewell with a grin. "I didn't expect to hear from you so soon."

"Hey, Duchess. How was your exam?"

"Pretty sure I aced it." I was touched he remembered. "Where are you?"

A fit of coughing interrupted his words. "At The Shop."

"Are you all right?"

"Yeah. I got 'Seem spraying a head on my left, and Suzika lighting incense on the right."

"You better open a window before you suffocate." I

96

glanced at my watch. "Guess you're going to be late."

"Late like tomorrow morning."

I hid my disappointment. Or tried to. "That's okay. Two days is plenty of weekend to burn."

"You sure?"

"Positively."

"Thanks, Duch. I'll be outside Meridian by 8:00 tomorrow. Is that cool?"

I crossed my fingers. "As long as I see you this weekend, it's beyond cool."

TWELVE

After Q-Tip rocked The Yard—which was dope but not the same without Tribe—the girls and I returned to Meridian. Bernie had an extra ticket to the Step Show and insisted I attend. Other HBCUs bragged about their step shows, and their confidence was adorable.

Nobody stepped like a Bison.

Each group had a distinct flavor and flair. One sorority moved with smooth femininity as another channeled an audacious verve making me want to grow a 'fro and raise my right fist. After the sororities hyped us up, the fraternities shut it all down. Stomping and kicking, their masculine energy was at once primal and precise, blending into something uniquely black.

After HU swept the awards, Bernie whisked us

from Constitution Hall to a brownstone a few blocks from the Towers. There was nothing like a good ol' fashioned house party, and this one would go down in history.

I huffed as Bernie readjusted her skirt in the vestibule. "Pink panties for an entrance fee?"

She shrugged. "I'm wearing nude tights under these. He ain't see nuthin."

The rest of the night flowed like mystery punch into red plastic cups. A popular student DJ kept us moving with a tight mix of old and new, East, West, and everywhere else on the map. High off their Step Show victories, the winning BGLOs wound through the throng every few minutes, whooping with increased fervor. And though The Chesty Cheetah's dance floor antics once again stole the show—who breakdances in a mini-skirt?—the only drama involved a dance-off between some Drew Hall freshmen and some women from the Annex. By show of applause, the guys won. But when the ladies started showing and shaking other things, the gentlemen from Drew happily conceded defeat.

Gotta love Homecoming.

Though staying out past two in the morning seemed a fine idea at the time, Saturday's sleep-deprivation headache exposed the folly of my plans. Knowing I would see Maurice in an hour did little to soothe my throbbing head, but it helped me smile through my morning toilette.

After a strong cup of coffee, I let my *Café Latte* soundtrack serenade me as I dressed. Yesterday's warm weather lingered, but Greene Stadium's winds required no less than my thickest HU hoodie. By 6:45, I was dressed and wondering why Maurice hadn't called when he left Philly. My call to Naseem's cell went to voicemail, but that wasn't unusual. I wouldn't be surprised if he left Philly with a dead cell phone and no charger. So I called Maurice, ready to apologize for disturbing him while driving, but he didn't answer.

Not at 6:56 or 7:19 or 7:43.

By 8:07, my churning nerves ignited my appetite. I finished my cereal, wiped the table, washed my dishes, brushed my teeth again, and watched 8:30 come and go without hearing from Maurice.

When my cell phone buzzed ten minutes later, I flipped it open as I came to my feet. "Are you all right?"

"Why wouldn't I be?" Cherrie asked.

I flopped on the bed. "I thought you were Maurice."

"You're not on campus yet?"

"No, I'm in my room. Maurice was supposed to be here at eight, and I haven't heard from him. If I don't leave soon, we won't get good seats."

Cherrie hummed in thought. "Tell him to call you when he's close to campus, and you'll meet him at the flagpole on The Yard. This way, you won't miss each other and Bernie won't catch a case holding our seats."

"Okay. I'll be down in a minute."

I swallowed disappointment when yet another call to Maurice went unanswered but left the message as instructed, grabbing last year's pompoms as an afterthought. The shuttles weren't running because of that parade on Georgia Ave, so Cherrie and I joined the Meridianites hoofing it to campus. Everybody represented HU with their chosen hues, though some revelers were decidedly underdressed.

"White blazers and navy Wonderbras?" I shook my head at a trio of ladies in front of us. "Really?"

"That's Jones New York." Cherrie knew brands like the back of her hand. "At least the quality is good."

Our brisk walk had me sweating, so I unzipped my hoodie as we showed our tickets at the Greene Stadium gate. Rumor had it a Tony Award-winning alum was singing *Lift Ev'ry Voice and Sing* after a local acapella group performed the National Anthem. The newly crowned Mr. and Miss Howard would also take their inaugural walk around the stadium, and the halftime show promised to be the stuff of future legend.

Hopefully Maurice would be here by then.

Our seats were located near the 20-yard line. The view of the field was nice, but any true Bisonette chose her seat based on who sat nearby. In this section, a group of upperclassmen led us in popular cheers like "Do It!" and "What's Goin' On?" to entertain us regardless of the score.

We reached Bernie, and she removed her blanket from the bench. She noticed Maurice wasn't with me but loved me enough not to comment. Tone leaned forward from Bernie's other side, offering cheese fries. "Have none?"

Cherrie declined for us. "Where did you get those at this time of morning?"

"Being an athlete has its perks."

"I hope you have some Tums," Bernie said. "Your stomach is gonna hate you, and I'm not running to Rite Aid."

"You see what I put up with?" Tone shook his head. "It's a wonder I stick around."

"This is why I don't need a relationship," Cherrie said. "I can live vicariously through you people."

"Look!" someone cried. "The Bison are taking the field!"

I checked my phone one last time and tucked it in my pocket, forcing my attention on the team and away from my absentee boyfriend.

Halfway through the second quarter, my headache returned with a vengeance. It may have been the constant cheering because the score was tied. Or the lively rendition of *I'm So Glad I Go to Howard U!* between quarters. Or the nonstop cackling behind me. If I heard "Girl, you know I ain't havin' it!" one more time, I was gonna scream.

I needed a beverage to take my ibuprofen and made a solo trip to the concession stands on the other side of the stadium. The lines were always long, so I told Cherrie to give away my seat if I weren't back in an hour. Besides which, Maurice still hadn't called, and my enthusiasm for the festivities waned with each minute of his absence.

After getting my lemonade, I dug in my pocket for my pills and bumped into someone in front of me.

"Dag, you just gonna plow into me? That's cold, D."

I looked up into the face of my second-favorite Philadelphian. "Naseem?"

"In the flesh." His bear hug suggested it had been years not days since he saw me. "What's up, girl?"

"What are you doing here?"

"I never miss Homecoming. Bet I've been to more of these than you."

"Probably so. But Maurice didn't say you were coming."

"That's because I'm here with my young buls from Forty-Seventh Street. I ain't talked to my cousin since yesterday." He watched my face fall. "What's wrong?"

"He was supposed to be here hours ago, and he's not answering his phone."

"I'd call him, but my battery's dead and I forgot my charger."

That made me smile. "I know what I'm getting you for Christmas."

"That's what Suzika says. Look." Naseem threw his arm around my shoulder. "I'm sorry about my cousin, but I'm here, so we gonna do it up right. Show me the sites, all your hangouts." He wiggled his bushy brows. "Introduce me to some stacked Howard young jawns."

"You dating one of my friends would be borderline incestuous."

"Is that a 'no'?"

"And I appreciate the offer, but I'm going home to wait for Maurice." I hugged Naseem, whispering in his ear. "I don't want to see y'all on the news, so behave."

"I always behave." At my smirk, he laughed. "All right, I got you. But when you hear from my cousin, tell him to call one of the brickheads to let me know what's up."

"The brickheads?" I noticed the boys behind him. "I suppose these would be they?"

"I could listen to you talk all day. But you sure you

103

gonna be all right?

"Yes. Enjoy Homecoming, and I'll have Maurice call you."

It took some convincing, but Naseem finally took his leave, a few brickheads waving in recognition as they departed.

Even without my headache, there was no way I would return to the game now.

ThirtEEn

The walk to Meridian was slow and painful. My body hurt from sweatin' to the oldies last night, but my brain couldn't process Naseem being here without Maurice. I replayed yesterday's conversation over and over again, remembering Maurice's promise to meet me outside Meridian this morning. He wouldn't have lied, so where was he?

Finding nothing on my dorm room's answering machine, I grabbed the phone and dialed The Shop. Maybe there was a work emergency, and he hadn't had time to call me. With that possibility in mind, I hung up after the first ring. I never brought personal business to Maurice's business, and I would not start now.

No matter how worried I was.

But my merciful God wouldn't allow me to suffer too long, and I thanked Him aloud when Maurice's ringtone graced my eager ears a few minutes later.

"Where are you?" I asked by way of greeting.

"Duchess?"

"Maurice?" His scratchy voice brought me up short. "What's wrong?"

"I'm sick. I…" Phlegmy coughing interrupted his reply, and I sat on my bed. "I felt it coming on last night, so I took some Nyquil, and…"

"You know Nyquil makes you comatose."

"But it works, and I wanted to see you." He coughed again. "I'm sorry I missed our weekend."

"I'm sorry you're sick." I looked at the clock. "But Amtrak could get me there in a few hours."

"You've got midterms next week, and I don't want you catching this."

"Is there anything I can do?"

"Yeah. Get up with 'Seem and…crap. You heard from him?"

"I saw him at the game. He's with the brickheads but forgot his charger."

"All right. I'm so sorry about this."

"Don't be. I'll be fine. But listen, throw away that Nyquil and get some generic cold and flu medicine. Do you have orange juice and tissues?"

"Mom is getting that stuff now. She hunted me down when I didn't call her from DC this morning. She had to slap me awake."

"I'll bet she enjoyed that a little."

He laughed and promptly started coughing. "You ain't right."

"Seriously, don't be a hero. Let her take care of you."

"Okay."

"I love you."

"I love you too, Duchess. And I'm…"

"Don't say it again."

"Yes ma'am."

He spoke his parting words with a smile, but mine faded when I hung up. My entire weekend centered on Maurice, and with the girls planning to go salsa dancing with some *amigas* from Bernie's Spanish class, I had no clue what to do tonight besides have a massive tantrum.

But the throbbing in my head solidified my immediate plans, and I turned off my ringers and curled up atop the covers. As I drifted off, I realized I hadn't removed my hoodie.

After a long nap, I rose determined not to let Maurice's absence ruin my weekend. There were any number of available amusements, from the academic to the outrageous. But as I analyzed my options, my dulled but persistent headache convinced me to stay put. Company would be nice in theory, but with no desire to bring in some third-string ringer, my ideal night would soon involve pizza delivery and *Café Latte*.

When I grabbed my binder of alphabetized menus, a commotion in the hallway got my attention. I opened the door to catch a horde of people in sweats and sneakers rushing to the front elevators. A door down the hall was open, and a head popped out to yell, "We're meeting in the park in ten minutes!"

I leaned against my doorjamb. "Is that how an RA should behave?"

Mordecai smiled. "Sorry. Did I disturb you guys?"

"No, and it's just me."

He stepped into the hallway. "What happened to Maurice? I saw the Visitation Requests for this weekend."

"The flu."

"I'm sorry." Someone called him from the other end of the hall, and he waved. "And your girls are busy?"

"Yep."

"So what are you going to do?"

"Pizza and a movie."

"During Homecoming weekend? You'll get expelled. Come with us."

"Who's us?"

"Those rabblerousing Negroes who brought you out of your room and myself. We're playing Capture the Flag across the street in an hour."

"Are you serious?"

"I never joke about recreation. Without it, we'd be savages."

"Yo, Cai!" A cornrowed boy pardoned his interruption, clapping Mordecai on the shoulder. "We need to abolish that whole 'jail' thing, man. I mean, don't we have enough black-on-black crime in these streets?"

"It ain't my fault you kept getting locked up," Mordecai said. "The jail stays."

"For all that, I should've gone to a white school." As I chuckled a second time, the boy smiled. "You coming tonight, beautiful?"

"Thanks." I rubbed my eyes. "But I've got a

headache, so I'm going to stay in and…"

"My bad." He backed up with his hands raised. "I get it. See you at the field, man."

"Why did he leave like that?" I asked when he was out of earshot.

Mordecai pointed at my left hand. "Because you blinded him with diamonds."

"Nice play on words."

"I learned from the best. So you aren't coming?"

"Next time, I promise. Right now, I want to crawl in bed and sleep until Monday."

"And I'll do my best to keep the ruckus to a minimum."

"Thank you."

He saluted me and jogged down the hall. I closed my door to find a spotless room sullied by the disappointment that Maurice wasn't here. We were supposed to start this new season together. Now I faced another lonely weekend with me in DC and him in Philly.

As though never the twain would meet.

Having turned down the best offer I was likely to get, I decided to stop moping and accept my lot. I grabbed my menu binder again and called Pizza Hut, ordering enough food for breakfast and lunch tomorrow. The thought reminded me of my breakfast plans for Maurice, and I picked up my cell phone.

"What a nice surprise," the warm voice answered.

"Hi, Mom McClain. How's your ankle? Maurice said you sprained it last week."

"It's fine, sugar. But you didn't call to talk about my ailments."

This was why I loved her. "Are you still with Maurice?"

"Not that he hasn't tried to kick me out. But my homemade broth has an appointment with his stubborn sore throat, and nothing he says will make me break it."

"I wanted to do something for him, and I would need…"

"Sure, honey. What is it?"

"Could you get him that cheap rainbow sherbet from the supermarket? It's his favorite thing in the world."

"And it would soothe his throat and help bring down his fever." I felt her smile through the phone. "My, my. You're going to make an excellent wife."

"What?"

"Oh, honey. I know you two are nowhere near that stage yet, so don't be alarmed. But you've got a selfless heart, and someday some man will be very lucky to call you his wife."

Mom's words frazzled me such that I barely said goodbye. Maurice never indicated anyone outside of Naseem and Suzika knew about the ring, and they never discussed his private life at work. I didn't think his family knew, but could I believe he hadn't told his mother, a woman who turned water into wine while walking atop the waves? And if he had, wouldn't he have made it clear that this was a promise ring and nothing more?

The house phone rang, and I stared at it in confusion. Could she be calling back to apologize? Could Maurice be calling to see if I was all right? Could Pizza Hut be calling to offer me free dessert because I was so polite when I called?

Probably not that last one.

But I didn't want the call to go to voicemail, so I took a cleansing breath and answered. "Hello?"

"Daria? Wow, hey."

I froze as anxiety deepening to annoyance. "Hi, Dad."

"Did I catch you at a bad time? I thought you'd be out with your friends."

"Not yet. But I do have plans."

"Sure, sure. It's Homecoming at the mecca, right?" He chuckled, his nerves creating strange tension. "How is Cherrie? Is she student body president yet?"

"No, but she'll be here soon, so ..."

"Right. Well, it won't matter now, but *Blazing Saddles* is on TNT tonight."

"Really?" I coughed to rein in my enthusiasm. "TNT, huh?"

"Yeah, which means commercials. So I guess you wouldn't want to record it."

"No, but thanks for telling me."

"You're welcome. Listen, Daria, I know things have been ..."

"Hold on, Bernie!" I called out. "Dad, I'm sorry. The girls are here early."

"Don't let me keep you then. Enjoy your weekend, and be careful, okay?"

"Okay."

"I love you, Daria."

"I know. Bye, Dad."

Not the kindest reply, but it was honest. And that was the best I could do.

With an hour's wait ahead, I grabbed my cleaning supplies and toiletry bin and headed to the hall. Scrubbing the stall would consume fifteen minutes, after which I would shower until the hot water ran out. Or someone banged on the door.

Unwilling to answer any more phone calls, I shuffled downstairs in my flannel pajamas and waited for my pizza. The delivery guy raised a brow at my fuzzy slippers but smiled at the generous tip. I locked my bedroom door without a sound, praying no one disturbed me. After washing my hands and setting my table, I grabbed a YooHoo from the fridge and served myself. As the television found itself tuned to TNT, I set down the remote with a sigh. For someone supposedly living it up in DC, my heart was tied up with the men I left in Philadelphia.

Fourteen

"After everything Sage did for her," Cherrie said. "Paying the car insurance, having her roof patched, taking her spaniel to the vet in the middle of the night, Scarlet wouldn't answer the door? That made no sense."

Dr. Treble leaned against the desk. "Was this poor decision-making on Scarlet's part or faulty characterization by the author?"

"Both." Bernie and Cherrie said together. "I don't know how this book was a bestseller," Cherrie added.

"I take it you don't like the book."

"No!" the class crowed in unison.

"It's all right," Tone said. "Better than that high school pamphlet on STDs."

"Antonio, your comments add such spice to these

discussions." Dr. Treble fought a smile as Bernie rolled her eyes at her boyfriend. "But your annoyance is worth exploring. Why don't we like this book?"

Bernie's hand shot up. "The amnesia. We get that Scarlet can't remember things. But aside from that, there's no tension. It's like, she can't remember anything, and we want to forget everything she says."

"Amnesia is a noun not a plot," I said.

"Well put, Ms. Nelson." I tried to take the compliment in stride, failing when Dr. Treble turned my way. "What do you dislike about the novel?"

"Honestly—and I hope I don't get a demerit on my 'Black Enough Card' for this—I can't stand all that phonetic talk."

"Ugh," Cherrie said beside me. "I know."

"Phonetic talk?" Dr. Treble asked.

"When she remembers her great uncle's farm in Alabama," I said. "All the dropped g's and 'de' instead of 'the.' "

Dr. Treble nodded. "The dialect."

"Yes. I understand how it distinguishes her uncle's voice and establishes him in a certain time and place. But it is so distracting it takes me out of the story."

"Real rap," Bernie said. "By the time I understand him, I've read the section four times and done forgot what was happening in the story."

"You said 'done forgot,' " Dr. Treble said. "We know you meant 'have forgotten,' but 'done forgot' amplifies your feelings. The act of code-switching is telling in and of itself."

"But imagine reading ten pages of me talking like that," Bernie said. "And not just the Ebonics—the Deep

South aspect also. You can't give me with a bunch of apostrophes and expect me to understand."

"Besides the contexts Ms. Nelson mentioned," Dr. Treble said. "Why else might the author have chosen to mark the great uncle's speech this way?"

"To juxtapose his blackness and Scarlet's," Cherrie said.

"Interesting." Dr. Treble said. "Elaborate."

"Scarlet fears not being black enough. Even with the amnesia, her subconscious is full of self-doubt on that point. By contrasting her uncle's dialect with Scarlet's proper English, the author supports Scarlet's self-perception."

Dr. Treble heard me scoff as I scribbled some notes. "You don't agree with Ms. Cummings, Ms. Nelson?"

"I agree with her assessment, and that's what bothers me. I'm sick of this idea that speaking proper English negates blackness."

"It's bad enough when a blonde journalist notes how 'articulate' a black politician or celebrity is," Cherrie said. "But we expect that kind of ignorance from them."

"Do you think they intend to be insulting?" Dr. Treble asked.

"No, and that makes it worse," Bernie said. "They mean it as a compliment, not hearing how surprised they sound or how jacked up their surprise is."

"But to hear it from black folks?" I shook my head. "That is the worst."

"We've internalized their ignorance," Cherrie said. "We believe the lie that proper English and 'real blackness' are mutually exclusive."

"So Ebonics must be our official language," Bernie said.

"Exactly," Cherrie and I said.

Dr. Treble laughed, the sound foreign to my ears. "That was a fascinating exchange. I can tell you three spend a lot of time together.

"You have no idea," Tone muttered.

"Let's get more into Ebonics." Dr. Treble closed her book, and we followed suit. "How does accepting it as a valid dialect confront the controversy in California?"

A collective groan filled the room, and Dr. Treble held up her hands. "Believe me, I feel you."

"I have a question about that." Tone's hand was at half-mast. "Why was it offensive to suggest teaching black students using Ebonics? I get it might be unnecessary or foolish, but offensive?" Bernie's eyes narrowed, and he shrugged. "I'm sorry, B, but if my early teachers had offered to teach me in Spanish, I'd've jumped at the chance."

Bernie formed her fist of frustration, and I decided to intervene. "The difference is the assumption that all black people speak Ebonics at home…"

"Which is false," Bernie said through clenched teeth.

"Plus the underlying assertion that black children couldn't learn otherwise," Cherrie said. "As if Standard English was as foreign to them as German or Hausa."

"Wow." Tone nodded. "That is different."

"Is it?" Dr. Treble asked. "Think of a child in a house in a neighborhood where Ebonics, slang, or other nonstandard English is spoken. If she hears Standard

English only in school, couldn't it be considered a foreign language to her?"

We looked at each other in silence.

"And if the school is in that same neighborhood," she continued, "wouldn't the odds of hearing the local tongue in school increase, furthering that child's indoctrination?"

"Are you saying speaking Ebonics is wrong?" Cherrie asked.

"Or that California was right?" I asked.

"No to both. But there are many black children who are never taught about code-switching or the potential implications of something as divisive and misunderstood as Ebonics. Though the Oakland school board's suggestion was profoundly problematic, we should not ignore the reality they sought to address."

No one responded, and Dr. Treble glanced at the wall clock. "Let's break now. Ten minutes then back to the book."

Cherrie went into the hall, and Bernie joined Tone at his desk, swiping his Snapple before he could take a sip. I smiled at their antics, missing Maurice all over again.

"Ms. Nelson?" Dr. Treble called. "A moment?"

I rose from my seat and approached her desk. She watched me with a not unfriendly eye over the top of her glasses, and I offered a small smile.

Or something close to it.

"I appreciated your honesty today," she said. "*Of Scarlet and Sage* is an acquired taste, and few are they who appreciate it."

"Thanks," I said, though it didn't seem the proper

response.

She picked up her leather satchel, dropping her gaze as she walked her fingers through it. "Have you decided on a field of focus yet?"

"I'm sorry?"

"On your first-day questionnaire, you indicated a lack of post-secondary plans. Has that changed?"

"No."

"And why not?"

"I…I just haven't decided yet."

"Hmm." Dr. Treble was a woman of a thousand hmm's. "I see."

I didn't know what she'd seen, but for the sake of my GPA, I hoped it wasn't me rolling my eyes as she opened a different compartment in her bag. She produced a dark green folder, retrieving a set of papers. Handing them to me facedown, she said, "If you need to use the restroom, you've got seven minutes."

I gaped at the papers to not glare at her, mumbling useless gratitude as I returned to my seat. I stuck the papers in the back of my folder without reading them and exited the room through the back door.

Thanks for nothing, Dr. Trebelenosa.

By the time we finished with Scarlet's mind-numbing memory loss, I had to hoof it to catch the 9:00 shuttle. Thankfully Dr. Treble's class had been moved from Just Hall to Douglass Hall for the rest of the semester, and there was a shuttle stop right behind this building, reducing the odds of me having to walk home. Trekking to Meridian on foot was time-consuming—and not my favorite thing to do alone at night—and I had little of that to spare.

My grades were good: a painstaking review of graded assignments and modest assessment of class participation confirmed it. But I often downshifted after midterms as my focus shifted to end-of-semester projects and earning my way out of final exams. I could handle the tests, but why take them if I didn't have to?

And yes, the sooner I finished, the sooner I'd get home to Maurice.

Without checking Caller ID, I knew he was calling when I reached my room. I wanted to answer the phone, but a potty emergency took precedence. I grabbed my disposable seat covers and headed out my door again.

"I'll call you back in ten," I told the ringing phone.

But ten minutes became thirty as every Meridian female in a three-floor radius invaded the bathroom at once. Though we'd gotten past the awkwardness of sharing seven stalls with a bunch of strangers, pleasantness could be tough to maintain. People were cranky, likely aided by a monthly visitor—it's not sexist if it's true—and when toilet paper ran low, a war almost broke out. Thank God for the girl who brought extra rolls and good incense, the latter saving us from a hazmat situation.

"That's why I don't go to the gym," Maurice said when I finished the story. "I ain't down with public pooping."

My laughter bounced against the walls in my room. "That was rank."

"This is your last year dealing with it, so treat it as a

learning experience."

"Why? You think I'm moving to The Towers?"

"I figured you and your girls would want one of those suites over there."

I thought about the three of us living together. "Now there's a scary idea."

"Here's a better one: Penn has an excellent Resident Life staff that would be…"

"Ha ha." I dug in my bag for the behemoth known as the *Norton Anthology of English Literature*. "I have an idea. Why don't you come down here and read *The Canterbury Tales* for me?"

"Don't they have CliffsNotes for that?"

"Blasphemy!"

"My bad. I miss you, Duchess."

"Me too." As I set *Of Scarlet and Sage* aside, Dr. Treble's rebuke came to mind. "But we might have to talk only on weekends for a while."

"I was only kidding about the CliffsNotes."

"It's not that. This is my busiest season and need to buckle down. And talking to you…"

"Gets in the way."

"Distracts me in the best way. And I want to finish strong so I can skip some finals and come home early for Christmas."

"What about Thanksgiving?"

"Um…" There was no avoiding it. "I'll be home but won't see you."

"Why not?"

My middle fingernail scratched the pad of my thumb. "August."

It took him a moment to connect the dots. "They're

still mad about me taking you out that night?"

"He is. Corina thought it was romantic."

"So he's forbidden you to see me?"

"Not 'forbidden.' Just made clear I wouldn't have time."

"When did he say this?"

"August."

Maurice was quiet, and I let him gather himself.

"It's cool," he said. "It won't be like this for long, so he can have it."

"Are you all right?"

"You know me, Duch. Always on to the next thing. So you go 'head, and I'll call you tomorrow night."

"I have to work, remember? So I'll call you when I'm done. But if I forget, it's because I decided to…"

"It's all good, baby. Do what you gotta do."

I could tell he was trying not to pout. "I love you."

"Look down and to the left. You know how I feel."

I hung up the phone angry at Adrian all over again. He didn't want me anywhere near my boyfriend during Thanksgiving, and he was all the way wrong for that. And though I resented his ridiculous reasoning, the thought of seeing my parents next month reminded me of a problem I hadn't considered.

A shiny, sparkly problem with a white gold band.

Fifteen

Concentrating in the Undergraduate Library was like threading a needle on a rollercoaster. Between the spontaneous fits of laughter and the balls of paper flying by, it was a wonder I'd written anything intelligible.

Happy Friday.

Someone knocked over a chair across the room, so my ringing cell phone went unnoticed. "Mom, I can't talk right now."

"Oh, no. Is that DC mugger roaming Howard's campus?"

"No, and stop eavesdropping on our news. It only upsets you."

"If you can't talk, jump on MSN for a minute."

"Be right there."

After finding a free computer and waiting for the glacial network to connect, I logged on and clicked on Mommy's name. She was already typing.

> *"...totally up to you, but I'd rather have a quiet night at home than brave those crowds. Then again, you might want a home-cooked meal after so many KFC nights. Are you eating all right? Do you need more Dining Dollars?"*

My mother's train of thought ran on several simultaneous tracks, and my ability to follow it was a resume-worthy skill.

> *"Breathe, Mom. You're gonna burn up all the bandwidth, and I haven't answered you yet."*

There was a pause while she likely pursed her lips.

> *"Is this why I sent you to Howard? To learn how to sass your mother? After all those hours I spent in labor, you should be grateful to be here. A lesser woman would have given up after the first 24."*

> *"I was hoping you'd've forgiven me by now."*

> *"Come home early for Thanksgiving, and I'll think about it."*

My spidey senses tingled.

> *"Define 'early.' "*

> *"You're an English major, Daria. Surely you know what 'early' means."*

> *"Now who's being sassy?"*

> *"Couldn't resist. Anyway, since you said Dr. Treble's class is only an hour that Tuesday night, Adrian could pick you up..."*

> *"What? Why would he do that?"*

> *"Because he misses you, Daria, and wants to reconnect on the drive home. I thought it was sweet."*

Sweet as a lemon stuffed with Sour Patch Kids.

> *"Mom, my next class is starting soon. Can we discuss this later?"*

> *"Nothing to discuss. Daddy won't be dissuaded, and he's more stubborn than both of us put together. So you might as well prepare yourself for a nice, long ride."*

I signed off with halfhearted hugs, a palpable foreboding permeating the rest of my day and my shortened stint at Borders. I traded shifts with a coworker who needed Friday night off, so I only had to work three hours tonight. But with Corina's conversation on my mind, I really just wanted to stay home.

At least Bernie and Cherrie's company might make the time pass faster.

"Adrian gets on my nerves." I moped as they looked on. "Who drives home for Thanksgiving when they can afford the train?"

"At least it's not Wednesday night." Cherrie lived on the silver lining. "That oughta save you a few hours in traffic."

"And a nice, long drive?" I grabbed more books from my cart. "That's what Tony says before sending Paulie and Christopher to the Pine Barrens."

Bernie chuckled. "It ain't that bad."

"Bernadette, I will be trapped in a car with a father I've spoken to once since August—and that accidentally—while trying to keep a secret."

"What secret?" Cherrie asked.

I held up my left hand. "My French manicure. He only likes American."

"Crap," Bernie said. "How are you going to explain that?"

"That's easy," Cherrie said. "Tell him you and Maurice are in love, and the ring symbolizes that love."

"Sure! One question: when did Maurice give me this ring?"

"Columbus Day weekend," Cherrie said.

"And how did he do that when I'm in DC, he's in Philly, and we haven't seen each other since the summer?"

Cherrie's mouth dropped open. "Oh."

"Why can't Adrian just let me take the train?" I buried my face in my hands. "I'll be home all weekend and not see Maurice. Isn't that enough?"

"Maybe he just wants to…" Bernie looked up, taking a long whiff. "Cinnamon rolls. I need to handle that."

"Handle one for me!" Cherrie called after her. "Bet you she forgets."

"You know Bernie would choose food over friends any day. Maybe I could bribe Adrian into staying in Philly with a week's worth of cocobread." I looked beyond Cherrie and spotted The Chesty Cheetah lurking across the aisle in Sociology. "And the hits keep coming."

Cherrie followed my gaze. "What's your problem with Imani?"

"Imani?" I barely kept my voice down. "You're on a first-name basis with The Chesty Cheetah?"

"You should stop calling her that," Cherrie said. "And anyway, she's nice."

"I'm so sure." I watched Cherrie's new best friend select a title from the end display. "I hope she puts that back where it belongs."

"Have you ever talked to her?"

I looked at Cherrie like she sprouted a second head with a neon mullet. "After she popped that bubble in Intro to Sociology, why would I?"

"Okay, she did some unfortunate stuff in class. The truth is you don't like her clothing choices and decided she's not worth knowing. Which is not only stupid but judgmental."

Like any card-carrying Christian, I bristled at the j-word. "I don't like how she thrusts her assets in everyone's face. Being more modest would keep people from getting the wrong idea."

"Even if it's the right idea, does that mean she can't be a good person?"

As if her ears burned, The Chesty Cheet—Imani looked over, smiling when she saw Cherrie. My kindhearted friend waved back, and my brain developed a serious cramp.

"As far as Adrian goes, try to be thankful you have a father who worries about you like that. Someone people go their whole lives without that sort of protection."

Sometimes I forgot Cherrie never knew her dad. "I'm sorry."

"I'm not even talking about me, so don't get all sappy. We're all guilty of forgetting how blessed we are sometimes. And once we realize it, we should try to be more grateful."

This was the result of being alone with Cherrie. She cut to the heart of the problem, cleared out the crap, and left nothing but the truth. A powerful asset during emotional crises.

An annoying habit when you didn't want to be exposed.

"I'll be done here in fifteen minutes," I said. "Go make sure Bernie left some rolls for the rest of us."

"Okeydokey." Cherrie grabbed a title with a suggestive cover image. "And I'll catch up on *Thick Hips, Loose Lips*."

I wiggled my eyebrows. "The sequel is better."

"I can't believe you bought that." I shook my head at Bernie as we walked back to Meridian from Columbia Heights. "That book is…"

"Filthy and poorly written," Bernie said. "I knew that five pages in."

"So why did you waste $14.99 on it?" I asked.

"One, I need to figure out why a publisher decided it was ready for print."

"Good question," Cherrie said.

"Two, it represents a new trend in African-American fiction…"

"Ralph Ellison just rolled over in his grave," I said.

"…the kind of books we'll see en masse…"

"And Dr. Treble had a stroke," Cherrie said.

"So I need to prepare myself," Bernie said.

"You are a warrior among women," I said.

Bernie shoved the book into her messenger bag as Tone's ringtone blared from her pocket. She silenced it quickly to our surprise. "I gotta answer his every call?"

Cherrie raised defensive hands. "I didn't say a word."

"Anyway," Bernie said. "If anyone should be reading these books, it's you, D."

"Hush," I said. "Mother Morrison might hear you."

"You're an English major at an HBCU," Cherrie said. "That kinda obligates you to get a well-rounded understanding of our writings, past and present."

"And some urban lit is the truth," Bernie said. "Remember *The Coldest Winter Ever*?"

"You finished that jawn in two days," Cherrie said.

"Yeah, that book was the truth." I led us up the Meridian ramp toward the front doors. "But don't expect me to be reading *Ridin' with Rafeek* anytime soon."

"Hey," Cherrie said. "Isn't that..."

I looked up to see a lone figure push off the wall when our trio came to a halt. My brows knit in confusion, convinced I was dreaming.

But all doubt disappeared when his face was fully in sight, hazel eyes aglow.

"Hey, Duchess."

Sixteen

The four of us stared in a triangulated pattern: Me at Maurice, Maurice at me and the girls, the girls at Maurice and me. No one spoke, though Cherrie was about to take care of that. She was allergic to awkward silences.

"Maurice, what brings you down here?"

"What else?" He smiled at me. "To see my girl."

I felt Cherrie looking at me, but my mouth refused to work.

Not that my brain fared much better.

"I'm Bernadette." She extended a hand. "Bernie, if I like you."

"Nice to meet you, Lady B."

"Lady B? I'm'a have to let that marinate."

He retained his smile. "No problem."

After more silence from me, Cherrie ushered Bernie into the building, wanting her to blend in with the fresh-off-the-shuttle crowd. Once alone, my mind quickened, and I found my voice. "Maurice?"

He lifted me off the ground. "It's me."

Despite my shock, I melted into him like twilight into dusk. "What are you doing here?"

"Cherrie asked me that. Weren't you paying attention?"

"I was distracted."

He grinned. "Still got that effect on you, huh?"

"You always have that effect on me."

"That goes both ways." He took my hands, pressing them to his chest. "I gave you a ring that weekend in Philly, but it's like you put a lasso around my heart. Got me listening to country music in The Shop."

"Are you serious?"

"The fellas say I'm whipped. Suzika thinks it's sweet, and Naseem sings along whether he knows the words or not."

"I can totally see that." I relaxed until I recalled our situation. "Crap."

"What's wrong?"

"We might have a problem with you being here this weekend."

"You got a big test or something?"

"No. But we have to give notice for overnight guests, remember?"

"Can't they use my approval from Homecoming? It's still me, just a week later."

"It doesn't work that way." I paced in front of the

door. "And I don't know what to do now."

"I could stay in a hotel or…"

"Let me see if I can figure something out. Stay here."

He nodded, though his heart wasn't in it. "I'm sorry."

"Don't be." I touched his cheek. "I'm glad you're here."

"Me too." Our gazes locked, and I forced myself to remember my errand. "Okay, I'm going."

Lord, I hope it's not wrong to pray about this, but please make a way for Maurice to stay this weekend. It was so sweet of him to come, and I'd hate for it to get ruined. And I promise to be a virgin when he leaves.

Where did that come from? Of course, I'd still be a virgin. Though I'm open to expanding my boundaries a little …

Fantasize about making out right after you pray. Real holy, Daria.

I found Mordecai behind the Meridian front desk. He waved me forward when the crowd dissipated. "What's wrong?"

I leaned on the counter. "I've got a beautiful problem."

"Those are the worst kind. Talk to me."

I explained my predicament, noting I was delaying the inevitable. "There's no way to get him in for a whole weekend," I said. "And I have no idea how to tell him."

"Where is he?"

"Outside. Waiting for a miracle."

Mordecai tapped his pen against the desk. "Hold on."

132

He disappeared into the back office, and I waited, having no idea why. I watched the wall clock above the mail slots, the second hand as good a distraction as any. Six full rotations later, with the Dorm Director behind him, Mordecai emerged from the back office. Though he smiled, his irate supervisor did not.

"Ms. Nelson, Mr. Hill says he misplaced your Visitation Request Form and never filed it." She glared at him. "Your guest is here?"

"Yes." I couldn't look at Mordecai. "He's outside."

"Then we have to let him in." She muttered something about absentminded RAs. "Does he have proper ID?"

"Yes. And he's not a drunk or drug dealer." They looked at me, though Mordecai was the only one poised to laugh. "I thought you'd want to know."

"I'm sure we're all relieved to hear that." She turned on heel, calling over her shoulder. "Mr. Hill, I'm not quite through with you."

He shrugged with another grin, waving off my mouthed thanks as he followed his boss. I skipped out to retrieve my man, who relaxed upon seeing my face. "We good?"

I motioned him inside. "We're good."

The third floor RA signed Maurice in, smiling at him more than was professionally necessary. I was used to female interest in Maurice but not in my own house.

"Thank you." My stern voice startled her. "If you need us, we'll be upstairs."

"Okay." She filed our IDs in the weekend visitation container. "Make sure he never leaves the dorm without you."

"Never that." Maurice laced our fingers together as the inner doors buzzed. "Wouldn't leave her for a second."

We boarded the empty elevator which provided ideal acoustics for my rant.

"Did she not see the ring?" I leaned against the metal hand bar as the doors closed. "For goodness' sake, have some pride before you sit there and…"

My feisty monologue was interrupted by Maurice's lips on mine. That silly girl fell away with the rest of the world, and I locked my fingers around his neck until the elevator chimed at the fourth floor.

"Better?" he murmured against my mouth.

"Much." We stepped off the elevator hand-in-hand. "And, uh, welcome to Howard."

"I'm sorry I missed Homecoming and didn't tell you I was coming today. But I hope to make all of that up to you this weekend."

His words worried more than warmed me, but I faked a smile. All the courage I'd summoned for last weekend had long since dissipated, and having Maurice all to myself in my suddenly-not-so-large room had my inner self hitting the panic button like a carnival kid at whack-a-mole.

"You all right?" he asked.

"Yeah. I was just thinking…"

"There you are!" Cherrie rounded the corner with Bernie in tow, the latter shooting lukewarm glances at my beau. "We went ahead and ordered two pizzas like we planned, but in light of your surprise"—she smiled at Maurice—"you guys can keep one. Is that cool?"

God bless Cherrie's quick thinking. "Perfect."

"And since you rushed to catch the shuttle this morning," she continued, "I figured Maurice could wait with us downstairs while you tidy up your room."

I turned to him. "Do you mind?"

" 'Course not." He caressed my fingers. "I wouldn't want to see your unmentionables or anything."

My face flamed, and Bernie snorted. "I assume you mean her Oxford English Dictionary."

Maurice grinned. "Of course."

"He'll be gone less than an hour." Cherrie pushed the button on the elevator. "So don't break out the buffing machine."

"Just keep him away from the sign-in desk," I said. "Some hungry heffa had her eye on him."

"As long as he keeps his eyes to himself, ain't no problem." Bernie looked him up and down. "Right?"

"Yes, ma'am." As the doors opened, he swiped his hands across his eyes. "Take these."

I caught the imaginary eyes in midair as Bernie nodded. "I'm starting to like him, D."

"Well, I love him, so be nice."

She stuck out her tongue as the elevator door closed, and I sprinted down the hall.

Though Cherrie created a fictional mess in my room, she knew I needed time to get myself together. It took two weeks to prepare for last week's non-visit; now I had mere minutes?

I closed my eyes and inhaled through my nose, feeling my lungs expand to the point of discomfort. Counting backwards from ten on the exhale, I felt the calm return. This was Maurice and me. We survived a weekend at his place without incident, so being together in my room was no different.

Except for the vast reduction in square footage and sleeping space.

But I could handle this. I had to. Maurice was downstairs, and that alone was an accomplishment. Last year it would have taken an Act of God for him to acknowledge Howard, let alone spend a weekend on campus. This was a good thing, an exceeding-above-anything-I-could-ask-or-think thing. And if I remembered that, I would be fine.

I turned on WHUR and changed my sheets as Eric Benet vowed to spend his life with Tamia. The romantic track was the perfect complement to my mood, and I hummed along with a happy heart. I dust mopped my floors, cleaned the mirrors, and set out a towel and washcloth for Maurice. After rewriting my weekend's to-do list, I had eighteen minutes to shower and slip into something more comfortable.

I'd always wanted to say that.

Fresh and dressed, I'd just finished setting my dinette table when there was a knock at the door. A pleasant shot of adrenaline coursed through my veins, and I gasped aloud. With one last glance in the full-length mirror, I went to answer the door.

"Who is it?" I asked sweetly.

"Who else?" he said. "Let me in, Duchess."

I threw open the door, grinning like a loon. "Hi there."

Maurice's mouth fell open, but there was no sound. His gaze traveled down my body, taking in my strappy tank and pajama shorts. "I hope you don't always answer the door like that."

I took the pizza box. "Never."

He whistled as I turned to set the box on the table, closing the door behind him. "Yooo ... when did you buy this?"

"After you gave me this." I held up my left hand. "I wanted to surprise you when you came down for Homecom—"

Maurice finished my thoughts with another kiss, and I forgot all about the pizza. His hands were around my waist, pulling me closer. Heads tilting, we deepened the kiss as though months not minutes had passed since the last one.

When we came up for air, Maurice gave me a sheepish smile. "I'm sorry I keep cutting you off. I just...I missed you. And I hope that's okay."

"Not okay." I stood on tiptoe to kiss him again. "It's perfect."

SEVENTEEN

I awoke this morning swaddled in warmth. Our arms and legs were entwined, and despite my innate shyness, I was surprisingly comfortable with our intimate position. Owing in no small part, I'm sure, to the absence of a certain morning male phenomenon.

I would still be red-faced had I experienced that.

After a quick breakfast, Maurice and I hit the road so I could give him the long-awaited tour of main campus. We started with Burr Gym and took the narrow path beside Cook Hall, where I pointed out Tone's window with the Transformers curtains.

"I might need to cop a set of those myself," Maurice said.

"And this is Greene Stadium where we slaughtered

the other HU in the Homecoming Game last weekend." We only won by a miraculous field goal, but he didn't need to know that. "This is also where last year's seniors pulled their prank."

"What did they do?"

"Bernie said I wasn't old enough to know."

As we crossed the street and passed Cramton Auditorium, Maurice snapped his fingers in recognition. "Isn't this where that big-haired actress with the weird name got booed off the stage?"

"Sort of. During a sneak peek of her last movie, half the crowd walked out and the remaining students jeered so much they had to turn off the film."

"Didn't she graduate from here?"

"Alumni means nothing without your A-game."

I pointed out Ira Aldridge Theater and the side entrance to Douglass Hall where most of my classes were held. We paused to appreciate a quartet of Fine Arts students who burst into harmonic song on their way into Childers Hall, and after a few steps forward, I came to a stop.

"And this." I stopped short of placing a hand atop my heart in reverence. "Is The Yard."

This was the moment I had waited for since first day freshman year: Standing hand-in-hand with Maurice on The Yard on a mild autumn morning as the trees offered a kaleidoscope of reds and golds against a perfect blue sky. Thanking God on the inhale, I closed my eyes to savor the memory, tucking it away somewhere safe.

"What's next?" Maurice roused me from worship, confused by my incredulity. "What?"

"What do you think?"

"About what?"

"About this." I indicated the bounty before him. "Don't you feel that?"

The lines in his forehead deepened. "The breeze?"

"Never mind."

"Wait." He grabbed my hand, preventing me from pulling ahead. "I'm trying to get it. The atmosphere, the legacy…I'm trying. But you know what I feel more than anything else?"

"Bored?"

"Proud of you."

I rolled my eyes, but my lips curled up anyway. "You're just saying that to hurry us along."

"I mean it. I know what it took to defy your father and come here based on a feeling, and I know I haven't made it easy. But you did it anyway. How could I be anything but proud?"

I grinned. "Then let's head to the bookstore and get you a T-shirt to show off your Bison pride."

Opening at the end of last year, the airy two-storied building still enjoyed much of its initial novelty and was a favorite student hangout spot. I found a "Someone I Love Goes to Howard University" tee on a rack and clapped my hands. "Gray, black, or blue?"

"I am not wearing that."

I showed my ring. "If I can wear this, you can wear a shirt."

"You're comparing a one-and-a-half-carat diamond with a Howard t-shirt?"

I fished out a blue one in his size. "But it's tagless."

He took the shirt with a shake of his head. "The

140

things I do for love."

"You'll need a hat too."

Speeding off alone, I headed toward the hats and got distracted by the New Books display. Despite working at Borders, I couldn't remember the last book I read for pleasure. Some titles looked promising, and I grabbed a few, reading their back blurbs.

"One of these days you're going to turn into a literary opus about country music and conjunctions."

"And you shouldn't quit your day job." I smiled at Mordecai. "Comedy is not your forte."

"You wound me, Ms. Nelson."

I set the books back in their place. "Thanks again for last night. Did you get in trouble?"

"Nothing I couldn't handle. After the first ten minutes of yelling, you tune her out."

"Still, thank you. We would have been stuck if you hadn't done that."

"Done what?"

Maurice's voice startled me. "Hey, you," I said.

"Hey, yourself." He looked at the book display where Mordecai stood. "This doesn't look like a hat stand."

"You must be Maurice." Mordecai extended a hand. "Good to meet you, man."

Maurice shook his hand. "I would say the same, but I don't know who you are."

"This is Mordecai," I said. "My RA. I was thanking him for risking his job to get you in last night."

"She's exaggerating," Mordecai said. "It was no big deal."

"It's a big deal to us." Maurice slid a hand around

my waist. "Any time I get with my lady is precious. I appreciate you making it happen."

Mordecai smiled. "Whatever I can do, you know?"

"Yeah, I know," Maurice said.

"What brings you in here?" I asked Mordecai.

"There's this book I saw about…"

"Duchess, we gotta go if we're gonna have lunch before the show."

I glanced at my watch. "Crap, you're right."

"What movie are you seeing?" Mordecai asked.

"It's a musical at Arena Stage," Maurice said. "After an early lunch in Dupont Circle."

"Enjoy." Mordecai picked up another book. "I'll see you around."

"I'm sure you will," Maurice said.

After the show, Maurice lay against my bed pillows watching television. We'd been back about an hour, and I was sneaking in some Brit Lit in preparation for Tuesday's test.

"I don't like him," he said.

I glanced at the screen. "It's un-American not to like Will Smith."

"Not him. West always respects West."

"Then who?"

"The bul from the bookstore."

"The bul from…Mordecai?" The last word came out on a laugh, and I faced Maurice when he didn't return my humor. "You're serious?"

"He's too familiar. Talking about some 'Whatever I

can do.' "

"He's an RA. That's their motto."

"Yeah, well, he needs to find somebody else to do it for. Where you know him from anyway?"

"He lived here last year. I used to see him on the shuttle or in the lounge, and we'd talk sometimes."

"About what?"

"I don't know. Classes, dorm drama, life."

"He know about me?"

"Obviously."

He snorted. "I still don't like him."

"Obviously."

He came over to the desk, leaning over my shoulder. "What are you reading instead of making me feel better?"

"William Wordsworth's 'Lines Composed a Few Miles above Tinturn Abbey.' Its pseudo-religious overtones make it a seminal work in his canon."

"Uh-huh. And you need this in your life because…"

"My professor says so." I marked the page and reached for my Dr. Treble folder. "On to the next thing."

Maurice lifted the folder out of reach. "You've done enough for one day."

"Give it!" I stood on tiptoe, barely reaching his wrist. "Why are you so much bigger than me?"

"It was part of God's plan to keep you from being too serious."

"Here's to His mysterious ways." I walked my fingers beneath his armpit, and he yelped and dropped the folder, spilling its contents all over the floor. "It's an English miracle!"

As we bent to pick up the papers, Maurice read one

with a frown. "You're thinking about studying abroad?"

I rearranged the handouts in chronological order. "I've got enough to do on this continent, thanks."

"Then what's this?"

I took the paper he'd been holding, stunned to discover it was an application for the junior year Study Abroad program, punctuated by a handwritten note encouraging me to think about it.

"Dr. Treble gave me this a few days ago, but I never looked at it."

"Let's pretend you didn't." Maurice laid the paper face-down on the desk. "If Adrian didn't want you in DC, Barcelona is out."

"Paris."

"What?"

"I would go to Paris." I thought of Josephine Baker and James Baldwin, imagining a place amid their regal ranks. "Corina would vote in my favor and wear down my dad."

"Maybe." Maurice took my hands and brought me to my feet. "But if it's Paris you want, we could honeymoon there. It's in my top five."

"Honeymoon? You've thought about that?"

He leaned in. "Every night."

"Not like that." I swatted his arm, and he laughed. "I mean, where we'd go."

"The Caribbean is a prime choice, if only to see you in a bikini. Then I thought of Mexico so I could hear you roll your r's when you talk. Paris is a given because it's romantic, and Vegas."

"Vegas?"

"A city fueled by luck. And someday when I take

you on our honeymoon." He kissed the tip of my nose. "I'll be the luckiest man on earth."

A dreamy smile ghosted across my face before Maurice kissed me. He began gently, a promise of more to come, and his arms enveloped my waist. Though already warm, I shivered as his hands slid up my back. As I stood on tiptoe to snuggle closer, Maurice walked us backwards to the bed. The moment he stopped moving, I realized where we were and broke our kiss, looking down.

"Don't hide, Duchess." His whisper prompted me to look up. "It's just me."

I studied his eyes and saw in them a reflection of my own budding feelings. This didn't have to be different than any other time we kissed and only would be weird if I let my fears get in the way.

I stepped around him and sat on the edge of my bed. Focusing on his face, I scooted backward, resting on my forearms to stay upright. Understanding lighted his eyes, and he leaned forward, placing a knee outside my leg. Cupping my cheek, he brought our lips together. With his hips askew, he lowered his body, bracing with one hand so only our lips were touching. Maurice had the size and positional advantage, but I knew he was letting me set the pace. And I was grateful for the reins.

As his lips continued their patient work, I slid my hand up his chest to his shoulder, bringing him closer. With every inhale, my chest pressed into his, sending unprecedented tingles across my skin. With every exhale, our breaths mingled such that I couldn't tell them apart. We were one heartbeat with one agenda: enjoying this rare time alone.

His mouth left mine to trail light, open-mouthed kisses across my jawline as he made his way to my throat. His modest mustache brushed against my neck, and I giggled, clamping my mouth shut as he raised head and brow in curiosity.

"Is something funny?" he asked.

"It tickles."

"Does this?"

He attacked my neck with a playful growl, causing more laughter than lust. I pushed him off of me, but he held on to my waist, rolling me on top of him. The change in position halted my humor, and I stared at him with wild eyes.

"Do you trust me?" he asked.

"Yes. But I don't know what to…"

"The only thing you have to do is be here with me." His hooded gaze dropped to my lips. "Just be here, Duchess."

He leaned up and kissed me again, softer, gentler than before. As I relaxed, his hands slid down my back and over my backside to grab my thigh. He pulled it forward, parting my legs, and with a shift of his hips, I was straddling him.

Holy Noodleroni.

"It's okay," he murmured against my mouth. "Just be here."

But that was the problem. I was here, and he was there, and we were together, and that was all I could think about. The here of it all.

"Maurice…"

"It's okay." He rolled me onto my back again. "This is better."

146

His lips found my jawline, and I wrapped my arms around his neck, determined not to be self-conscious. I trusted Maurice, even though I was nervous, and I didn't want to ruin our weekend with doubts. I brought his face back to mine and kissed him, enjoying his sigh of satisfaction. He slipped a hand beneath my shirt, and I deepened our kiss in response. His warm palm rested against my bare torso, and I became aware of the precious inches between his pinky and my bustline. The thought of him touching me there tantalized and terrified me, and the confusing combination caused me to sit up. "Wait."

His eyes slowly opened. "What is it?"

I laid a hand on his chest. "We need to stop."

"What's wrong?"

"Nothing's wrong." I emphasized the word as I fixed my shirt. "I just think we should stop."

He ran a hand down his face, hiding his immediate reaction. When he didn't respond, I tucked my legs beneath me, shaking my head. "This is what I was afraid of."

"Afraid?" He glanced at me. "You're afraid I was going to…"

"No. I just…this is awkward."

"We're adults, Daria." His use of my full name got my attention. "We should be able to talk about anything."

"You're right." I steeled myself and faced him. "I want you and trust you, but I don't want to cross a line now that I'll back away from later."

"Oh." He folded his hands in his lap. "I get it."

"Do you? I know you gave me the ring after I asked

147

you to come here, but now you're here and I'm wearing it. And I know that makes everything different."

"Is different bad?"

"No, but different matters." I reached for his hand, covering it with my own. "I love you, Maurice, and I like spending time alone with you. But I don't think this is a good idea, and I hope asking you here didn't lead you to believe otherwise."

Though tempted to further explain, I held my peace, trusting him to understand. I thought Bernie was wrong about Maurice's agenda this weekend, but the longer he remained mum, the greater the possibility loomed in my mind.

"You're right," he said eventually.

"Really?"

"Yeah. My loins strongly disagree." He kissed the back of my hand. "But every other part knows you're right." At my silence, he frowned. "What's up with your face?"

My lips were clamped together, fighting a smile. "Loins?"

"It's better than the word I was going to use."

"You're terrible."

"But you love me." He pulled me onto his lap, and I settled into his arms as he kissed my temple. "And that's what matters."

We sat in easy silence, and I glanced at the clock. "What do we do now?"

"I would suggest *Café Latte*, but that boardroom scene would be too much for me and my loins right now."

I glanced at the window. "You feel like taking

another walk?"

"Where?"

"My favorite DC place other than The Yard." I came to my feet. "Adams Morgan."

EighteEn

Having overcome the sexual awkwardness, Maurice and I took to the streets in high spirits. We walked all through Eighteenth Street and U Street, holding hands and counting the number of boozed-and-buzzed street dancers. On the way back, we popped into Tryst for quesadillas and nachos, catching the final set of a local jazz band. After showering and changing (in different stalls, of course), we tumbled into bed, snoring within minutes.

The next morning, I awoke to find Maurice perched on the edge of my bed, a hand pressed to his forehead while the other held his phone to his ear.

"Yeah, I'm getting dressed now ... An hour and a half if I gun it. How far are you from...Well, could you do that later? Thanks."

By now, I was upright in bed. "What's wrong?"

"There was an incident at The Shop."

"When?"

"I don't know." He crossed the room to grab his boots. "Suzika was running late this morning, and when she got there, the front window was broken. When she went inside, the place was trashed."

"Is there anything I can do?"

"Just this." He leaned in and kissed me, and I didn't have time to worry about morning breath. I scooted forward and he pulled me onto his lap, wrapping his arms around my back. All too soon, he pulled back with a groan. "You keep that up, and I won't leave until tomorrow."

"Would that be so bad?" Watching him grab his things messed with my insides, leaving me bereft. "At least get some breakfast before you go. I've got cereal, Pop Tarts, oatmeal…."

"You're adorable." He zipped his bag, noting my sad eyes. "I hate this as much as you, Duchess. Maybe more. But I gotta go take care of business."

I forced a smile. "Let me get dressed so I can sign you out."

Mordecai wasn't at the front desk, but neither was our flirty foe from Friday night, so the process was quick and conversation-free. Maurice set down his bag, and I jumped into his arms.

"I had the best time with you," he whispered into my neck. "Thank you for sharing your world with me."

"Thank you for wanting to see it." I squeezed him tighter. "That means everything."

"You mean everything." He met my eyes. "I love you, Daria."

My face crumbled, and he kissed me, ignoring the stupid moisture on my cheeks. I had officially become *that girl*, the one who cries when her boyfriend leaves town.

He swiped my tears with his thumb. "And somehow we'll make it work for Thanksgiving, okay?"

"Okay."

"So can I get a giggle?"

A soggy chuckle was my first reply. "You can get a giggle."

"How much for two?"

"A moogle and a boo. Because I love you."

"That goes for me too." He held my gaze. "You and only you."

He kissed my forehead, cheeks, and the tip of my nose.

"Drive safely."

"I will." And with a peck to my lips, he walked out of the double doors.

I don't know how long I stood there, but when I heard the shuttle arrive outside, I turned to go upstairs. My Sunday plans were shot, but there was no shame in spending the rest of the day clutching his pillow and watching *Café Latte* on repeat. No shame and a whole lot of sense.

As the elevator doors opened on the main floor, Cherrie rushed out in sweats and on her phone. The sight of her so casually dressed alarmed me enough to wipe my face and follow her to the lobby. When she stopped beside a chair to dig in her purse, I tapped her shoulder.

"Where are you going?"

She ended her call, startled. "CVS."

I nodded in understanding: Girls only hoofed it to CVS first thing in the morning for one reason. Cherrie was private about such things, so I didn't ask if she wanted to raid my considerable supply. "I'll come too."

"Why aren't you upstairs with Maurice?" she asked.

"He left."

Her eyes widened as we went outside. "Did something happen?"

"Somebody vandalized The Shop." Maurice's car was already gone, and I swallowed my sadness as we passed its former parking spot. "So he had to go home."

"That stinks. But how was your weekend otherwise?"

"No."

"That's not a grammatically salient response, Ms. English Major."

"I'm saying 'No' because I want to talk about you for a change."

Cherrie shrugged. "Nothing much to tell."

"We're college sophomores at the premier HBCU in the world. There is always something to tell."

Cherrie laughed. "Touché. Let's see."

For someone who had nothing much to tell, there was a lot going on in Cherrieville.

First up was her strong consideration of adding a second subject to her already demanding biology major. With all her extracurricular activities on and around campus, she found her dreams of being a doctor strongly challenged by a social justice component.

"It's one thing to get my MD," she said. "But quite

153

another to have the multi-disciplinary background to use that degree where it's most needed."

"Let me find out you're going to quadruple major."

She laughed as we crossed the street. "I know. I'm crazy."

Next we discussed the drama in the Philly Club, and I chose not to mention that the infighting was why I'd declined to join. The chattiest person never did any of the real work but thought her perspective was valid.

"I was all for the Krispy Kreme drive because there's no way to get that many Tastykakes down here without busting the budget," she said. "But this one chick wanted to use the proceeds to charter a bus to Freaknik. And of course she had all this support from the other dumb young jawns in the group."

"A soft-core trip to Hotlanta with your name attached to it? That is so not going to happen."

"And they need to understand that with the quickness."

"How are Momma and GiGi?"

"Two peas in a crazy pod. Last night, Momma signed up for Tai Kwon Do at the Mt. Airy Learning Tree. I asked where GiGi was, and she said, 'Her happy place.' "

"GiGi loves that gun range."

"Let's pray that basement arsenal remains a pipe dream." Cherrie held the door for a woman with a stroller leaving CVS. "Enough about me. How was your weekend with Maurice before he left?"

My smile was immediate. "Wonderful. Amazing. Fantastic."

"Tell me how you really feel."

"He let me take him around campus. We walked Adams Morgan, saw a play at Arena Stage…"

"And slept in the same tiny bed."

"Why you say it like that?"

"Just to see your face to do that. Anything I need to know?"

I started to answer her question until I noticed which aisle we were in. "Um, Cherrie?"

"Yeah?"

"You want to tell me why you're buying a pregnancy test?"

Cherrie turned and met my gaze. "It's not for me."

Bernie was pacing her studio floor when Cherrie and I arrived, her locs in a sloppy ponytail. "Why aren't you cuddled somewhere with Maurice?" she asked.

I closed the door behind me. "I got a better offer."

"That's crap, and you know it."

"He had to make an impromptu return to Philly," I said. "Shop trouble."

"Bummer." Bernie grabbed the bag from Cherrie and peeked inside. "Where are my Reese's Pieces?"

Cherrie snapped her fingers. "I knew I forgot something."

Bernie rolled her eyes and walked down the short hall. "Good help is so hard to find."

"We'll get you some," Cherrie called out as the bathroom door slammed. "Or not."

Cherrie and I sat in Bernie's mismatched chairs, looking around. There was nothing to say or do but wait for Bernie to come back out.

And do so quietly to avoid her potential wrath.

"Do you think she's okay?" Cherrie whispered.

"I don't know, but I'm not going back there to find out."

"If any of us should go, it's you."

"Why me?" I leaned forward. "You met her first."

"Yeah, but she calls you first whenever she needs something."

"Not today."

"We thought you were busy!"

"You two can't whisper for crap." Bernie emerged from the bathroom. "And I didn't need help peeing on a stick." She flopped on the couch, training her gaze on me. "Any problems this weekend?"

It would be easy to deflect, but she needed a distraction. "There was some weirdness with Mordecai at the bookstore."

"You didn't tell me that," Cherrie said. "What happened?"

"Maurice made something out of nothing, that's what happened." I unzipped my jacket. "He doesn't trust Mordecai."

"Mordecai's a puppy," Bernie said. "I wanna pinch his cheeks and give him treats."

"Why doesn't Maurice trust him?" Cherrie asked.

"I have no idea," I said. "Mordecai risked his job so Maurice could stay this weekend, but that didn't make things better."

Bernie snorted. "Isn't it obvious? Maurice doesn't trust Mordecai because he's a guy who lives in your building and sees you more than your boyfriend does."

"So he's jealous?" Cherrie laid a hand over her heart. "That is so sweet."

"And stupid. He should spend less time worrying about Mordecai and more time keeping things smooth." Bernie leaned forward. "Anything else?"

I shook my head. "Nope."

"Good." The timer dinged in the bathroom, and Bernie's eyes widened before she recovered. "If you'll excuse me."

I came to my feet. "Do you want us to come with you?"

"I know where the bathroom is."

As Bernie walked through the valley of the shadow of maternity, Cherrie and I grabbed hands, praying God would have mercy on our fearless friend. And us by extension.

Bernie pushed open her bathroom door and disappeared inside. We heard a loud gasp, and she ran out of there with frantic eyes. "I don't believe it. I don't believe it!"

"Oh my god!" Cherrie's gaze darted between me and Bernie. "Does this mean…"

"Here." Bernie shoved a wad of cash in Cherrie's hand. "Get three more, all different brands. I won't believe anything until you do."

"Bernadette." Cherrie covered Bernie's hands. "I know you must be scared, but an unexpected pregnancy doesn't have to…"

"Pregnancy?" Bernie cried. "What are you talking about?"

My voice recovered. "Wasn't the test positive?"

"No." Cherrie and I released a heavy breath as

Bernie kept talking. "But I need confirmation in triplicate. So get three more tests. If they're all negative, I'll relax." When we didn't move, Bernie put her hands on her hips. "Do I need to try that again in Philly slang?"

Cherrie and I blinked to life and headed to Bernie's front door. As I passed her, Bernie grabbed my arm. "I'm glad things went well with you and Maurice, but listen to me very carefully. Don't have sex. With anyone. Ever!"

"Okay."

"Or at least until you're 21. Or married. Whichever comes first."

"Okay."

"Now go." She shoved me out the door. "And don't forget my candy!"

NinEtEEn

Five hours, four negative results, and three packages of Reese's Pieces later, Bernie accepted the truth. She tossed out the used tests with the garbage, swearing us to silence. By the time Cherrie and I returned to Meridian, it was well after dark. With a weary wave goodbye, Cherrie continued on the elevator to the seventh floor, and I trudged to my room where Brit Lit homework and an unmade bed awaited.

But no messages from Maurice.

Monday's calls to his house and cell went unanswered and unreturned, so I figured things at The Shop were worse than we thought. Tuesday, Maurice didn't call to walk me home from work, and that was of concern. It was only on the third day I finally heard from someone and not the person I expected.

"Naseem?" I stopped to answer his call on the Douglass steps. "What's going on up there?"

"Whatchu mean?"

"Didn't you see my missed calls?"

"Naw cuz Suzika was drawin. She took my phone Sunday cuz I left it in The Shop. Just gave it back to me this morning."

"I'm liking Suzika more and more. Wait. The Shop was open yesterday?"

"Every day except Mondays."

I set my bag on the ground. "What about the break-in?"

"What break-in?"

"The one Sunday morning."

"Oh, when them knuckleheaded young buls from Spruce Street threw some rocks through the door? That was nothing."

I rubbed my forehead. "So nobody stole anything?"

"Just Suzika's candy stash and some *Vibe* magazines. I can't even be mad at that Nia Long one though." He let out a long whistle. "Shorty is phyne."

Cherrie appeared beside me, tapping her watch face, and I nodded. "I gotta go, 'Seem."

"A'ight," he said. "And don't worry. The Shop is fine, busier than ever."

"Guess I misunderstood what happened."

"Or Suzika exaggerated. People who hold other people's phones hostage do that. She play too much."

"Take it easy, Naseem."

"I'm'a do my best. See you, D."

After Naseem hung up, I was tempted to call

160

Maurice and straighten out my confusion. But there was no time with my presentation waiting.

As Dr. Treble entered the room, I settled in my seat and realized Bernie wasn't here. I glanced at Cherrie, and she shrugged. Bernie never skipped class, but after the near-miss this weekend, today would make a logical exception.

"Definitive Black Speeches," Dr. Treble began. "Three powerful words that when combined could mean any number of interesting things. Last year's class enjoyed this project, so I cannot wait to hear your choices. Mr. Torres, set up the A/V equipment, please."

As Tone busied himself with the VCR, Bernie came in through the back door. She nodded at Dr. Treble, who seemed unsurprised by her tardy entrance, and chose a seat beside me. And on the other side of the room from Tone.

"You all right?" I whispered.

She nodded. "Just tired."

"Ms. Cummings?" Dr. Treble said. "You're up."

Cherrie started us off with Congresswoman Shirley Chisolm's speech to the House of Representatives, her timeless words on equal rights resonating in our female-dominated classroom. Other students chose gems by Sojourner Truth and W.E.B. DuBois, and another read a few lines from a rare interview of Lucille Clifton.

Antonio surprised us with Sofia's epic speech in *The Color Purple* and shared how that scene touched him as a child.

"It was the first time I realized women have it hard and men are often the reason why." He glanced Bernie's way, but she was taking notes. "And I promised God to

161

be part of the solution."

"Well, thank you for recognizing the male role in the female struggle, Antonio," Dr. Treble said. "And to those who know the speech by heart, thank you for keeping your recitations to yourselves. Ms. Price?"

To our collective surprise, Bernie read an excerpt from the "I Have a Dream" speech. Dr. King's words never failed to inspire, but they seemed a pedestrian choice for the mistress of the unexpected. And when Bernie excused herself from class shortly thereafter, I was hard-pressed to focus on the next two presenters.

"Ms. Nelson?"

I paused my concern for Bernie and cued up my videotape. "This is from my favorite daytime drama, *Never Ever After*."

Cherrie burst into applause then stopped. "Sorry."

"In this scene," I said. "High school senior Denzel defends his choice of an Ivy League school over his parents' HBCU."

"Why did you choose this speech?" Dr. Treble asked when the scene concluded.

"Because I chose Howard over my father's Ivy League alma mater, and to some, that yields me a higher degree of blackness. But if having the freedom to be ourselves was the point of the Civil Rights Movement, then assigning levels of blackness based on collegiate choice, manner of speech, or other arbitrary details only indulges the same stereotypes we sought to overthrow."

"Preach!" cried a girl on the other side of the room.

"I know my education would have been different had I gone to Penn," I said. "But does different constitute racially inferior?"

"What do we think?" Dr. Treble asked the class. "Do these parents have a point in wanting this boy to attend an HBCU?"

I resumed my seat as the discussion swelled around me, observing it all with no small measure of pride.

Indelibly black pride.

I left my tape on top of the VCR, so I was late leaving class. I passed Dr. Treble's desk where she was making notes in her grade book.

"Nice choice, Ms. Nelson." she said. "And very well defended."

I adjusted the straps on my bookbag. "Thank you."

"Have you had the chance to review those papers I gave you?"

"Yes. I'll discuss them with my parents the next time I go home."

"See that you do."

I could have floated downstairs. That was the second time in as many weeks Dr. Treble gave me a compliment. A student could wait four years for one.

"No one knows Bernie better than you," Cherrie was telling Tone as I came outside. "You know she needs space sometimes."

"But why now?" Tone asked. "Everything has been great, and now she's freezing me out. She won't return my calls. She's ignoring me in class. I don't know what to do."

"Just be easy," I said. "Isn't that the N-Y-son motto?"

Tone half smiled. "Something ain't right, Daria. And I wish she'd tell me what."

Cherrie and I refused to look at each other. "If Bernie has anything to tell you, she will when she's ready," I said. "But get to practice. It'll take your mind off things."

Cherrie patted him on the back. "Score a hoop shot for me."

"You have got to raise your basketball IQ," I said to her.

Tone walked away with a laugh. "For real."

"Nice diversion," Cherrie said when he was out of earshot.

"I am good for something."

Cherrie checked her watch. "I've gotta run to Blackburn before the Campus Pal office closes. See you at home?"

I walked-ran toward the shuttle stop at Cramton, pulling out my phone to call Bernie. I didn't want to talk to her about Tone, just wanted to hear her voice.

And I did. On her voicemail.

Maybe I needed to take my own advice and let her recover in peace. And if I didn't hear from her by Thursday, I'd camp out in front of her apartment building Friday morning.

Mordecai approached on my right side. "Penny for your thoughts?"

"Thinking about Bernie."

"Yeah, Tone said she's being weirder than usual." He glanced at me. "And you know what it is."

"My lips are sealed. But I told him to give her some room, and that's what we all should do." We reached the vacant shuttle stop at Cramton. "Thanks again for signing Maurice in."

"Good weekend?"

"The best."

"Hey!" Someone called from across the street. "Are you waiting for the shuttle?"

"Yeah!" I called back.

"You just missed it."

"I was at Douglass," I said to Mordecai. "I would have heard it pass."

"Thanks for telling us!" Mordecai yelled back.

"You think she's right?" I checked my watch. "It's only quarter after."

"Maybe we should walk. It's not cold and not that far."

"Why not?" We headed down the back steps of the School of Business. "How do you know Tone?" I asked.

"We were roommates in Drew for two weeks my freshman year until he was transferred to Cook with the other athletes."

"But he's a year ahead of you."

"Long live the geniuses in Resident Life."

We crossed Georgia Avenue. "What were you doing in the bookstore Saturday?"

"You mean, why was I shopping at a non-Borders store? Do you own stock yet?"

"Working on it. And I buy books from the HU bookstore, but I didn't think visual arts people needed them."

"You think we only use the crayon aisle at Toys R Us?"

"Are you denying it?"

"I was actually researching a Christmas gift for Mel. She's, uh ... she's been asking about our mother."

That was about the last thing I expected him to say. "Oh."

"She was only two when Mom left, so she doesn't 'miss' her or anything. But I think she wishes she remembered her."

"I know you talk to your mom sometimes," I said carefully. "Have you told her about this?"

"Nah. It's not like Mel wants to meet her, at least not yet. She just wants a special connection, something uniquely hers. So I want to tell the story of Mel's birth in picture book form."

"I think that would be amazing."

"Yeah, if I can pull it off." He stuffed his hands in his hoodie. "I can draw the pictures and can probably come up with a good title. But I want the story to be good too."

"How about a poem? You only need a few lines on every page, and the rhymes would help her remember the story."

"If I'm a bad writer, I'm a terrible poet."

"Hello? English major here."

"I can't ask you to do that. You've got work, a full course load, and a long-distance relationship to maintain."

"One, you didn't ask. Two, I can handle all that and help you give Melody the bestest gift anyone has ever gotten."

"Bestest?"

"Poetic license." We stopped at the red light on Thirteenth Street. "Tell me about her birth, and we can

166

get started tonight."

After a moment of hesitation, Mordecai told me about the freak snowstorm the week of Mel's birth. How the city was completely shut down and they needed a police escort to get off their Greenbelt block. He smiled, remembering how his mother stuffed her face with Christmas cookies and egg nog because she wouldn't be able to eat at the hospital. As his story took shape, certain words and phrases stuck out, and I made note of them for Melody's poem.

"I can see why you'd use this story. It shows how much your mother loved Melody."

"Yeah. I'd never seen Mom so happy."

His wistful tone made me want to give him a hug or buy him a pony, but neither seemed particularly practical. So I sent up a prayer instead.

"So tell me about your weekend," he said after a moment. "You were heading to a show when I saw you in the bookstore, right?"

Grateful for the distraction, I told Mordecai about *Play On*, an African-American adaptation of *Twelfth Night* featuring the music of Duke Ellington. The colorful costumes and jazzy dialogue well suited Shakespeare's play, to say nothing of the vocal virtuosity of the cast.

"Maybe I'll take Mel this weekend," he said. "She has an old soul."

"You'll both love it."

We entered the Meridian lobby and found Cherrie in the seating group, rummaging through her briefcase.

"How'd you beat me here?" I asked.

"I took the shuttle," she said.

"Some girl leaving the School of B told us we missed it," I said.

"Did she say it was the Meridian shuttle?" Cherrie pulled some flyers out of her bag. "Cuz she could have been talking about a different one."

I shook my head as Mordecai laughed. "At least it was a nice walk."

"Yes, it was." I caught an orange paper in the abdomen. "What's this?"

"The flyer for the Thanksgiving Soup Servers Event I'm organizing," Cherrie said. "With so many people traveling home, it's hard getting commitments." She looked at Mordecai. "You're local, right?"

"But we're going to North Carolina to see my pop's family."

"Crapenstein!"

"But I can help with the food drive."

"Yeah, yeah."

"Ignore her," I said to Mordecai. "But if you still want to, I'll see you in an hour."

"My room?" he asked.

"Are there snacks?"

"Of course."

"Your room it is." I turned back to find an uber-curious Cherrie watching me. "He's working on a special Christmas gift for his sister Melody. She doesn't remember much about their mother, and he wanted to…"

"Aww!" Cherrie hugged herself. "That's the kinda guy I need for this event. Farfegnugen!"

"You know that's German for 'driving-pleasure,' right?" At her glare, I asked, "Momma and GiGi are letting you skip Thanksgiving for this?"

"It's a grassroots effort to help needy families during the holidays. How could they object?" She scanned the lobby, spotting a group of new arrivals. "Will you help me hang these upstairs?"

I stared at the flyer in my hand. "Let me make a quick call first."

As she flitted into the crowd, I pulled out my cell phone and put on contrition.

"Mom? Sorry to bother you, but I have news."

Corina was all ears. "Oooh, tell me!"

"I, uh ... I won't be home for Thanksgiving."

There was a long pause, then my mother inhaled all the air in the tristate area. "What?"

Twenty

Though I avoided going home for Thanksgiving thanks to Cherrie's well-timed event, Christmas could not be delayed. So after my last final exam—my stellar grades emancipated me from only one of them—I packed my things for the return trip to Philly. My ring kept catching my eye, and I reconsidered Cherrie's suggestion to take it off and figure out in Philly how to explain it to my parents. But I hadn't removed the ring since Maurice slid it on my finger and refused to do so now to appease my father.

Bernie and I brainstormed for an hour last night, and she came up with a brilliant idea: I would feign sickness on the ride home and keep my gloves on. Because of my illness, Corina wouldn't expect me to eat dinner, and I could go to bed early and undisturbed. Maurice would sneak over tonight to cheer me up and "give me" the ring, answering the all-important questions of when, where, and how I got it.

Bernie should be a professional problem-solver.

Cherrie and I wondered if Bernie would create similar success in her relationship with Tone over the break. Things between them were better, but he still didn't know about her pregnancy scare. We hoped she would confess when he visited her family around New Year's, but it wasn't our place to ask. Lawd knows I had enough drama on my own plate.

Though excited to see my mom, I dreaded driving home with Adrian at the wheel. The very thought of talking to him made me feel like a Grinch, so I planned to find an all-Christmas music station and hear those sleigh bells jingling, ring-ting-ting-a-ling all the way home.

That or get out and walk.

I unplugged my television set, and the dorm phone rang. The short tones let me know it was the front desk. "This is Daria."

"Ms. Nelson, there's a gentleman down here who looks just like you," Mordecai said.

"I was here first," Adrian said in the background. "She looks like me!"

"I stand corrected. There's a girl in your room who looks like the gentleman to my left."

I rolled my eyes at their laughter. "I'll be right down."

Checking for the traveling copy of my renter's insurance agreement one last time, I zipped my bag and locked my door, praying for the strength to honor my father.

When I pulled my rolling suitcase into the lobby, I spotted Adrian looking at Mordecai's gift to Melody.

"There's my favorite writer now," Mordecai said as Adrian beamed beside him.

"Hey, you!" My father wrapped me in a hug which I had no choice but to return. "You look great! And this is awesome." He looked back at the book. "You really are talented."

"That she is." Mordecai smiled. "Melody is going to love this."

"It started with your illustrations," I said. "All I did was narrate."

"However it happened, you two created something beautiful and unique." Adrian clapped Mordecai on the back. "And if that isn't the essence of Christmas, I don't know what is."

I hoisted my bag on my shoulder. "Can we go?"

"Can I take your bags to the car?" Mordecai asked.

"I appreciate it, son, but that's why Daddy's here." Adrian took my luggage, giving Mordecai the once-over. "Tell me again about your major."

"Dad, we need to go. Traffic at this time of day is horrendous."

"All right." He extended a hand to Mordecai. "It was great to meet you, Mr. Hill. I hope to see you again soon."

"I'd like that." Mordecai grinned. "Merry Christmas, Daria."

I punched his arm. "And a Crappy New Year to you, too."

Adrian smiled a little longer until I shoved him through the double doors, Mordecai's amusement at my back.

"Nice guy," Adrian said. "Not as good as a Penn man, but nice."

I rolled my eyes in amusement. "Your bias is ridiculous."

"Would you ever say any woman is better than a Bisonette?"

I tilted my head in thought. "Touché."

We loaded the car, and Adrian reached for my hand. I was startled until I recalled our family ritual. "Lord," he said. "Grant us traveling mercy as we head back home. Protect us from fools, drunkards, and the irresponsible, and protect them from themselves. In Jesus' name, Amen."

"Amen."

"All right, driver controls the radio," he said. "But we're in your neck of the woods, so I'm deferring to you."

"Even country?"

He laughed. "Would you believe I missed you enough to hum a few bars of *A Thousand Miles from Nowhere*?"

"No, I wouldn't."

"Well, I missed you just the same."

I couldn't say it back, but the words were sweet.

"Snacks are in the glove compartment," he continued. "I got those cheesy pretzel things you like and chocolate bars. Do you need anything else before we get on the road?"

"Actually, my throat's been scratchy." The raspy

cough was a nice touch. "Could I get some hot tea with lemon?"

"Sure. Do you need organic honey too?"

I stuck out my tongue and turned to the country station. Brenda Lee was rockin' around the Christmas tree, and I joined in as Adrian tapped his fingers against the steering wheel. He hummed his way through *Silver Bells,* and his twang-heavy rendition of *O Holy Night* was a hilarious surprise. By the time Grandma got run over by that reindeer, I felt like a kid on Christmas morning.

"If they don't have lemon, I'll live without it," I said. "This is our third stop, and Mom will have a conniption if we're late."

He pulled into the 7-Eleven parking lot. "Ten-four, good buddy."

Three sugars and two lemon wedges later, we pulled back onto to New York Avenue and were officially on the road to Philly.

"How were finals?" Adrian asked.

"Long." I sipped my tea. "Dr. Treble's final assignment was an in-class essay about the importance of black literature in a multicultural society. I liked what I wrote, but I don't know if she will. And my Brit Lit professor must have pulled his questions from some Middle English textbook."

"Sounds about right. I remember during sophomore year, my….Slow down, stupid!"

Dad slammed on his brakes with a muttered curse as a certified doofus in an Escalade ran the red light and nearly swiped our car. My seatbelt held my body in place, but my hard-won tea sloshed out of the cup and onto my lap and gloved hands. "Ow, crap!"

"All that to get a whole block ahead? Way to go, genius!" Adrian tried to calm down as he turned to me. "Are you all right?"

I shook my wet hand. "Yeah, but my tea bit the dust."

"We'll get you another one." Adrian pulled over and put on his blinkers. "I'm sorry."

"It's okay. Could've been worse."

"Give it here." He held out his hands for the empty cup while I removed my damp gloves. "If you set them on the dash, they'll be dry by the time we...." Dad fell silent, his eyes narrowing. "What is that?"

"What is what?" I followed his gaze and noted the one-and-a-half-carat cat I just let out of the bag. Er, glove. "I can explain."

He didn't reply, but that telltale vein popped in his forehead.

"Or maybe I should just be quiet."

"Oh, I think you'd better start talking." His glare sent a chill across my hand. "Right now."

"Why should I talk if you won't listen?" I said again.

"I'll listen when something you say makes sense!"

So went the past 50 miles. Every time I tried to explain myself, Adrian derided my words, rendering them useless.

"Is this really surprising?" I asked. "Maurice and I have been dating for four years, and..."

"You have been dating for one year, which is not

enough time to warrant an engagement ring."

"It's not an engagement ring!"

"Ever heard that expression about walking, quacking ducks?"

I clenched my fists, determined to remain respectful. "Maurice and I spent last year apart, and that was hard. But I maintained a 4.0, The Shop is thriving, and everything between us is fine. That means something."

"It means there's a lot you don't know."

"What?"

He sighed. "I think you're naïve when it comes to him."

"I get that you don't like Maurice, but you don't know him."

"And you do?"

"After four years, how could I not?"

"You were a child most of that time and didn't spend that much time with him."

"I was a teenager, and whose fault was it that I didn't spend much time with him?"

"I had my reasons." He glanced at me. "And I still do."

"Dad, listen. Maurice may not be your choice for me, but could you at least try to like him? I mean, everyone else has: Mommy, Cherrie, Bernie ..."

"Bernadette doesn't even know him!"

"Well, when he came to visit after Homecoming, she said he was ..."

"When he came *where* after *what*?"

Crap.

Crappity crap crap-crap!

"Dad, I think we're getting away from the main…"

"Came where? After what?"

I swallowed hard. "He came to visit the week after Homecoming."

His jaw clenched as he changed lanes. "You mean he got a hotel room, met you on The Yard, and never came past the Meridian front doors?"

I kept my eyes on the road. "Nothing happened."

"That boy spent the night in your dorm room?"

"We made a deal after I came home for Columbus Day weekend that he would …"

"Columbus Day?" I feared his shout would shatter the windows. "You spent an entire weekend with him in West Philadelphia?"

"That's when he gave me the ring."

Lips tight, my father looked at me. "Are you having sex?"

"Are you serious?"

"Is that your answer?"

I folded my arms. "I cannot believe you asked me that."

"Is that your answer?"

"No, we are not having sex! Not even close, if you must know." I was stunned to feel my eyes welling. "I can't believe you trust me so little."

"How can I trust you when you drop these bombs on me with no regard for what they mean? You're wearing an engagement ring, and…"

"It's not an engagement ring!"

"We're two weeks from the dawn of the Twenty-first Century, Daria. Do young black men give promise rings anymore?"

"I thought it was a nice gesture."

"A charm bracelet is a nice gesture. Twenty tulips on a Tuesday is a nice gesture. A gigantic diamond in a velvet box is statement of intent."

"You are so wrong about him."

"That diamond alone would run him two grand. Where would he get that kind of money? Did you ask him?"

"He couldn't have saved it?"

"Did he?"

"I don't know!"

"Did you ask him?"

"No." I looked out the window. "And I won't because I trust him."

"Then I hope your trust isn't misplaced."

Neither of us spoke another word until we pulled into our driveway. Dad yanked the keys out of the ignition and shoved them in his coat pocket. "You can tell your mother. I'm sure you don't trust me to explain it properly."

Despite my deliberate dallying, Adrian and I walked into the house at the same time, greeted by my mother's angelic smile. "How was the ride home?"

Adrian dropped my bags in the vestibule and went back outside.

"Peachy," I said.

Twenty-One

Safe and alone in my bedroom, I called Maurice and told him the jig was up. And with Adrian so upset, coming over that night would have been the wrong answer.

"What about Christmas day?" he asked.

"No good." Although angry, I wasn't trying to ruin my favorite holiday. "But pick me up the day after. He'll have to make nice because Corina won't tolerate rudeness."

That settled Christmas but not the few days between. And after deciding not to work at Borders during this break, I lost my daily excuse to escape the cold war at home. My father and I hadn't spoken since our argument, and I refused to be the one to crack. He was the adult, so it was up to him to mend fences.

And soon, so I could get my presents.

Because Corina walked on water, she invited me to come to work with her. She may as well have invited me to Great Adventure because my mother's shop was the happiest place on earth.

CoCo Davenport Designs was a modest but thriving furniture boutique on Germantown Avenue near the top of the Hill. Specializing in custom pieces and unique decorations, it was the go-to spot for that something special for your home. Cherrie required every Christmas and birthday gift be a CoCo original, and I couldn't blame her. My mother had a flair for blending the dramatic with the practical, and the results were nothing short of spectacular.

December was her busiest season and my favorite time to be here. Retail was in my blood, it seemed, as I was happiest in crowded stores with long lines at the registers. Being the point of calm for stormy shoppers satisfied me, but watching Corina in her store was like watching an Olympic swimmer glide through water. She moved with grace and spoke with kindness, treating each client like a VIP. No request was dismissed out of hand, and if she couldn't meet the need, she had no problem referring someone to an artisan who could. Her relationship with nearby business owners made her a local gem, and I'd yet to find anyone who didn't adore her.

But, as I often pointed out, I loved her first.

"Fifteen minutes to close," Corina announced from the middle of the sales floor, and everyone laughed. At CDD, "fifteen minutes to close" meant "fifteen minutes until I start thinking about not letting anyone else in." In reality, she closed an hour after this announcement, making sure everyone left satisfied with their experience. I wouldn't be surprised if she made a few deliveries on our way home tonight. "It's Christmas," she'd shrug as though she wouldn't have done it otherwise.

"Have a blessed holiday!" She waved at the final duo of ladies. "And I'll have those door knockers by mid-January."

Per her custom, she stood in the doorway for another few minutes in case a departing customer needed one last thing. When no one appeared, she locked the door and turned off the overhead lights. But with the festive holiday greens in the window and twinkle lights throughout the showroom, the store was as bright and beautiful as ever.

"Take the till in the back and lock it up." She joined me behind the registers. "I'll count it tomorrow morning."

"Really?" This was unprecedented. "Can I at least make sure the bills are all facing the same way?"

"Tomorrow." She took the money from my hands and headed toward her office. "Let's go eat."

Corina drove us down the hill to Yu Hsiang Garden where we ordered seafood wonton soup, house lo mein, and tsing tao duck. As I sugared my third cup of tea, my mom set down her spoon and smiled.

"Here it comes," I said.

"What?"

"Mom, I've been studying you my whole life, and I know that look. You've been waiting three days to discuss this situation between me and Daddy, so out with it."

"What makes you think I have anything to say?"

I cocked an eyebrow. "I'll be here all night."

As I stirred and sipped, she sighed. "You're both right and both wrong. You feel your father has stopped giving you the benefit of the doubt, that despite your legal adult status, he treats you like a child."

"Thank you!"

"But he feels your insistence on keeping secrets suggests you're not as mature as you think." She lowered her voice. "I understand why you didn't tell us about your two weekends alone with Maurice. But those omissions don't inspire confidence."

"Nothing happened, Mom."

"You say that because you think only sex is significant. But sharing a bed with a man in any capacity creates binding intimacy. And I assume that did happen."

I had no good reply, so I was grateful when the server interrupted with our food.

"You get used to him being there," she continued after Amen. "His warm body and strong arms around you, and you start to crave that feeling. And that craving invites all that 'nothing' that hasn't happened yet."

"But Daddy was wrong to assume it had happened."

"Yes, he was. But as he tells it, he didn't assume anything. He asked a question, and you got defensive. Why is that?"

"Because he doesn't trust me. No matter what I do, he sees me as the girl who broke his heart by getting a boyfriend or going to school or whatever it was I did that was so bad."

"You're half right. No matter what you do, he sees you as a girl, his little girl, to be exact. And it's difficult for him to let go of her. Believe me, I know."

"But you never treat me like a child."

"Because you don't treat me like the enemy. Usually."

She stole a shrimp from my plate, and I cut my eyes at her.

"I see a lot of me in you, Daria. Your sense of adventure, your passion and independence. I admire those traits and want you to cultivate them to create the life you dream about. But I also want you to be careful, to count the cost of your decisions before you make them. Accepting Maurice's ring was your choice, but confusion about that choice made you lie for two months and skip Thanksgiving."

"But you married Daddy young. And after quitting school senior year to take an apprenticeship with that craftsman in Olde City."

"And after starting a business as a single woman barely old enough to drink," she added.

"Exactly."

"But your father asked my father's permission to seek my hand." She stirred her tea. "And I didn't quit school: I withdrew, speaking to all my teachers and advisors beforehand to protect my GPA and transcripts. And I discussed the possibility of withdrawal and starting CDD with both parents before making the decision because I wasn't ashamed."

I looked up. "I'm not ashamed of Maurice."

"Something prevented you from coming clean."

"I didn't tell you guys because you don't like

Maurice, and I didn't want you freaking out at the idea of us getting married."

"Why would we do that if it isn't an engagement ring?"

"Because I'm the only one who doesn't think this is an engagement ring."

The words were intended to support my case, but saying them aloud had the opposite effect. Corina didn't reply, but her expression spoke volumes.

"Maurice and I are not getting married," I said. "At least, not now or based on this ring."

"Then we don't need to discuss this anymore."

"Good. And I don't want to discuss Daddy either, if that's okay with you."

"Fine by me. But I hope you remembered to get him a present."

I paused my noodle-laden fork in midair. "Crap."

She reached for the soy sauce. "There's still tomorrow."

Ordinarily I preferred shopping on Christmas Eve. My chronic indecisiveness was rendered moot by knowing if it wasn't on the shelves, it wasn't in the store. I'd head to the mall with snacks and a paperback, high on chaos and carols. But with the paternal strain in my life, I had no desire to shop or brave a bastion of strangers.

Which left but one shopping option.

Besides being my home-away-from-home and frequent place of employment, Borders Book Shop in Chestnut Hill was the perfect place for last-minute shopping. Boasting more than books, their journals, picture frames, and budding music section offered viable possibilities. The café's jumbo cinnamon rolls didn't hurt, and the benefit of my discount was the whipped cream atop my Holly Holiday Smoothie.

Already weary of discussing my ring since coming home, I kept on my leather gloves as I greeted my former coworkers and friends. They chastised me for not helping them out this holiday, one of them begging me to jump on the registers to help clear the line. I waved them off and roamed the first floor, noting the changes since summer. Calendars of all shapes and sizes had replaced the Summer Reading tables in the back and reminded me to get a Strawberry Shortcake day planner for Bernie (huge closet fan).

Our cold war aside, I wanted to get Adrian a gift he would like. My odds of success would improve upstairs, so I climbed the curved staircase to the second floor. Inspirational books were out as the Bible was the only such title he read. He enjoyed the occasional game of chess but not enough to read about it. And I would grab a desk reference set only in case of a closing-time emergency.

Wandering over to History, I perused the titles on the two World Wars. Adrian was a huge fan of movies like *Lawrence of Arabia* and *Legends of the Fall*, the latter of which we saw together the day it premiered. Though admittedly interested on account of Brad Pitt, I was touched by its depiction of the clandestine effects of war over time, and it remained one of our favorite films. Perhaps I could find the short story on which the movie was based downstairs in Fiction.

Though I didn't find that book, *All Quiet on the Western Front* was another beloved film, and a hard copy of the novel would make a nice gift for my father. Satisfied with my choice, I joined the checkout line where it snaked beside the audio books beneath the stairs. I finished all my shopping for Corina in DC, but another present for the world's most amazing woman could never be ruled out.

As I skimmed the audio fiction offerings, I spotted a title that made my stomach turn. Despite my revulsion, I grabbed it from the shelf.

"I still cannot believe Dr. Treble made us read this," I muttered.

"Isn't it an odd book? I forgot Meredith was teaching it this year."

The comment came from a honey-toned African-American man with a bald head and green eyes, idly scanning the endcap titles. I didn't want to be caught staring, so I forced my brain to catch his comment.

"You know Dr. Treble?" My hackles rose as he nodded. "How did you know I was a…"

"Howard student? Your hat. Those were new to the bookstore last month, which I know because I bought a blue one." He held out his hand with a warm smile. "James Maddox, Professor of Afro-American Studies."

I accepted his hand, touched in more than one way. Dr. Maddox's reputation preceded him, and the news was all good. Lauded for intellect and accessibility, Dr. Maddox could connect the cultural significance of Marcus Garvey, Colin Powell, and Teena Marie in one digestible nugget. His dual devotion to Howard and our hometown inspired his daily commute from Philly to

DC, and with all of that going on, his aesthetic appeal was a superfluous bonus, something so-called "Maddox Addicts" had no problem appreciating.

"I've heard a lot about you," I said.

"Only the crazy stuff is true." He looked at the title in my hand. "So you didn't like *Of Scarlet and Sage*?"

"That's an understatement. How long have you known Dr. Treble?"

"Since grad school." He put the offending audio book back on the shelf. "She's always been an odd duck, but that's part of her charm. Which of her motley crew are you?"

"Daria Nelson."

"Serendipity!" We moved forward in the register line. "She speaks highly of you, admires your nuanced thinking."

"She does?"

"Yes, ma'am. So much that I wonder why you haven't taken one of my classes."

"They're usually full, and I hate fighting for overrides."

"So pick a class and time, come on the first day, and I'll sign your form. No brawling necessary."

"Wow. Thanks!"

"Don't thank me until you see the syllabus. In some ways, I'm worse than Meredith." He checked his watch. "Got a lunch meeting. Great meeting you, Ms. Nelson. I'll see you in class."

He strolled away, whistling a happy carol. And I hummed along through the checkout line and out the doors into the frosty air. Though my spring schedule would be three credits heavier once again, I could not pass up the chance to take a Maddox class. Especially when an override was guaranteed.

I was so thrilled by the news I decided to pad my father's proverbial Christmas stocking. Heading across the street to the music store, I found a John Coltrane and Miles Davis jam session on vinyl. Kitchen Kapers had one grill masters tool set left, and at Jos A. Bank, I scored on a men's cashmere pullover thanks to a holiday associate's pricing mistake.

It was beginning to look a lot like Christmas, and I couldn't wait.

Twenty-Two

Early the next morning, my bedroom phone rang. I rolled over without opening my eyes, smiling as I realized what day it was. "Hello?"

"Merry Christmas, Duchess."

"Merry Christmas, you." I covered the receiver to hide my yawn. "Why are you up so early?"

"I wanted to be the first voice you heard this morning."

"Aww." Though his sleep-laden baritone was barely intelligible. "Now my day is complete, and I can go back to bed."

"Like Corina would allow that. I'm surprised she hasn't stormed your room yet."

I glanced at the clock. "I've got ten minutes to

189

present myself or there will be consequences."

"Such as?"

"I'll miss her famous cocoa. And I love you, but not that much."

"Now the truth comes out. You think you know a person until she sells you out for hot chocolate."

"Did I mention the white chocolate shavings?" He chuckled, and I imagined him lounging against his headboard. "Are you going to be all right today?"

"What do you mean?"

"I'll be here all day, and we're not seeing each other until tomorrow. Is Naseem coming over or something?"

"Don't worry. I'll be sure to find some fun."

"Okay." The opening strings of *The Christmas Song* floated beneath the door, and I sat up. "That's Nat King Cole. Gotta go."

Maurice gasped. "You cheating on me?"

"Only once a year."

"Guess I can live with that. Merry Christmas, Duch."

"You, too. Love you."

Humming as I hopped out of bed, I brushed my teeth and headed downstairs, taking my time to appreciate the decorative touches that made this my favorite time of year. Corina rehung our family photos in red and gold frames, perfectly coordinated with the poinsettias on each carpet-free stair. Clusters of round red, gold, and silver ornaments hung from the ceiling by velvet ribbons of varying length, selected groupings accented with mistletoe. From the hand-stitched monogrammed stockings above the family room fireplace to my second-grade popsicle stick tree on the side table, every inch of our home reminded me of how blessed I was to have such loving, devoted parents.

Including the one speaking to me for the first time in four days.

"Merry Christmas, honey," he said. "The cocoa's almost ready."

"Merry Christmas, Dad. Can't wait."

"I tried something different this year." My mom set down the tray of creamy hot chocolate and hugged me tightly. "Hope you like it."

"If you made it, I'll love it." My ring clinked against the ceramic mug as I picked it up, drawing Adrian's attention to it. He kept his smile in place as he grabbed his own mug, and we took our first sip together.

"Wow, Mom." I licked a dollop of whipped cream from the corner of my mouth. "This is incredible."

"You like it?" She frowned, unsure. "I didn't know if this new blend of mint would work."

"It does," Adrian and I said together, and he winked at me. "Jinx."

After another healthy sip, I joined my mother on the loveseat, and Dad opened his grandmother's gold-leaf Bible to that precious passage in Luke. Though Linus did a bang-up job in the annual Peanuts special, no one read this sacred story like my dad. His rich voice never failed to put me right beside those awestruck shepherds, and we sat in reverent silence after he finished.

"All right." I rubbed my hands together. "What'd you get me?"

Mommy retrieved boxes from under the tree. "Such manners. Were you raised by wolves?"

"I'm not an animal, so I wasn't 'raised' anywhere." She handed me my gifts and swatted my arm. "But I was reared by an abusive woman with excellent taste in wrapping paper."

My parents didn't give each other Christmas gifts anymore. They were more into creating memorable experiences, so they were taking a four-day Alaskan cruise in January. The idea of my parents being intimate was slightly nauseating, but it warmed my heart to see them so in love after twenty-plus years. I could only hope for similar felicity in my marriage.

My someday-but-nowhere-near-today marriage.

Corina loved the jewelry and the year's worth of flowers from Robertson's, but she squealed when she saw the cashmere pashmina. She couldn't believe I remembered, let alone that I found it in DC. "And in my favorite shade of purple."

"Whoa-ho!" My father unwrapped the jazz album in shock. "Where did you find this?"

"Hideaway at the top of the hill." I was thrilled he loved it. "It was misfiled in the country section, so I doubt anyone knew it was there."

"The other gifts are great, but this." He read the back cover. "This is a gem."

Corina nudged me with a warm smile. "Open your gifts."

The book-scented candles were a delightful surprise as was the wall poster featuring the full text of Shakespeare's *Hamlet*. And though I was excited by the compilation CDs from Patty Loveless and Dwight Yoakam, it was the small rectangular jewelry box that caught my attention. With a bit of hesitation, I opened the box and was stunned to find a pair of teardrop diamond earrings.

"As soon as I saw them, I knew they were for you." My father joined me on the couch. "They were…I mean, I wanted them to be your first diamonds."

My left ring finger throbbed at the news, as did my daddy-loving heart. I put the earrings in my ears immediately and threw my arms around my father. "They're perfect, Daddy. Thank you."

"You're perfect." He patted my back. "And you're more than welcome."

Corina clapped her hands, about to burst. "All right, kids. It's waffle time!"

Every Christmas morning, the three of us made breakfast together. My dad and I made whole wheat banana walnut waffles while my mom braved the outdoors to grill chicken breasts on the back patio. It was the only time Adrian let Corina use his precious grill, and she swore he only did so to spend time with me in the kitchen.

As I touched my diamond-studded ears, I believed her.

"You wanna sift?" my father asked as we set the ingredients on the counter.

"Your hands are stronger."

"You're younger."

Cocking an eyebrow, I put out my hand. "Rock, paper, scissors?"

He rolled up his sleeve. "Best out of three."

Younger hands or not, my expert sifting made for some delicious waffles. Mom used a secret spice on the chicken and kicked the meal up a whole 'nother notch.

With dad's new favorite album in the background, we reminisced about classic holiday stories, most centering on Dad's eccentric relatives.

My sides ached with laughter. "I cannot believe she didn't thaw the turkey first!"

"That's what happens when eccentric aunts run the kitchen." Mommy winked at her husband. "On the plus side, we had the back corner of that Roy Rogers to ourselves."

"What was that green stuff Cousin Cal used to chew? He never spit it out, and it smelled like I-don't-know-what."

My dad smiled. "You're too young to know."

"You said that about why Aunt Greta and Aunt Patrice aren't speaking."

"And that's still true," my mother cut in. "I wish I was too young to know that story."

"What's next?" I finished my orange juice and took my plate to the sink. "Scrabble tournament? Parade watching? Movie marathon?"

"Movie marathon!" My mother ran into the family room. "I get first pick."

"No musicals!" Adrian called out.

"And nothing with subtitles," I added. "No reading during Christmas break."

Adrian put up his hand for a high-five. "Hear, hear."

As we proceeded to the family room, I heard the phone ringing in my bedroom. Everyone knew I was spending the day with my folks, so the caller would have to leave a message. Grabbing a throw from the basket beside the coffee table, I tucked myself on the couch beside my father. He put his arm around me and kissed my temple.

"All right, woman." He patted my mom's leg as she snuggled on his other side. "What are we starting with?"

She poked him in the stomach. "You'll have to wait and see."

The house phone rang as we huddled under the blanket, and we let it go to voicemail, the moment too sacred to disturb.

But halfway through Corina's second pick, which she earned with a stellar opening choice, the doorbell rang. It was early afternoon, and we weren't expecting anyone.

"Carolers?" I suggested.

Corina jumped up from the couch. "Wouldn't that be fun?"

My father paused the movie. "Only if they can sing."

We went to the door with various levels of excitement for the would-be revelers. But when we opened the door, our joy splintered into surprise, confusion, and outright hostility.

"Hey, family!" Maurice smiled. "Merry Christmas!"

Twenty-Three

"Oh my gosh!" I ran off the porch and into his arms. "Maurice!"

He enveloped me in warmth, well, as much as his bulky coat allowed. "Merry Christmas, Duchess."

"What are you doing here?"

He set me down with a grin. "Surprising you."

"And letting out all the heat." Adrian's tone was as chilly as the front step.

"It is rather nippy out here." Corina said. "Why don't we all go inside?"

I grabbed Maurice's hand, and he griped it in response. "Gladly."

My mother steered my father toward the living room, and I turned to Maurice as he shut the door behind us. "I can't believe you're here."

"You think I'd miss the chance to spend Christmas with my girl?"

"Why didn't you tell me you were coming?"

"Because I love to see that look in your eyes."

"What look?"

"That one that means I've done good."

"And you have." I laced our fingers together. "Better than good."

He leaned down and pressed his frosty lips to mine, and I shivered in delight. His arms went around my waist, and I almost forgot where we were.

"Maurice?" My mother called from the kitchen. "Would you like some cocoa?"

"Uh, yes." He stifled a laugh as we jumped apart. "Thanks, Ms. CoCo."

"Coming right up!"

"Why don't you come in here?" Adrian didn't sound as friendly. "Instead of hiding in the vestibule."

I rolled my eyes. "Dad, we're not ..."

"It's okay," Maurice whispered as he took my hand again. "Let's just go before he accuses me of abusing the mistletoe."

I swallowed my annoyance, knowing he was right. "Okay."

Hand-in-hand, Maurice and I entered the living room and chose the loveseat, leaving my former spot beside my father vacant. Though Maurice and I left appropriate space between us as we sat down, that didn't stop Adrian from glaring at our joined hands as we waited for CoCo's cocoa. I wanted to recover the goodwill we'd enjoyed before Maurice's arrival and scanned my brain for safe subjects.

"How was the drive over?" I asked Maurice.

"Not too bad. But some of the side streets are still slick from the flurries last night.

"Really?" Adrian picked up his mug. "Then maybe you should have stayed home."

"Dad, is that really ..."

"Here you go!" My mother came in holding a steaming, reindeer-themed mug. "I hope you like whipped cream."

"Love it, thanks." Maurice took the cup and a long sip before turning to me. "You like my new mustache?"

I swiped the white foam from his top lip with a laugh. "I love it."

"Here." Adrian passed me a tissue from the box on the end table. "Don't get whipped cream on the furniture."

I took the tissue from my dad, doing my best not to snatch it.

"Speaking of furniture." Maurice said as I wiped my hands. "Is that a new lamp on the console?"

"Yes," my mother said. "It's from a new collection at the store."

"It's beautiful," Maurice said. "The matte finish was a great choice."

"I thought so too. Do I detect an increasing interest in interior design?"

Maurice laughed. "I wouldn't go that far, but I know a quality piece when I see it."

"Speaking of quality pieces," I said. "Mom, you should see the new table in his ..."

"Bedroom?" my father asked.

"Living room," I said. "It has these cool compartments for a remote and books and stuff. And beneath it is a rug with Howard's colors."

Maurice looked at me. "What?"

"H-U blue and white." I sat back, enjoying his surprise. "Didn't even notice, did you?"

"Nope. Must've had you on my mind when I bought it."

Adrian cleared his throat rather loudly, and my mother admonished him with a sharp look. Maurice took another long sip of his cocoa as an awkward silence descended, and I glanced at the front window.

Where were those blasted carolers when you needed them?

"So what movie were you watching?" Maurice indicated the paused television. "I thought the game would be on."

"Why?" Adrian asked.

"I just know what a huge basketball fan you are."

"You also know how much I value spending time with my family," my father replied. "Private, quality time."

"I didn't mean to intrude," Maurice said. "But I don't get to see Daria that often and ..."

"Yet somehow she managed to see your new rug and coffee table."

My mouth dropped open, and Corina pursed her lips. "Adrian, I don't think ..."

"It's okay," Maurice said. "I deserve that."

My father folded his arms across his chest. "Well?"

"Mr. Nelson, I am sorry you feel I've disrespected your rules by ..."

"That's your idea of an apology?" Adrian leaned forward. "You're sorry about the way I feel and not what you did?"

"He didn't do anything!" I said. "He didn't force me to come up for Columbus Day or invite him to DC ..."

"Or accept that obnoxious ring behind our backs?"

I blinked at my father. "Obnoxious?"

"Okay, everybody calm down." My mother held up her hands. "None of this is helpful. And we can't change what's already happened."

"No, we can't change it, but some of us should be sorry for it." My father shook his head. "But he doesn't even have the decency to do that."

"Dad, come on! "What do you want from him?"

"You know what I want?" As my father looked at me, his expression shifted from hostile to something I didn't understand. "I want to enjoy my holiday in peace."

"Meaning what?" Corina asked.

He came to his feet. "I'm going to watch the game in the den."

"You can't watch it out here with your family?" I asked.

His back stiffened. "I'd rather not."

He didn't look at Maurice, but he didn't have to. And as I watched my father gather his things from the coffee table, something inside me gathered as well.

"You don't have to do that," I said. "We'll leave."

"Daria, no."

"It's fine, Mom. I'd like to see the McClains today anyway."

Corina looked at my father with wide eyes, her gaze darting between him and us. But Adrian just grabbed his mug and turned away with a muttered, "Be careful on the road."

I turned to Maurice. "Can you give me a half hour?"

"Sure. That'll give me time to get some gas and see if they need anything over there."

"Make sure you take them a gift from the closet, Daria." My mother sighed as she rose out of her chair. "The Christmas-themed gift bags are in the marked drawer."

"Thanks, Mom."

She nodded before following my father out of the room, her soft pleas for civility falling on stubborn ears. And as I climbed the stairs to my room, I told myself not to stomp.

At least one of us could behave like an adult.

Once in the safety of Maurice's car, however, I gave full rein to my attitude.

"It's Christmas, a day of hope and reconciliation," I said as we turned off the Expressway. "And he turned it into the Thrilla in Manila."

"It's all right." Maurice patted my hand where it rested in my lap. "He was more upset with me than you."

"He was being mean to you to punish me. And either way, he was wrong."

"I should have known he would mention our secret visits this semester. My bad."

"I'm the one who mentioned your new furniture. That was my fault."

Maurice squeezed my hand. "I'm sorry just the same."

"And I'm sorry he ruined that really good thing you did."

He glanced at me and smiled. "There's that look I love so much."

The parking on his parents' block was nonexistent, so Maurice found a spot around the corner. The large twin homes in the McClains' Cobbs Creek neighborhood were all decked out with Christmas spirit, and mine gradually returned as we passed each festive display.

"So what did you tell your family?" I asked.

"About what?"

"About this obnoxious ring you gave me."

He squeezed my left hand with a light chuckle. "I told them I gave you something special for Christmas and not to make a big deal about it."

"Do they know it's not an engagement ring?"

"Of course. Mom knows you're in school and trying to figure things out. She's very proud of you." He kissed my cheek. "As am I."

The merry sounds of Donny Hathaway greeted us as we reached the front walk. As Maurice pushed open the door, the clamor inside the house mellowed to a dull roar.

"Ho, ho, ho!" he called out.

"Mook!" came the general cry.

"I told y'all to stop calling me that in front of my lady."

"That ain't no lady," Naseem yelled from the far end of the room. "That's just Daria."

"And you're just jealous," Maurice yelled back.

"Nah." Naseem crossed the room and swept me up in his trademark hug. "That ain't it."

"Naseem, get your own girlfriend." Mr. McClain's baritone filled the silence between songs as he made his way toward us. "This one is spoken for."

"Merry Christmas, Mr. McClain."

"Daria, I told you to stop calling me that."

"Leave her alone, Martin. She was brought up right." I hugged Mom McClain and handed her a large gift bag. "See?"

"But she's still got her coat on." Mr. McClain helped me out of it. "Stay awhile, why don't cha?"

"I think I will." I removed my gloves and tucked them in my purse. "Should I hang this in the…"

"Oh my god!" someone shouted. "What is that?"

I looked behind me, thinking the Christmas tree was on fire. "What is what?"

A gray-haired woman grabbed my left hand. "This huge diamond on your finger!"

"Diamond?" came the chorused reply.

"Oh, this?" I smiled, holding my hand to my chest. "It's a …"

"Now just hold on here." Mom McClain wiped her hands on her apron. "Daria, honey. Let me see that hand."

I shot Maurice an alarmed look as his mother inspected my finger. Someone had turned off the music, and the room fell so silent I heard the kitchen timer ticking away on the stove.

"Maurice Horatio McClain," she whispered. "You said you gave Daria a special gift."

"It's very special." He joined me on my other side

and slipped his arm around my waist. "But I also said ..."

"I'll say it's special." She released my hand, her face exploding into a wide grin. "Because you're getting married!"

The family erupted in shouts and squeals, and I was pulled away from a protesting Maurice and sucked into an aggressive group hug. "Wait! It's not an engage ..."

"Ooh!" Mom McClain danced in place, clapping her hands. "Wait till I tell the ladies at the church! Or maybe I should call Reverend Randolph first and get a peek at his summer calendar ..."

"Mom, listen." Maurice stepped in front of her. "You don't need to call Reverend Randolph because ..."

"... course that all depends on what sort of wedding Daria has in mind." Mom McClain turned to me with bated breath. "Did you set a date yet?"

"No, ma'am." I pulled away from the surrounding crowd. "Because this is not an engagement ..."

"Did you ask her father's permission first, son?" Mr. McClain asked. "These may be the last few days of the Nineties, but respect is still respect."

Naseem's loud guffaw reached me from the other side of the room, and I narrowed my eyes at him. He sipped his egg nog undaunted, enjoying our discomfort.

He would pay for that later.

"Dad, no, stop. And Mom, come here." Maurice brought his parents together in the center of the room, taking my right hand as I returned to his side. "Listen. Daria and I are not engaged."

"Not engaged?" his father asked as the room gasped.

Maurice shook his head. "No."

"You gave her a diamond, but you're not engaged?" Mom McClain fixed her incredulous gaze on me. "Then what is this?"

I smiled at her son. "It's a promise ring."

"Say word?" A teenager with waist-length braids peeked over my shoulder. "That's some promise."

"Yes." Mom McClain turned down the wattage on her smile. "And a lovely gesture."

"Guess the show's over," Naseem crowed from the corner.

"Well, in that case, I'll go check the sweet potato pie." Mom McClain headed toward the kitchen, and Maurice rested his hand on my lower back.

"I'm gonna go talk to Mom," he whispered. "You go kick Naseem for leaving us hanging."

I kissed him. "You got it."

I turned to give Naseem the stink eye, and the bearded boy looked for a way out. "Uh, Uncle Mar, didn't you need me to take out the trash?"

Mr. McClain scratched his head. "Uh, I don't think you need to ..."

"Great! I'll do it right now."

He ran past me, catching a punch on the arm, and I beelined for the cushy chair he'd vacated. I sank into the chair and grabbed a handful of Christmas candy, hoping to tide myself over until dinner. Hopefully the hullaballoo surrounding our non-engagement would die down by then, and Maurice and I could eat in peace.

"How's school?" A forty-something with green talons for fingernails leaned over me. "You're at Howard, right?"

I nodded, finishing my fifth piece of candy.

"Sophomore year."

"I used to go to Homecoming all the time. Mmm-mmm! Y'all got some phyne brothas down there." She scratched the bridge of her nose, and I feared she'd put out an eye. "What are you studying?"

"English."

A crowd gathered behind her, led by the girl with the braids. "You wanna be a teacher?" she asked.

"I'm not sure. So I might study abroad next year and get some…"

"Oh, no, no, no." Green Talons waved me off. "You want to spend your first year of marriage in a different country?"

"As Maurice said, this isn't an engagement…"

"But if Reese goes too, you could honeymoon at the same time," she concluded.

"Mmm-hmm." Long Braids popped her gum. "That's what I'd do."

"Do those braids cause deafness?" Maurice tugged on one of them as he parted the crowd. "I told you we're not engaged."

Long Braids rolled her eyes. "Don't be dissin my hair, Maurice."

"And give my girl some room." He sat on the arm of my chair. "Y'all drawing too much heat."

"But I don't understand," Green Talons said. "Why would she need to study abroad if she's already got you?"

I tried and failed to see her logic. "What does one have to do with …"

"And for real for real," Long Braids said. "She don't need to be all the way in DC if her man is up

206

here."

"All right." Maurice helped me out of the chair. "If you people are finished minding our business, we're going upstairs."

"For what?" Green Talons said. "You ain't honeymooning yet."

Maurice sighed. "We're not eng ..."

"I'm just messing with you." Green Talons chuckled as we passed her, bending to Maurice's ear. "But leave that bedroom door open. I don't want no nieces or nephews."

TWENTY-FOUR

By the time we got on the road to my house, it was well after dark. Mom McClain cooked enough food to feed the whole block twice, and I ate more than my fair share. I missed the sweet potato pie while fielding an apologetic call from Corina, and by the time I came back, the pickings were slim. Green Talons kept offering me dessert, and though I never decline a sweet treat, that night I made an educated exception.

"Fruitcake pudding?" I asked as we pulled off.

Maurice shuddered. "I still have the taste in my mouth."

"Why did she serve that?"

"Because her love-struck husband makes her think she's B Smith or somebody."

"That's sweet."

"Then I'll have her make some jello jubilee for your birthday."

"No, you won't either." I adjusted the angle on my seat. "On the plus side, that culinary abomination got people to stop staring at my finger."

"What was with our families today?"

"At least yours was happy to see us. Nice change from what happened at my house."

"Yeah, but Mom knows I would have told her we were engaged. Once she freaked out and made the announcement, of course everyone believed her."

"I should have kept my gloves on, pretended I had circulation problems."

Maurice chuckled. "Well, that's the last family gathering for a while, so you should be good."

"Yeah." I studied the ring as we approached a red light. "Can I ask you something?"

"Of course."

"Why did you get me a diamond? You know opals are my favorite."

"I thought about that," he said after a moment. "But I ... I mean, I wanted you to know this ring wasn't just another piece of jewelry."

"A gift from you could never be just another anything."

"Do you want me to exchange it?"

"You would do that?"

"If you wanted me to."

I stroked the smooth band of the ring with my thumb, loving the fluttery feeling it gave me. "Nah. I wanna keep it. But ..."

"But what?"

"I wonder if you want me not to study abroad, like they said, and transfer to Penn instead."

"Honestly?"

"Hopefully."

He turned on his left blinker. "I can't deny wishing you were home and mine in every way."

"You mean sex?"

He gaped at me. "Um, what?"

"Never mind. Forget I said that."

"Not a chance. You wanna tell me where it came from?"

"Well ... because you said 'in every way.' "

The silent seconds ticked by, and I set my hands in my lap, resisting the urge to wring them. Traffic slowed to a stop again, and Maurice turned down the radio.

"I wasn't talking about sex. But denying those desires would be a lie."

"So how are you okay without it?"

"What?"

"I understand that you had a life before we were together, that you weren't sitting alone watching *The Jamie Foxx Show* at night."

"But?"

"You're older and more experienced, and sex is a non-option for us. And with me living in DC most of the year, I just wonder how you're okay with all that."

"Duchess." He brushed my cheek with the back of his hand. "I'm 'okay with all that' because loving you makes me patient. I mean, I'm always willing to do more, but I'm content to wait."

"Are your loins content too?"

He smiled. "My loins don't get a vote. I actually need to apologize for being so aggressive in DC. I just got overwhelmed being in your room for the first time, finally seeing this life you have that I'm not a part of. And with Busta Rhymes being all familiar and…"

"Busta Rhymes?" I pulled away. "You mean Mordecai? What does he have to do with anything?"

"He's into you."

I rolled my eyes. "I doubt that."

"He's too nice to you."

"That's his job. He treats everybody that way."

"I doubt that."

"I love you how protective you are, but there's no need." I turned in my seat to face him. "Mordecai may share my address, but you have my heart no matter where I am."

"I know. But I wish you didn't live so far away."

"I'm not far away now." I leaned in to kiss him. "So why don't we make the most of it?"

He brushed his lips against my mouth. "Best idea I've heard all day."

A car honked behind us, and I smiled. "To be continued."

Corina must have convinced Adrian to keep a low domestic profile, for I only saw him a few times for the rest of Christmas break. I even earned permission to skip Watchnight Service and spend New Year's Eve ice skating with Maurice at the UPenn rink. I suspected major concessions were being made, and I took full advantage of my newfound freedom.

I spent most of my time with Maurice in West Philly, stopping short of sleeping over. The Shop open every day except Mondays and holidays with never a dull moment between them. The guys kept the conversation flowing and varied, hitting every subject from crazy Y2K people expecting digital Armageddon to personal romantic crises. They asked for advice I was wholly unqualified to give, but Suzika had no shortage of opinions, making the fellas laugh and think. Naseem rolled his eyes whenever she spoke but couldn't feign disinterest.

If they weren't dating by Valentine's Day, I'd shave my head.

I even received a phone call from Mom McClain on New Year's Day as Maurice and I were heading to the movies.

"I'm so sorry for putting you on the spot at Christmas," she said. "I saw that diamond on your hand and lost my mind for a minute."

"It's okay."

"We just love you so much and were excited about the idea of you officially joining our family."

"Well, I already consider you guys family. And I hope you feel the same about me."

"Oh, we do, honey. Thank you for being so understanding."

If only my father had displayed similar contrition.

Having not spoken to me since Christmas Day, Adrian only knocked on my door this morning to offer me a ride to 30th Street Station. I declined with as much respect as I could muster, for until he changed his tune on Maurice, I had nothing to say to him. And the train ride back to DC was peaceful and quiet, exactly what I needed after a blockbuster Winter Break.

Per our tradition, the girls and I gathered for post-break brunch to chat and chew about our lives back home.

"Wow." Beside me, Cherrie shook her head when I finished my tale. "That's heavy stuff, D."

"Yeah, well, that's Adrian." I cut up my Cobb salad. "Who's next?"

"Let's see." Cherrie crumbled crackers in her soup. "Momma and GiGi took me to New York to see the tree and the Rockettes, which made me want to buy a pair of tap shoes."

Bernie reached for the salt. "Switching your major again?"

"Ha ha. And no, because my advisor would kill me and it doesn't fit my life plan."

"Not to mention you're two feet tall."

"And just when I thought the trip couldn't get any better," Cherrie said. "Guess who I saw at Penn station!"

Bernie bit into her Reuben. "Elmer Fudd?"

I looked at Bernie. "Is your blood sugar low?"

"Nope," she mumbled around her sandwich. "Just missed her, that's all."

Cherrie rolled her eyes. "Guess, Daria!"

"Rudy Giuliani?"

She frowned. "Why would seeing the mayor be amazing?"

"Maybe he usually takes the bus."

"I'll just tell you." She paused for effect. "Caprelle."

"Caprelle? Who is...wait! Caprelle from *Never Ever After?*"

Cherrie grinned so hard I thought her teeth would shatter. "And she wasn't alone."

I gasped. "If you say she was with Canyon, I will fall out."

"If y'all don't stop talking about this, I will fall out."

"Shut up, Bernie," we said together, and Cherrie dropped her voice to a whisper. "Rasool. And I talked to them."

I slapped Cherrie's arm. "Shut up!"

"Ow!" She rubbed the tender spot. "I haven't missed that at all."

"Would you just tell her what happened before she beats you up?" Bernie cried.

For her own safety, Cherrie recounted her conversation with Caprelle and Rasool, not bothering with their real names. Unlike his character on *Never Ever After*, Rasool was polite and personable and gladly posed for pictures. Caprelle was subdued on account of a sinus infection.

"They're like brother and sister in real life," Cherrie said. "Have known each other since childhood."

"Wow." I leaned back against the seat. "Now I want to see them together on the show."

"Right!" Cherrie said. "I mean, Canyon is phyne, but the Rasool-Caprelle connection is so obvious."

A loud snore from across the booth drew our attention. "Oh, I'm sorry," Bernie said. "I drifted off."

"You would think spending the entire break with her boyfriend would improve her manners," Cherrie said. "So much for Christmas miracles."

Bernie hid her smile behind her root beer. "It wasn't the entire break."

"So things are good with you guys?" I asked.

"Yep."

"And everything is out in the open?" Cherrie asked.

"Everything that needs to be there."

As Bernie slowly dipped her fries in mayonnaise, Cherrie sighed. "Oh, honey. You didn't tell him."

I looked at Bernie. "You didn't?"

"I couldn't find the right time," Bernie murmured. "He was getting along with my dad and brothers, my mom only told four embarrassing stories, and I couldn't wreck it. Not even for the sake of the truth."

"But if you can't be honest with him…"

"It's not that I can't, Cherrie. I don't see the point. Two months ago, I didn't get pregnant, so what's the point in telling him now? You feel me, right, D?"

"I understand your hesitation," I said. "But if the positions were reversed, would you have wanted him going through something like that alone?"

"But I wasn't alone. I had you two yokels."

"And if it was important enough to tell us," I said. "You should tell him."

"Like you did?"

"What do you mean?"

"Did you tell Maurice straight up that you're not getting married or transferring to Penn?"

"He knows that." She met my eyes, and I stared right back. "He does."

"Good." She turned to Cherrie. "Wanna split the double banana split?"

215

"Sure." Cherrie glanced at me. "You want in?"

"No, thanks." I turned to Bernie. "And what does a banana split have to do with you telling Tone the truth?"

"Nothing." Bernie wiped her mouth with a napkin. "But I was done talking about it and wanted something sweet. Any other questions?"

"Just one." I went back to my salad. "Why are you such a pain in the butt?"

"Oh, that's easy." She drained the rest of her root beer. "Because it's fun."

Twenty-Five

Dressed in sweats on the 9:30 shuttle, I wondered if I was insane. Despite the madness of that Brit Lit final, I earned another 4.0 last semester and planned to take it easy in the spring. But thanks to Dr. Maddox, I was now taking six classes: his seminar, two core requirements, and three courses for my major. I also kept the same work schedule at Borders, hoping the decision wouldn't be a GPA-crushing mistake.

The final group of riders boarded the bus, but I thought I was hallucinating when I saw Bernie among them. She stopped beside my seat and frowned. "Are you gonna move that bag sometime today?"

She sat down as I set my bookbag on my lap. "Why are you riding our shuttle?"

"Why walk if I can ride?"

"And why are you wearing sweats?"

"I'm going to class with you."

"You're taking Aerobic Dance Fitness?"

"The next question will cost you $5.00," she said as the bus pulled off.

"I didn't think people in the School of B took those electives."

"Well, we do, and this was the only tolerable option. Cherrie almost died last year."

"But she lost twelve pounds and three inches off her waist."

"I ain't worried about that." Bernie pulled out a Milky Way. "I love every one of these 197 pounds. And before you open your mouth, I'm in the 53rd percentile for my height."

"I didn't say a word."

Bernie bit into her breakfast of champions. "You'd better not."

"That woman is crazy." Bernie had not stopped complaining about our instructor since class let out. "I don't know what she thinks this is, but it isn't."

I pulled my wool hat over my chilly ears. "It wasn't that bad."

She stopped to gape at me. "Who expects 50 push-ups, pull-ups, sit-ups, sit-ins, and whatever else that was, and then makes us take five laps around the building on the first day? I'll say it again: that woman is crazy."

"So drop the class."

"Never." She huffed ahead of me. "I won't give her the satisfaction."

We stopped at the food trucks outside the School of B, needing to rehydrate. As I pulled out my wallet, Tone appeared on my left side. "Allow me."

"Thanks, dude." I unscrewed the cap and downed half the apple juice without tasting it. "I thought I was going to pass out."

"I am about to pass out." Bernie collapsed against Tone as we moved away from the line. "Carry me to my next class?"

"Gladly." He buried his face in her neck. "Mmm, I love how you smell."

"Huh?"

"Even through all these layers." He took a deep whiff. "I can catch your natural scent."

"My what?" Bernie shoved Tone away. "Ugh, I need a shower. Maybe three."

"What about your next class?" Tone called after her. "You gonna cut on the first day?"

"Don't have a choice!"

As Bernie disappeared around the corner, Tone turned to me in confusion. "I think she smells like a meadow on a sunny spring day."

"And I think you need to learn how to compliment a woman who feels sweaty and disgusting."

Tone checked his watch. "You heading back to Meridian?"

"Negative. I've got Contemporary Afro-American Studies with Dr. Maddox. His class fills fast, and I don't want to be stuck in the back with the slackers."

"I sit in the back."

"No comment."

The classroom was half full when I arrived at Locke Hall, but I found a seat on the front row. Other overachievers joined me there, and palpable anticipation hovered in the air. I pulled out my red notebook and fine point black rollerball pen when someone sat beside me with a chuckle. "Nice sweats."

"Mordecai? You're taking this class?"

"Am I that obvious?" At my smirk, he smiled. "Did you get the card I slipped under your door?"

"Yes! I'm so glad Melody likes her book."

"Likes? She takes it everywhere, sleeps beside it, and couldn't wait to write you that note. I swear she thanks me every time I see her."

"I couldn't be happier to hear that. You're such a good brother."

"I'm all right. But what about you? I didn't know you were a Maddox Addict."

"I'm not. But I saw him in Borders on Christmas Eve, and he invited me here."

"You would spend Christmas break at Borders."

"I was shopping."

"Yeah, sure."

A hush fell as Dr. Maddox strolled into the room and tossed his beat-up leather knapsack onto the platform. He blew into his hands for warmth and rubbed them together before addressing a brown-skinned girl leaning against the wall. "Why are you here?"

She stopped biting her nails. "What?"

"Why are you here?"

She looked around. "I don't know."

"Now there's an A-plus answer." He smiled. "I'll

come back to you."

"Why are you here?" he asked Mordecai.

"I'm taking a class in my minor."

Dr. Maddox folded his arms. "Ms. Nelson, do you know this gentleman?"

"More or less."

"Will you accept responsibility for his participation here?"

"Absolutely. If he doesn't behave, I'll snitch to his little sister."

"Brilliant black woman! I'll need to keep my eye on this front row."

He repeated his question around the room and received standard answers: It fulfills a requirement. They wanted to learn. They heard it was fun.

"Why are you here?" Dr. Maddox asked The Chesty Cheetah who'd arrived in the row behind me. I fought the urge to suck my teeth.

"I'll know by the end of April," she said.

He shook his head. "Imani, you promised to behave this semester."

Her light, pleasant laughter surprised me. "Come on, Doc. You know I got you!"

I wondered at their camaraderie as he returned to the platform.

"Let me tell you why I am here. I believe I have a divine appointment with your lives. Some of you will hear one fascinating fact you will never forget. Some of you detest serious scholarship and will drop the course tomorrow. Some of you will discover something about yourselves which will change the trajectory of your lives. And some of you will leave the same way you came.

"Here's what I promise. I promise you will work hard. I promise you will be challenged. I promise you will disagree with me at least once, perhaps enough to consider fisticuffs, a passion I respect but will not allow. I promise what you learn will help you no matter your course of study. And I promise if you stick with me, you will be rewarded.

"That's my opening day spiel. I wanted to give you the low-down before the first lesson. Those who want to drop, feel free. You'll make room for those who wish to stay. And don't feel bad for leaving—different people want different things, and you shouldn't waste time on what you know you don't want. Thanks for listening, and I'll see some of you Wednesday. Overriders, come to the front."

"What should we bring on Wednesday?" someone asked.

"A notebook, a pen, and an open mind," Dr. Maddox replied. "You'll get the syllabus and book list then."

"I like this guy already," Mordecai said.

"Yeah." I closed my notebook. "We're gonna have a blast."

Friday afternoon, I boarded an afternoon shuttle and collapsed into my seat. The first week of spring semester was over, and I somehow survived with my sanity intact. My fitness class with Bernie was more work than I bargained for, but watching her grumble through every exercise was worth the price of pain. As a reward, tonight's dinner would consist of the last of Corina's barbecued chicken and cheddar mashed potatoes with her apple crumb cake for dessert.

As I entered Meridian, I realized I hadn't checked my mail since returning from Christmas break. The flirty girl who ogled Maurice was behind the desk, but she didn't seem to remember me when I gave her my room number. Most of the mail was unremarkable, but a large manila envelope got my attention. Its penmanship was vaguely familiar, but the return address gave little clue of the package's contents.

Once I returned to my room, though, curiosity became incredulity.

Inside the envelope was an assortment of bridal brochures covering everything from venues to menus. Also included was the latest issue of *Philadelphia Wedding*, its glossy pages flagged with Post-its in Mom McClain's flowery handwriting. Clipped to the magazine cover was a thin envelope bearing my name with a "Read me first" note beneath it. I set the magazine aside and opened the letter, hoping Mom McClain hadn't forgotten her promise not to pressure me.

Daria, dear ...

Now don't be alarmed—this isn't what it looks like. But I have some exciting news, and you're the first person I wanted to share it with.

Pop noticed how excited I was about the idea of a wedding, so he's decided to let us renew our vows for our anniversary this fall! We got married almost thirty years ago at City Hall, and I wore a cream suit from the sale rack at Penney's. I never got to do any of the fun and fancy wedding stuff, and I can't believe I'll finally get the chance!

Now, Maurice doesn't care about such things, and that's fine. But I was hoping you could help me make some choices. And ... well ... I was also hoping you'd be willing to be part of my bridal party. Do they still call it that these days? I'm so out of the loop!

No pressure if you aren't sure. I know you're busy with school and all, but if you wouldn't mind, I would love your advice and to have you stand up with me. You're like the daughter I never had, and I couldn't imagine doing this without you.

I sent you copies of everything I have with the same notes I've made. Maybe we can talk next week after you've looked over everything? No matter what you decide, thank you for just letting me share this news with you. I feel like a schoolgirl preparing for her first dance!

Love,

Mom McClain

I set the letter on my bed with a happy sigh. Mom McClain said she wanted me in her family, but to ask me to stand up at her wedding was a whole 'nother level of inclusion, and I was deeply touched. I picked up the magazine again with renewed interest, envisioning her smiling face as she wrote the many notes.

Do you like this aisle runner?

This neckline is too low for me, but the skirt is beautiful.

Would these colors work for a fall wedding?

For someone who claimed to be out of the loop,

Mom had amassed a crap-ton of information in the past few days. She had thought about every possible detail of the ceremony and reception, and if I was going to keep up with her, I would need to get organized.

I opened my supplies drawer and rubbed my eager hands together. Let Operation: Mom McClain's Wedding begin!

Twenty-Six

My American Lit professor was dumb late, which was unlike him. Students could leave without penalty if a professor was fifteen minutes late, but half this class had already exercised that right. With my luck, I would run into him on the way out and have to come back anyway, so I might as well wait the required time.

As another student came to his feet, the door opened, admitting a surprise visitor and a collective groan in the room.

"And good afternoon to you." Dr. Treble set her briefcase on the front desk. "I see my reputation precedes me."

I hid my smile as the protests simmered. Even without the 'A' I'd earned in last semester's seminar, Dr.

Maddox's favorable report rang in my ear, banishing any apprehension I might feel about another class with the notorious Dr. Treble.

After announcing our former professor had returned to his home state for a family emergency, Dr. Treble pulled a folder from her attaché. It was identical to the one from which she pulled my Study Abroad application, and I made a mental note to complete and return it to her next week.

"According to the syllabus, you're scheduled for a unit test." She adjusted her glasses. "I don't think I'll be doing that."

Tearing that syllabus in half, she dropped it into the can beside the desk. The room sighed with relief, one student muttering she'd forgotten to study. The boy beside her cosigned the admission, adding that Dr. Treble might not be as bad as they thought.

The intrepid woman looked his way with narrowed eyes. Her expression was impossible to read, but her gaze lingered on him before she retrieved different papers from her bag.

"Instead of a unit test today, you will submit an essay next week." She paused for disappointment as she distributed a handout. "I need to know what you know, and this is the best way to determine that."

I intended to review the assignment details later, but the murmuring around me suggested I do so now. The essay was due next Thursday and required examination of two early-American writings covered so far. There were no additional details about topic or length, so I set down the paper and raised my hand.

"Yes, Ms. Nelson?"

"Could you please clarify?"

Dr. Treble laid the extra papers on her desk. "Clarify what?"

"The requirements for this essay."

"Did you not receive a handout?"

"I did." I offered a smile which was not returned. "But I wondered if you could elaborate on what it says."

"Certainly." She leaned against the front of the desk, crossing her feet at the ankles. "The directions are written in clear, grammatically correct English. If they are not elaborate enough for you, perhaps you should head downstairs for a Freshman English refresher course."

Dr. Treble's arctic reply brought the room to a complete halt. The incredulous stares of my classmates singed my face, but with Dr. Treble watching, I could not react. I swallowed hard, hoping my expression was neutral enough, and nodded.

"Any other questions?" Silence was the only reply, and Dr. Treble nodded. "Good. Now open your textbooks to page 27. Our discussion will begin there."

Though the remaining hour proceeded without incident, I could not get Dr. Treble's censure out of my head. Not during Egyptian Mythology where I probably failed the pop quiz on symbols. Not on the shuttle ride to Shaw/Howard Metro station where a local drill team rehearsed its routine on the platform. Not even when I got to work and found a fresh batch of peanut butter cookies in the café. No matter how I repackaged her comments, I was left with one disheartening truth.

Dr. Treble thought I was stupid.

There could be no other explanation for her curt response. She knew the class was confused, saw the darting glances as she passed out that ridiculously vague assignment, yet she treated me as if I were the village idiot complete with dunce cap and jester's cloak. The last time I'd been embarrassed like that in school, I was in third grade and Corina had to bring me a new pair of pants. Compared to this humiliation, that incident was an evening stroll on The Yard.

Not in the mood to deal with people, I asked to spend the bulk of my shift at Borders in the Receiving Room with the new arrivals. Our back shelves were crowded with post-holiday arrivals that needed sorting and boxes that needed opening. It was a task no one on the fiction team wanted and the type of mindlessness I needed. As I worked, I hoped to unearth the courage to face Dr. Treble again.

Or figure out how to drop the class without losing face.

With WHUR playing on the small radio in the back, the first two hours of my shift flew by. I was about to tackle mystery paperbacks when the phone on the receiving desk rang.

"This is Daria."

"Why you hiding in the back?"

"Bernie, what are you doing on an employee-only phone?"

"Telling you to get out here. Ain't it time for your break?"

"Yeah, but I was…"

"Good. I'm in Self-Help."

She hung up, and I straightened my pile of books before exiting through the rear door. I found Bernie where she said she'd be, her full lips curved in a smirk.

"*Help Me Help You Help Me.*" She flipped over the book. "Who writes this stuff?"

"Don't judge." I filed the hardback book alphabetically. "Some people need all the help they can get."

She gave me a sidelong glance. "Who spit in your latte?"

"Dr. Treble took over one of my classes and decided playing me was her first order of business."

"That sucks."

"She assigned an essay next week, and I have no idea what to write."

"I find that hard to believe."

"I don't write well for Dr. Treble." I reshelved a book that was upside-down. "My in-class essay for last semester's final exam was a mess."

"I thought you said you aced it."

"Even so, if her attitude today was any indication, I should take the 'F' now."

"Don't be so dramatic." Bernie straightened a book that lay sideways. "Maybe she's going through menopause. Them hot flashes can make you wanna smack somebody."

"I know the feeling." I remembered I was on break and decided we should both leave the books alone. "You never told me why you're here."

"And you never asked." At my unamused stare, she sighed. "I'm hiding from Antonio."

"Why?" My gaze dipped to her stomach. "Do you think you're…"

"Be late one time, and this is what people think of you." She walked out of the aisle and flopped into a cushy wingback in the nearby seating area. " 'No, I don't,' to answer your question. But it's in that neighborhood."

As she twirled an errant loc around her finger , I waited on the adjacent sofa.

"I told him," she whispered.

"Wow." I leaned closer. "What did he say?"

"He was upset I kept it a secret so long, hated that I went through it without him. And…"

"And?"

"He said we should leave each other alone."

"What?" I covered my mouth, hearing how loud I was. "He broke up with you?"

"No. He said we should stop doing things that could lead to pregnancy."

"Things? As in …"

"As in he thinks if we only stop doing the main thing, we could do other things that would tempt us to do that thing, so we're stopping everything."

"Everything?"

"Ev-er-y-thing."

"Couldn't you go on the pill? I'm not advocating premarital sex, but if pregnancy's your issue, there are ways around it."

She shook her head. "I forget to lock my front door at night, so taking a tiny pill every day won't make the short list. And now that Tone and Christ rekindled their relationship on New Year's Eve, he wants to abstain for other reasons."

"Good for him." My comment earned a frown. "Bad for you?"

"No, I'm glad he's getting closer to the Lord, and I want us to be chaste. But wanting it and living it are two different things." She slapped my leg with a smile. "And that's where you come in."

"I don't follow."

She raised her right hand. "I hereby declare you my Holy Coochie Coach."

"Don't ever call me that again."

"Good Girl Guru?"

"Slightly better."

"Invent the title of your choice." She joined me on the sofa and put her arm around me. "But you and I are going to spend some serious quality time together."

"For how long?"

"When is his graduation?" I groaned into my hands as Bernie rubbed my back in circles. "Oh, cheer up, Charlie. It's gonna be a great semester!"

Twenty-Seven

True to her word, Bernie spent the entire weekend in my room. Though she thwarted my plans to catch up on *Never Ever After*, it was nice having someone to talk to when the mood struck and a steady hand to polish the nails on my right hand.

She was no help, however, in the essay writing department, so I was on my own figuring out what the higgledy-piggledy Dr. Treble wanted. After spinning my wheels for the better part of the weekend, I developed some semblance of a thesis statement. She gave no length requirements, but less than five pages would surely earn the Sandman's hook. When my thoughts dissolved at the top of page seven, I tacked on a logical conclusion, printed out my essay, and rewarded myself with two packs of Twinkies.

But this perfectionist couldn't leave well enough alone, so I pored over my paper Monday afternoon during a break between classes. Red pen out and PunchOut combo to one side, I read my work with a critical eye, looking for thin arguments, conflicting evidence, and glaring grammatical errors. Dr. Treble seemed the type to tack a bad essay to the front door for all to see, and I wasn't trying to be the first example.

I was searching my glossary for clarification on a literary term when Tone slid across from me in the booth. "How can you concentrate in here?"

"Ignoring the chaos helps me think." I looked up in time to catch him stealing one of my fries. "Is that on your coach-approved diet?"

"No, so don't tell anyone." He leaned forward, peering at my essay. "What's your topic?"

" 'Revisiting the Revolutionaries.' You can only analyze colonial literature so many ways, you know?" Tone nodded, steepling his hands on the table. "But I'm sure you didn't come here to discuss Samuel Adams."

He tapped his fingers on the table. "I need to talk to you about something but not if you think it's going to be weird."

I capped my pen and closed my folder. "I won't know if it's weird if I don't know what it is."

"Right."

"But if it's about the holy state of affairs between you and B, it won't be weird."

"For real?"

"As long as you keep it PG."

"Thank you." He sighed. "What did she tell you?"

"We're here to discuss you."

He stole another french fry, dipping it in my ketchup cup. "I know this is the right decision, and I want to stick with it. I really do."

"But…"

"It's killing me, D. I miss Bernadette so much I can't sleep at night. I miss her eyes, her laughter, that thing she does with her…"

I held up both hands. "PG, remember?"

"That thing she does with her nose when she thinks too hard. Now who needs to keep it PG?"

I moved my fries after he swiped three more. "So why can't you spend time together in public?"

"I don't want to risk it. I'm not saying I can't control myself, but Bernadette and I went there after our first real date, so we don't know to behave without it. I can't hold her hand without wanting more."

"Wow. Maurice and I have never been anywhere close to there."

"Not even during Homecoming? Why not?"

"It's easy not to do something you've never done."

"Exactly! This sexual siesta is like…it's like when someone tells you not to laugh and suddenly everything is funny." He slumped against the banquette seat. "And lately, whenever I see her…"

"Everything is funny. Yeah, that's tough. Have you ever considered trying to…" My cell phone buzzed in my bookbag, and when I saw the home number, I wondered why Corina was there in the middle of the day. "Mom? Are you okay?"

"Daria, hey."

I bit back a mild expletive. "Hi, Dad."

"Am I disturbing you?"

"Yes, I'm on my way to class. I only answered because I thought it was Mom."

"Right. So, uh, listen. I'm coming to DC and want to take you to dinner."

"Tonight's no good, and I work tomorrow night."

"I'm not coming until tomorrow. And you're off Wednesdays, right?"

Crap. Why did I give Corina such a detailed schedule?

Adrian interpreted my silence as acquiescence, and his excitement rang through the line. "So what time should I pick you up from Meridian?"

The only positive outcome of talking to Adrian was the reduction in anxiety over my American Lit essay. Tone excused himself after the call, deciding my problem was bigger than his, and I fought the urge to invent an illness, request Corina's intervention, or leave my father hanging when he showed up.

But considering those options gave me spiritual indigestion, so I came straight home Wednesday afternoon to shower and change for my daddy-daughter date. Adrian never cared what I wore, but my rebellious streak chose a cute HU sweater instead of something neutral. Daddy's earrings stayed in my jewelry box—for safety reasons, of course—so the only diamond on my body was my gift from Maurice. That one hadn't returned my calls in three days, but Adrian didn't need to know that. I would give every appearance of a proud

Bisonette-slash-cherished girlfriend tonight no matter what it cost me.

I was in no mood to watch him yuck it up with Mordecai in the lobby, so I went outside fifteen minutes before pickup time, donning my thickest scarf for warmth. When his silver sedan pulled up, I jumped in the passenger seat as soon as the car stopped.

"You didn't have to do that," he said as I buckled my seatbelt. "I would have come in."

"It's fine." I favored him with a quick smile. "I had an early lunch, and I'm really hungry."

As we drove to the restaurant, Adrian steered our conversation toward his recruitment efforts in DMV area high schools. Penn wanted to increase its out-of-state minority enrollment, and with so many of these students opting for local schools, he had his work cut out for him.

"I hate to admit it," he said, "but a lot of them set their hearts on Howard in middle school. Convincing them otherwise is no easy feat."

"Guess our senior year conversations were great practice."

"Not really, seeing how that turned out." He glanced my way. "But Penn can offer them something Howard can't."

"Student loan debt?"

"A new environment. Many of these kids have seldom traveled more than 25 miles from home. Attending an out-of-state university offers an opportunity to discover a new place, see what the world has to offer."

Though I'd never admit it, location was one of Howard's biggest selling points. Not that there was anything wrong with my hometown, but the idea of embarking on my collegiate journey somewhere other than Philly was enticing.

"Our reservation is at six, but being early couldn't hurt," Adrian said in the restaurant parking lot. "I went with Chinese because Mom said you went to Yu Hsiang over the break. Is that okay?"

"Sure." I pulled my scarf around my ears as the trees swayed outside my window. "I wish I'd have brought my earmuffs."

"Glove compartment."

I pulled the indicated handle and found a pair of fluffy white earmuffs in their protective plastic cube. When I looked at my father, he shrugged. "Some things never change."

I pressed them against my chilly ears. "How long have these been here?"

"I was preparing for Thanksgiving. Better late than never, right?"

"Right."

Bamboo plants, jacquard wallpaper, and tinkling music greeted us as we entered the restaurant, along with a prompt and friendly host. After we ordered our food, our waitress removed the menus with their gilded Chinese characters, and my father poured the tea.

"If a new environment is so important," I asked. "Why did you choose Penn?"

He flicked the sugar packets before tearing them open. "I enjoyed living in Philadelphia and wanted nothing more than to study there. It's why I went to grad school at Penn and work there now. If you're happy where you are, there's no need to leave."

"Can't you be happy where you are and crave new experiences?"

"Yes." He sipped his tea, wincing at its temperature. "But running away out of fear or insecurity is a different matter."

"Is that what you think I did? Ran to Howard because I was afraid to stay in West Philly?"

"I didn't say that." He set his spoon on his saucer. "But I find it interesting that you did."

"That's not why I left." I stirred my tea with more vigor than necessary. "In fact, I'm studying abroad next fall."

"Where?"

"Does it matter?"

"Very much. Different cities offer different experiences. You want to reach your academic goals and ensure your personal expectations are also met. What are your options?"

"Why do you care?"

His eyes widened, but he remained calm. "Because it's an important decision, and if you want to talk about it, I'm all ears."

"Based on your reaction to Howard, I didn't think you'd support me."

"Believe or not, I will always support you, even if I disagree with your choices."

"And you don't disagree with me studying abroad?"

"Not at all. I think you'd love it."

I returned his smile as the waitress arrived with our pupu platter. The assortment of savory appetizers made my stomach growl, and I set my napkin on my lap. Our server set the tray on the table and struck the match to light the oil in the center plate.

But when the flame ignited, a horde of tiny roaches crawled out from beneath the plate, scurrying toward our saucers.

I screamed and fled the booth, and Adrian joined me in the aisle beside the table. As our server smashed the vermin with napkins and apologies, Adrian grabbed our coats. "I am not paying for that!"

Twenty-Eight

Shaking off considerable heebie-jeebies, we returned to my neck of the woods and got some Cluck U to go. My room was clean enough where we could eat off the floor, but the dinette table sufficed.

Adrian licked atomic sauce from his fingers. "Do we have Cluck U in Philly?"

"Nope. Another reason locals don't want to leave DC."

"No doubt." He wiped his mouth with a napkin. "I'm gonna need another order before I head home tomorrow morning."

"Don't you have afternoon appointments?"

"My last school visit was today, but I wanted to have dinner with my daughter."

"I'm glad you did."

We finished our meal with easy conversation and washed the dishes together. When the last plate was dry, I grabbed my phone. "Bernie and Cherrie would love to see you. They should be in Cherrie's room."

Adrian checked his watch. "Bernie's visiting Cherrie at this hour?"

"She's creating new habits. It's a long story."

"What about that Mordecai?" he asked after I left Cherrie a voicemail. "Is he around?"

"Is that why you lingered in the lobby earlier?"

"Seeing him again wouldn't have been the worst thing. He seems like a great guy. Any chance you two might be…"

"Good friends but nothing more? Absolutely."

"Can't blame me for trying." He wandered toward my desktop bookshelf, scanning the titles. "A backwards dictionary? Where'd you get that?"

"Borders. My inner geek gets so happy when I use it."

"Inner?" I slapped his arm, and he laughed. "Let me check this out."

As he reached for the dictionary, the bookends slid the wrong way, and everything on my top shelf fell off the desk to the floor. "We seem to cause accidents everywhere we go," he said. "I wonder if there's a…"

Adrian crouched down mid-sentence and picked up something I couldn't see. Stepping around him, I prepared to make light of my penchant for pocket thesauri. But every sensible word flew out of my brain when I saw what was in his hand.

It was my copy of *Philadelphia Wedding*.

His voice was taut. "What is this?"

"It's not what you think."

"And what do I think?"

"You think it's proof I'm marrying Maurice this year, and you're wrong."

"Am I?" He came to his feet, turning the magazine on its side. "Seems well-marked. Lots of colors and symbols."

"Those post-its aren't mine."

He flipped to a random page and pointed at its note. "This isn't your handwriting?"

"Let me see it."

"Why do you need to see it?" He closed the magazine. "Either it's your handwriting or it isn't."

"Let me see the one you mean, and I can tell you if…"

"Are you thinking a Spring Break wedding?" He tossed the bridal book onto the bed. "Penn's break is a week before yours, and if I need time off to give you away, I'll need two weeks' notice."

"Dad, stop it."

"Then again, maybe you don't want me there." He folded his arms. "Is that what this is about? You're planning a wedding behind my back and have no intention of inviting me?"

I copied his stance. "Why should I answer? You're going to cut me off and tell me what I mean anyway."

"What choice do I have? Every time I think I make progress, you spring something crazy on me."

"I didn't spring anything on you! The books fell, that magazine spilled out, and you jumped to the wrong conclusion as usual."

"Is this not a bridal magazine, Daria?"

"Yes." I sighed. "Mom McClain was asking me if ..."

"Why is Maurice's mother sending you a bridal magazine?"

"If you would let me finish, I would explain."

"Were there satin swatches? An appointment for cake-tasting on President's Day? Maybe you can sneak home for that too."

"This is why I don't talk to you. All you do is joke and judge."

"You think I would joke about this? My barely-legal daughter is wearing a diamond ring purchased by a boy I don't trust and hiding wedding books between her *Norton* anthologies. There is nothing funny about any of that."

I closed my eyes. "I don't know what you want me to say."

"Say whatever you want. It's not like you'd tell the truth."

The words forced me to open my eyes. I waited for an apology or clarification, but he stuffed his hands in his pockets. His downturned gaze moved across the floor and landed on the hapless pile of books. "I'll pick these up."

"Don't bother." I grabbed my keys off their wall hook. "I have to go study."

"That's probably best."

He gathered his coat and left the Cluck U menu on the table. I locked my door with furious force, standing as far away from him as the empty elevator allowed. The desk clerk returned our ID cards, and I walked away without a goodbye or backward glance. A girl from the fifth floor jumped in the elevator at the last minute, and as the doors closed, I swallowed the scream threatening to break loose.

"I cannot believe him." I reloaded my spoon with frozen comfort as Cherrie looked on. "He came all the way down here, wooed me with Cluck U, only to make me feel worse than I did at Christmas."

"I'm sorry," she said.

"And what's worse? He doesn't think he did anything wrong. As far as he's concerned, this is my fault." I paused to swallow my spoonful. "He called me a liar. Stood right there and called me a liar. I don't know how we're supposed to recover from this." As I dug my spoon into my bowl once more, I looked up at Bernie. "Why are you looking at me like that?"

"Who drowns their sorrows in sherbet? The fat content is laughable."

"We have another fitness assessment Monday."

"And?"

I turned back to Cherrie. "For all that, why did he bother coming in the first place? I should have followed my first mind and pretended I wasn't home."

"So you could feel guilty until summer break? Not worth it." Cherrie intercepted my spoon and sampled my wares. "Neither is this. Where's the rocky road?"

I pointed at the Microfridge. "Why is everything so hard with him?"

"Because he's your father and cannot accept your

new identity as a consummating, engag—uh, promised woman." Bernie smiled. "See? I didn't say it."

"How were things before the magazine fell?" Cherrie asked.

"They were great. We were laughing, talking about Study Abroad. He supports me on that. At least, he did."

"Then the night wasn't a total wash." Cherrie grabbed a bowl and spoon. "Give it a few days, call him up, and just…"

"I'm not calling him because this wasn't my fault. Maurice's mother asked me to help her plan her vow renewal ceremony, and Adrian sullied the sentiment with suspicion and sarcasm."

Bernie gave me a thumbs-up. "Nice alliteration."

"Daria, can I ask you something without you getting mad?"

"Not the best way to begin, Cherrie."

"Do you want to marry Maurice?"

I looked up. "What kind of question is that?"

"A fair one." She scooped some ice cream into her bowl, doubling the amount when Bernie grabbed a spoon. "Do you want to marry him?"

I carried my bowl to the sink, unwrapping a new sponge. "Not this summer as Adrian seems to think."

"Next year?"

I laughed. "No."

"The next?"

"Try again."

"After graduation?"

I turned to face Cherrie. "Do you want to marry him?"

"I'm trying to understand why you accepted his ring

246

if you have no intention of marrying him."

"Because it's…"

"Not an engagement ring, I know." She passed her bowl to Bernie. "But you know that ring represents more than some vague hope for your future. It means something serious to Maurice, and no matter what anyone else thinks, you need to figure out what it means to you."

I set the dried bowl in its assigned spot. Tonight was supposed to be about repairing my relationship with my dad, not defining my romance with Maurice. And from the look of it, I wasn't equipped to do either.

"Does she have to decide right now?" Bernie glanced at her Strawberry Shortcake watch. "*Soul Food* is coming on, and D has clearer reception and better snacks."

"Gee, thanks," Cherrie said.

"I call 'em like I see 'em."

As Bernie adjusted my guest pillows to her specifications, Cherrie joined me at the sink. "Don't be mad at me."

"I could never be mad at you. But I've had it with all the men in Philadelphia."

"Good thing you're 100 miles away."

I rolled my eyes. "Until one of them pops up for a visit."

"In that case, just remember." Cherrie hooked her arm in mine. "Visiting hours always end."

Twenty-Nine

With my mental attention focused on not thinking about my father, I had nothing left for school the next day. So when Dr. Treble called for essays at the end of class, I laid mine atop the pile without a hint of trepidation. She didn't look up and I didn't linger, leaving the room as soon as was polite.

My cell phone buzzed in my pocket on the front steps of Locke Hall, but I didn't answer. If the earlier calls were any indication, Corina was fulfilling her marital duty to defend my father. He must have called her first thing this morning, likely spinning last night's events to cast me as the naughty daughter with a willful streak and innate inability to tell the truth.

Good thing I also had a mobile phone I could

ignore.

A follow-up buzzing interrupted my thoughts, indicating yet another voicemail. This would be the third, and though not in the mood to talk to my parents, I could listen to a message.

> "Good morning, Daria. This is your mother, you know, the one who always has your best interests at heart and would never say or do anything to hurt you. I just got off the phone with your father, and…well, I don't know what to say, but that's never stopped me before! Maybe that's why you're so reluctant to talk to your father: you never know what to say because you don't know what he's going to say. It's like the two of you are playing conversational chicken, and no one understands …"

The message cut off, and I wondered if she stepped into a bad spot. I went on to the next message.

> "How rude of your machine to cut me off! I was in the middle of a very good point. And I can't remember what it was now…oh, soda crackers! It'll come back to me, I hope. In any case, you should call your father. He feels terrible about what he said, and though he stands by his belief that Maurice is wrong for you, he…"

I deleted the message, hoping she would change the

subject in her third voicemail.

> "Daria, it's me again. I hope you've had time to consider what I said. Your father is only looking out for you, and though his mouth sometimes gets ahead of him, you can't deny his intentions are good and right, as they always are toward you. This isn't really about Maurice, and I hope you soon come to see that. I love you both so much and hate to see you fighting. Could you call me to let me hear your voice? I just want to know you're okay. Love you."

With a heavy sigh, I closed my phone, grateful for the Metro shuttle's arrival. Slumping into my seat, I promised to call Corina during my break at Borders, hoping she would offer comfort not counsel.

Though based on what awaited me at Pentagon City, I needed both.

With two call-outs and one cashier going home sick, my plan to spend the evening alone in my section was totally derailed. I was stuck on the register with only the store manager available for backup, and that only on occasion as the cappuccino machine also decided to malfunction.

I expected a clogged toilet any minute.

"Would you like your receipt in-hand or in the bag?" My customer held out her hand, smiling as I handed her the slip of paper. "Thank you for shopping at Borders and have a great evening. May I help the next person in line?"

I stretched my back as the next customer struggled with her overflowing basket. As she set some of the titles on the counter, I spotted three without prices and one with coffee rings from her trip to the café. She had a similar stain on her white sweater but said the book was damaged when she found it.

Would this night ever end?

As I rang up her stickered purchases, I heard my manager on the loudspeaker. My customer matched my name tag to the name my manager called, and she frowned. "I shouldn't have to wait to buy overpriced books."

I forced a smile. "No, ma'am."

She huffed and grabbed an assortment of Lindor balls. "How much for ten?"

"They're three for a dollar, so…"

"Never mind." She tossed all the candies into one bin, ruining the color-coded display and activating my dormant OCD. "I can get a Hershey bar for 50 cents."

I sped through the rest of her order, taking her word for the prices of the unmarked books. "Your total is $168.47."

"For five books?" Her inaccurate tally earned an eye roll from the customer behind her. "I'll just go to the library. Two hundred dollars—this place is crazy!"

I set her loaded bags behind the counter, rubbing my eyes as my manager paged me again. I asked the next customer to excuse me and picked up the nearest phone.

"Hey, sorry." I said to my manager. "I need you to void this order."

"The lady from the café? Saw that coming. Switch

to register three, and I'll be there soon. And your fiancé is on line two."

That was a surprise. "I told you I'm not engaged."

"Tell him. That's how he introduced himself, saying it was an emergency."

"What?"

"Take it after you clear your line. I hope everything is okay."

After my last customer took his receipt and bags, I picked up line two with my heart in my throat. "Maurice?"

"Duchess! Thank God."

"What's wrong? Is Mom okay?"

"What? Yeah, she's fine."

"Is everything all right at The Shop?"

"Business is booming."

"Then what's the emergency?"

"Emergency? Oh." He laughed. "My bad. I didn't think they'd give you the phone otherwise."

I pinched the bridge of my nose. "Maurice, I asked you not to call me at work. I'm going to get in trouble."

"I'm sorry. But I miss you."

"I miss you too." I leaned against the counter. "I've had a craptacular week."

"School kicking your butt?"

"Among other things. When can you visit again?"

"I don't know. Things at The Shop are crazy busy, and I'm not ready to leave Suzika in charge. Naseem would lock the keys in the safe, and no one else is qualified."

"What about a day trip on a Monday?" I played with the phone cord. "The Shop is closed, right?"

"Usually, but I've been accepting some high-profile clients who want a more private experience. It's really paying off."

"I'm glad." And tried to sound like it. "Could you pencil me in for a Monday next month?"

"I'll see, Duch. I was hoping you could come up for spring break."

"I don't know about that. My course load is full, and I'm already struggling." My manager approached the registers to void my last order, eyeing the clock behind us.

"I'm so glad I got to hear your voice, but please don't call here again unless it's a true emergency."

"Missing you doesn't count?"

I could feel my cheeks warming. "Not according to the employee manual."

"Don't worry. If you get fired, I can carry you."

"Maurice…"

"All right. But call me tonight so I can escort you home."

"I will. Love you."

I apologized to my manager as another line formed at the register. He logged in beside me and waved the next group of customers forward. A mohawked blonde with a cheek piercing set a stack of CDs on the counter, and I smiled. "Did you find everything you wanted?"

After two straight hours as cashier, my manager had mercy and let me shelve awhile. I grabbed my cart of mass market paperbacks and headed to science fiction.

At a glance I saw the need for alphabetizing, so I rolled up my sleeves and started with Douglas Adams. I was negotiating space around Tananarive Due when Mordecai walked up my aisle. "There you are."

I wiped my weary brow. "Here I am."

"You look beat. Can I get you something from the café?"

"We're not allowed to drinks on the floor, but thanks for offering." I sat on a stool to reach the bottom shelves. "You came all this way to see me?"

"Yes and no. I'm catching a movie with some Fine Arts folks across the street, but I wanted to run something by you, and I remembered you worked tonight." He sat on the floor beside me. "My next door neighbor loved Mel's Christmas gift and asked if we could do something similar for his wife for their 40th wedding anniversary in late March."

"How sweet!"

"He said he'd pay us too."

"Even sweeter."

"I told him I'd have to check with you, so if you can't…"

"Don't be silly. We can start this weekend."

"You sure?"

I cocked an eyebrow. "Do I need to tell you a third time?"

"No, ma'am. Thanks."

"None needed. I love these books. They remind me writing is more than essays and chapter reviews."

"And give me the chance to draw something I actually like." He checked his watch and came to his feet. "Need a hand getting up?"

"No, I'll be fighting with this section until quitting time at eleven."

"My movie will be over by then, so I'll pop by to escort you home."

"You don't have to do that."

"I know, but I want to. Gotta make sure you're safe."

"Protecting your investment, huh?"

"You know it."

"Go enjoy your movie. I'll see you at Meridian."

He bowed, tipping an imaginary hat. "Whatever you say, partner."

Mordecai left, and I turned back to my stubborn shelves. The time passed without interruption, and before I knew it, my manager announced there were fifteen minutes to close. His words reminded me of CoCo's store at Christmas, and I decided to leave a message on her private work line tonight. It was better than an email and eliminated the possibility of speaking with her. My wounds from Adrian's antics were too fresh to endure mom's attempts at reconciliation, no matter how well-intended.

After last call, I rolled my full cart to the restocking area. I clocked out, accepting my manager's thanks for my help, and called Maurice. The phone rang seven times, so I hung up, went to the bathroom, and checked the freebie bin for quirky books or country CDs. After scoring a classic George Strait collection, I tried Maurice again. This time, it rang twice then disconnected. When a third call went straight to voicemail, I turned my ringer off and put my phone in my bookbag.

As I took the mall exit out of the store, I saw

Mordecai sitting on a bench across from Linens n' Things. He stood at my approach with a sheepish shrug. "I'm old-fashioned."

"Good." I returned his smile. "Looks like I need an escort after all."

Thirty

Two weeks later, I was in the fifth floor kitchen when Cherrie appeared in the doorway. "There you are!" She collapsed against the wall beside me, fanning her flushed face. "I've been looking all over."

"What if I was still on campus?" I stirred my ramen noodles. "You'd be breathless for nothing."

"No time for logic. I have a meeting in a half hour but wanted to talk to you about Valentine's Day."

My stomach soured. "Why?"

"Because I've spent the past four nights with Bernie, and she's freaking out. The coitus embargo is going well, but she's afraid to spend the holiday with Antonio. Too many overtones."

I caught that gleam in her eyes. "What do you want

to do?"

"I want to throw a platonic co-ed get-together in my room. We'll be there, Tone will invite a friend or two, and everything will be chill. Unless you have plans with Maurice."

"Nope." If my answer surprised her, she didn't show it. "So what do you need me to do?"

"Show up and be your pleasant, charming self. Oh, and prepare to dance."

"What?"

She grinned before scurrying out of the room. "Just kidding!"

Her enthusiasm followed me to my room but dissipated at the door. I would do anything for Bernie, especially when she was trying so hard to be chaste. But with the way things stood between Maurice and me, I wanted to spend this Valentine's Day alone, watching *Café Latte* like I'd never seen it before.

Like most girls, my relationship with Valentine's Day evolved over the years. At first Cherrie and I had sleepovers where we did each other's nails and made popcorn-and-candy necklaces. In our early teens, we upgraded to bowling parties with other single gals, attending the occasional co-ed game night.

But Maurice's arrival changed things, and junior and senior year, my pseudo-beau and I watched movies in my living room under Adrian's watchful eye. No, they weren't romantic films—*Imitation of Life* and *The Power of One*—but we spent Valentine's Day together, and that's what mattered. Last year, I attended a PunchOut poetry slam with Cherrie while Maurice left me a sappy voicemail apologizing for my gift being late.

With things finally going in the right direction, Maurice and I would do much better this year.

I was almost sure of it.

Well, I should have been sure of one thing, and that was the gift of Corina's signature Valentine's Day gift box. Nobody sent care packages like my mother, and this year's bounty was better than ever. Among the goodies were butterscotch Krimpets and oatmeal raisin cookie bars—God bless Tastykake—freesia body wash with matching lotion and loofah, three pairs of fuzzy pink socks, and a greeting card filled with heart-shaped confetti and five-dollar bills. On top was a handwritten note reading, "I Corinthians 13:6, 7. It goes for parents, too."

Subtle, huh?

On the subject of my boyfriend, I could say that his gift arrived on time this year. When I returned from class, the front desk attendant flagged me down to pick up a heart-shaped box of chocolate and a giant vase of two dozen long-stem red roses. Sitting beside the holiday standards was an equally large but far more adorable stuffed frog with a snazzy red bowtie. My female RA had to help me bring everything upstairs, and I got a lot of jealous stares in the elevator.

Can't deny enjoying that a bit.

The floral arrangement was too big for my tiny dinette table, and I would have to share all that chocolate with the girls. But the frog looked right at home on my bed, and I couldn't wait to snuggle him after Cherrie's party. And select the perfect name.

"What about Kermit?" Bernie suggested when she came in.

"Too obvious."

"Toadie?"

"Toadie the frog? He'll have an identity crisis."

She shrugged, stealing two candies from my chocolate box. "Red roses? Doesn't Maurice know pink tulips are your favorite?"

"Roses are classic." I adjusted the cowlneck on my red sweater. "Besides, they smell amazing."

"And this room could use the help." She headed toward the door. "Come on. We don't wanna be late."

Bernie would never admit it, but all the snarkiness was a sign of her nerves. This would be the first Valentine's Day where she and Tone were attempting celibacy, and that couldn't be easy for her.

"What did you get Sr. Torres for Valentine's Day?" I asked as we crossed the hall to Cherrie's room.

"Underwear." At my stare, she shrugged. "All his socks have holes, and his white tees are on the other side of beige."

"Where'd you get them?"

"Hustle Man was having a special. They came with free deodorant."

"Please don't tell me anything else." I knocked on Cherrie's door. "You know Hustle Man makes Cherrie break out in hives."

"But she buys her snacks from the so-called store on the seventh floor." Bernie shook her head. "Gotta love her."

"Happy Valentine's Day!" Cherrie threw open her

door. "You gals look great!"

"You look hot too, *Mami*." Bernie admired Cherrie's sleeveless white tuxedo blouse and red capris. "Are those Ann Taylor?"

"You know it." She noted the large gift bag in my hand. "Is that for me?"

"You know it." I kissed her cheek, avoiding the tiny pink hearts she'd painted there. "Happy Valentine's Day."

She accepted the bag. "You guys didn't have to get me anything."

"For throwing this party, it's the least we could…" I glanced around her room, losing my train of thought. "Wow."

Red and black balloon bouquets filled the far corners of her room, and heart-shaped streamers looped above us. Her daybed boasted red accent pillows and a candy-striped duvet that filled me with instant jealousy. Under the bright center light was her dining table complete with a black tablecloth, red and white settings, and a bowl of colorful chocolate kisses.

"What do you think?" I turned to find Cherrie watching me with nervous eyes. "I added black accents for the guys, but should I get rid of the streamers?"

"Are you kidding?" Bernie asked. "Tone might try to buy them off you. He probably has his heart-shaped nightlight plugged in by his bed."

"Are you going to be okay?" I asked. "Because we could give Tone and his friend some money and send them to the movies."

"Slumber it here and watch every gushy movie Lifetime can offer," Cherrie added.

"Thanks, but ..." Bernie grabbed a handful of Hershey's. "As long as you keep these coming, I'll be fine."

"A monogrammed leather portfolio?" Cherrie squealed as she opened the gift bag. "You shouldn't have!"

Bernie grabbed some Hawaiian Punch. "We can take it back."

"Ignore her." I hugged Cherrie. "Happy Valentine's Day, sweets."

A knock on the door got our attention, and Bernie raised her glass, er, plastic cup. "All right, kids. Let's get this party started!"

I went to the door expecting Tone, so seeing Mordecai threw me for a loop. "What are you doing here?"

"And a Happy Valentine's Day to you too," he said. "Do I need a password to get in?"

"No, I'm just confused." I looked past him to Tone. "He's your date?"

"I wouldn't go that far." He lifted the three pizza boxes in his hand. "Could we continue the interrogation in there? My hands are burning."

"Sorry." I stepped aside. "Put them on the table."

"Glad you could come." Cherrie hugged Mordecai. "I figure two RAs are enough to control this crowd."

"I resent that," Bernie and Tone said in unison, smiling at each other.

"On second thought, we might need backup," Mordecai said. He joined me at the food table while Tone admired Cherrie's decorating skills. "Is it weird that I'm here?"

"No. I just didn't think you and Tone were that close."

"Outsiders can never understand the eternal bonds of Drew Hall. A day there is a year anywhere else."

"You sound like y'all were in Desert Storm."

He put his hand over his heart. "We survived. That's what matters."

"Can we eat now?" Bernie asked from her seat beside Tone on Cherrie's bed. "Chocolate is nice, but hot cheese is better."

"We're still waiting for someone," Cherrie said.

"D and I are here, so who else do you need?" Bernie looked at the guys. "No offense."

"None taken," Mordecai said.

"I'm used to it," Tone said.

"But seriously," I said. "Who else could it be?"

"Am I late?" came the question from Cherrie's opening door. If Mordecai's presence was a surprise, there wasn't a word big enough to describe the newest arrival.

"Hi, Imani!" Cherrie waved her in. "You're just in time."

"Oh, good." The Chesty Cheetah closed the door behind her. "I missed the shuttle and decided to walk."

"In those heels?" Bernie stared at her leopard-print boots. "I couldn't walk from here to the closet."

The Chesty Cheetah laughed, and I tried to stop frowning. "It's a balancing act," she said. "But when you take five years of ballet, stilettos are a piece of cake."

"I only survived two," Bernie said. "Much respect."

"Wow." Tone laid his head on Bernie's shoulder. "Please tell me there was a tutu."

"That's for me to know." Bernie batted her lashes. "And you to want to know."

"I'll take your coat," Cherrie said to The Ches—uh, Imani. "And I think you know Daria and Mordecai."

"Contemporary Af-Am Studies, right?" She smiled. "Isn't Doc the best?"

"It's my favorite class," Mordecai said. "But mainly because Daria lets me cheat off her."

I elbowed him. "You wish."

"Now that we're all here." Cherrie took my hand. "Daria, will you bless the food?"

The question dragged my attention from our guest. "Why me?"

"Because you're the most spiritual person I know, and I want to start this night right."

Her guileless expression didn't fool me, but my smile didn't fool her either. As Mordecai appeared on my other side, I took his hand with a smile. Tone, however, was not as gracious.

"I gotta hold his hand?" he asked.

"You oughta dance with the one who brought ya," I sang.

Tone squirmed. "This is no time for a country song, D."

"No, it's time to pray," Bernie said. "We've got the Lord on the line, and you're making Him wait. Now grab Mordecai's hand."

"Act like you're in Drew Hall," I said. "Behind enemy lines."

Tone shot me a dirty look, and I laughed, sobering when Cherrie squeezed my hand. "Okay, okay. Dear Lord, thank you for our friends and loved ones near and far. We ask you to bless this food and the fun we'll have tonight. And help us behave like we remember you're here. In Jesus' name, Amen."

I opened my eyes to find Cherrie smiling at me. "Amen."

Despite my concerns, we had a bang-up time. Cherrie played hostess as only she could, keeping an inconspicuous eye on Bernie and Tone without behaving like an uptight school marm. The Chesty Cheetah divided her time between my two best friends, and though I resented the intrusion, my eavesdropping suggested she wasn't as obnoxious as I thought.

With everyone else accounted for, I spent most of the night with Mordecai. We hadn't started the anniversary gift for his neighbor, and he borrowed supplies from Cherrie to sketch some preliminary ideas. Once she realized we were working, she confiscated the paper, promising to return it at the end of the night, and put on *Coming to America* for our viewing pleasure. As Bernie and Tone regaled us with their word-for-word recitation, Cherrie set out pound cake, strawberries, and whipped cream for a final sweet treat. By time I got back to my room, it was almost 11:30.

I set my take-home container of strawberry shortcake on the table beside my roses. After a night of good food and good friends, I only needed to hear Maurice's voice to make my night complete. I sat on my bed to remove my shoes before calling him and noticed the red light flashing on my answering machine.

"Duchess, hey. I was going to say I'm sorry for calling so late, but you're not there. Are you studying? Hanging with your girls? Whatever you're doing, I hope you're enjoying yourself and liked your gifts. I'm sorry I haven't been in touch much. My stupid phone was acting up, and I had to get a new one. Oh, and thanks for the Iverson jersey. Naseem said he wants to steal it, so you know you did good. Anyway, I'm about to turn in so don't call me back. I mean, you could, but you know I won't remember our conversation tomorrow. So I love you, and ... Happy Valentine's Day."

I saved the message with a smile and picked up the phone. "What Maurice doesn't remember won't hurt him."

Thirty-One

"Though arguably the most famous writer from the Seventeenth Century, you can see why some find his work derivative and uninspiring." Dr. Treble paused for comment and received none. "I would dive into the next part of his essay, but I long ago learned the futility of covering new material the day essays are returned."

She fished a thick, black folder from her infamous satchel. Her expression was unreadable as she glanced at the top paper, and a cramp formed low in my belly.

"You'll find your grades on the last page. Rewriting is optional and will result in an average of both scores."

"What if we have questions about our grade?" asked the boy beside me.

"Your grade is based on academic standards

befitting a college-level English course at a prestigious university. Any questions about those standards should be directed inwardly." She handed him his paper face-down. "Okay?"

Blanching despite his deep brown skin, he nodded, eyeing the paper with suspicion.

As Dr. Treble roamed the room like a shark in bloody waters, the rustle of papers was followed by deep groans and muttered curses. I glanced at the girl on my left, a fellow *Scarlet and Sage* survivor, and took some comfort in her muted reaction to her grade. Noticing my stare, she gave me a thumbs-up. The small gesture comforted me, and I breathed easy for the first time in the past 80 minutes.

But when I flipped to the last page of my essay, my heart skipped a tragic beat.

C-minus.

She gave me a C-minus.

I blinked at the paper, unacquainted with this combination of letter and symbol. In all my years of education, the lowest I'd ever gone was a C-plus, and as I had no artistic talent whatsoever, I expected as much in seventh grade art. Me getting a C-minus on an English essay was like a culinary major failing a spice test. A music major not knowing the scales.

An overachiever kissing her 4.0 goodbye.

"By the looks on most of your faces, you expected better. So did I." Dr. Treble had returned to the front of the room and stood with her arms folded. "I cannot clarify the assignment any further, but I suggest you seek whatever academic help you can. Because if these papers reflect your best work, I grieve for the future of the

Howard University English Department." She grabbed her briefcase and headed for the door. "See you Thursday."

With that benediction, she walked out, stunned silence enveloping the class like a wet cloak. One by one, we straggled from the room in shell-shocked dejection. No one made eye contact or conversation, and had onlookers described the scene, they would have assumed someone died.

I made it to a bench at the edge of The Yard, plopping down with a weighty sigh. The chapel bells sounded, reminding me of my evening Borders shift, and I called out without feeling guilty ... which made me feel guilty. I didn't want to move, didn't want to think, didn't want to face the fact that I was back to square one with a woman who once upon a time seemed to like me.

Not that I expected special treatment as a result. Had my paper been subpar, I would have agreed with her assessment. But her comments seemed nitpicky, as if she were searching for reasons to give me a low mark.

"Incoherent conclusion," I muttered, recalling her favorite criticisms. "Insufficient literary support. Comma splice. Who flags an essay for a comma splice?"

"Talking to yourself aloud is the first sign of insanity." Mordecai hoisted his backpack on his shoulder as he stopped by the bench. "Sitting on a metal bench on a frosty day would be the second."

"Guess you're insane too," I said as he sat down.

"Can't have you going crazy by your lonesome. So what gives?"

I told him about Dr. Treble trashing my essay, and he laid a hand on my shoulder. "I'm sorry. I know how hard you worked on that paper."

"She'll never sign off on my Study Abroad application now. And my actual advisor is a virtual stranger, so he won't do it. She killed my junior year traveling dreams and foreshadowed the destruction of my 4.0 with one red C."

"Can you rewrite for a higher grade?"

"Yeah, but I don't understand the assignment, and she's disinclined to clarify it. So what would be the point?"

"Because you're brilliant. And you won't give up until you figure out what she wants."

I didn't share Mordecai's confidence, but it was nice to hear.

He came to his feet, pulling his hat over his ears. "I've gotta run, but I'll check on you tonight at work."

"No need. I already called out to get cozy with a bucket of ice cream and bad TV."

"Then go home and get out of this cold. Frostbitten fingers can't flip channels."

"Thanks, Mordecai."

"I'll put it on your tab." He winked. "See you around, Ms. Nelson."

Mordecai headed toward the Fine Arts Building, and I made my way toward Sixth and Howard, the warmth of the shuttle calling my name.

Calmer after a long hot shower, I put on some flannel pj's and put Dr. Treble of my mind. French bread pizza and vanilla fudge ice cream offered comforting sustenance with a possible cameo by a salty snack. With Cherrie and Bernie at a movie, I might get to spend the night in total isolation and comfort.

Thank God for small blessings.

Café Latte would be the main feature, but I couldn't pass up a *Golden Girls* marathon. I was in the middle of the second episode when my cell phone rang, its soulful tones making me smile. "Hey, you."

"What's up, Duchess?"

"My mood, thanks to you." I muted Dorothy's snarkiness. "It's been a rough day."

"Wanna come up this weekend and get your mind off it?"

"That the last thing I need to do. Not because I don't want to see you, but I've got a lot of work to do and can't afford to slack off."

"When have you ever slacked off anything?"

"I haven't, but I don't think a weekend in Philly is the answer. But I love that you asked."

"Right."

"How are things in The Shop? Has Naseem lost his phone this week?"

"Same old, same old. And no, Naseem hasn't lost his phone."

I suppressed a sigh. "Maurice, try to understand. Things are tough for me right now."

"How bad can they be? The semester just started."

"I got a C-minus on a paper today."

"A what?"

"A C-minus. The first of my life."

"That's why you won't come to Philly? Because you got one bad grade?"

"It's not just one bad grade."

"So you got more than one C?"

"No, but it's more complicated than that. This is from Dr. Treble."

"Who?"

"Dr. Trebelenosa. That professor who told the other professor she thought I was smart? The one who gave me the Study Abroad application as a sign of her belief in my potential?"

"Okay, so she changed her mind and gave you a bad grade. You don't need to study abroad anyway, so what's the big deal?"

I covered my mouth, not that I needed the muzzle. His words had stunned me into silence.

"Duch? You still there?"

"Yeah. But someone's at my door, so can I call you back? It's probably Bernie."

"I thought you worked tonight."

"I forgot something so I had to come back to Meridian."

"Then call me tonight."

"Bernie's going to work with me, and she's got mace and a mean left hook, so I'll call you tomorrow."

"All right. I'll talk to you."

I ended the call in disbelief. I didn't put the phone back on the cradle, assuming Maurice would call back and apologize for being so insensitive. But when ten silent minutes passed, I realized he meant everything he said exactly as he said it.

I didn't know what to do with that information.

That might explain my fabrication about Bernie and work. I never lied to Maurice unless in the name of a happy surprise. But the peace of not speaking to him later eclipsed my concern about the little white lie, and I grabbed my small baking tray and box of deluxe pizzas, unmuting the television to hear Rose begin a story about St. Olaf.

Two French bread pizzas and three episodes later, there were no new voicemails on either phone, and I determined not to care. I washed my plate and was about to select dessert number one when there was a knock at my door. Drying my hands, I opened the door to find no one there. I glanced left and right and only saw a girl exiting the shower down the hall. I thought some bored soul was playing games until I looked down and saw a small yellow gift bag bearing a tag with my name.

With a squeak of surprise, I brought the bag inside and found a three-pack of microwave kettle corn, a handful of mini peppermint patties, and a greeting card. On the front of the card was a wide-eyed owl with large black-rimmed glasses saying, "Heard you were having a rough time in English class." Inside it read, "There, their, they're."

The card was signed, "Your Friendly Neighborhood RA."

I shuffled into my slippers and headed down the hall. Mordecai didn't answer his door, so I used the dry-erase marker from his board to write "Thank you. From Me, Myself, and I," adding a curly-haired smiley face for good measure. Whistling back to my room, I shelved *Café Latte* and grabbed *Clue* instead. The hilarious whodunit was the perfect complement to my sweet and salty snack. And when my cell phone rang ten minutes later, I ignored the familiar ringtone and let the call go to voicemail.

Thirty-Two

Despite the trouble with Dr. Treble, I slept like a baby that night. Maurice's voicemail was full of longing but lacked the desired apology. I called him this morning as promised but ended the call in a rush, citing lateness for the shuttle.

Mordecai sat beside me in Dr. Maddox's class. "Good morning, Ms. Nelson."

"A very good morning. How did you know kettle corn was my favorite?"

"Lucky guess. I'm glad you enjoyed it."

"We sure did."

"We?"

"The grammatically-challenged owl and I. He ate most of it."

"This is why you don't invite owls to dinner parties."

I covered my mouth to stifle my laughter as Dr. Maddox started class.

"Today we're gonna do a Roundtable: discuss a given topic in hopes of sharing and learning from one another. You won't be tested or graded on this. I just want to know what you think."

He stepped off the podium. "What is the greatest obstacle facing black couples today?"

"White women!" shouted a female in the back.

People laughed, but Dr. Maddox raised his hand. "All opinions must be defended, so if you can't own your answer, keep it to yourself. Let's start again."

Soon mentioned were the effects of slavery, black male incarceration, and pessimistic feminism. Though never shy with my opinions, the state of affairs between Maurice and me left me content to yield the floor to others. Including Mordecai who raised his hand.

"Fear," he said.

"Interesting," Dr. Maddox said. "Elaborate."

"People are so afraid to be honest no one's getting real about their needs."

"I got real before," a girl behind me said, "and I got played."

"I've applied for jobs and wasn't hired before," Dr. Maddox said. "That doesn't mean I stop looking if I want to work."

"Losing a job and losing your heart are two different things," she replied.

"But isn't it worth the risk to find the right job, the right person to share your heart with?"

Yes, I thought. *No matter what Maurice and I are going through right now, the joy of being with him is worth it.*

"But how do you find the right person?" asked a boy in a camouflage do-rag. "Most of my boys just wanna get in where they fit in, but I want someone special. How do I find her?"

"That is a thoughtful question deserving a thoughtful answer." Dr. Maddox chuckled at the rustling papers. "If you want to take notes, be my guest. But this is one man's opinion. You can't sue me if it doesn't work.

"Before you look for the right person, you need to know who you are, what you value and want out of life. So spend some time getting to know yourself. Because if you don't know you, how can you know when you have found the perfect person for you?

"And when I say 'perfect,' I don't mean literal perfection because that doesn't exist. Which reminds me, some of y'all need a reality check. Ladies, stop holding out for the Kobe look-alike with the bad attitude. Fellas, if that foxy freshman gave you a wrong number four different times, take the hint. Y'all laughing, but I'm trying to hip you to the truth! When I say 'perfect,' I mean the perfect partner for you—someone who lights you up inside, who you like even when he gets on your nerves. Someone who likes you when your manicure is chipped and your knobby knees are ashy. Sometimes we can't see that person because we're distracted by the superficial.

"Anyway, as you learn more about what you want, you'll also discover what you don't want. But focus on what's important. Some of you only date inside your race, others only outside. And if that's about attraction, fine. If not, you're limiting your options. You should never date anyone who doesn't respect and appreciate who you are, and that goes for people of all colors and creeds.

"And redefine your definition of 'date' to mean 'get to know someone non-sexually.' No one mentioned this yet, but one of our biggest problems is sleeping together too soon. We bump bellies before knowing each other's last names and think we're in love. That ex you can't leave alone no matter how many times he hurts you, what connects you to him? I'll give you a hint: it's below his waist and above his knees. Ideally, dating should focus on our hearts, our minds, and hopefully our souls."

"Is that how you date?" The Chesty Cheetah asked. Just when I forgot she was in this class, she sat on the front row.

"I don't date at all anymore, but I have had relationships of varying length and success. And the best ones were with people I liked, respected, and enjoyed outside the bedroom. Crazy physical chemistry is incredible, but nothing surpasses the connection between two people who know and care about each other on a deeper level."

"And if you have crazy chemistry and genuine affection?" Mordecai asked.

"Then you have everything."

As other people offered opinions, I mulled over Dr. Maddox's words. Maurice and I had our problems, but we loved each other. Our bedroom activities were minimal, but they always set my soul on fire. Long-distance relationships were especially difficult, but Bernie and Tone proved dating on campus wasn't simple either. Love was work no matter where you found it, and Maurice and I just needed to roll up our sleeves and get it done.

"You all right?" Mordecai asked as we walked out of Locke Hall. "You seem distracted."

"I'm fine. I was thinking about how Maurice and I were...is that snow?" I looked up with everyone else, stunned to see small white flecks blowing around.

"Yeah. But it never sticks, so I wouldn't get too excited."

But for the first time in our friendship, Mordecai was wrong.

Flurries fell all afternoon and evening, and when I awoke the next morning, the ground was covered with a shimmering white blanket. Cars and tree branches boasted a few inches of coverage, and the skies remained gray. Compared to Philly snow, this was nothing, so I was surprised by the neon signs on the walls by the bathrooms and elevator.

SNOW EMERGENCY – UNIVERSITY CLOSED – CLASSES SUSPENDED.

"Are you serious?" I said aloud. "It's a dusting."

"You would protest a day off." Bernie came around the corner in a black bathrobe. "Can't you be grateful like the rest of us?"

"Snowed in?"

"I had two touch-ups last night and decided to stay

with Madame Cummings. What are you doing today?"

"Going to the bathroom." I stopped short of dancing in place. "But I'll call you later. Maybe we can have that Upwords rematch."

"Not until you people acknowledge 'crickaden' is a word."

I stepped around her. "Pictionary it is."

"Y'all are cheating!" she yelled as the bathroom door shut behind me.

Once my immediate needs were addressed, I returned to my room and found a voicemail from my boss. Concerned about the state of local roads, he gave me the day off.

"No book is that important," he said. "And they can drink coffee at home."

With the entire day at my disposal, I glanced around my room and grinned.

It was time for some fun.

After a quick breakfast and change of clothes, I donned my red cleaning scarf, shuffled three country CDs in my stereo, and grabbed the glass cleaner. Frost couldn't mask filth, and I wanted to enjoy the first snow of my collegiate career. Once the windows were clean, I tossed the curtains in the washing machine with my tablecloth. I dusted my desk and dresser and rearranged the books on the shelf, shaking my head at Mom McClain's bridal magazine. Corina recently abandoned her efforts to repair my relationship with Adrian, but seeing that magazine always reminded me of our estrangement. So into my bottom drawer the bridal book went.

I set my wastepaper basket in the hallway so I could

dust-mop my floors. As I dragged the desk chair beside it, I heard a gasp behind me. "You are not doing this."

I turned to face Mordecai. "Doing what?"

"Spending this unprecedented snow day cleaning." He peeked inside my room. "Though the windows do look great."

"See? This is a good idea."

He grabbed the kitchenette chairs before I could. "What am I, a barbarian?"

"I'm not cleaning all day. I'm also working on the Dr. Treble essay and getting ahead on my Dr. Maddox reading."

"At Homecoming, you promised to come out with us next time. I'm calling in that favor today."

"But I have to…"

"Don't make me pull rank as your RA." He folded his arms. "Wouldn't want this to get ugly."

"Fine. But I need to get some work done first."

"Fine. Be ready at 2:30."

"Where are we going?"

He walked backwards down the hall. "Somewhere awesome."

Our awesome adventure began with a walk to campus…or a trudge as the weather allowed. There were five inches of snow on the ground, and everyone was beyond excited. Even Bernie and Cherrie joined in, linking arms so we wouldn't fall.

"I'm surprised you're not spit-shining your shoes today," Bernie said.

"Thanks to my bossy RA," I said. "I made time for work and play."

Mordecai turned around. "Bossy?"

"But in a good way."

When we hit campus, I expected us to head for The Yard. Instead we made a left turn toward the stadium.

"Is there a game today?" someone asked.

Mordecai lead us through an unlocked back gate. "Something like that."

When I saw the field, I realized what he meant.

Dozens and dozens of students in wintery attire hurled snowballs at each other. Debutantes and derelicts alike laughed and squealed as they were chased in every direction. There didn't seem to be one side versus another—just a good old-fashioned neighborhood snowball fight.

"All right!" Bernie clapped her gloved hands. "Let's do this!"

As if waiting for that signal, our group rushed the field and joined the fray. Before we could gather any ammo, we were bombarded with snowballs. Cherrie got hit in the face, and Bernie laughed so hard, she slipped and fell. Cherrie took that opportunity to retaliate, gathering an armful of snow and dumping it on Bernie's head.

"That's no way to treat a lady." Tone came to help Bernie get up. "Apologize."

Cherrie swiped snow from her knees. "No way."

Tone stroked an imaginary villain's beard. "Then prepare to die."

"Oh, no, you don't!" I threw a snowball at the back of Tone's head, diverting his attention. Cherrie ran away, and Tone turned around as Bernie came to her feet.

"Did you just hit *mi papito* with a snowball?"

"*Si, señorita.*" I put on my thickest accent. "And what are you gonna do about it?"

Bernie cracked her knuckles. "I'm gon' turn this mutha out."

"Gotta go!"

"Get her, baby!" Tone yelled as Bernie ran after me.

With the wind at my back, I zigzagged through the melee, getting pelted with ricocheting flurries as I searched for Cherrie. To my left, a boy from my fitness class assembled an arsenal while his buddies formed a protective shield around the ammo. I heard a random scream, followed by peals of laughter, and covered my head just in case.

Reaching a point of safety behind a friendly battle between the Ooh-La-La girls and the cheerleaders, I bent to my knees and tried to catch my breath.

"Admit it." Mordecai strolled toward me, nose in the air and hands behind his back. "This is better than snuggling with a thesaurus."

"It is. I'm glad you called me out."

"I hope you feel that way in a minute."

"What do you—"

My words were cut off by a snowball to the face. As I blinked through the powdery puff, he chuckled. "Know thine enemy, Ms. Nelson. Men of Drew Hall always stick together."

"Is that right?" I swiped snow from my face and gave my darkest glare. "Well, Drew hath no fury like Meridian women scorned."

He grinned. "I am so scared."

Mordecai hit me in the stomach with another snowball, and I gave immediate chase. He was taller, but I was faster, gaining ground as he stumbled and slipped. Falling to the ground, he rolled onto his back with his hands up.

"Now, now, Ms. Nelson. Would you kick a man when he's down?"

"Now there's an idea." I kicked a nearby pile of snow all over him, smiling when Cherrie arrived. "Perfect timing, my sista."

Together we buried Mordecai in a drift of snow, waiting until he was good and coated before taking off running.

"Have I told you lately that I love you?" I asked.

Cherrie ducked as a boy took aim with a snowball the size of a cantaloupe. "Tell me tomorrow when you spring for manicures."

"Done."

"Have I told you lately I'm glad you came to Howard?" she asked.

When she shielded my face as a snow grenade exploded above us, I grinned at her. "I think you just did."

As we weaved through the expanding crowd, Cherrie grabbed my arm and pulled me to a stop. "We should make a snowman!"

"What?"

"Over there." She pointed to the stands. "All that pristine snow can't go to waste. We'll call them 'snow-fans' because they're in the bleachers."

I chuckled. "We should tell B we're forfeiting."

A huge cascade of snow rained upon our heads, accompanied by a short, familiar laugh. "No need," Bernie said.

Tone and Mordecai followed us, lending their hands as we climbed into the stands.

"Does this mean you forgive me for that snowball to the face?" Mordecai asked me.

"We'll see." I elbowed Tone in the side as he passed. "Never know what you Drew men might be up to."

"I was being chivalrous." Tone swept snow from the stairs toward the pile for the snow-fan's base. "Defending my woman's honor."

Bernie kissed his nose. "And she thanks you."

Cherrie and I let them have their moment and met Mordecai at the bottom of the stairs.

"Do you know what you're doing, Mr. We-Only-Get-Snow-Once-Every-Five-Years?" I asked.

"I've seen *Frosty the Snowman*," he said. "Made me cry as a kid."

"I know!" Cherrie patted the snow on her side of the huge ball. "When he melted in that greenhouse…"

Mordecai sniffled. "Please. I can't."

I patted his back. "It's all right, little guy. He comes back on Christmas Day."

As the bottom layer took shape, a bright light shone on the middle of the field, illuminating our unauthorized activities. Having a snowball fight on the gridiron wasn't an expellable offense, but no need being on the front of *The Hilltop* because of it.

Mordecai grabbed my hand. "Time to go."

"Come on." I grabbed Cherrie who patted the snow-fan's side. "Edgar will be all right."

"But he doesn't have a head," she said. "He won't be able to see anything."

We stopped to look at her, and she wrinkled her nose. "Yeah, I heard it too."

As students poured out of Greene Stadium, their whoops and whistles created a childlike song of happiness that seeped into my soul and warmed me from head to toe.

I'm so glad I go to Howard U.

Thirty-Three

Monday night, I broke with tradition and accompanied Bernie to one of Tone's home games. The irony of an HBCU having a lackluster basketball was not lost on me, but there was no denying Tone's talent. He hadn't been scouted, but his coach had mentioned the NBA draft more than once.

"I don't think he'll do it," Bernie said as we snacked on snuck-in Snickers. "He wants to play professionally but doesn't think he'd get picked up. That disappointment would be devastating." She came to her feet as Tone drained a three-pointer in double coverage. "That's what I'm talkin' about!"

"Have you discussed other plans?" I asked as she sat down. "He graduates in three months."

"Tough to do while we're spending less time together. Our conversations are strained, like we don't know how to be us anymore."

I knew the feeling. "I'm sorry."

"We made a choice, and it's the right one. So that's something."

"Is it getting easier?"

"If by 'easier,' you mean 'more unbearable,' then yes, it is." A whistle signaled a coach's timeout. "If I'm not with you or Thing Two, I'm in here sweating on the treadmill until I smell rank enough to go home."

"That's why you completed today's fitness gauntlet so quickly." Our aerobics class was killing me. "I thought I was going to pass out."

"At least this abstinence thing is good for something." The players hit the court again, and game play continued. "You're a soldier for resisting Maurice."

"The two and a half states between us help a little."

"But you survived two weekends alone, and that's nothing to sneeze at. Though I wonder."

"What?"

"Not to make everything about that ring, but because you're wearing it, I'm sure he'll expect to spend more time with you this summer. And with two years of college under your belt, your parental units might loosen up on them reins." She glanced at me. "Do you think you can handle that?"

"At the moment, I don't know what I....wait, hold on." I pulled my buzzing phone out of my pocket, recognizing Maurice's number. "Hello? Hello?"

No one answered, but I heard an irate woman in the background yelling, "Then mind your business, yo!

Ain't nobody ask you nuthin."

I couldn't understand the man's reply, but his annoyance was clear.

"What's that line about Vegas?" the woman snapped. "A'ight then!"

As I couldn't make heads or tails of it, I hung up and called The Shop, forgetting it was Monday, and no one would be there. But a woman answered on the second ring. "We closed."

That's when I identified the voice from before. "Suzika? It's Daria."

"Hey, girl. Hold on." Her voice was muffled. "It's Daria."

"Duchess?" Maurice was on alert. "You all right?"

"Yeah, you just called me."

"It's this stupid Nokia. I'm going back to the store and getting another flip phone." Then he chuckled. "Sorry about the language. They got a little rank with it."

"All I heard was how pissed Suzika is."

"Yeah, all her and Naseem do is argue lately."

"Because she ain't right!" Naseem cried.

"I ain't make nobody do nuthin!"

"Yo, can y'all just…" Maurice sighed. "Forget it. I'm going home. Lock up and try not to kill each other."

Bernie tapped my knee. "What's going on?" she mouthed. I rolled my eyes as Maurice came back to the phone.

"My bad. Ain't much I can do when they get like that."

"What's wrong?"

"Some people just rub each other the wrong way."

"I don't know about that," I said. "They seemed

pretty *simpatico* Columbus Day weekend."

"Sorry if I don't remember. I was distracted by something more important." I felt his smile through the line. "So how are you? Ain't heard from you in a minute."

I didn't point out the phone works both ways. "Busy with school, work, and avoiding people with my last name. But we had a snow day last week."

"For real?"

"Yeah. They're not equipped to handle snow down here, so a few inches shuts down the city."

"And that's where you want to go to school? Nice."

"It was nice. I got in a snowball fight and built one-third of a snow-fan."

"A snowman?"

"No, a snow-fan. A snowman who watches football games." I chuckled. "Cherrie was so annoyed we didn't finish it."

"So it was you and Cherrie?"

"Among others."

"Any Milli Vanilli wannabes?"

My smile faded. "I don't know anyone fitting that description."

"You know who I mean."

"And you know his name." I lowered my voice. "So if you're going to insult him, you should at least use it."

"Don't be difficult, Daria."

"I'm not being…" I took a deep breath. "You know what? I only called because I thought you called me. But this is a waste of time, so I'm gonna go."

"No, don't. I'm sorry." The line was silent while we gathered our wits. "I'm just…he wants you."

"Just because he's nice doesn't mean he wants me. And even if he did want me, why would that matter if I'm yours?"

"You're right," he said. "You are mine."

I didn't know what to say to that, so I used a convenient roar from the crowd to justify ending the call. I closed my phone without putting it away, and Bernie stopped cheering to sit beside me. "What's going on in Philly?"

I looked at her. "I have no idea."

"I'm surprised," Cherrie said. We were on the Meridian shuttle catching up. "Maurice never seemed like the jealous type. Possessive, yes. But not jealous."

"It's weird, right?" Two weeks later, Maurice's attitude hadn't changed. It didn't help that when he called last night, I was about to meet Mordecai in the lounge to work on our next book. "Can you see why I lied?"

"Yeah, but no good can come of it. You're a terrible liar."

"What do you mean?"

"Remember when I got finger waves before the Soph Hop?" She raised an eyebrow as I put on my best poker face. "You made that face when I asked if they looked good on me, and I washed them out that same night."

I gaped at her. "You said they made your scalp itch."

"And that's how you lie convincingly."

We got off the shuttle, shivering against the wind as we headed inside the dorm. "Enough about me and Maurice. What's going on with you?"

"Same old, same old. The Philly Ski Trip is this weekend, and I don't even want to go. After all that drama with the planning committee, I'm tempted to push a few folks down a mountain."

"Then stay here. We can catch up on *Never Ever After*."

"I don't trust them heffas." We went to check our mail. "And if anything goes wrong, my name is all over it."

"It's a shame none of us are pre-law. You might need an attorney with that group."

"Tell me about it." She looked at my mail. "What is all that?"

I inspected the large white envelope in my pile, turning it to read the return address. "University of Pennsylvania?"

"Maybe it's from your dad."

"He wouldn't use company stationery to send me anything." I tore it open and pulled out the top page. "This is a letter from the Office of Student Transfers."

"Student transfers? Why would they be..." Cherrie's eyes widened. "Oh, wow. Would he do that?"

I stuffed the papers in my bag. "Apparently so."

"Guess you need to make a phone call."

"Apparently so."

But that call would have to wait, for there was also a voicemail upstairs from the same oh-so-helpful Transfer Admissions Officer, asking if I received the package I requested.

I requested?

Humming a calming hymn under my breath, I deleted the message from one phone and dialed The Shop with the other.

"It's Tuesday at The Shop."

"Is Maurice there?"

"And hello to you, too, Daria." Suzika chuckled at my rudeness. "He stepped out."

"Will he be back soon?"

"Yeah, but if it's urgent, I can send…"

"No, it's fine. Ask him to call when he gets back, please."

"You all right?"

"Just need to talk to him. Thanks."

Watching the clock wouldn't speed up matters, but it was all I could do. That or glare at my bookbag where the offending papers were stashed. When my phone rang fifteen minutes later, I flipped it open. "Maurice?"

"Hey. Suzika said something was wrong."

"You could say that. Why am I being contacted by a Transfer Admissions Officer from the University of Pennsylvania?"

"That happened today?"

I folded my arms, not that he could tell. "Yes."

"I didn't think they'd send it that fast."

"That's your response? You didn't think they'd sent it so fast?"

"I hope you're not expecting an apology. Because I'm not sorry."

I closed my eyes and counted backwards from thirty-five.

In Spanish.

"You'd be closer to me, so you wouldn't need to study abroad," he continued. "And you'd be away from that teacher who doesn't believe in you anymore. It's a win-win."

"You really believe that, don't you?"

"Duchess, it is my job to get you out of situations that are over your head. You tried the out-of-state school thing, and it didn't work. There's no shame in scrapping that plan and coming back home where you belong."

"Would you do it?"

"Do what?"

"If you had a bad week or month at The Shop and I made arrangements for you to uproot everything and go somewhere else, would you decide…"

"You can't compare the two."

"Why not? I have a life down here just like…"

"A life? I've been sweeping these floors since I was six, watched myself become a man in these mirrors, held back tears when my uncle put my name on the door three months before he died. This is more than my life, Daria. It's my legacy."

"I know," I said as calmly as possible. "And that's what I'm building here at Howard."

"No, you're playing in the snow and watching cheap soap operas, and you could do that here. I mean, if you don't even know what to do with your degree, why does it matter where you get it?"

My mouth dropped open, but his words kept me silent.

"Listen," he said after a few moments. "I was only trying to help. You were upset about that mean teacher, missing me, and having trouble with your dad. I just thought you coming home would solve all those problems. Even Suzika thought it was a nice gesture."

"What?"

"She called Penn to get the information. Said it was fun pretending to be you, except having to speak proper all the time."

"Right."

"I need to get back to work. Are we good?"

"Yep." I rolled my eyes and tossed the package on the floor. "We are just fine."

Thirty-Four

When the line went dead, I closed my phone, clamping my mouth shut to hold in the expletives. As a Christian wordsmith, I didn't curse outside of dropping something heavy on my foot. Or watching the Eagles lose to the Cowboys. But as I stared at the picture of Maurice and me on my desk, dazzling combinations of profane phrases flew into my mind, and I almost laughed at how much fun my brain had creating them.

Almost.

But this situation was anything but funny, and once the urge to call and cuss out my boyfriend passed, I grabbed my shower caddy, robe, and slippers, preparing to wash my anger down the drain. With an arsenal of menus at my disposal, I was sure to find an unhealthy-but-satisfying meal to comfort my soul. And though *Café Latte* was out of the question, I knew my movie collection wouldn't let me down.

"There you are." Bernie was waiting at my door when I finished my shower. "Just the woman I wanted to see."

I pulled out my keys. "What's wrong?"

"Nothing. But I need a favor."

"If this involves eavesdropping on the shuttle, count me out."

"No, no." She closed my door behind me. "Though I still think that girl stole my best comb when I braided her hair last month. Anyway, Antonio and I are going on a date tonight."

Finally some good news. "Where?"

She turned away while I disrobed and lotioned. "We haven't decided yet."

"Well, wherever you go, I'm sure you'll have a good time."

"I'm so glad you feel that way."

"Do you need help with outfit ideas? Because dark-wash jeans and a cute top look great no matter where you're going."

"I'm also glad you feel that way."

It was then I remembered her opening statement. "What do you want?"

"We want to go on a date but not by ourselves, so…"

"A third wheel? Thanks, but no thanks."

"But Tone is bringing somebody for you. Well, not 'for you,' but somebody to round out the group." She waited for a question I didn't ask. "Mordecai."

"That's nice, but the last thing I want to do is go out."

"Why?" She turned around, unfazed by my state of undress. "Did something happen?"

"No. I just want to stay in tonight."

"Stay in tomorrow night." She flopped on my bed as I went to my pajama drawer. "Antonio and I are in a good place right now, and we could handle a date with chaperones. I trust you, and he trusts Mordecai, and you know Mordecai, and Mordecai knows you, and…"

"Fine. I'll throw something on."

"Great!" She crossed the room and closed my drawer. "But no sweatpants."

A pair of jeans and striped t-shirt later, I banished Maurice to the back of my mind as Bernie and I went outside to wait for Tone. He was borrowing a friend's car to take us to Jillian's in Arundel Mills Mall. I would have preferred a large pepperoni pizza and *The Five Heartbeats*, but I couldn't deny Bernie the chance to spend time with her boyfriend.

Especially when he was a rational human being who respected her choices and supported her dreams.

Shaking off the thought, I forced a smile as Mordecai came down the walk. "Ms. Nelson."

"Mr. Hill. Did you have to scramble to get the night off?"

"When you offer to work the weekend, everyone wants to switch with you. Have you been to Jillian's before?"

"No, but I think Dave & Buster are her cousins. Did you get any sketches done last night?"

He snapped his fingers. "That's what I forgot. I wanted you to see my idea for the last page. I can't decide if it needs more pizzazz."

"Just hearing you use the word 'pizzazz' is enough for me."

"I'm full of pizzazz. And panache. And pluck. And…"

"Problems," I said as Tone pulled up. "A prime pick for purposed prayer."

Tone honked the horn, and we met him at the curb. He opened the passenger door for Bernie while Mordecai opened the back door for me with a flourish. "Alliteration addicts first."

The ride to Jillian's was long but full of laughs. Watching Tone and Bernie bicker about directions was hilarious as Bernie had no working knowledge of Maryland's roadways. Mordecai and I added play-by-play commentary in our best Marv Albert voices. Or worst, depending on whom you asked.

"You talk a lot of crap, Torres." Bernie removed her knitted aviator hat when we walked into Jillian's. "Let's see you back it up."

"What's your game, Price?" Tone asked. "Pinball? Skeeball?"

She stabbed his chest with a finger. "Billiards, baby."

"You asked for it."

"You want in, D?" Bernie asked as Tone paid for three games. "I know you're a secret shark."

I stuffed my gloves in my coat pocket. "I'd rather

watch y'all go at it."

"You, a secret shark?" Mordecai raised an eyebrow. "I don't believe it."

"Believe it, buddy. Adrian has a pool table in the basement and insisted I learn."

His smirk spoke volumes, and Bernie took issue with it. "You doubt my girl's skills?"

"Never that. Just confident in my own."

"Then put your money where your mouth is." Bernie marched toward the empty table. "Guys versus girls. Losers buy dinner."

"I'm already buying your dinner," Tone said.

"Yes, but this way Daria gets a free meal too," Bernie said. "And her greedy behind won't turn down free wings and onion rings."

As it turned out, those wings and rings came with a side order of jalapeño poppers and astonishment. Bernie did her best, but I had the hot stick. And though I should have enjoyed my two straight wins over the boys, my stupid mind kept drifting to my stupid boyfriend and his stupid stupidity.

Which made me feel really stupid.

Mordecai crumpled a used napkin on his plate. "I think I got hustled by an English major."

I sipped my Shirley Temple. "I think I'm insulted."

"I think I need to reclaim my manhood." Tone swiped the last popper. "You need to let me win at something."

"If I let you win," Bernie said. "How does that help your manhood?"

"A win is a win, baby. And Dance Party USA is calling our name."

Bernie drained the last of her milkshake. "Let's get it."

They left the booth, and Mordecai glanced around. "Where to, Ms. Nelson? I still have a small morsel of pride somewhere in my coat pocket."

"You go ahead." I played with my straw. "I'm going to chill for a minute."

"I'm not leaving you here. So tell me what's wrong."

"I don't want to ruin your night."

"Unless you plan to announce my defeat at next week's dorm meeting, I'll be all right."

I moved my empty cup to the side. "If you say so."

Mordecai and I seldom talked about Maurice, but he knew we barely survived last year. I tried to be brief as I caught him up on this year's drama, but the more I talked, the more I wanted to say.

"I mean, it's not all bad. He's been calling more often and only dissed Howard because Dr. Treble hurt my feelings. And the fact that he chose Mr. Darcy shows how well he knows me."

"Mr. Darcy?"

"The stuffed frog he sent for Valentine's Day." At Mordecai's chuckle, I pursed my lips. "Are you judging me for naming my stuffed animal after a fictional character?"

"No. I think it's great that Mr. Darcy makes you so happy."

"Okay. Then you think I'm being unreasonable and judging this Penn situation too harshly."

"No. I just ... I know how much your relationship means to you, and I don't want to upset you by saying

301

the wrong thing."

"You won't. I value your opinion."

Mordecai leaned forward, folding his hands. "If I loved a woman enough to give her a diamond, I wouldn't want her in another state three-quarters of the year either. So the whole Penn thing? I get that."

"I smell a 'but.' "

He smiled briefly. "But loving her means I would support her no matter what, no matter where. I would put her wishes above mine and respect her choices. And if she could deal with the distance, then so would I."

"You'd never try to force me to change schools, would you?"

"I would never force you to do anything, Daria." At my answering smile, his gaze drifted behind me. "Except..."

"Except what?"

"Give me a chance to redeem myself." He rose from the table, extending a friendly hand. "I won't be able to sleep with this loss hanging over my head."

"I wouldn't want to give you insomnia." I accepted his help getting up. "Thanks, Mordecai. For...you know."

"Don't thank me yet." He rubbed his hands together. "I'm the reigning air hockey champion of Greenbelt."

Thirty-Five

I survived the rest of that week with my good humor intact, a feat aided by my decision to ignore Maurice for a while. We'd never had a major argument before, and I was in no mood for a spring debut. Besides, if he still didn't understand why I needed to be here, no amount of talking could change that.

As for the other frustrating Philadelphian in my life, my wall calendar recently put him back on my radar. Adrian's birthday was in a week, and despite the current nonsense, I couldn't allow myself not to send him a card.

So during my lunch break on Saturday afternoon, I went across the street to Pentagon City Mall for a birthday card. The Hallmark Gold Crown store was the only choice, and I expected to find something suitable with time to spare for a good meal.

I hated being wrong.

Every card I picked was too generic, too sappy, or too juvenile. The covers had pictures of grown women hugging their fathers or little girls sitting on daddy's lap, neither appropriate for the current state of affairs between Adrian and me.

Maybe I should buy some construction paper and crayons.

A rumble in my stomach suggested better luck after a bite, so I went downstairs to the food court. My bourbon chicken smelled divine, but I couldn't bring myself to eat.

When did everything become so complicated? When did Adrian go from being my best friend to the bane of my existence? Why couldn't he respect my independence and give me the benefit of the doubt? And why did Maurice have to be so negative about my path? Why couldn't he accept Howard the way I accept The Shop? Why did he have to be such a Neanderthal?

"Why are you sitting there frowning at your food?" The familiar voice silenced my inner monologue, and I blinked twice before realizing I was staring at her. "Too much bourbon in your chicken?"

"Dr. Treble? What are you doing here?"

"Am I not allowed to leave campus grounds?"

"No. I mean, yes. I mean…"

Her throaty chuckle was somehow comforting, and she indicated the chair across from me. "May I?"

I nodded, unable to do much else. Her full afro looked kinder in the cavernous food court, and I relaxed.

A bit.

"Other than your unimpressive lunch, what's on your mind?"

Though her tone was kind, her *her-ness* left me wondering what I should say. With everything else going on, the last thing I needed was a weaponized version of my life exploding in our classroom next week. And I didn't know if I trusted her not to do that.

"I've got a lot going on right now," I said.

"That the best you can do?" She removed her creamy leather gloves, setting them in her lap. "Come on, Ms. Nelson. I don't bite."

I didn't quite believe her, but time was running out, and I needed help.

"It's my father. Not just my father, but it's easy to start with him. He's upset with me."

"Because…"

"Because I'm carving out a life he doesn't like."

"You really think that's the reason?"

"What else could it be? I'm not doing drugs or failing school." I looked up for confirmation, but she only stared back. "I'm not pregnant or on the lam. But because my choices don't line up with his perfect plan for me, he's angry."

"Why does his opinion matter?"

"What?" I caught myself and cleared my throat. "I mean, I don't understand."

"You're old enough to crash and burn without his permission. He's allowed to be upset with you, but you're choosing to let his feelings govern yours. Why?"

"Because he's my father."

"But if he's as indifferent and out of touch as you claim, then why would you want someone like that in your life?"

As I stumbled over her logic, my reply was slow in coming. "It's not that simple."

"Life is precisely that simple. You are an adult or at least becoming one. And the greatest lesson you can learn is how to determine if someone is for or against you. People seldom agree with everything you do, but anyone who disrespects your choices, invalidates your feelings, or belittles your concerns deserves not a tick of your time. If there's anyone in your life like that, I'd suggest you reevaluate their necessity." Her gaze dropped to my left hand. "No matter who it is."

"What do you mean by..." I looked down to find myself twisting the ring. "It's a habit."

"I'm sure it is." She checked her watch. "I'm meeting a colleague for lunch, so I must leave you now."

"Thank you, Dr. Treble. This was surprisingly helpful." My eyes widened, and I covered my face with my hands. "Oh, God."

"Yes. Perhaps more prayer would help." I looked up as she grabbed her gloves. "Oh, and nice job on your rewrite. I was impressed."

With a wink, she lost herself in the crowd. I took a few bites of my tepid chicken and headed back to Hallmark. Loath though I was to admit it, I knew Adrian's objections were rooted in love, and I couldn't fully fault him for that.

I had ten minutes left on my lunch break and needed to find the right card with the quickness. Ignoring the previously rejected ones, I moved a misfiled anniversary card to its proper place and found a promising option underneath.

Daddy...

When I was a little girl, you were my whole world.

I thought you were perfect, and you made me feel perfect too.

As I've matured, I've come to see you not only as my father but as a man

A man with dreams, flaws, and opinions of his own.

We don't always see eye-to-eye

But one thing has never changed:

You have always loved me.

I may not say it often, but I want you to know how much I love and respect you.

And I thank God all the time you are my father.

Happy Birthday with Love from Your Daughter.

There was no picture of Adrian and me on the front, but the earthy swirls would suffice. I purchased and signed the card, deciding against a personal message, and dropped it in the mailbox outside my job with three minutes to spare.

When I returned to Borders, my manager was in the lounge munching on leftover Valentine's Day candy.

"Howard's spring break is coming up, right?"

"In three weeks." I rummaged through the goodie basket. "I can't wait."

"Do you need me to take you off the schedule? Because I'd have to do that today."

I had no current travel plans—and the way Maurice was acting, that was unlikely to change—but with the semester I was having, a week off might be just the recharge I needed.

I unwrapped a chocolate heart. "Don't mind if you do."

Thirty-Six

And how did my blockbuster spring break begin?

With laundry. Loads and loads of laundry.

For three weeks, I'd written essays, worked on the anniversary book with Mordecai, and tried not to obsess over my romantic problems. Catching the flu didn't help, and when the fog cleared, every stitch of fabric in my room was dirty.

The thought nearly made me break out in hives.

So bright and early Monday morning, I ignored a call from Corina—I sent the man a birthday card. Couldn't that be enough for now?—and separated my laundry. Few Meridianites were awake at this hour, so I could be finished by the afternoon. After some Egyptian Mythology homework, maybe I'd go solo to an artsy independent film. I hadn't talked to Bernie and Cherrie all weekend and could make plans to see them tomorrow.

As I hauled bag one into the laundry room, someone was pulling clothes out of the dryer.

"I hope you cleaned the lint filter," I said.

Mordecai looked up. "What are you doing up this early?"

"Need you ask?" I set the laundry soap on the table. "What about you?"

"Last stop before a road trip."

"Road trip?"

"An actor friend is answering an open call for an off-off-Broadway musical, and a bunch of us are going for moral support. His family lives in Mt. Vernon, so we're gonna crash there for a few days."

"Sounds fun."

"You haven't made plans yet?"

"No." I pulled out my laundry card. "But I'm sure Bernie will cook up something fun."

"If she doesn't, have some without her." He held up a pinkie. "Promise?"

"Is this legally binding?"

"Does it matter?"

"No." I linked pinkies with a solemn nod. "I promise."

A little bird must have squealed to Bernie because the next morning, she called me in her frantic voice. "I've got to get out of here."

"You wanna come over? I'm working on a Dr. Treble assignment now, but..."

"No, I mean away from Howard. We need to go

somewhere, do something."

"We can go to the Harbor, find a hotel," Cherrie said.

"We're on three-way?" I asked.

"Easiest way to get something done," Bernie said. "And I like the harbor, but it's not warm enough to be near the water."

"What about Busch Gardens?" Cherrie asked. "It's not that far away, and there's plenty to do there."

Bernie gasped like a little kid. "D, you in?"

"Book it." I found myself grinning. "We'll leave tomorrow."

"We're leaving this afternoon." Bernie shushed our protests. "If you two heffas can't be ready in four hours, something is wrong."

"Why we gotta be heffas?" Cherrie asked.

"I'll make the arrangements," Bernie said. "We'll have to stay in a cheap hotel, but…"

"No, we won't." I remembered a seldom-used card in my wallet. "This trip's on Adrian."

Five hours later—Cherrie had a meeting she couldn't reschedule—we pulled out of Enterprise and headed toward our four-day vacation. Colonial Williamsburg was three hours away, but LeadFoot Price got us there in two.

And Cherrie got a cramp in her neck checking for sirens.

We dropped our bags at the hotel and headed straight for the park. We played Rock, Paper, Scissors to pick the first ride and groaned when Bernie won. Cherrie and I wanted to ease into the day with the swings or the Scrambler, but Bernie was having none of it.

"Apollo's Chariot, baby!" she said. "Put up or shut up."

"I just hope I don't throw up," Cherrie said.

We all survived with our stomach's contents intact, and Cherrie suggested we get the high-flying stuff out of the way. So we endured a 40-minute wait for the Alpengeist, which was totally worth every second, and a similar line for the Griffon. But when she steered us toward the Loch Ness Monster, I feigned a headache. A 114-foot drop from six stories high at 60 miles per hour?

No thanks. I value my life.

Bernie clowned me until we left the park, but I didn't care. I held onto my dignity and lunch and considered that a triumph.

Once in the room, Cherrie opened her suitcase. "Are we in for the night? There's a new *Trading Spaces,* and I forgot to set my VCR."

"Yep, I'm done." I grabbed the channel guide to find the right channel. "After that, let's order a movie and room service. *To Have & To Hold* is on pay-per-view, and I want to try the cherry cheesecake."

"Way to make it a five-star night, D," Cherrie said.

"Don't thank me. Thank Adrian and six months' worth of untouched money."

"Do you think he'll say anything about you using that debit card?" Cherrie asked.

"Please. He'll be so glad to be useful he might replace what I spend, especially since this trip had an educational component."

"Like learning how much funnel cake Cherrie can eat before she barfs?"

"Shut up, Bernie. And I didn't barf. I choked."

"I meant the conversation with the actors from that other resort," I said.

"That was deep," Cherrie said. "I never thought about the racial issues such an exhibit could create."

"They're pretending to be slaves," Bernie said. "Some buttmunch is bound to take that literally."

"But little white children ordering them around, demanding snacks and favors?" I shook my head. "That must be humiliating."

"I loved the one girl's attitude though," Cherrie said. "Being grateful that she could clock out of a life our ancestors couldn't escape. It really is all about perspective."

I raised a fist. "To the ancestors."

The girls did the same. "To the ancestors."

"And I will further honor my ancestors by taking a luxurious soak in that ginormous tub." Bernie headed toward the bathroom. "Unless you need to go first, germaphobe."

"I'm not a germaphobe," I said. "I just prefer to clean things myself."

"Is that an answer?" Bernie asked as my cell phone buzzed on the nightstand. "Guess that is."

"It's her booooyfriend." Cherrie made kissy noises. "Maybe we should leave them alone."

"Shut up." I answered the phone with a smile. "Hey, you."

"Why aren't you answering your phone?" Maurice asked.

"I just did, silly."

"Not this one. Your dorm phone."

His tone deflated my cheer. "Because I'm not

there."

"Where are you?"

"Virginia."

"What?"

"Bernie, Cherrie, and I took a road trip…"

"Road trip!" they called out.

"…to Busch Gardens for spring break."

"And you couldn't tell me that?"

"It was a last-minute thing. You said you'd be busy all week, so I figured I'd call you tonight. I'm sorry I worried you."

"I'm not worried. I'm here."

"Where?"

"In the Meridian lobby. I came down to surprise you because you said you weren't going anywhere for spring break."

I didn't remind him about the perils of surprising me. "That's really sweet, but we're already here and not coming back until Friday night."

"This gets better and better." I waited out his attitude, ignoring the amused looks from my roommates. "Guess I'll head back to Philly."

"Okay. Again, I'm…"

"Sorry. Yeah, I got that. Have fun, I guess."

"We will. I love you."

He muttered the same and hung up, and I set my phone on the desk.

"So Maurice is at Meridian?" Cherrie asked.

"Mmm-hmm."

"After being a jerk for the past few weeks, he drove all the way there to surprise you," Bernie said. "But you're here?"

I rocked on my heels. "Yep."

The silence stretched as Bernie and Cherrie looked at each other.

"Guess the surprise was on him," Bernie said.

Before I could reply, the dam broke, and the three of us fell out laughing.

Thirty-Seven

Though Maurice remained the butt of many jokes for the rest of the week, I called him when we left Virginia. And though he still seemed annoyed, I got an intelligible "I love you" when the call ended.

Hooray for progress.

All in all, Busch Gardens was the bomb. We laughed, relaxed, and had plenty of souvenirs to show for it. Bernie went all out with T-shirts, while Cherrie got mugs for herself, her Momma, and GiGi. Though disappointed in the stationery, I was impressed by the quality of their ink pens. Never met a fine point I didn't like.

Bernie dropped us off and took the car back to her apartment, where I would meet her Saturday morning to return it to Enterprise. When I rolled into Meridian's lobby, my female RA waved me over to the reception desk.

"Did your fiancé find you?" she asked.

"Yes. We had our signals crossed."

"Thank God. For a moment, I thought we were going to have to call security."

I set down my shoulder bag. "Was he that bad?"

"That concerned. He insisted you were upstairs, and when someone from your floor said she saw you with a rolling suitcase, he snapped at her."

"Good grief."

"Like I said, I think he was worried because he didn't know you were leaving town." She retrieved my mail from the slot. "Oh, and he left something for you. Should I get it now or will you come back?"

"I'll take it now."

"Sure thing."

When I opened the small, padded envelope upstairs, I couldn't believe what was inside. Grinning from ear-to-ear, I picked up the phone immediately.

"Did you notice I'm calling from my dorm?"

"Yeah, yeah." I could tell he was smiling. "You'd better not go to the bathroom next time without telling me first."

"Yeah, yeah. I got my present."

"Do you like it?"

"I do. Especially the LOVE Statue key ring."

"They represent the keys to my heart, but they also work on my front door."

"Thank you." I twirled them around my finger. "And I really am sorry we missed each other this week."

"Maybe you can make it up to me."

"Maybe I can." I checked my calendar. "What are you doing two weeks from today?"

"Same old, same old. Why?"

"The Bison Ball is that Friday night, and I'd like you to be my date."

"The Bison Ball, huh?"

"It's an annual HU event honoring outstanding student organizations."

"Oh."

"We just see it as a college prom."

"Oh." His voice warmed. "As I recall, we always had a great time at the prom."

"You recall correctly." I glanced at our senior prom picture on the wall. "Are you in?"

"You know it. Does that mean I can pick your dress? I'm thinking short and backless."

I laughed, glad things were back to normal. "Don't press your luck, homie."

I was taking the final load of clothes from my mini vacation out of the dryer when someone tsked behind me. "Tell me you didn't spend the entire week in there."

"Shows what you know," I said to Mordecai. "I left DC."

"You went to Borders for a part-time shift?"

"Ha ha. The girls and I went to Busch Gardens."

His eyebrows shot up in surprise. "Now that's how you spend spring break."

"Did your friend get the part?"

"No, but we had fun anyway." He checked his watch. "Well, I'm sure you're knee-deep in your notes, so I won't keep you."

"My notes?"

"Studying for that test in Dr. Maddox's class tomorrow." As my eyes widened, he sighed. "I should have reminded you before I left."

"No, it's on my calendar. I just forgot." I slammed the dryer door shut. "This is why I don't make spontaneous plans."

He checked his watch. "You've still got plenty of time to study tonight."

"Yeah, but I'm a terrible crammer."

"Well, cramming is my undeclared minor, so let me help you."

"You sure you want to do that? I get cranky when I cram."

"I have plenty of chocolate in my room."

I folded my arms. "Are you saying that because you think I've got some sort of female issue or because you know chocolate keeps me calm?"

"Obviously the second one."

"Good answer." I grabbed my laundry basket. "I'll see you in a half hour."

Once in his room, I settled in my favorite spot on the floor with my lap desk. Working on the books for his sister and neighbor developed our camaraderie, and we fell easily into it as he pulled out his notebook for Dr. Maddox's class.

"According to the syllabus, we'll be tested on the past three weeks." He set the bowl of M&Ms between us. "Which covered intraracial conflict."

"Such a happy topic." I grabbed a handful of candy. "I'll be glad when we get to the next unit."

"You just want an excuse to talk about *Café Latte* in class."

"Am I that bad?"

"Not bad. Just devoted."

"You always put such a positive spin on things."

"I do what I can. By the way, my neighbor's wife loved the gift. She cried."

"How sweet!"

"And…she asked if we could do one for her best friend."

"Shut up!"

"The friend recently completed her first marathon, and my neighbor wants to celebrate how hard she's worked. She understands if we were too busy, but…"

"Of course we will. Though at this rate, we might need business cards."

"And a brochure."

"And a tray of mini-muffins in the waiting area."

"It always comes down to food with you, doesn't it?"

"You know it." I added the new book project to my long-term to-do list. "Speaking of which, are you going to the Bison Ball?"

"That's not my scene." He pulled a folder from his bag. "And what does that have to do with food?"

"There's a catered three-course meal."

"I'll pass. What about you?"

"Maurice is taking me."

"Good. You deserve to do things like that."

"So do you." When he looked up, I tilted my head

to study him. "Why aren't you in a relationship?"

He rifled through his folder in a panic. "Is that on tomorrow's test?"

"You're cute, kind, smart, and funny. The total package."

"Well ..." His eyes darted back and forth. "I tried to holla at the PunchOut lady with the red glasses, but she said I was too skinny for her."

I narrowed my eyes. "Is that true?"

"Would I lie?" I tossed some M&Ms at his smirking face, and he caught a few in his mouth. "Again!"

"Are you going to give me a useful answer?"

"Sure. A flashlight, snacks, and clean underwear."

"What?"

"Things you should keep in the glove compartment. That was your question, right?"

When I reached into the candy bowl again, he held up his hands in protest. "Okay, okay. Stop threatening my precious chocolate."

"You sound like Willy Wonka."

"And you're acting like Veruca Salt." I pursed my lips, and he chuckled. "Listen, most jokes aside, I can't be with anyone right now."

"Why not?"

He uncapped his yellow highlighter. "Let's just say I have my reasons."

"That's all I get?"

"For now. But if you stop hurling food at me, maybe I'll elaborate."

I studied him then reached into the bowl again. "No deal."

Thirty-Eight

After my last class on Bison Ball Friday, I walked home from campus, too excited and impatient to wait for the shuttle. All the arrangements for my weekend with Maurice were set, and I had serious shivers in me timbers. Instead of staying together in Meridian, we had a room in a Dupont Circle Marriott for the weekend. Not only did he request double beds in case I wanted the option, but Maurice assured me his reasons for booking the room were about privacy not passion.

"Yes, I want you alone," he said. "But mainly I don't want people in our business, especially overzealous RAs who can't seem to help themselves."

"You don't have to worry about Mordecai," I said for the umpteenth time. "He's not interesting in dating anyone right now. He told me so."

Maurice muttered something I didn't catch, and I returned to the safe subject of our time together. He would arrive in DC around 5:30 and call me then.

So when my cell phone rang two hours early, I was pleasantly surprised. "Couldn't wait to see me, huh?"

"You know that's always the case."

I didn't like the sound of his voice. "What's wrong?"

"There's been another incident at The Shop."

I stopped walking, causing a logjam in the Meridian lobby. "What happened?"

"Suzika didn't give details, but there's a lot of damage, and one of my guys got injured."

"What is going on up there?"

"I have no idea, but I need to deal with this."

"Of course." As his words echoed in my ears, I realized what they meant. "Oh."

"I am so sorry, Duchess."

"You don't have to apologize." I flopped onto a sofa in the lobby seating area. "It's not your fault folks have no respect for other people's property."

"If Suzika could handle this, I would let her, but..."

"Maurice, it's okay. This is your business. There will be other balls."

Next year.

"But I don't want you to miss it," he said. "It won't be the same, but go with your girls and do it right."

"Sure."

"Promise you'll have a good time without me."

"Okay." I wouldn't let my worsening mood make him feel guiltier. "I'll save you a dance."

"That's my girl." A car horn sounded in the background. "I gotta go. I pulled into a rest stop to call you."

"I'm sorry about The Shop, and I hope your friend is okay."

"He'll be fine. I'm just sorry I can't be there tonight. I'm gonna make all of this up to you, baby. I promise."

"I know."

"I love you, Duchess."

"I love you too. And it's okay." I closed the phone and sighed. "Except it's not."

I hung my head, counting backwards from forty-three to keep calm. There was no sense in having a fit. Maurice wasn't coming, and there was nothing to be done about it. I didn't know what in heckfire was going on in West Philly, but couldn't the foolishness have waited until next weekend? Didn't they know we had a date?

A date I was now expected to attend alone.

"I'm sorry, Maurice," I said aloud. "I can't do it."

"Do what?" Cherrie stood beside my chair. "And why are you rubbing your neck? Are you sick?"

"Only of West Philly Negroes and their shenanigans."

"I don't follow."

"Something happened at The Shop. Windows broken, barbers injured, chaos a-go-go."

"Oh, no." She sat beside me. "Is Maurice all right?"

"Yeah. He's on his way back to Philly now to deal with it."

"On his way back to…oh." She covered her mouth.

"He's not coming."

"Nope. So I'm not going."

"But you have to go!"

"Why? So I can spend the whole night wishing Maurice was there? Sitting with you when the slow jams come on?"

"We could dance together. GiGi taught me how to lead for that jitterbug competition."

"You are not funny."

"But I am serious. Come on!" She huffed to her feet. "You can't not go to the ball."

"You're not going?" Mordecai approached on my other side. "What happened to Maurice?"

"Problem at The Shop. There was a break-in or something."

"In broad daylight on a Friday afternoon?"

I shrugged. "Wouldn't be the first time."

Mordecai paused. "That doesn't mean you can't go to the ball."

"That's what I'm saying," Cherrie said. "Lots of people go alone. I am."

"You're going with the Campus Pals," I said.

"But we can leave Meridian together."

"So I can get there and sit by myself? No thanks."

"What about Bernie?" Mordecai asked.

"This is her busiest week outside of Homecoming," Cherrie said. "She's been doing hair all day and plans to do her own tonight."

"It's fine." I tucked my cell phone into my bookbag. "I've got a stocked fridge and full movie bin, so…"

"No," Mordecai said. "You're not eating Stouffer's

and watching *Café Latte* again."

"Their lasagna is tasty, and Mr. Darcy will keep me company."

"No disrespect to that fine gentlefrog, but you've been excited about the ball for weeks and you should be there." He sat beside me on the couch. "Let me come with you."

I smiled. "No."

"Why not?"

"For one thing, you work tonight."

"I'm off at eight," Mordecai said as Cherrie scurried away. "I can be dressed in half an hour."

"I wouldn't want you to rush."

"It's for a good cause. And a real meal."

I chuckled. "The ribs were slamming last year."

"And would you really deprive me of such deliciousness?"

"But what would you wear?"

"Last year's Halloween costume. How do you feel about Darth Vader?"

As I shook my head at him, Cherrie grinned her way toward us. "The Grad Assistant agreed to start her shift at seven, giving you plenty of time to get ready." At my surprised expression, she shrugged. "This is what I do."

"Now there's no reason you can't go," Mordecai said. When I didn't reply, he lowered his voice as Cherrie pretended not to eavesdrop. "I know you had other ideas about tonight, but I think we could have a good time together."

"We always do."

"Then what's the problem?"

"I just ... you said this wasn't your scene, and I wouldn't want you to be uncomfortable."

"It would only make me uncomfortable to know you stayed home tonight." He leaned back on the sofa. "I'll even let you throw chocolate at me."

"Only if you're sure."

"I'm positive. Though I hope to keep the candy carnage to a minimum."

"Well." I pursed my lips in thought. "I make no promises on that."

He came to his feet. "So you'll go?"

I looked up and smiled. "I'll go."

Cherrie clapped her hands. "Yay!"

Checking my reflection in my full-length mirror, I smoothed the front of my dress, tugging at the mid-thigh hemline. Maurice would never have expected me to take his suggestion, but when I saw this shimmery gold dress, I couldn't say no. The creative draping kept it from being truly backless, and the long poet sleeves provided enough modesty to keep me from blushing all night.

Theoretically.

Not only was I bummed to miss the grown-up redo of my senior prom, but I was steeped in guilt about my stand-in date. Maurice told me to have fun without him, but I'm sure that invitation didn't include his Chocolate City nemesis. Maurice would definitely feel some type of way if he knew I was going with Mordecai, and I wouldn't feel right if I didn't tell him.

But when I called Maurice's cell after my shower,

the phone rang seven times and the voicemail never came on. I figured he was busy with the police and tried again later. But after three more calls and no answer, I was unsure what to do. If I brought my phone to the ball and Maurice called, the rest of the night would be disastrous. Maurice would be angry, Mordecai might be offended, and I would be caught in the awkward middle. The more I thought about it, the more I realized the futility of telling Maurice anything tonight. Mordecai and I were friends, and Maurice would have to trust there was no more to it than that.

Tucking my cell phone in a top drawer, I tabled my thoughts of Maurice and heard three soft raps on my door.

"Coming!"

I grabbed my black and gold clutch, triple-checking for the tickets, and cut out my room light. But when I opened my door and saw Mordecai, I blinked in confusion.

His dark, shoulder-length locs were held back by side strands and fell neatly on his shoulders. He wore a white shirt and black tie with pinstriped black slacks and vest. And two never-before-seen dimples were on prominent display.

When a full five seconds passed in silence, he frowned. "Is something wrong?"

"No. I just didn't expect you to look that good."

I covered my foolish mouth as he laughed. "I think there was a compliment in there somewhere."

"I'm sorry. I must be nervous."

"Fortunately I planned for such an event." He produced a small gift bag from behind his back. "Now play nice."

I peeked inside and found a small bundle of colorful Tootsie Pops. "This beats a nosegay of roses any day."

"I'll have to take your word for it."

We took the back elevator downstairs and walked through the lounge to the front of the building. I noticed several girls craning their necks to gawk at Mordecai—the sharp suit a suave departure from his crewneck tees and cargo pants—and I chuckled to myself. I also noted the pointed scoffing they aimed in my direction and took it in stride, stopping short of sticking out my tongue.

Jealous heffas.

"Why the smirk?" Mordecai asked as we reached the lobby doors.

"Girls are funny, and they've got their claws out tonight."

"Don't worry." He tapped his vest pocket. "I have mace."

When we reached the lobby, the helpful Grad Assistant whistled as she walked around the desk. "Mordecai in slacks? I need a picture of this."

I stepped aside, but he grabbed my hand. "You got me into this, so you're not going anywhere."

"Hold that pose!" The Grad Assistant clicked away. "Mordecai, if you don't smile, I'm going to wallpaper the lounge with these."

"And she's got the authority to do it," I said through my smile.

He looked at me. "That's the last time I buy you a candy bouquet."

As other partygoers arrived, they clapped and whistled on their way to the shuttle. A few joined our picture, and soon we were pressed together in the center of a group shot.

"This was not part of the deal," Mordecai muttered as a freshman filly pushed up on his other side.

"Aww." I pinched his cheek. "Is someone wearing his grumpy pants beneath that suit?"

He shook his head. "You are so going to pay for this."

The photo shoot concluded, we followed the other revelers outside in high spirits. For his share in the fun, the shuttle driver hung colorful lights inside the bus and put on a mixtape. Mordecai sat in the aisle seat beside me as The Ohio Players serenaded our send-off. I snapped my fingers and tried not to lose my rhythm laughing at Mordecai lip-syncing his way through their greatest hits.

It was a clear crisp night in DC, and the weather was warm enough that I didn't miss my coat as we got off the shuttle. Though based on some of the fashion choices, clothing may have been altogether optional.

"I feel like I should cover my eyes." Mordecai held the door as we entered Blackburn. "That dress may as well be made of air."

"Don't stare or you'll turn into a pillar of salt." The line for ticketholders was halfway down the stairs, and as we waited our turn, it was my turn not to stare. "Oh my wow."

"What?" Mordecai looked around. "That girl from the lobby isn't behind me, is she?"

"No, but look who's in front of us."

"Dr. Maddox and Dr. Treble?" Mordecai stood on tiptoe for a better look. "Holding hands?"

"Did you know they were together?"

"Not at all." The line moved, and we followed suit. "Rumor had it that Dr. Maddox married last summer, but no one believed it. And Dr. Treble…"

"… doesn't seem like someone's wife." I thought back to winter break. "He used her first name the day we met, but I figured they were good friends and thought nothing of it."

"And in class he said he doesn't date anymore."

"But married to her?" I shook my head. "They don't match."

"Sometimes opposites attract," he said. "Like chocolate and celery."

My stomach churned as we climbed the stairs. "What is it with you and chocolate?"

"It makes the world go 'round. Besides, those two are more alike than different. They're both professors and both passionate about cultivating the next generation."

"That's true."

"And she didn't seem so bad with you that day in Pentagon City Mall, right?"

"No, she was actually quite helpful. So yeah, I guess everybody has more than one side." I watched them enter the ballroom. "I just wonder why they don't wear rings."

"Some people don't need rings to prove their love."

"What?"

"Different relationships have different priorities," he said. "My great uncle just got married, and instead of getting rings, he paid for a week-long honeymoon. That sounds like something Dr. Maddox would do."

"And I bet Dr. Treble would choose a flight to Zimbabwe over a box from Zales." I handed the tickets to the attendant, remembering we weren't talking about me. "So maybe rings aren't everything."

"Nope." He held open the ballroom door. "Sometimes they're just glorified pieces of jewelry."

Thirty-Nine

This year's theme was "Midnight Elegance," and the ballroom expressed that sentiment with school-spirited style. Sheer fabric in HU navy and white billowed in layers from the ceiling, while balloons and decorative topiaries in coordinating urns held down the floor. Round eight-person tables were graced with tall arrangements of blue and white flowers accented by tea lights, and a lively duet by Ella and Louie jazzed up the audio atmosphere.

"The electric blue delphiniums are gorgeous." I set my purse down as Mordecai pulled out my chair. "And I love these white dendrobium."

"Ahh, yes." He bent to sniff the flowers and turned into a Frenchman. "And ze green symposium is ze perfect accent."

I looked at him. "Symposium?"

"Uhh ..." He stroked an imaginary beard. "Magnesium?"

"There you are!" Cherrie arrived in a gust of lavender chiffon, coming to a halt when she saw Mordecai. "Holy crap."

He rolled his eyes. "I will never wear a suit again."

"And deprive us of such yummy eye candy?" Cherrie snapped a quick flick. "Don't you dare."

"Where did the camera come from?" he asked.

"She keeps it on a holster." I passed it to him. "Now be nice and take our picture."

Cherrie and I defaulted to our favorite poses from high school, save one where we frowned to show how much we missed Bernie. During the individual shots, she noticed the back of my dress and grabbed the camera from Mordecai.

"D, that open back is seriously sexy! Turn around so I can send a picture to Maurice."

"You know what?" I stepped out of the frame. "I'd rather show him in person."

She wiggled her eyebrows. "You mean after a certain early summer event?"

"A little formal for the Penn Relays, don't you think?"

"I hate you." She glanced behind me. "I gotta say hi to Imani."

She fluttered away, and I took my seat beside Mordecai. "You didn't steal candy from my purse while I wasn't looking, did you?"

"Not my style." He examined his empty water

glass. "Was she talking about your wedding?"

"She's talking crazy. A summer wedding? I'm not even engaged."

"Right."

"You don't believe me?"

"I believe you believe that."

His tone filled in the blanks. "But you don't think Maurice believes that."

"I didn't say that."

"Or maybe you don't believe that."

"It doesn't matter what I believe."

"It matters to me."

"I believe…" He glanced at the stage where the HUSA president approached the podium. "We should finish this conversation eleven nevers from now."

"And I believe you suck."

As Mordecai tucked his laugh into a cough, the president gave a brief history of the Howard University Student Association and highlighted its major accomplishments during the current school year. She explained the selection process and requested we hold our applause until the nominees in each category were announced. The eager crowd ignored the directive as expected, and I admired her poise during the constant interruptions. I paid attention through the first three awards, but when Philly lost State Club of the Year, I lost interest.

Mordecai leaned in. "I wasn't trying to upset you earlier."

"I know."

"I'm just…I'm the last person who should talk about your relationship with Maurice."

"Why? You know I value your…"

My reply was drowned out by uproarious applause from the room. I came to my feet with everyone else and watched Dr. Maddox receive the award for Professor of the Year. He never mentioned the nomination in class, and his modesty only sweetened his triumph. I cheered with the rest of my table and turned to Mordecai.

"Look at Dr. Treble! She is so adorably proud of him."

"And that's what matters," he said. "Being supported and being with someone who makes you smile. If you've got that, it doesn't matter what anyone else thinks."

Dr. Maddox's win was the climax of the ceremony, so the remaining awards were received with much less fanfare. After the Campus Pals accepted Student Organization of the Year, the HUSA president took the stage once more.

"And now." She rubbed her hands together. "Dinner is served!"

The buffet was set up in the hallway, and patrons closest to that area were instructed to rise first. Though we weren't too far away, I braced myself for the wait. Curiosity made me grab the menu card on our table, and as I surveyed the options, my stomach growled in anticipation.

"Do you need a Tootsie Pop while you wait?" he asked.

I opened my purse. "Would that make me greedy?"

"Not greedy," he said. "Prepared."

I took out two red pops, handing one to him. "Good answer."

When they finally called our table, Mordecai insisted on getting my plate, and I used that opportunity to go to the bathroom. A few girls from Dr. Treble's fall seminar were at the mirror, and we admired dresses as we waited for empty stalls.

"Did you see Dr. Treble with Dr. Maddox?" A girl in a turquoise dress checked her lipstick. "My jaw about hit the floor!"

"I didn't know they were married either." I turned to check the back draping on my dress. "But it was great to see them so happy and in love. And looking good while doing it."

"He always looks good," her friend with the nose ring added. "Wanna-sop-him-up-with-a-biscuit good."

"Mmm-hmm, and he can do so much better," Turquoise Dress said. "She's obnoxious, mean, and nobody likes her. To snag him, she must have worked hard on that night shift."

Behind us, a toilet flushed, and Dr. Treble stepped out of the center stall. Nose Ring paled, and Turquoise Dress averted her gaze as the intrepid professor approached the sink.

"You both should worry less about my overtime." Dr. Treble pressed the lever on the soap dispenser. "And more about your grades."

"Yes, ma'am," they said in unison.

"I think I'll use the bathroom downstairs," Turquoise Dress said.

Dr. Treble smiled. "Good idea."

"Bye, Daria," Nose Ring added as the door closed behind her.

Dr. Treble dried her hands and tossed the paper

towel in the trash. Adjusting the gardenia in her gorgeous 'fro, she met my gaze in the mirror. "Good to see you, Ms. Nelson."

"You too, Dr. Treble. Have a wonderful time."

"Oh, I will." She walked toward the door. "Especially when I see those heffas on Monday."

"She said that?" Mordecai asked after I relayed the story. "She is vicious."

"They were foolish." I sipped my sweet tea. "Don't ever talk about someone in a public bathroom without checking under the stall first."

"Sounds like you're speaking from experience."

"I don't know what you're talking about."

He took my fork. "Confess."

"You're coming between me and a plate of yams? Negro, you done lost your mind."

"I've got all night."

I rolled my eyes and grabbed my fork. "My high school chemistry teacher gave me an undeserved B on an exam…"

From there we swapped embarrassing stories from childhood and beyond, stopping only when the DJ played a funky tune that transcended age and musical tastes. Dr. Maddox walked hand-in-hand with Dr. Treble to the center of the space and kicked off the Electric Slide. In a matter of seconds, the dance floor was full.

"I know this isn't your scene." I pushed away my empty dessert plate. "But tell me you do the Electric Slide."

"I've been known to slide from time to time." He stood with a smile. "Let's go."

We joined the rest of our friends, finding space in the back of the line. Dr. Treble surprised us with her variations, including a 360-turn on the third pass. Her bathroom nemeses were nowhere in sight, but if they knew like I knew, they'd be putting in for a transfer.

The Electric Slide gave way to that song Carlton made famous on *The Fresh Prince*, and anyone still seated filled the floor to capacity. It was refreshing to see Mordecai so relaxed, and as the DJ played hit after hit, he loosened up even more. Cherrie and Imani joined us, and the latter didn't attack Mordecai for once. Though he refused to dance beside her, the four of us had a great time.

When the music's tempo slowed to a crawl, Cherrie sighed. "If only Canyon were here."

"I thought you were rooting for Rasool," I said."

"After what he said to Caprelle? Never again." She patted my shoulder before walking away. "But you kids have fun."

"What did Rasool do now?" Mordecai asked me.

"It's a long story. But after yesterday's episode, I don't think Caprelle can forgive him."

Imani paired up with a boy from Dr. Maddox's class, and Mordecai and I looked at each other. He was only here to keep me from staying home alone, and I appreciated the sacrifice. But after surviving the first round of dancing, a slow jam might be too much to ask.

He leaned in to be heard over the music. "Are you tired?"

I shook my head. "But you don't have to do this if

you don't want to."

"No, I'm good."

"Okay." I moved closer to him. "Don't step on my feet."

"I wouldn't dare."

He put his arms around my waist while I cinched mine behind his neck. The song was sweet not sexy, and as it played, I realized I was happy. And why wouldn't I be? I was in a beautiful dress on a lovely night with one of my very best friends and a tummy full of home-cooked goodness. I had a purse full of chocolate I didn't have to share and won the raffle at our table for the centerpiece.

As the song changed to a Roberta Flack ballad, I laid a hand on Mordecai's shoulder. "Thank you."

"For what?"

"For doing this. I'm having a great time."

"Good. This dress wasn't made for Stouffers and sitcoms."

I looked up. "Is there a compliment in there somewhere?"

"Very much so."

An overeager couple twirled by us, and I pressed against him to get out of their way.

"I'm glad you came," Mordecai said.

"Me too. Even Maurice thought I should."

"What?"

"He wanted me to come without him, suggested I go with the girls. But you're as good a friend to me as they are." I looked up at him. "So thank you for that as well."

He nodded. "You're welcome."

Heatwave's eternal anthem came through the speakers, and we fell silent. But midway through the song, Mordecai stepped back. "I need to leave."

"What's wrong?"

"My stomach is acting up. I think I ate too much."

"It was that second piece of cobbler." I wagged my finger at him. "I knew you couldn't keep up with me."

"I'm sorry to do this to you." He looked around. "Could you stay with Cherrie?"

"I think we made our point. Besides, Cherrie will be here until the last balloon deflates."

We made our way off the dance floor and out of the ballroom, and the Meridian shuttle picked us up from Cramton within minutes. Mordecai was quiet as he stared at the back of the seat in front of us, and I couldn't stand to see him embarrassed.

"Just so you know, these heels were killing my feet. You actually did me a favor."

He didn't look at me. "Score one for the rookie."

When we got to Meridian, Mordecai walked me to the front elevators and excused himself. His parting smile was more like a grimace, and I waved goodbye as the doors closed between us.

I slipped off my shoes as soon I hit my bedroom, grateful to be home. The food, folks, and fun made me giddy, so I took a lengthy hot shower to relax. Despite the initial disappointment of my boyfriend's absence, I had no complaints and couldn't wait for next year's ball. Maurice hadn't called, and as it was almost eleven, I wouldn't call him now. No news was good news as far as the wilds of West Philly were concerned, so I assumed his barber was recovering and any shop damage was covered by insurance. Everything else could wait.

I walked to the door to turn off the overhead light and was startled by a soft knock.

"Who is it?"

"Mordecai."

I opened the door with an easy smile. "Feeling better?"

"Not really."

"Do you need medicine? I've got Pepto, antacids, Midol…"

"Midol?"

"Don't knock it 'til you've tried it."

He rubbed the back of his neck. "I want to apologize for cutting our night short."

"Don't. It was just about perfect."

"Yeah, it was."

"Besides, you can't control how you feel."

"No, I can't."

"But if you're not better by tomorrow morning, you might want to go to the…"

Though the rest of that sentence formed in my brain, it never left my lips because it was interrupted by something else, something tangible and powerful and unexpected.

Something like Mordecai's lips pressing against mine.

Forty

The kiss lasted five seconds, forever or fleeting depending on your perspective:

First I wondered what was happening. I didn't see him move or feel a shift in the air. There was no warning or prologue. Only shock and awe.

Wonder demanded answers, so sensation filled in the blanks: his hands cupping my face, his lips sampling mine, communicating desires I didn't know he had.

Sensation yielded to surprise which lingered for two seconds, unable to do much else.

Surprise finally melted into reaction, and I recognized the need to do something.

But before I got the chance, Mordecai pulled away, his voice hushed as he stroked my cheek with soft knuckles.

"This is why I can't be with anyone right now, Daria. Why I'm the last person who should ever comment on your relationship with Maurice. Why every time I'm with you, I'm the happiest and most miserable person alive, why our friendship means everything to me yet isn't enough. I just…"

He shook his head with a heavy sigh, and I held my breath, expecting more. But without another word, he dropped his hand and turned away. By the time I found the courage to open my eyes, I was alone.

Alone and struck dumb.

The elevator dinged in the distance and snapped me out of my trance. I shut my door and locked it, leaning against the back of it to catch my breath. The longer I stood there, the more confused I became, and for fear of falling, I made my way to the bed and sat down.

"What just happened?" I asked aloud. My lips tingled in response, and I brushed them with tentative fingers. "What on earth just happened?"

The room remained mum, and I folded my hands, preparing to pray. But when I closed my eyes, a replay of recent events sauntered past my lids, dragging my attention from the sacred to the sensual. And I opened my eyes again, having no choice but to face what happened.

Mordecai kissed me.

He knocked on my door, apologized for ruining our night, and kissed me.

I stopped short of repeating it aloud, preferring to keep the crazy inside my head.

Mordecai and I were friends, best friends even. So

how did this happen? Had he always wanted more but feared polluting the platonic waters? Did his feelings surprise him like they surprised me tonight?

I thought back on the past two years: every talk on the shuttle, laugh in the lounge, and moment in the hallway. I remembered his eyes and smile, his humor and wisdom. And I saw nothing suspicious, not even a hint of flirtation. Not during the snowball fight, Valentine's Day, our work on the gift books, or the double date with Bernie and Tone. We didn't cuddle while watching movies in his room or hug hello on The Yard. Tonight was the most physical contact we'd ever shared by far, not including the kiss.

I fell back on my bed, running my hands through my hair. I couldn't believe Mordecai kissed me, couldn't believe his confession. How could I be the reason he was single? I saw the looks he got tonight, the number of females interested in him. He could have any one of them if he chose. How could he hold out for me? How long had he held out for me?

Was he holding out for me still?

What did this kiss mean? Was he asking for a beginning or saying goodbye?

And how could I ask him any of this? Did I want to ask? Did he want me to ask? I couldn't be sure, especially after he mentioned my relationship with Maurice.

I sat up with a gasp.

What on earth was I going to tell Maurice?

How could I tell Maurice that while he was in Philly dealing with a vandalized business, Mordecai was in my doorway, standing in his place, kissing me? How could I admit that for all my protests to the contrary, Maurice was right: Mordecai wanted me and had conveyed that desire tonight in no uncertain terms?

Maurice told me to have fun tonight, but this was in no way what he meant. I was worried enough about telling him I attended the ball with Mordecai. Now I had to tell him that Mordecai kissed me, and I...

And I did what exactly?

I didn't stop him or push him away.

I didn't turn my head or close my mouth.

Which means Mordecai kissed me, and I let him.

I let Mordecai kiss me.

And if I let him, could he have kissed me so long without my participation or consent?

Holy crap. Did I kiss him back?

That last question swirled around my frazzled brain enough to give me a headache. I popped some Tylenol PM and buried myself under the covers with Mr. Darcy. I wouldn't get any answers tonight, so at the very least, I wanted to get some sleep.

But that didn't happen either.

All night long, I dreamed about my dilemma: Mordecai swirling me around the dance floor at Blackburn, dipping me under a spotlight with a kiss as Maurice storms away. Maurice in a tux on one knee offering a bigger diamond while Mordecai cowers in a corner with sad eyes.

Thanks for nothing, Tylenol PM.

Cranky and groggy, I rose after eleven with no greater clue of what to do. Every time I picked up the phone to call Maurice, guilt stalled my fingers and I hung up feeling worse than before. And for fear of running into Mordecai before understanding my feelings, I resolved to stay in my room all weekend, save stealthy trips to the bathroom and shower.

Comforted by a hearty bowl of oatmeal, I pulled out my journal and tried to outline my concerns. How to tell Maurice hovered at the top, followed closely by what to say to Mordecai the next time we met.

But there was something else nagging at me, something on the edge of my mind I couldn't quite grasp. Mordecai kissed me, and I didn't stop him, but what did that mean? Nothing had to change. We were still friends, neighbors, classmates, and colleagues working on a book project. Our friendship could survive this hiccup, whatever it meant, and someday we might look back on it and laugh. It wasn't like we had an argument or I was upset with him.

I shoved my spoon back into the bowl as my mouth dropped open.

Why wasn't I upset?

Mordecai, a really good friend and nothing more, kissed me last night, and I wasn't upset. I wasn't angry or disappointed or feeling any type of negative way about it. I felt guilty because I was with Maurice and confused because I didn't know what the kiss signified about Mordecai's current feelings. But as for me and my house, we weren't upset.

Why wasn't I upset? Did I have romantic feelings for Mordecai?

Did I?

Though the knock on the door was gentle, it made me jump, sending my oatmeal-laden spoon clattering to the floor. Warm, gooey mush splattered on my rug and dresser, and if that weren't enough, my brown suede boots also took a hit.

I came to my feet, stepping over the mess, and waited. Hiding from Mordecai wasn't my finest moment, but it was all I could do until I sorted out my feelings.

"Daria?" came the soft voice. "Are you in there?"

My visitor's tone amped up my concern, and her expression put me on high alert. "What's wrong?"

"I'm sorry for coming so early." Bernie looked at my floor. "What happened?"

"I dropped my spoon." I grabbed my cleaning bucket as she sat on the bed. "Is everything okay?"

"Something happened last night. Something bad." I waited as she sighed. "Tone and I slept together."

"That's not so bad." I fished out my rubber gloves. "I know you were trying to be celibate, but messing up once doesn't mean…"

"Then we broke up."

"What?" I left the gloves on the floor and joined her on the bed. "Why?"

"Because we slept together."

"You're not making any sense. Walk me through it."

"Okay." Bernie leaned back against my guest pillow. "After my last client last night, I gave myself a deep conditioning treatment, expecting not to see Antonio because he was at a Wizards game. But they were down by 33 at the half, so he called and asked to hang out for a while, not to spend the night. I still had two hours left on my treatment, so I thought I was safe. Until he washed my hair."

I waited for the rest. "Okay…"

"Hair-washing is an intimate, almost sacred act between lovers, especially with locs because they are warehouses of energy."

"They are?"

She waved off my question. "He washed my hair, oiled my scalp, retwisted my locs, and put me under the dryer. I should have asked him to leave, but I didn't."

We were silent while she gathered herself. There was no need to fill in the rest of those blanks. "But why did you break up?"

"Don't you get it? We can't stay away from each other because that's too difficult, but when we're together, we can't control ourselves. There was no other option."

"There's got to be another option. It doesn't make sense to break up with someone you love because the chemistry's too good. You need to find a balance."

"It's more than the chemistry. Did you know there are European teams interested in him? He's thinking about it but hates the idea of us being so far apart. And based on what you go through with Maurice, I don't blame him."

The mention of my boyfriend stole my breath, and I was grateful to be seated already.

"I want Antonio to make his important decisions without worrying about me," she said. "And he can't do that if we're together."

"Are you sure this is what you want?"

"What's done is done." She patted my hands and noticed my sparkly stilettos on the floor. "Wow, I have no home training."

"What do you mean?"

"I didn't ask about the ball. Cherrie told me about the Maurice-Mordecai swap. How was it?"

I looked at my shoes. "It was nice. We had fun."

"Nice and fun." She went to my fridge and pulled out the milk. "I'll ask again, are you sure you should be an English major?"

"What's done is done." I returned to my bucket and gloves. "Your Cocoa Krispies are in the bin."

Putting her favorite bowl on my table, she smiled. "You always know what to do."

I looked at the mess I'd made. "I wish."

Forty-One

Bernie stayed with me until Sunday night, and her sadness distracted me from my woes. She didn't say much about Tone, but I knew she was thinking about him. Cherrie met us for Sunday brunch at The Diner, and we kept the conversation flowing with tales from the ball.

I kept one particular story to myself.

But Cherrie doesn't miss anything, so when Bernie went to raid the dessert counter, Cherrie asked if I was okay. She didn't believe my smiling answer but let it go.

I wished I had as much freedom.

No matter what else happened all weekend, my thoughts ping-ponged between Maurice and Mordecai. My boyfriend didn't call, and I battled more guilt for being relieved by his silence. Lies of omission were easier to stomach, I reasoned, and as long as Maurice didn't ask about the ball, I was safe. Dealing with Mordecai could only be put off so long, and as I crossed The Yard Monday morning, I prayed God would give me strength.

Because it was sunny and more than 60 degrees, I dodged a few Frisbees and frat brothers before reaching the safety of Locke Hall. I didn't see Mordecai in the crowd outside Dr. Maddox's classroom and considered that a good sign. On my way to the front row, I kept my head down, raising it only when Dr. Maddox took the podium. He noticed the empty seats to my left and right and raised a querulous brow. I shrugged and smiled, hoping he didn't ask for clarity.

I was barely holding on as it was.

"Okay, party people," he said. "We're having an Audio Encounter today. For those who have only been to class twice, I'll review it. I'm going to play an audio clip—could be a speech, a commercial, anything—and I want you to tell me what you hear. And I don't mean 'A conversation about unemployment.' Describe its mood and undertone, its possible purpose or contradictions, how it signifies on something we have discussed in class—listen with a critical ear. There are no wrong answers; you will be graded on how well you defend your position.

"Today's Audio Encounter requires you to consider two tracks. Here is the first."

Instantly recognizable was *Queen of His Kingdom* by hip-hop trio Kinky Kurlz, a number one hit in which the audacious lead brags about being her philandering man's main jawn. I scoffed at the notion, wondering how anyone could laud such a distinction, and remembered my current predicament. Was I not in a relationship with one man and the object of affection for another? Where did I get the nerve to be judgmental?

I shook off my problems and wrote my initial impressions of the song.

When track one ended, Dr. Maddox announced the second would soon begin. "And ladies, try not to cheer too loudly."

"Aw, Dr. Maddox," the do-ragged boy in the back said as *Sloppy Seconds* by the same group filled the silence. "That ain't fair. You gotta redeem us next time."

"I'll see what I can do," Dr. Maddox said.

Before I knew it, Dr. Maddox called for all papers. I filled five pages about Kinky Kurlz' complex relationship with men in their music but felt I barely scratched the surface. If Dr. Maddox assigned us a final project, maybe I would focus on them.

I handed in my paper and spotted Mordecai packing his bag in the back row. Though oddly relieved to see him, my nerves tripled and I considered making a run for the side exit.

But when our gazes met, his expression pinned me to my spot. I could only watch as he hoisted his bag on his shoulder and walked out, leaving me more confused than ever.

Was he expecting me to say something? Should I have followed him? Was the ball in my court or was the game over?

What was I supposed to do?

As I pondered these matters on my way to Douglass

Hall, my jacket pocket buzzed. With the ringer off, I had no clue who was calling, and I held my breath as I pulled out my phone. Relief filled my lungs when I saw the number, and I answered with a smile. "I'm so glad you called!"

Naseem's deep laughter rumbled over the line. "Miss me that bad?"

"You know it. And I wanted to know how things were going after the break-in."

"What break-in?"

"The one at The Shop Friday night. What, it's so bad out West, you can't keep track no more?"

He huffed a short laugh. "You know how it is. Here a crime. There a crime. Everywhere a crime, crime."

"But everyone is all right?"

"I guess. Haven't heard from Maurice all weekend."

"Was The Shop closed?"

"I had the weekend off."

"But he was supposed to be down here. I figured he would have left you and Suzika in charge."

"I can't stand being in the room with her, let alone run The Shop together for three days."

"Guess you haven't settled your differences yet."

"Huh?"

"Maurice called me by accident a few weeks ago, and I overheard you and Suzika arguing."

"Right." He sighed heavily. "I'm sorry about that."

"It's none of my business. But the way you got worked up, I wonder if you secretly love her."

"Never that." He snorted. "Females today can't be trusted."

I froze on the Douglass steps. "What do you mean by that?"

"Nothing."

"Naseem?"

"It's nothing, D. Really. I'll holla at you later, a'ight?"

The line went dead, and I clutched the phone to my beating chest. Naseem couldn't possibly know about Mordecai, yet he called me for no discernible reason and made a point of talking about untrustworthy women. Either that was a huge coincidence or God was trying to get my attention.

Either way, I was freaking out.

I sat on the Douglass steps, thinking of blowing off my next class, when I heard faint singing to my right. It was timeless and rich, the sound of earth and its elements on the morning of creation. Curious students trickled out of Douglass Hall, and I wondered what was going on.

A flood of women poured onto The Yard dressed in identical colors, balloons and symbols following. They carried the song with them, their collective voices raised against the cloudless sky. In the center of the throng were a different group of uniformed ladies wearing the same colors, stepping and chanting in elegant unison. Their cadence carried them to the center of The Yard where they moved into a set formation. Among them was Imani from Dr. Maddox's class, and I was stunned to be happy for her.

But as I got a closer look at the line, I recognized someone else. With her head high and gestures precise, Cherrie Cummings stood fourth from the front.

I waved like a crazy person. "Oh my god, Cherrie!"

I doubted she heard me with everyone else cheering for their friends and family, but I yelled anyway. Though Cherrie never harped on her interest in Greek life, I knew this moment was the culmination of hard work, perseverance, and patience. To the unacquainted, sorority life seemed to be about colors, calls, and choreography. But watching this ocean of sisters welcome their newest members, the weight of the moment pressed upon my heart. They were women of every shade and size, steeped in solemn pride in themselves and each other. Unified beyond their coordinated clothes, these sorors now shared an identity, a heritage, and a destiny.

I blinked and bit my lip, suddenly on the brink of tears. I could not have been any prouder of Cherrie, but another emotion bubbled its selfish way to the surface, sullying the celebration.

Jealousy.

Not of her accomplishment or the benefits that would surely follow. Nor did I feel a sudden aspiration for affiliation. No, it was the same problem I always had with Cherrie, magnified by my current problems: her certainty versus my shakiness. She knew in sixth grade she wanted to be a doctor, revealed her specialty two summers later. If she was in a club, she was an officer. If she supported a cause, she raised money and awareness. And she did it all while flirting with the 4.0 about which I obsessed. Things didn't come easy for Cherrie, but she never met a challenge she wouldn't accept.

And I couldn't confess to my boyfriend or confront my best friend.

I backed away as the whistles and well-wishes swelled around me, no longer in the mood to go to class. When I saw Cherrie at Meridian that night, I tucked away my sadness and greeted the visiting Momma and GiGi with genuine excitement. Cherrie gushed and giggled as only she could, and they whisked her to dinner before she combusted with joy. I didn't see Mordecai in the lobby or elevator, and I didn't know whether to be relieved or disappointed.

Once in the sanctity of my room, I dropped my bookbag and sat on my bed. As I reached for Mr. Darcy, the red blinking light on my answering machine filled me with fresh dread.

Somehow I knew who it was. And I prayed the sound of his voice wouldn't rip me apart.

Forty-Two

All things considered, it wasn't as bad as it could have been.

Maurice's voicemail had been cheerful and quick, saying everything was fine at The Shop and he was sorry he hadn't called sooner. When he asked about the ball and hoped I'd had a good time, I deleted the message with a guilty groan. Naseem's words came back to me once more, and I cried myself to sleep, clutching Mr. Darcy for solace.

With bleary eyes, I faked my way through Brit Lit II Tuesday morning, grateful my professor let us out a bit early. Phoning it in with Dr. Treble wasn't an option, so I grabbed a soda from a vending machine, grateful when the caffeine kicked in. When class ended, I pulled out my phone and rushed out of the room to avoid possible conversation. Dr. Treble could unravel me with a well-timed word, and as I was holding onto my sanity by a shaky thread, I couldn't spare the fabric.

With my cell phone in my hand, I considered a quick call to Maurice. But speaking to him voice-to-voice was out of the question, so I left him a message on his home phone. I don't remember what I said, but I ended with "I love you" and hoped it would be enough. The thought of his voicemail reminded me of another I'd yet to return, so I headed to the I-lab to email Corina. I hit the highlights of the Bison Ball—focusing on the peach cobbler instead of my boy problems—and promised to mail copies of the pictures once Cherrie got them back.

After surviving Egyptian Mythology, I sat on The Yard and weighed my evening options. I could go to work, lose myself in mindless shelving, and treat myself to a cinnamon roll for each cart I cleared. But with new releases from two New York Times Bestselling Authors, the odds of that outcome were slim. More likely, I'd spent the entire night behind the register or stuck at the info desk answering mind-numbing questions about the Computer Programming section.

No thanks.

Doing my best impression of a girl with the flu, I called out of work. Maurice and I had long ago abandoned the walk-home phone call, and somehow the thought made me sad. The leftovers in my Meridian Microfridge were even sadder, so I grabbed a three-piece dark from the KFC on Georgia Avenue. Stuffed to the gills, I headed up the hill to wait for the Meridian shuttle and was joined by a familiar face.

"Hey, Daria."

"Imani, hi! Congratulations on making line."

"Thanks!" She glowed with pride. "I still can't believe it. Are you heading to the Showcase?"

"The what?"

"The Not-My-Major Showcase in Ira Aldridge tonight."

I'd seen the signs around campus but paid them no attention. "Is that where Fine Arts people perform in areas outside their major?"

"Yes, and it's hilarious. Especially when people with terrible voices try to sing. I have an extra ticket if you want."

Mordecai hadn't mentioned it, so I assumed he wouldn't be there. And some harmless entertainment would be the perfect end to an otherwise stressful day. "Yeah, thanks."

We filed into the crowded theater where freshmen handed out programs. Imani was swept into eager hugs and high-fives, and I prepared to leave her with her sorors.

"Come on." She waved me forward. "There are seats up front."

I hadn't thought I wanted company, but it was nice not to be truly alone. Imani found me a seat two rows in front of her, and I flipped through the colorful program. Put on by Fine Arts freshmen, the showcase was a lighthearted last hurrah for graduating seniors. The program only listed last year's acts, so the mystery of tonight's performers was half the fun.

The house lights blinked, and a cornrowed Mistress

of Ceremonies stepped into the spotlight, accepting the applause with a curtesy. After quieting the rowdy crowd, she welcomed us to the third annual event and promised it would be better than last year. She reviewed some ground rules—no booing or throwing things, no climbing on stage, and no audience participation beyond clapping or call and response.

"There are no winners or losers tonight," she said. "Only hard-working, creative professionals about to take the world beyond our borders by storm. Are you ready to send them off right?"

We roared our assent, and she consulted her clipboard, announcing the first performer. I relaxed into my seat, cleared my mind of personal drama, and waited for the magic to begin.

The acts were diverse and diverting. A trio of photography majors lent an accidentally comedic tone to their scene from *Two Trains Running*, and a well-meaning design student mangled a Negro spiritual. Between the cracked notes and botched words, we were grateful our ancestors hadn't witnessed the sacrilege.

But some of the performances roused us for better reasons. A nervous theater technology student stirred our souls with an elegant flute solo, and a group of childhood friends-turned-music education majors set it off with a dance routine set to a New Edition classic. After taking their bow, they flashed their sorority's hand signs, prompting Imani and company to cosign with its call. Imani tapped my shoulder to say goodbye before heading backstage, and the female MC tapped the microphone to get everyone's attention.

"Though only a junior, this next performer stepped

in today when a friend got sick because that's the kind of guy he is. He had no time to prepare, so we can give him some extra love, right?" The crowd gave its approval, and the MC nodded. "Then give it up for visual arts major, Mordecai Hill!"

I froze in my seat as Mordecai appeared on stage, giving a friendly hug to the announcer. Though I saw him in class yesterday and from a distance on The Yard this morning, his presence here seemed oddly intimate. I was too close to the front to leave without being seen, so I resolved to get through it as best I could.

"Yeah, Cai!" someone called out from behind me.

Mordecai looked up, and as he scanned my side of the room, his gaze fell on me. He blinked in surprise but recovered before anyone noticed.

Anyone but a petrified me, that is.

"This was a bit last-minute," he said. "But in some ways, I guess I've been preparing it for a while."

My heart hammered in my chest, and I reconsidered bolting for the rear exit.

He cleared his throat, closed his eyes, and said, "Excuse me, pretty lady. Please let me bend your ear."

The crowd went wild and clapped in time, and I could only stare as Mordecai recited the very familiar words.

> *I need to put this out there*
> *Don't want to lurk and leer*
> *You didn't think I seen'd you*
> *But how could I ignore?*
> *Girl, I ain't missed a moment since you*
> *walked on through that door*

I remember every word
Every syllable and sigh
I memorized your laughter
And your beauty makes me high
Forgive me, pretty lady
For changing up my lines
I ain't sorry that I want you
I'm only sorry 'bout this rhyme.

There's a scene in *Café Latte* where main character Stephon catches sight of Alicia during pre-show sound check and gets inspired. He enlists the help of the crew, grabs a microphone, and spits this earnest old-school rap about his feelings for her. Stephon's impromptu lyrics are the cutest kind of corny, causing Alicia to blush despite her attempts to be indifferent. When Stephon finishes, Alicia gives him a standing ovation and says, "Now for that, I'm taking you to lunch," thus beginning their delicate dance.

I sat in stunned silence as Mordecai recreated this seminal moment from my favorite movie. He was bold and brilliant, and the audience loved him, coming to their feet as his words flowed with increased ease. During the last verse, he removed the microphone from its stand to move around the stage more freely. His voice was raw with surprising passion, and when he reached the last line, the audience joined in and shouted, "I'm only sorry 'bout this rhyme!"

As the hyped-up crowd whistled and cheered, Mordecai looked right at me, and all I could do was let him. Where did my shy, unassuming friend go? And who was this confident man in his place who rocked an infamously critical Howard crowd with little preparation or trepidation? This dapper dude who escorted his best friend to the Bison Ball last week, showed up at her door, and...

I shook off the final thought, refusing to remember that kiss. No good could come of it, especially with Mordecai leaving the stage with earnest cheers at his back. If I wanted to avoid him, I needed to leave now. I grabbed my bookbag and scurried up the aisle to the rear doors, wondering how much more my heart could take.

Forty-Three

When I got back to Meridian, I took a shower and locked myself in my room with the lights low and both ringers off. I didn't think Mordecai would be bold enough to knock on my door, but after what happened earlier, who knew anymore?

Focusing on my homework proved more challenging than usual, and when I reread the short Walt Whitman poem a fourth time without understanding it, I closed the book and my eyes for the night. I could catch up on the shuttle if needed.

But Meridian was abuzz with Mordecai's performance Wednesday morning, so I opted out of the shuttle and hoofed it to campus on foot. Though I had to share Dr. Maddox's class with him, there was no way I could concentrate if he were somewhere behind me. Ignoring my inner overachiever's protests, I took the right aisle seat on the back row of the lecture room, stopping short of skipping class altogether.

I watched the opposite door to know when Mordecai arrived, but I needn't have bothered. The earlier fanfare followed him to class, and people chanted the words to *Sorry 'Bout This Rhyme* as he made his way to the front row. I considered hiding behind my bookbag then thought the commotion would prevent him from noticing me anyway. But as Mordecai took off his jacket, he spotted me, and his expression changed. Before I could react, Dr. Maddox entered the room, and I had never been happier to see him.

Through the end of the semester, we were covering African-Americans in the media: commercials, news programs, and the like. Last week, we covered misogyny in music videos, and Dr. Maddox had to negotiate a cold war between two students with profoundly different views on the subject. Monday began our treatment of blacks in movies, and as I pulled out my notebook, I remembered what we'd be discussing today.

And didn't know whether to smile or cry.

"*Café Latte*," Dr. Maddox said. "The most popular African-American film of the last two decades. What do we think?"

"Loved it," Imani said from the front of the room. "Funny story, great dialogue, tangible heat between the two leads."

"Hated it," a boy in an orange headband said. "Shorty was always trying to get the upper-hand. Steph shoulda dropped her when she showed up at the Daytime

Emmys with that dude from the soap opera."

"She did that because he waited until the last minute to invite her," said the girl with the annoying laugh. "If he wanted her to be his date, he should have asked her in advance."

"If she was feeling him, she would have said 'yes' no matter when he asked," Orange Headband said.

"Okay." Dr. Maddox held up his hands. "Let's not have an encore of last week's dispute. Other thoughts?"

"The movie had not one but two Howard alumni?" Imani gushed. "Can I get an 'Amen'?"

"Amen!" half the room replied.

"Yeah, it was good to see family doing big things," Orange Headband said. "But ol' girl's character irked the crap out of me."

"Why?" Dr. Maddox asked.

"She gave mixed signals," Mordecai said. "One minute she wanted to keep it professional, the next she struts in his office after-hours wearing a trenchcoat and a smile. What was he supposed to think?"

"He didn't give mixed signals?" Imani asked.

"Yeah," Orange Headband said. "But no man can refuse the naked trenchcoat. It's the 11th Commandment."

The class laughed at his sincerity, but I was stuck on Mordecai's comment. Was he talking about the movie or me? Did he think I encouraged the kiss by asking him to the ball? And if I kissed him back, could I blame him for believing that?

Did I kiss him back?

"Bebe was my girl," Annoying Laugh was saying. "A strong, intelligent sista who held it down without

367

losing her femininity? I really dug that."

"And that actress is stacked," Orange Headband added.

"Because that's what matters, right?" Dr. Maddox chuckled as he solicited comments from the back of the room. Meeting my gaze, he raised his brows in surprise. "Ms. Nelson?"

I smiled through my nerves. "I liked Bebe's friendship with Derek. It was nice to see a dynamic yet platonic relationship between a man and a woman."

"I think Bebe had feelings for Derek," Orange Headband said. "But she was afraid to admit them."

"Me too!" Imani said. "That green room scene said it all."

"I swore he was going to kiss her!" Annoying Laugh said. "That would have been amazing."

"If he tried," Mordecai said. "I wonder if she would have let him."

"Interesting question," Dr. Maddox said. "If a kiss can happen, is the relationship truly platonic?"

The class disagreed on that point, and Dr. Maddox let them defend their positions as he made his way to the front of the room. Mordecai kept his focus forward, but I felt his energy everywhere. Though the story was fictional, the current topic hit too close to home, and I couldn't take it anymore. Grabbing my bag while Dr. Maddox turned away to dig in his knapsack, I snuck out the back door for the first time in my HU tenure.

I rushed out of Locke Hall, collapsing on the nearest bench. My head throbbed with unanswered questions, and without talking to Mordecai or Maurice, I saw no relief in sight. As my ability to remain rational around Mordecai was compromised, I focused on having an actual conversation with Maurice. I didn't know what I would say if he asked about the ball, but I hoped something intelligible would occur to me by the time he answered the phone.

But he didn't answer. His cell phone rang several times, but his voicemail never picked up. When I called right back, the message indicated he was on the other line. Determined, I broke with protocol and called The Shop.

Suzika answered on the second ring. "It's Wednesday at The Shop."

"Where's Maurice?"

"Daria?" The buzzing of clippers faded. "What's wrong?"

"I need to talk to Maurice. Is he there?"

"I haven't seen him today. Did you try his cell?"

"He didn't answer." I tapped my foot in thought. "Is Naseem there?"

"No. Do you want me to…"

"That's okay. Thanks."

I hung up and hoped Naseem had his phone for once. It rang five times before he picked up.

" 'Sup, D?"

"You know where Maurice is?"

"Why? What's wrong?"

"Why does everyone think something is wrong?"

"Who's everyone?"

"Suzika asked me that when I called The Shop."

Naseem paused. "So Reese ain't at work?"

"No, and why aren't you?"

"I close tonight, so I go in at noon. What'd Suzika

say?"

"That he didn't come in. And that makes no sense because..." My other line beeped. "Never mind. That's him now."

"Call me back, a'ight?"

"Yeah." I took a deep breath and clicked over. "You're a hard man to find."

"Hey, Duchess." His voice was hoarse and nasally. "Sorry I didn't click over. I was on the phone with the pharmacy."

My traitorous heart dropped into my stomach. "You're sick."

"Yeah." He broke off into a coughing fit. "It came on after I closed last night. I was going to tough it out, but I'm too weak to get out of bed."

"Do you need anything?"

"Just some rest." He sniffled. "I'll call you tonight."

"Don't worry about that. I'll send a care package to The Shop, so have Naseem bring it to the house. Sleep till you feel better, and I'll check you on tomorrow night, okay?"

"I love you."

"Love you too."

I closed the phone, tapping it against my knee. I spent five days obsessing about Mordecai and avoiding Maurice, and now my boyfriend was sick with no one to care for him.

Just when I thought I couldn't feel any worse.

The Rankin Chapel Bell chimed the time, and I got an idea. If I caught the next Metro shuttle, I could be at Union Station in an hour. With Adrian's credit card in my wallet, a last-minute one-way ticket was well within budget.

Hold on, Maurice. The Duchess is on her way.

Maurice's block was quiet for a mild spring afternoon. It was that peaceful hour between lunchtime and school dismissals, and I stood at the bottom of his steps to appreciate it. It was also the beginning of my next class, but that could not be helped. After everything Maurice endured this week, most of which he knew nothing about, the least I could do was nurse him through the flu. I pulled out my LOVE Statue key ring and unlocked his front door, closing it quietly behind me.

Setting my bookbag on the couch, I unzipped my hoodie and went into the kitchen. Based on the quantity of leftovers, he and Allegro's on 40th Street had recently spent some quality time together. I pulled out the writing pad in the top drawer and made a modest list of get-well essentials. Spotting the stew pot on the top shelf, I decided to try my hand at Corina's hearty chicken soup. I'd never made it before, and the thought of doing so for Maurice made me smile.

As I put the notepad back into the drawer, I heard a banging sound above me. Instinct propelled me toward the stairs, but Maurice didn't know I was here, and I didn't want to scare him. Tucking the list in my back pocket, I grabbed my cell phone and dialed Maurice's house number. The shrill sound filled the silence, and I kept still to keep from spoiling the surprise.

But the surprise was on me when the phone kept ringing. Two, three, and four times before the machine picked up. I hung up without leaving a message, wondering if I should check on him. Then I realized if he didn't answer the phone, he was likely asleep. Which meant he probably knocked the stereo remote off the bed by accident, and I was glad my phone call didn't wake him up.

Hopefully the savory soup aroma would later do the trick.

But I needed to make sure he was okay, so I tiptoed up the carpeted stairs, grateful they didn't creak. Just before I reached the landing, a different sound graced my ears.

Laughter.

Husky, mocking female laughter.

It must have been the stereo. When Maurice knocked the remote off the bed, it must have turned on Power 99FM, and the DJs were telling a crazy joke. That had to be it.

Except I recognized the voices.

And they weren't local radio personalities.

"Why you ain't answer the phone?" Suzika snorted. "You too sick to talk to your boo-thang?"

"Shut up." His laryngitis had disappeared. "You don't have to be rude."

"You like me rude."

"I don't like you at all unless you're on your back. Roll over."

"Make me."

Then there were sounds: telling, tantalizing sounds lovers make when no one is around. The kind I had yet to experience with Maurice or anyone else.

The kind Maurice should not having been making

with Suzika.

I covered my mouth as chunks of my Union Station lunch rushed to the surface. Gripping the railing as I trudged silently down the stairs, I grabbed my stuff and crept out of the house, locking the front door without using my key. Pulling my jacket's hood over my head, I managed to cross the street and make a sharp left at the corner. One traffic light became three, one block blended into another as aimless turns took me on a brokenhearted tour of West Philadelphia.

Blinded by tears, I ambled into a small playground at the corner of Duped and Devastated. I flopped onto the bench, lost and turned inside out. I couldn't move, couldn't breathe, and couldn't spare the energy to do anything else.

But through the haze of my sadness, I recovered my cell phone and selected a seldom-used contact. After two rings, the call was answered.

"Daria?"

"Daddy?" My voice cracked. "Can you come get me?"

Forty-Four

Adrian said nothing as I climbed into the backseat of his luxury sedan. I met his gaze in the rearview mirror, and his eyes widened. Looking away, I buckled my seatbelt, and he pulled off. I didn't tell him where to go and didn't care where we went. The earth could have swallowed me whole, and I would have considered it a blessing. The unthinkable had happened, and there was no getting around it.

Maurice cheated on me.

I shook my head, balling my trembling hands into fists.

Maurice cheated on me with Suzika.

Shutting my eyes, I forced back my tears, refusing to fall further apart in front of my father. Up front, he turned on the radio and let KYW's newscasters give us the world in the 22 minutes it took to reach his parking spot on Penn's campus.

"Is this okay?" he asked. "I have a short meeting at three, but after that, we can…"

"It's fine." I wiped my face. "Thanks."

Adrian took the back way to his office, avoiding his colleagues and their good-natured curiosity. The gesture touched me so much I almost cried all over again. But I couldn't. Not about Maurice, not in front of him.

As it was, I didn't know why I called him. Corina was the logical choice as her empathy was guaranteed. But she also came with questions and quoted Proverbs, and I had no stomach for either. I just needed the pain to subside, and for that, I needed silence.

The one thing Adrian and I did well.

"I'll be back soon." He unlocked his office door, and I noticed his work bag in his other hand. "You know where everything is?"

"I'll be fine."

He studied my face, focusing on my eyes longer than I wanted, and walked down the short hall. I waited until he turned the corner to open the door to his office.

It was smaller than I remembered, full of standard-issue office furniture. His orderly shelves teemed with binders, folders, and pamphlets, and there was enough Penn paraphernalia to choke the most enthusiastic alum. Even the woolly sofa was red with a Quaker-themed throw and pillows.

I walked toward the couch, tempted to lose myself to sleep, and noticed the frames on Adrian's desk. You could guess a man's priorities by what he kept on his desk, and I prepared for photos of him with the University president, the mayor, and other important people.

But when I inspected the first frame, my mouth dropped open.

It was our first Penn Relays. I didn't remember the occasion because I was too young to walk, but the story was as familiar as my name: my beaming dad in a Penn sweater with me and my giggly, gummy self on his shoulders. Our smiles were identical, the joy infectious, and the lump in my throat tightened for a different reason.

I swallowed hard and surveyed the snapshots of my life peppering the room.

My first and only dance recital, annoyance with the loud tap shoes etched on my face. A construction-papered Father's Day card complete with stick figures and lopsided penmanship. The elementary school Father-Daughter dance where he taught me how to bop. The city-wide middle school spelling bee where I finished in the Top 20, the satiny ribbon pinned to my lapel. My induction into the National Honors Society, my excitement doubled by Cherrie's presence beside me. And my high school graduation photo bookended by dueling images from junior and senior prom.

I picked up the latter photo, remembering this moment. My dad had kissed my cheek after the oohs and aahs over my Grecian gown subsided. He put his arm around my waist and asked Corina to take our picture. Though Adrian looked at me, I was gazing at Maurice, the love in my eyes now making me nauseous.

I set down the photo and blinked away the sadness.

I couldn't remember the last time I visited my dad's office, but none of these mementos had been here. Did Corina put him up to it?

As I was about to return to the sofa, I noticed another frame behind Adrian's desk. When I realized what was in it, I dropped into his office chair in disbelief.

It was a color copy of my acceptance letter to Howard University.

"This letter ruined everything between us," I murmured. "Why would he want to see it every day?"

"Because you were so excited." My father's voice made me whirl around. "More enthusiastic than you'd ever been about following my footsteps to Penn. How could I not want a daily reminder of that feeling?"

"But you were so upset with me."

"Yes, I was." His sigh was heavy. "I learned you weren't going to Penn because a colleague in Admissions told me she hadn't received your application. And I was deeply disappointed..."

"That I chose a different school."

"No. That you didn't tell me yourself." He took my hands. "I never imagined you could make such a huge decision without telling me. I thought we were closer than that."

"I couldn't..." My eyes watered. "I thought you wouldn't want me to go."

"I never want you doing anything to remind me you're growing up." He crossed the room and grabbed a tissue from his desk. "Going away to school. Getting your license. Dating. I worked so hard to help you grow up, but no one taught me how to let you grow up."

"It's okay." I dabbed the tissue on my face. "I didn't do such a great job with it either."

"Like father, like daughter."

"Yeah." I crumpled the tissue and tossed it in the wastebasket. "You never liked Maurice, did you?"

If he was surprised by the subject change, he didn't show it. "No, but I would have resented Christ for trying to date you."

"But you knew." I sat on the couch. "You saw something in Maurice I didn't see, something I wish I had known."

"And what was that?"

"I…I can't bring myself to say it."

Adrian dropped to a crouch in front of me. "Did he hurt you?"

"Not physically. But he's too cliché to be inventive, so I'm sure you can guess what he did."

He sighed. "Sweetheart, I…"

"Don't say 'I told you so,' Dad. I couldn't take it."

"I would never say that, but I must say something else."

"What?"

"I…" He exhaled harshly. "I really want to kill him right now."

I huffed a laugh. "Get in line."

"So…do you want to talk about it?"

"I don't know. My head has been a mess, which is why I came up here in the first place, but this? I did not expect this."

"You did not deserve this." He lifted my chin. "Never forget that. You are too kind, too loyal of a person to have someone like him…oh, honey, don't cry."

I fell into my father's arms, guilt spilling all over his crisp white shirt. He joined me on the couch, cinching me at his side as I cried my heart out. When at last the tears subsided, he handed me the box of tissues and smoothed back my hair.

"Better?"

"Getting there. Thank you, Daddy."

"That's why I'm here. And always will be." He went to his refrigerator and brought me a bottle of water. I unscrewed the cap and took a small sip. "What do you want now?" he asked.

My stomach growled in answer. "A turkey hoagie with everything on it. And a chocolate and cherry Gelati from Rita's."

He patted my knee with a smile. "Coming right up."

Daddy went to South Street for our early dinner and left me on the couch, locking the door behind him. I must have fallen asleep, for the next thing I knew, his office radio was on and our food was spread out on his small meeting table.

"You had five more minutes before I was claiming that water ice for myself," he said.

"You would have died trying." I stretched awake. "How long have you been back?"

"A while. I returned some emails, reviewed my notes from that meeting, and talked to your mother."

I sat up. "What?"

"She asked when I'd be home, and I told her I had a

student in my office who needed to talk some things out. She told me to take my time."

"Thanks for not snitching."

"Figured you had the right to tell her what you want, if you want." He chuckled at my expression. "I can be rational on occasion."

I unwrapped my hoagie. "Can I get that in writing?"

We passed the next hour in evolving conversation, wading through the muddy waters of our recent relationship. He apologized for overreacting about the bridal magazine, and I admitted that I default to defensive whenever he disapproved.

"You're an adult, Daria," he said. "Loath though I am to admit it. Other people's opinions shouldn't govern your decisions."

I stirred what remained of my Gelati. "I don't want to study abroad."

"I thought you did."

"I didn't know what I wanted to do. I was flattered by Dr. Treble's suggestion and resented Maurice for telling me I couldn't go." I stumbled over his name, but my dad didn't comment. "His opinion doesn't matter so much now, but I respect Dr. Treble."

"And if she respects you, she'll accept your choice. That goes for anyone in your life."

"That's what Mordecai said."

"How is good ol' Mordecai?"

I stared at him. "What do you mean?"

"I mean, how is he?"

"He's fine."

He chuckled at my tone. "Are you sure?"

"As sure as I can be."

When I looked away, my dad cleared his throat. "Is he part of the mess in your head?"

"A big, unexpected part."

"What happened?"

I paused the mental replay. "Things have changed."

"I thought you guys were friends."

"So did I. But that's not all he wants."

He didn't seem surprised. "What do you want?"

"What do I want?" I looked out the window, seeing the high walls of Franklin Field in the distance. "I want to sit on your shoulders and watch the Penn Relays."

"I don't know about my shoulders, but the seat beside me has your name on it."

"Sounds good."

After dinner, I declined his offer to escort me inside 30th Street Station, fearing a daddy's girl meltdown at the escalator, but promised to call when I reached Meridian. He hugged me tight, promising everything would be all right. And for the first time in a while, I believed him.

Adrian insisted I take a cab from Union Station to campus, and in a half hour, I was on the fourth floor of Meridian Hill Hall. It was almost midnight, and I just wanted to shower, sleep, and forget most of this day ever happened.

I unlocked my door and saw a manila folder on the floor topped by a post-it note.

> *After you left, Dr. Maddox gave out an assignment for Friday's class. I wouldn't want you to miss it and jeopardize your 4.0, knowing how hard you work to maintain it.*

I feel like I should say more ... and like I've already said (and done) too much. So I won't say anything and just hope to see you again soon, smiling.

Even without recognizing the handwriting, I knew the heart behind the words. Mordecai knew I left class early and probably guessed the reason. Yet he put aside his confusion and our awkwardness and did this. Because that's the kind of man he was.

Maurice pretended to be sick so he could hook up with his business associate without being interrupted because that's the kind of man he was.

And I went home to take care of one man because I couldn't deal with my ambiguous feelings for another but still didn't know what kind of woman I was.

I scooped up the folder and hugged it to my chest, hoping my tears didn't cause its ink to bleed.

Forty-Five

Thursday morning a headache roused me from sleep. A glance at the clock revealed I could catch the shuttle for Dr. Treble's class if I hustled, but the memory of Maurice and Suzika's hushed voices pinned me to the bed, and I vowed to stay there until semester's end.

I felt so stupid. Stupid, naïve, and complicit in his crime. Maurice cheated with Suzika, but was I any better for kissing Mordecai? I could no longer deny my participation in the act, and the admission released only a modicum of pressure from my heart. Because yes, I kissed Mordecai, but Maurice didn't know that, so he didn't do this to retaliate. And the more I noodled on what I heard in West Philly, the more I realized it wasn't the first time.

And from all indications, it wouldn't be the last.

But why would he do that? Was sex that important to him? We discussed it at Christmas, and he said he could wait. Was he sleeping with her then? Was that the source of his saintly patience?

My thoughts drifted back to Columbus Day, but I dismissed the possibility. Even if there had been an attraction, there's no way they were sleeping together back then. Not if Naseem had anything to do with it.

Naseem. God bless him.

After last night's shower, I discovered a voicemail on my dorm phone. I checked the time-stamped caller ID and matched the message to the number for The Shop. It took an hour to summon the courage to check it, and when I did, my tears began afresh.

> "Hey D. I just heard the craziest thing. One of our regulars said he saw a girl who looked just like you wandering around West Philly today. I told him to leave the cheap stuff alone, but it made me want to call you. I...I hope you're doing all right down there, living it up and getting everything you want. You deserve nothing but the best, no matter where it comes from."

I listened to the message over and over again, and by the fifth time, I heard the confession between the lines: Naseem didn't believe I was in West Philly yesterday, but he knew what I would have learned had I been there.

Because he knew about Maurice and Suzika.

That voicemail crystallized so much else. The argument with Suzika I overheard two months ago. What he meant the other day about girls who can't be trusted. Why he seemed confused when I asked about the most recent break-in. Poor Naseem felt obligated to keep the secret, and I couldn't blame him. If anything, I felt sorry for him.

I picked up the phone to tell Naseem what I knew but set it down again. Beyond the lingering confusion of my kiss with Mordecai, I didn't know how to speak to Naseem without crying nor did I want him to feel more trapped than he already was. Maurice was his cousin and boss; I was just a friend. Whatever relief he might feel knowing I knew the truth would fade in light of my devastation and duplicity. I could hardly discuss Maurice without mentioning Mordecai, and what could I say when I didn't know how I felt?

And though Mordecai reached out with a sweet gesture, things between us were still a mess. We hadn't spoken since the night of the ball, and after his performance at the showcase, I had no idea what to say. Stuck at a stalemate, I set Mr. Darcy on the pillow beside me and shut out the world once more.

The next time I rolled over, it was nigh noon, and my stomach rumbled in agitation. With minimal appetite, I forced down yogurt and granola, hoping to calm the beast. Skipping Dr. Treble's class required me to skip everything else, the guilt of which was duller than expected. I clicked on the TV, hoping to get lost in a feel-good film.

But when the opening titles for *Café Latte* cut

across the screen, I stormed to the television and cut it off. My fury landed on the DVD in the rack, and I dropped it behind my dresser, satisfied by the audible *crack* when it hit the ground. I made a note in my calendar to retrieve the movie at the end of the semester but had no clue what to do with myself until then. So when my dorm phone rang, I let the machine get it, keeping up the volume so I could hear.

> "Okay, so you left a message that you made it to Meridian safely, but I've yet to receive confirmation that you're accepting my previous offer. With everything you've got going on, I think it could help. No pressure; just wanted you to know it still stands. I understand you might not want to talk, but I'm going to call anyway, just to let you know you're loved. And if you don't answer, that's okay, as long as we keep our date in two weeks. And if you're good, I might let you sit on my shoulders. Daddy loves you, Junie."

My cheeks were damp again long before the beep.

Adrian hadn't called me "Junie" in years, not since Maurice arrived on the scene to be exact. It was short for "Junior," a testament to everyone saying I looked and acted so much like my dad. During my teen years, the sobriquet reeked of paternal pressure, a desire that I conform to his preferred image, and I resented it into retirement. For him to resurrect it while I longed for a simpler time was the kindest, most beautifullest thing he could have done.

The least I could do was accept his offer.

Wiping my face with the back of my hand, I picked up the phone and called my job, asking to speak with the general manager. He wasn't surprised by my call and made the potentially awkward conversation easy.

"We have several on-call staffers looking for more hours, so no worries," he said. "If you want to make last Thursday your last day, I can reflect that in your file."

"That would be great, thanks."

"I hope everything is okay."

I sagged against my pillows. "It's not, but it will be."

With no obligation to leave the dorm for the rest of the day, I considered burying myself under a mound of chocolate chip cookies and *Never Ever After* reruns. But I refused to let dejection ruin my afternoon, so I dusted off my cross-country sneakers, grabbed my Discman, and decided to hit the DC streets running. Despite what my toned legs suggested, I was neither a great athlete nor a frequent runner. But on the rare occasions when words failed me, running helped. I always felt as if God and I were alone in creation, and with every exhale, He bent to hear the cry of my wounded heart.

Dodging a reckless cab driver, I crossed Euclid Street and entered Meridian Hill Park, better known locally as Malcom X Park. The weather was cool for early April, but stubborn sunshine peeked through the budding trees. Despite my turmoil, I was grateful for the simple pleasures of dandelion fluff and patches of vibrant grass, for tulips and gerbera daisies in cheery shades.

And for over-the-counter allergy medicine.

I jogged down every path in the park, careful of the serious runners and their coordinated gear. Down the steps and around the fountain, letting the soft breeze and music soothe my muddled mind. As I worked up a modest sweat, my problems with Maurice and Mordecai faded into the background, and I emerged at Florida and W Street in better spirits.

As a reward, I walked to The Diner as a cool-down, ordering a grilled chicken salad with balsamic vinaigrette on the side. The lunch crowd was out in full force, so the wait was longer than expected. I returned to Meridian an hour later and caught Bernie getting off the shuttle.

She frowned at my attire. "Casual Thursday?"

"I'm taking a personal day. What are you doing here?"

"Inviting you to dinner next Monday."

"For what?"

"Do I need a reason?" She shook her head. "Black folks."

"Should I bring anything?"

"A bucket of Popeyes, spicy. And don't skimp on the strawberry jam for them biscuits."

I rolled my eyes. "Black folks."

"What did you bring?" I asked Cherrie as we walked the few blocks to Bernie's place.

"Paper and plastic. You know B don't do dishes."

"She's so random." We waited for a car to pass. "A

dinner party on a Monday night?"

Cherrie laughed. "I hope she never changes."

"I never congratulated you on making line! I was so glad I skipped class that day."

"I'm sorry I couldn't tell you. There's strict protocol, and I didn't want anything jeopardizing my chances."

"I don't see how anything could. You're smart, active in the community, and more determined than anyone I've ever met. They would have been crazy not to accept you."

She shrugged. "It happens."

"What would you have done?"

"Tried again next year. Then waited until grad school because pledging senior year is an unofficial no-no."

We stopped outside Bernie's building. "The rejection wouldn't have crushed you?"

"It's not rejection. It's a chance to learn and do better next time."

"This is why I admire you." I rang Bernie's bell. "Nothing gets you down."

"Nothing keeps me down." She pulled the buzzing door. "There's a difference."

We let ourselves into Bernie's apartment, unsurprised to find it messy. Bernie was in the back, likely arguing with her locs, so Cherrie and I washed our hands and got to work.

"Is there something to go with the chicken?" I yelled.

"Pasta salad in the fridge," Bernie yelled back. "Cookie dough in the freezer."

"Ice cream?" Cherrie asked.

"No, actual cookie dough." I pulled out the container. "Double chocolate chip."

We set the table and had time to organize her hair magazines and book collection before she emerged. Dressed in frayed sweatpants and a ratty t-shirt, Bernie looked ready for bed not dinner with her best friends.

Cherrie inspected her own attire. "Guess I should spill something on my shirt."

"I could cut a hole in my jeans," I said. "Cherrie, get the scissors."

"You are not funny." Bernie pulled out a chair. "Can we eat? I haven't had anything since breakfast."

After Cherrie blessed the table, we passed around the food. Bernie commandeered the jam packets, and I split the honey with Cherrie.

"Did you see the flyer for the 'Born in April Listening Party' in the Lounge next week?" Cherrie asked.

"Al Green, Babyface, Herbie Hancock." I reached for my iced tea. "I'm gonna need a playlist."

"Mordecai can do it," Cherrie said. "He's good for that kind of thing."

I kept my gaze down. "Right."

"So what's up, B?" Cherrie asked. "Did you ask us over because you knew we'd clean?"

"No, but thanks for that. Can't beat cheap labor."

I wiggled my honey-coated fingers. "I'm gonna leave streaks on your bathroom mirror."

"Antonio and I got married this morning."

I stopped mid-wiggle as Cherrie gulped down her last bite. "What?" we cried.

"Antonio and I got married this morning."

Cherrie and I looked at each other, and she looked at Bernie. "Bernadette Ujima Price, are you telling me you snuck off and got married without as much as a how-de-do to your best friends?"

"Yep."

"Without your family present?" I asked.

"We called them on speakerphone."

"And without a pre-nup?" Cherrie asked.

"As if. Besides, we in this for life and don't need one."

Cherrie stood up. "In other words…"

Bernie put down her fork. "I's married now."

Cherrie screamed, and we ran around the table to bear hug Bernie. She indulged us for a moment then told Cherrie to lay off her eardrum. "Antonio ain't marry a deaf woman."

"I can't believe you let me come here without a gift!" Cherrie swatted Bernie's arm. "I feel so triflin'."

"And I can't believe you got married." I took Bernie's left hand. "Where's your ring?"

"Didn't want one."

"Why not?"

"Not everyone needs a ring to prove their love." She glanced at me. "No offense."

The echo of Mordecai's words from the ball pulsed through my head. "None taken."

"What did you wear?" Cherrie asked.

"Jeans and an HU hoodie." Bernie grinned. "The justice of the peace liked that we matched."

Cherrie shook her head. "Was there cake?"

Bernie reached for her glass. "We split a pack of

chocolate cupcakes on the way back."

Cherrie groaned. "I can't believe I'm hearing this."

"Look, isn't the point that I'm happy?" Bernie asked. "That I know I made the right decision?"

"Yeah, yeah." Cherrie waved her off. "But you should have had more! A nice dress, witnesses, a catered meal."

"If it makes you feel better, we're going to have something next summer in Detroit." Bernie broke a piece of her biscuit. "I may even wash my face."

"But how did you know you were ready?" I asked. "Loving Tone is one thing, but marriage is everything."

Bernie held up a finger while she chewed. "I love Antonio and hated being away from him. I thought sleeping together would squash the pain of separation, but it didn't. Because we're bigger than sex or our few years together. We're the stuff you build a life on, the stuff my parents and grandparents have after so many decades. And I didn't want to be without it any longer."

Cherrie dabbed at her eyes. "That's beautiful. B."

"I know it won't be easy with him overseas somewhere, but ..."

"Is that definite?" I asked.

"Three European teams are interested." She wiped her mouth with a napkin. "Basketball is his passion, and I want him to play as long as he can."

"Long-distance marriage?" I sipped my soda. "That sounds difficult."

"No more difficult than what you and Maurice are doing. For real for real, you were a huge part of my decision."

I almost choked on my chicken. "What?"

"Watching you hold it down three states away inspired me. The distance and lack of physicality will be a challenge for us, but you guys survived, and that gives me hope. If I can be half as good to Antonio as you are to Maurice, then I'll be....girl, why are you crying?"

"I'm sorry." I covered my face, ashamed of my outburst. "It's just wrong. Everything is all wrong."

Forty-Six

"Wow," Cherrie said when I finished my tale. "I can't believe you kept all that to yourself."

"And let me blah blah blah about my marriage when your heart was torn up." Bernie flicked my knee from her position beside me on the couch. "Don't do that again."

"But we inspired you," I mumbled. "And now that's ruined."

"The only thing ruined will be Maurice's face if I see him again," Bernie said. "Don't give that another thought."

"So this Mordecai thing started the night of the ball?" Cherrie passed me some tissues. "I saw you guys but only noticed how phyne he looked in that suit.

Although ..."

"Although what?" I asked.

"Well, I have the pictures we took that night, and there's one of you that's much different than the rest."

I sniffled and held out my hand. "Let me see it."

Cherrie pulled out a Kodak pouch from her bag, flipping through the photos until she found the one she wanted. She set the picture in my nervous hands, and when I finally looked down, I frowned.

"This is just a headshot." I gave the picture back to her. "So what?"

"The picture was supposed to show off your dress." She passed the picture to Bernie. "But Mordecai was only interested in your face."

"Your glowing, happy face," Bernie said. "You don't look like you miss Maurice at all."

"I did, but I wasn't going to frown all night. It was bad enough that when I mentioned Maurice ..."

"Why would you do that?" Bernie asked.

"I don't remember. But when I did, Mordecai said he shouldn't comment on our relationship." I took the picture from Bernie to study it. "Now I know why."

"So let's break it down." Cherrie tucked her legs beneath her on the couch. "Put Maurice aside."

"Gladly," Bernie said.

"How do you feel about Mordecai?" Cherrie asked.

I closed my eyes. "I can't answer that."

" 'Can't,' 'don't know how,' or 'won't?' " Cherrie asked.

"All of the above." I tucked the picture in my purse. "Things with Mordecai were complicated before I found out about Maurice, and now? They're a bona fide mess."

"I get that," Cherrie said. "But even without the Maurice of it all, you've got to have some opinion about Mordecai."

"Because, and no offense," Bernie said. "You don't seem angry. Surprised and confused but not angry. And if a male friend kissed me out of nowhere, I'd be pissed. And punch him in the face."

"D wouldn't do that," Cherrie said.

"D didn't do anything," I said. "I just let it happen."

"How was it?"

"Bernie!" Cherrie said.

"It's a fair question," I said. "But I'm ashamed to answer."

Bernie leaned forward. "That good, huh?"

I buried my face in my hands. "I can't stop thinking about it."

Bernie looked at Cherrie. "That good."

"And that's bad. Because I have a boyfriend…"

"A cheating boyfriend," Bernie said.

"…and I let my best friend kiss me. Now I don't know how I feel, and every time I try to deal with one, I get distracted by what the other did. What does that make me?"

"Human," Cherrie said. "And capable of making mistakes."

"This is more than a mistake. I cheated on Maurice…"

"Who cheated on you first," Cherrie said.

"We don't know that."

"Does it matter?" Bernie asked. "Let's say last week was his first time with Skanky McTrampenstein. Does that make his treachery any kinder? Mordecai kissed you, not the other way around." She held up a hand. "Even if you enjoyed it, you didn't set out to deceive Maurice. But he lied about being sick to enjoy his afternoon delight, and I bet he ain't steeping in guilt right now."

"Not very comforting but true," Cherrie said.

"So you have the right to figure out this thing with Mordecai," Bernie said. "If you want to."

I rubbed my eyes. "I'm trying."

"There is no 'try,' duckie." Bernie took my hands. "Eventually you'll know how you feel."

"I already do: rotten."

"We can't have that." Cherrie walked to the freezer and pulled out the tub of cookie dough. "Time for the big guns."

By the time I left Bernie's, the scarlet letter on my chest burned a little less. Bernie and Cherrie convinced me to ignore the past, stop worrying about the future, and just live in the present moment.

"This isn't some Maurice-versus-Mordecai battle royale." Bernie said as she hugged me goodbye. "So no matter what you decide, you win."

Her words rolled around my head all night long, echoing Adrian's advice. When I came home and found three voicemails from Maurice, I deleted them without bothering to listen. I heard enough noise from him last week, and anything more would have to wait.

But Dr. Treble's class the following morning would not wait, so I arrived early. After skipping last Thursday,

I wanted to remove the stench of slacking. She noticed my presence but said nothing of it until class was over and she summoned me to her desk.

"Class is different when you aren't here, Ms. Nelson." She erased the blackboard. "And by 'different,' I mean 'boring.' "

"I apologize. It won't happen again."

"I have no doubt."

I pulled out the blank Study Abroad application. "I've decided not to do this."

"Okay." She brushed her hands together to remove the chalk. "May I ask why not?"

"It's a great opportunity, just not for me."

"I respect that." She put the application in her folder. "Thank you for telling me."

"I'm actually thinking about spending spring semester at Penn instead."

"Isn't that your father's Alma Mater?"

"As a matter of fact, it is."

She grabbed her trusty briefcase. "Tell me more."

Dr. Treble and I walked and talked across The Yard, and she seemed pleased with my ideas. She even offered to help me select my courses.

"That would be great!" I said. "Guess it's too early to make a fall appointment."

"I'll add it to my calendar just the same." She stopped on the steps of Douglass Hall. "If I may say so, Ms. Nelson, I'm proud of you."

"That means a lot coming from you. And thank you."

"For what?"

"For, um…for being you."

She laughed, startling some nearby students who didn't know she had it in her. "That's the best compliment I've ever received. Enjoy your weekend, Ms. Nelson."

I smiled all the way to Cramton, heedless of who stared. My dad was right about Dr. Treble, and I was right about me. And that realization felt good enough to walk on. With my Egyptian Mythology class canceled today, I passed the shuttle stop and headed to Meridian on foot, enjoying the pleasant weather and the peace of trusting my instincts.

My night at Bernie's had ignited my sweet tooth, and as I neared my dorm, I thought of walking straight to Safeway. Ice cream was on sale, and Corina mailed me a bunch of coupons last week. A sale was good, but a sale with double coupons was God at work.

I turned up the path for Meridian, wondering if I should ask Cherrie to come with, and came to a stop.

Maurice sat on the wall, smiling at me.

I was tempted to turn away and head anywhere but here. But as he rose to greet me—his tender expression giving no indication of his recent activity—something in me solidified, and I held my ground.

"There's my girl." His gaze traveled up and down my body as he approached, and I recoiled inside. "I've been calling you."

"I know."

He frowned at my tone but opened his arms to hug me. "I missed you."

I stepped back. "Don't touch me."

"What's wrong, Duchess?"

"And don't call me that."

"Duc—Daria, what's up? You're not acting like yourself."

"And you're acting like…" I folded my hands in front of my mouth. "You know what? I don't want to do this. You need to leave."

"Leave? I just got here. Daria." He reached for my arm, and I pulled away. "What is going on? Are you mad about the Bison Ball? I told you I was sorry about that."

"That's what you're sorry for?"

"Look. Something is going on, and I'm not leaving until you tell me what it is." He folded his arms. "I drove all this way to see you, and I deserve that much."

I met his gaze with a sad smile. "And you should get what you deserve."

Forty-Seven

I led him across the street to the park and away from meddling Meridianites who witnessed our awkward greeting. Despite the beauty of the day, my stormy thoughts vacillated between angry and annoyed, neither fully capturing the breadth of my feelings. I'd been avoiding Maurice for a multitude of reasons, and now he was down here demanding we talk?

I hoped we wouldn't come to regret it.

Once in the park, I spotted a bench beside a tree with an overhang of cherry blossoms. I took off my bookbag and sat down, folding my hands in my lap. "This is far enough."

Maurice chose to stand, hooking his thumbs in his belt loops. "So what's up?"

For a while, the birdcalls of spring were the only sounds, and I let their joy override the silence my confusion provided. I wouldn't rush this—whatever it was—not when the stakes were this high and my confidence in us was this low.

"Still nothing?" The question suggested I'd been quiet too long. "You're making me nervous, Duch."

"I asked you not to call me that."

"And I asked you to tell me what's up. I mean, we ain't seen each other in months, you ain't been answering your phone, so I figured I'd come down. Now I'm here, all up close and personal, and you can't even look at me?"

No, I couldn't look at him: not with these words burning behind my lips, these questions with answers I was afraid to get. He wanted to know what was up? How could I tell him that when everything between us was upside down? I was so leery of saying the wrong thing that I almost said I'd had a fight with Adrian and wasn't in the mood to talk, just to buy me some time to think.

But when Maurice assaulted me with another sigh, my reticence receded, and I raised my head to look at him as he so desired.

"It's funny you coming all this way to see me. Funny because I didn't want to see you, even funnier because I had the same idea last week. You sounded so sick and miserable, and I felt bad being so far away and…"

"But Duch, I knew you had to…"

"Please let me finish."

"Sorry."

"You were sick, and you needed me. So I hopped

on a shuttle, two Metros, and a Metroliner, and took a cab to your block. I used the key you sent me and let myself in. It was so quiet in the house I thought you were asleep. So I crept into the kitchen, careful not to wake you, and heard something fall upstairs."

His sharp inhale was a knife in the heart, but I kept talking.

"After all those episodes of *Never Ever After,* I should have known what was going on. But no. I thought you had dropped the remote, and I headed upstairs to check on you. Good thing she started laughing before I made it to the hallway. Otherwise I would have seen just how much you like her when she's on her back."

"Oh Jesus…"

"Suzika's a pro; I'll give her that. She was always cool when I called The Shop. And Columbus Day weekend, I thought she was interested in Naseem."

"Daria …"

"And you? I don't even have words for you. But let's just say 'never saw it coming' is an understatement."

"Daria…"

"What?"

"I know it seems bad. But if you let me explain…"

"Explain what? That what I heard isn't what I think I heard?"

"No. Yes, but not like that." He followed me as I stormed away. "Just give me a chance. You owe me…"

I whirled around. "I owe you?"

"No! I mean … after all these years together, I would think you'd give me a chance to explain."

I grumbled my way back to the bench, crossing my

legs with a huff. "Well?"

His lips moved without sound, and I watched him with narrowed eyes, waiting for this glorious explanation he was so eager to give. But after ten wordless seconds, I shook my head and grabbed my bag.

"See? You can't excuse the inexcusable. And I'm not going to sit here while you …"

"Wait! I just ... I didn't know you were there."

I rolled my eyes so hard I got a headache.

"And I can't believe you did that," he continued." I mean, it's such a 'you' thing to do, but I can't believe you skipped class to come to Philly and … okay, okay!" He held up his hands to stop me from leaving again. "Listen. What you overheard wasn't personal. It was business."

"You paid her?"

"No, 'business' because it wasn't personal."

"Sleeping with her wasn't personal?"

"Exactly. See …" He folded his hands in front of his mouth. "You're here. And I'm up there. And I ... I didn't expect you to be here this long."

"For spring semester?"

"For college. Period."

"This again? I told you I wasn't transferring to Penn."

"No, you didn't."

"Well, I thought choosing Howard two years ago was a pretty clear indication."

"But you chose me first. And I thought you loved me enough to come back to Philly."

"Like you loved me enough not to sleep with Suzika?"

"But that's my point! The thing with Suzika...it wasn't about not loving you or wanting somebody else. It was just a simple arrangement."

"A business arrangement."

"Yes."

"When did this arrangement begin?"

"What?"

"You heard me."

"I know. I just ... does it matter?"

"Yes, it really does."

He took a deep breath, his puffed cheeks slowly deflating as he exhaled. "After work one night, a bunch of us went out: me, Naseem, Suzika, the old-head from Walnut Street ..."

"When, Maurice?"

"The day after Valentine's Day, but it's not what you think!" he rushed to add. "Suzika's birthday is February 15th, and we were all drinking and having a good time when the conversation turned to relationships and sex and ..."

"And what?"

"How long it had been."

"How creative."

"And Suzika said ..."

"How many times were you with her?"

He flinched. "Why would you ask me that?"

"I have a right to know if this was a regular occurrence or a treat for special occasions."

"Special occasions?"

"Yes, like her birthday or Easter or ..." A sobering thought crossed my mind, and my eyebrows furrowed in dismay. "There was no robbery, was there?"

"When?"

"The night you missed The Bison Ball."

"She called and said there was."

"But when you got back, you found out she was lying, didn't you?"

He toed the ground with his boot. "Yeah."

"So why didn't you call me or fire her?"

"It's complicated."

"I thought your little arrangement was simple."

"Look, Suzika is our best braider and has exclusive clients. She pretty much co-runs The Shop since Naseem don't halfway show up no more, and ..."

"You don't fire simple sex," I muttered. "Even if it ruins your plans with your girlfriend."

Maurice looked up but didn't deny it, and a rush of anger forced me behind the bench to put more space between us.

As if such a thing were possible.

"I should have fired her," he finally said. "And I'm sorry I didn't."

I turned to the trees. "That's what he's sorry for!"

"But this thing with Suzika ... it was nothing, okay?"

"Right."

"And I know that sounds like an excuse or something I'm just making up right now, but it's true. No matter what it looks like, she was just a means to an end all along."

Though I tried to tune him out, the last part of his statement lingered in my mind. "What do you mean 'all along'?"

"What?"

"You just said, 'she was just a means to an end all along.' "

"So?"

"So if this arrangement just started two months ago." I turned to face him. "Why would you say 'all along'?"

"You judgin' my grammar?" He forced a laugh. "You really are obsessed with that 4.0."

I ignored the feeble jibe, noting instead his sudden urge to fiddle with his collar and his utter refusal to look at me. And another piece of the puzzle fell into devastating place.

"That wasn't your first time together."

"Last Wednesday? No, I told you we went out on her birthday and ..."

"And that wasn't the first time, was it?"

He looked down. "Daria, I don't think ..."

"Was it?"

A deafening moment of silence passed before Maurice raised his head. "No."

Tears sprang to my eyes. "Then when?"

"In March." He swallowed hard. "1996."

"March? But we met in October."

"I know. But February was the first time in a long time, I swear."

"How long?"

"What?"

"Before February." I licked my lips and tasted saltwater. "When was the last time?"

"Daria ..."

"Please don't make me ask again."

He closed his eyes. "Your 18th birthday."

The words stole the breath from my lungs, and I feared I might actually vomit. With one hand over my mouth, I reached for the bench with the other, needing it to hold me up. I closed my eyes on a strangled sob, refusing to let the floodgates open.

"Dar ..."

"Shut up."

"I just ..."

"Shut up!" My hands clenched into fists as I came to my feet again. "Haven't you said enough?"

"No. Because I want you to ... I mean, you gotta see it like it was, not the way you want it to be." He approached me slowly. "We weren't in a relationship back then, remember? Your father ..."

"You're blaming him for what you did?"

"I'm reminding you of what he said. You were underage, Daria, and until you turned eighteen, we were not officially together, so I didn't cheat on you."

"So it's not infidelity on a technicality?"

"Call it what you want." He stopped in front of me. "But I'm just being honest."

"No!" I wiped my face with the tips of my fingers. "Honest would have been telling me about Suzika when we met. Honest would have been breaking up with me if sex was that important to you."

"And honest would have been not accepting my ring if you didn't want to get married."

I jerked back as if slapped. "You told me this wasn't an engagement ring."

"Because you were terrified! I saw your face when you saw that box. I thought you were just surprised, but once you saw the ring, you still looked like you wanted to run away or hide. So I told you it was a promise ring."

"But I asked you on Christmas why you bought me a diamond, and you said ..."

"What was I supposed to say? My family thought we were engaged, and you looked like you were about to pass out."

"Because we weren't engaged! Why would I pretend otherwise to appease your family?"

"Because it wasn't about them! It was about seeing if you wanted to marry me."

"Why would you think I was ready for marriage? We'd never talked about it, not once in four years. I'm still in school and ..."

"And there it is! You're so busy living it up down here you're not thinking about our future."

I pursed my lips. "Is that what you were doing last Wednesday?"

"I already explained that ..."

"And the first two years of our relationship?"

"There was no relationship then, but what about you?"

"Me?"

"How do I know what you're doing down here?"

"I'm not doing anyone else. I can promise you that."

"Maybe not, but you rejected all my ideas to bring us together: getting married ..."

"You never proposed!"

"... transferring to Penn, not studying abroad, staying away from Mordecai."

I froze inside. "What does he have to do with this?"

"He wants what's mine, so he has everything to do

409

with this."

"I'm not talking about Mordecai with you."

"Why not?"

"Because he's not why we're here right now."

"How do I know that? He lives right there and probably saw you more this week than I have in four months. For all I know, something already happened."

"No."

" 'No, nothing's happened'?"

" 'No, I'm not talking about this.' You cheated, lied, and undermined every decision I've made in the past two years, then gonna to stand here and grill me about Mordecai?"

He spat on the ground. "And the fact that you won't let me just proves there's something to talk about."

I didn't bother responding as I grabbed my bookbag from the bench.

"Where you going?"

"To my room."

"But we need to talk."

I secured the straps on my back. "I'm done talking."

"Daria, wait." Maurice took my hands, the warmth of his caress soothing me against my will. "I know things are a mess right now, and I ... well, there's enough blame to go around. But can we just stop and go back to the place where none of this stuff was in the way? Can we just, I don't know, move on and be done with all this?"

A cool breeze blew through the park, and I shuddered against the sudden chill. Maurice's hazel eyes watched me intently, but I barely noticed him. All I saw were the many decisions that led us here, the roads not taken and the signs I ignored. And as his last question echoed in my mind, I closed my eyes in receipt of its answer.

"Daria?"

"Yes?"

"Did you hear me?"

I blinked back to life. "Yes."

"So are we done?"

"Yes." I nodded once. "We're done."

"Good. Okay." He released my hands to check his watch. "It's a little late for lunch now, but I think we can ..."

"No."

"You're not hungry?"

"No, but that's not what I mean."

"Then what?"

"I mean." I twisted the ring off my left hand. "We're done."

Forty-Eight

As Maurice stared at the ring, his nostrils flared. "Don't play with me."

"I'm not playing."

"Then what are you doing?"

"Making things right. I shouldn't have accepted this, no matter what you called it. But I loved you and I thought…"

"Loved me? So, what? Now you don't?"

"I…I do love you, Maurice. But I don't want to be punished for choosing Howard and loving my life here. I don't want cruelty when you disapprove or infidelity for your convenience. And I don't want to be with someone who needs me to explain all of that to him."

"And what about Mordecai?"

"Stop making this about him! No matter he wants or how he feels, I was your girl, and you cheated on me."

"I told you that was nothing!"

"Which time? You know what? It doesn't even matter." I held out the ring. "Please don't make this harder than it is."

He folded his arms. "I didn't come here for that. I came so we could figure things out."

"And I figured out that we're done."

"We are not done."

"Yes, we are."

"Well I'm not done with you. So I'm not taking that."

"I'm sorry you feel that way."

"Don't be sorry." He ran a hand across his mouth. "Because I'm not buying this either."

"What?"

"This little performance of yours. What, you a drama major too?"

I turned back to the bench, focusing on it as I set down the ring.

Maurice scoffed. "Nice touch. But that ring will still be there in an hour when you decide to stop playing."

With a heavy sigh, I headed toward the same gravelly path that led us here. Maurice continued to insist I was joking, but his blustering faded from my hearing as I left the park and crossed the street. The closer I got to the Meridian double doors, the more I expected Maurice to take my departure seriously.

So I was surprised to hear him shouting my name, demanding I face him again. I turned around in time to catch his near-miss with a speeding sedan as he fumed up the ramp toward me.

"Are you crazy?" he asked.

"I don't know what you mean."

"Leaving this!" He thrust the ring in my face. "Leaving me?"

"Maurice, please."

"Please what?" His voice bounced off the walls of the arched driveway. "I'm sorry for yelling. I just ... I don't understand."

"I think I made myself clear."

"I know. I mean, I heard you, but I can't believe you're really doing this."

"What did you think I would do when I found out the truth?"

"I ..." He blinked at me. "I honestly didn't think about it."

"Of course you didn't." I closed the ring in his hand. "And I don't want to think about it anymore."

"Duchess ..."

"Maurice, please. If you ever loved me the way you claimed, accept what I'm saying and just ... let me go."

I held his gaze and my breath, hoping some measure of remorse would compel him to be gracious.

Instead he shoved my hands away, stuffing the ring in his pocket. "Go 'head then. Go inside and be with Mordecai. That's what you've wanted to do this whole time anyway."

I turned away as the rebuttal died on my lips. "Goodbye, Maurice."

The front doors opened behind me, and I went inside before he could say another word. I kept my head down as I passed through the lobby, ignoring the whispers of the gathered witnesses. An empty elevator waited on the ground floor, but I declined its offer, the dull thud of my footsteps echoing in the stairwell as I trudged to my room. My hands trembled as I pulled out my keys, but I managed to get the door open on the second try.

As I locked it behind me, the dorm phone rang, startling me so much that I tripped over my trash can. The special tone indicated the call was coming from the lobby, and my heart raced in my chest as I stared at the phone. I was too afraid to answer and too stunned to move, and as the phone rang a third time, I expected my answering machine to soon do its work.

But the call ended in the middle of the fourth ring, and I was both relieved and disappointed by the sudden silence. I righted my trash can and dropped my bookbag beside my dinette table. Collapsing on my bed, I flung myself face-down in Mr. Darcy's chest as the truth washed over me.

From the very beginning of our relationship, Maurice had been sleeping with Suzika.

When he took me on my junior prom, Maurice had been sleeping with Suzika.

When he took me on my senior prom, Maurice had been sleeping with Suzika.

While I was underage and impatient for the day that would change, Maurice had been sleeping with Suzika.

And on the day when that finally happened, Maurice slept with Suzika.

And the worst of it was that he never apologized.

Not for the sex.

Not for lying about the ring.

Not for trying to me force back to Philly.

And not for breaking my heart one piece at a time for the last four years.

Another wave of nausea rolled in my stomach, and I clutched Mr. Darcy tighter, blubbering all over his clothes. His happy little vest and tie always made me smile, but when I remembered who sent him to me, the second round of tears began.

I was reaching for the tissues on my windowsill a half hour later when my cell phone rang. The startling sound made me knock over the box, but the cheery ringtone encouraged me to answer the call.

"Cherrie?"

"Daria? What's wrong?"

I replied on a sob. "I dumped Maurice."

"Oh, honey. Are you home?"

"Yes."

"I'll find Bernie. Unlock your door."

Within the hour, the cavalry arrived with compassion and hugs abounding. They asked no questions, but I volunteered the answers, needing to purge my soul of its sadness. Bernie received the truth about the engagement ring in admirable silence, but the details about Suzika were more than she could take.

"I know people in Philly." She cracked her knuckles. "It would be slow and painful."

"Violence never solves anything," Cherrie said. "Let's have The Shop audited."

Bernie nodded. "That too would be slow and painful."

From there, Bernie's tea and sympathy took the form of milkshakes and wisecracks. The bawdy barbs were an odd balm for my heart, and I loved her ability to conjure laughter from my tears. Mother Cherrie cleaned my preferred shower stall while I picked at my pizza, and she changed my sheets while I bathed. By the time I returned to my spotless room, the air mattress was on the floor, and my girls were clad in jammies.

"I'm going to sing you a lullaby," Bernie said. "It has twelve different verses!"

I shook my head and slid between the cool, clean sheets with Mr. Darcy. The last thing I remembered was Bernie butchering the second chorus.

The next morning, I awoke to Bernie folding their sheets, teasing Cherrie about an alleged recording of her snoring. They planned to change for class at Cherrie's—Bernie had a second wardrobe there—and bunk with me for the rest of the week. Bernie waved off my protests with Cherrie cosigning, and before I could insist I was fine, my dorm phone rang.

We all froze, and I considered a dash for the closet.

Bernie looked at Cherrie. "If it's Maurice, hand me the phone."

"Bernie…" I said.

"I'll behave." She crossed her fingers. "Promise."

I grabbed Bernie's hand for strength as Cherrie squared her shoulders and grabbed the phone. "Daria's room."

It was so quiet you could hear a housefly bat an eye. I studied Cherrie like there would be a final exam and only relaxed when she smiled. "Hi, CoCo!"

I sagged against Bernie, and she rubbed my arms. "Go talk to Mommy. We'll see you later."

"… sleepover last night …" Cherrie was saying.

"Yes, we got our work done. You think your daughter would have it any other way? Yes, she's here....Okay, I will...Love you too, CoCo." Cherrie passed me the phone, mouthing her goodbye. They gathered their things with minimal noise, closing the door with air kisses.

As their footsteps receded, I put the phone to my ear. "Hey, Mom."

She gasped. "I know that voice. What's wrong?"

"It's Maurice." I sat on the bed, tucking my feet beneath me. "We, um...we broke up yesterday."

"Do you need me to come?"

"No, that's why Bernie and Cherrie were here. They're staying with me."

"This is why I love those girls. What happened?"

"All the best clichés. He lied, cheated, took me for granted, didn't care about my dreams, and hated my friends."

"My poor baby! How could he hate your friends?"

"That's what you're focused on?"

"It's the only thing that won't make me drive to that shop and kick him in the crotch with my steel-toe boot."

"Don't catch a case, Mom."

"It'd be worth it, hurting my baby like that! Where's my tire iron?"

"Mom..."

"I've got a flat."

"In the house?"

"On my rolling suitcase."

"You're insane." I played with Mr. Darcy's red bowtie. "He only hated one of my friends."

"Bernie?"

"Mordecai."

"Oh. And I assume you don't hate Mordecai."

Silence was my reply.

"Did something happen there?"

"Yes."

"Was it something major?"

"Yes. And it changed everything."

"Bet that made breaking up with Maurice harder."

"It really did." I walked to the window, watching the drizzle. "Not just because I felt guilty for not telling Maurice the truth, and I do feel guilty. But because I still don't know where things stand with Mordecai and me. He's my best friend, and I miss him so much. But we can't pretend that kiss didn't happen."

"What does he say about it?"

I remembered his performance at the showcase. "I don't think he regrets it, but I don't know what he meant by it. And I can't bring myself to ask him."

"Then don't. After everything you've been through, you've earned some time and space to think."

"Yeah, but Mordecai made two pretty clear declarations, and I haven't spoken to him since. Friend or more, he deserves better than that."

"Well," Corina said. "I guess you know what you have to do."

And if knowing was half the battle, "doing" was the half I was unprepared for.

Forty-Nine

Mom and I soon abandoned the boy talk and picked up a subject we could both enjoy.

My reconciliation with Adrian.

I spared no details as I described him riding to the rescue that fateful afternoon. Corina was stunned to realize I was the student in his office who needed help, and I was stunned Daddy hadn't told her about our Penn Relays date.

"I knew something was up because he kept talking about this year's race," she said. "But he didn't specify, and I didn't pry, figuring he'd tell me when he was ready."

We reminisced about Relays past, pausing to laugh about me spilling my cherry Slurpee all over Daddy's creamy sweater, and I stood up when I glanced at the clock.

"I should get to class." Though the thought of seeing Mordecai made my stomach churn. "I think we're watching a documentary today."

"Well, I love you, and promise your next care package will be in the mail before you finish lunch today. And I'll send extra Koffee Kake."

"You're the best."

"I do what I can. And that's my advice: do what you can, always remembering…"

"I can do all things through Christ who strengthens me."

I felt her smile through the phone. "That's my girl."

That verse became my mantra as I dressed for class, and it carried me to Locke Hall where I spotted Mordecai in the front row of Dr. Maddox's class. I let some students in ahead of me while I gathered myself, and by the time I entered the room, the front row was full. I found a seat three rows back and found Mordecai looking at me when I sat down. I offered a small smile which he returned with a wave, and as Dr. Maddox started class, I blew out a slow breath.

So far, so good.

For the next two weeks, Mordecai and I exchanged silent pleasantries in class and on the shuttle. We seemed to be time-sharing the front row, never sitting there on the same day, and if Dr. Maddox noticed, he didn't comment.

By the time the last week of school rolled around, I believed I could approach Mordecai and have an actual conversation.

Either that or leave a note under his door in Meridian.

My artful dodging also continued on another front, as I had not spoken to Maurice since the day I returned his more-than-a-promise ring. When his calls and voicemails went ignored, he upped the ante by sending rose bouquets every other day. The front desk appreciated the free flora, but Maurice wasn't finished. On day five, I came home from class to a voicemail from Mom McClain apologizing for her son's stupidity and asking me to reconsider. I wanted to return her call out of respect, but I chose to return the bridal magazine and Maurice's door key instead, hoping they'd both get the point.

But a week after I left Maurice outside of Meridian, I got a call I could not ignore. And when his name popped up on my cell phone, I answered on the second ring, anxious to hear his voice. "Naseem?"

He opened with a long apology, hating the need to keep his cousin's secret but loath to share the painful truth with me.

"I'm sorry you're hurt," he said. "But glad you finally know everything."

The news about the engagement ring shocked him, but Maurice's true feelings about my life at Howard did not. They only cemented a decision Naseem had been wrestling with since Suzika's birthday.

"I'm leaving The Shop," he said. "One of the brickheads got a sister with a salon out Southwest, so I'm'a see if he can hook me up there. Anything is better than working with somebody I don't trust."

"I'm sorry. I know this must be hard for you."

"Nothing was harder than lying to you all this time, and I'm sorry for that. I hope...I mean, I'll understand if you don't wanna mess with me like that no more, but I wanna stay friends, if that's cool."

"Come on, 'Seem. You know you'll always be my young bul."

"That's what's up, D." The smile in his voice warmed my heart. "That's what's up."

That was my last phone call from West Philly in the past week-plus. The lack of contact was painful, but I accepted its necessity. If I wanted to heal and move on, then I had to learn not to expect to hear from Maurice anymore, how to embrace the space his absence would create.

And I could do that, one silent night at a time.

PING! PING! PING! PING!

The irritating clang of the fire alarm jarred me awake, much to my weary body's chagrin. Classes ended tomorrow, and with a final test looming in Egyptian Mythology, I needed all the rest I could get.

PING! PING! PING! PING!

But the blasted alarm was right outside my door, so sleep would be impossible until it stopped. I threw on some sweats and my denim jacket, noticing Mr. Darcy waiting by the door. He'd been sitting there for three days while I harnessed the courage to finally throw him away. I scooped him up with a heavy heart, murmuring apologies as we headed into the hallway.

Girls in satin scarves and boys in do-rags filled the

hall, the most annoyed faces belonging to stowaways from other dorms. And as our moody mob lumbered downstairs, we learned this was not a scheduled drill.

"I am so moving to the Towers next year," someone said aloud.

"Real rap," came the reply. "This never happens over there."

Maybe not. But late-night pranksters couldn't separate me from free HBO and Showtime.

The crabby crowd exited the building, and I crossed the driveway to sit on the other side of the stone wall. Copping a squat in the grass, I tuned out the negativity and cleared a spot beside me for Bernie, uncertain if she were staying at Cherrie's tonight. Madame Cummings herself would meet with the other RAs, their duties usually keeping them indoors during such late-night foolery.

Which was why I was surprised to look up and find Mordecai standing in front of me.

He knew this was my preferred hiding spot, though in two years, I'd seen him out here only twice. I couldn't read his expression in the dark, but I knew the time had come to talk.

So I started with something easy. "Hey."

He put his hands in his pockets. "So it worked."

"What worked?"

He glanced at the building. "There's more than one way to get you to talk to me."

"You pulled the fire alarm?"

"I'll never tell."

The ensuing silence was awkward but bearable. It was my turn to speak again, and though my mind raced,

I couldn't catch a clear thought. "Want to sit down?"

He hesitated then settled in beside me. The night was clear but cool, and I shivered.

"Where's your scarf?" he asked.

"Upstairs keeping my closet warm." I rested the back of my head against the wall. "At this rate, I'm gonna oversleep and miss my train."

"Right, the Penn Relays."

"How'd you know?"

He shrugged. "Everybody knows that."

"I doubt it." I plucked a blade of grass, flicking it away. "I've been avoiding you."

"As well you should."

His sincerity confused me. "Why should I avoid you?"

"Why shouldn't you? I kissed you, Daria. You were missing your boyfriend, wishing I were him, and I kissed you."

"I didn't wish you were…"

"Then I declared my feelings in front of a few hundred strangers in Ira Aldridge without considering how that might make you feel." He shook his head. "I'm surprised you haven't moved out."

"You're being too hard on yourself."

"Am I?" He scanned my eyes. "What kind of friend does what I've done to you?"

"What kind of friend lets all that happen without talking about it? I haven't spoken to you since the ball, and that's…that's not who we are."

"I know."

"And so much has happened since then, and you should know about it." I paused before wading into the deep. "Maurice and I broke up."

"I know."

"You do? How?"

"The dorm director told us not to accept any calls or deliveries from, uh, from him." He looked away. "Do you want to talk about it?"

"Not tonight."

"Okay. But was it because...I mean, did I..."

"Have something to do with it? Yes, but not the way you think."

"Right. Of course not."

"But not the way you're thinking now."

"I think I don't know what to think."

Someone behind us announced the building was safe to reenter. The murmuring residents headed inside, leaving Mordecai and I alone with the night. The thought of confronting everything between us made me nervous, and I held Mr. Darcy tighter.

Mordecai chuckled. "You forgot your scarf but remembered Mr. Darcy?"

"Yeah, but I only brought him to say goodbye."

"Is he leaving you for Eliza Bennett? The scoundrel."

"Well ... Maurice gave him to me, so he has to go." Mordecai made an odd noise, and I looked up. "What?"

"Are you only getting rid of him because you think Maurice gave him to you?"

"What do you mean 'think'? On Valentine's Day ..."

"Your roses and candy were sitting on the back table behind the reception desk," he murmured. "And Mr. Darcy was beside them. But he didn't arrive with them."

"I don't understand."

Mordecai paused, glancing at me from the corner of his eye. "Mr. Darcy was from me."

My mouth fell open. "What?"

"I was in Beltway Plaza Mall right after New Year's and ..."

"New Year's?"

"... and I saw him in a toy store window. He looked so happy sitting there, and I just ... I had to get him for you. But I couldn't figure out when or how to give him to you without making things weird between us."

He paused again, and I bit my lip to keep from begging him to continue.

"Then on Valentine's Day, I went behind the front desk to check my schedule—okay, that's a lie. I wanted to see what he got you." He plucked a blade of grass, tearing it in pieces. "I saw the roses and candy—the typical roses and candy—went back upstairs, and set Mr. Darcy next to them when no one was looking."

"So why ..." I swallowed past the lump in my throat. "Why did you let me think he was a gift from Maurice?"

"Because it didn't matter that I bought him. When you told me at Gillian's how much you loved Mr. Darcy, that was all I needed to know." He shrugged. "So you don't have to give him up now. I mean, unless you think ..."

I shook my head and held Mr. Darcy tighter. "I wouldn't dare give him up now."

"Then I'm glad I told you."

The silence between us changed shape, and I closed

my eyes to savor it. What Mordecai did ... the words didn't exist to describe it. But as I sat there holding the gift he'd given me, I realized the time had come for me to give him something equally precious in return.

"Listen. It's only been a few weeks since Maurice and I ended, and I'm still processing it, trying to understand how he could love me but do what he did. And I know you don't know what he did, but it really hurt me. I'm recovering as best I can, and that's going to take time. And none of the bad names I've called him have made it any better."

"What if I call him a few? I have a highly developed imagination."

"I know you do." Our eyes met, and I couldn't look away. "You have a highly developed imagination and the most amazing heart that seems to know me better than just about anyone."

"I smell a 'but,' " he said.

"But I'm a mess right now. I mean, Maurice and I were together for four years, and I can't get over that in two weeks. Then there's you, the kiss, and…you shouldn't have done that, but I let you, and I'm still reeling and dealing with what all of that means. Now you tell me about Mr. Darcy, and I'm overwhelmed all over again. But…"

His eyes widened. "A second 'but'?"

"Yes. In spite of everything, there a second 'but'."

"A big but?"

"It's big enough."

"Okay, it's my turn now." He laid his hand atop my mine where it rested on the grass between us. "Big or small, firm or squishy, I want whatever 'but' you're offering."

"Even if it takes a while to get?"

"Doesn't matter. Your 'but' is well worth the wait."

A slow smile spread across my face, and I gave it full rein. "Mr. Hill, are you still talking about conjunctions?"

"But of course." He came to his feet. "What kind of rogue do you take me for?"

"Oh, I don't know. The kind who'd walk Mr. Darcy and me to The Diner for some ice cream?"

"You know me so well." He extended a hand with a smile. "But the frog is buying."

Epilogue

I smiled at a butterfly outside my window.

A cheerful, speckled, free-floating butterfly.

She seemed to follow us from Fourteenth Street, taking that tight turn onto Euclid with surprising deft. Adrian paid our escort no attention as he was more concerned with the congestion of cars making their way toward our destination, but I considered her the perfect ambassador for the final leg of our journey.

The magnificent Monarch lighted upon the passenger's side mirror as if winking at my thoughts and disappeared behind our minivan as we pulled to a tentative stop. As I turned to watch it flutter across the street—at a safe distance above traffic, thank God—the familiar sound of acoustic drumming caught my ears.

The Sunday drum circle was a celebrated staple of the neighborhood and the best excuse for a summer stroll through Malcolm X Park. Though my last memory of that place was bittersweet, its current offerings made me tap my fingers against the dashboard in perfect time with the infectious, audacious rhythm.

It was so good to be back.

"We're here." Adrian cut the engine and checked his watch. "And in good time too."

"Cherrie will be pleased." I snuggled into the passenger seat, not ready to part with the air conditioning. "Can I just sleep while you move everything in?"

"Sure, Junie. As long as you don't mind illogical zones of non-sorted supplies. And forgive me for forgetting how to use your buffing machine …"

I unclicked my seatbelt. "You are a horrible man."

"So your mother tells me." He looked out the window toward the driveway. "On second thought, stay here. I want to know how long we'd have to wait for a cart."

"God bless you."

Adrian winked. "He has."

He closed the door and headed inside, and I settled into the comfort of where we were now.

Going home for the Penn Relays was the start of a new season for my dad and me. Corina stayed away for the first two days, content to let us reestablish our bond alone. Some of the races we spent in amicable silence, enjoying the inspiring athleticism of the contenders. Other events we missed altogether as we were caught up in spontaneous but meaningful discussions about the past few years. I learned just how alike we were and how much I'd missed our closeness.

By the time I came home for the summer, I couldn't wait to spend as much time with him as possible. We went on daddy-daughter dates, debated current events and historical oddities, and developed an overstuffed breakfast crepe recipe without burning down the kitchen. Corina joined us for weekly Bible study at church and for Gin lessons on the back patio, happy we were a gleesome threesome once more. And after my part-time shift at Borders, every night with my family was the best time of my day.

Every night but one.

Adrian had picked me up from work, and the three of us were pouring over takeout menus in the dining room, refusing to use the oven during Philly's first heatwave. When the doorbell rang, Daddy joked it was an angel with a surprise pizza delivery, and Mommy guessed our neighbors were looking for their runaway retriever again.

So when Adrian opened the door to find Maurice there, no one knew what to say. My father's hand clenched around the doorknob, and I expected him to slam the door in my ex's face. Instead, Adrian turned to me with kind eyes.

"What do you want to do?"

Corina laid a hand on my shoulder as she leaned in to whisper, "There's no wrong answer, honey."

I looked at Maurice and sighed. "I'll talk to him."

My parents retreated to the den to stay out of earshot, and though I appreciated their discretion, they needn't have bothered.

It was a short conversation.

"Thank you for seeing me," Maurice said. "I know you didn't have to."

His mouth kept moving, but I didn't hear anything. I just studied him—his handsome face and familiar frame—and in doing so, I realized something.

I felt nothing.

No anger or curiosity.

No belated sadness or sentimentality.

Nothing.

Staring at the former love of my life for the first time since walking away in DC, I felt absolutely nothing. And I gasped at the wonder of it, covering my mouth with folded hands.

"What's wrong?" he asked. "Are you sick? Do you need me to get you something?"

"No." I straightened myself. "But I want you to do something."

His eyes lit up. "Anything."

"Go away."

"Go? No, Duc—ah, Daria. Just give me a chance to …"

"Maurice, enough. This is …" I shook my head. "I said everything I had to say eight weeks ago."

"But if you've been counting the weeks since you saw me, that's a sign."

"Yes. A sign that after all that time, we are still done."

"Daria, please …"

I had closed the door on his babbling and met my parents in the den. Adrian stood with folded arms by the window, watching Maurice's car drive away. After a

433

moment, he faced me with a deep frown, and I braced myself for his reaction.

"That's it," he said. "We're getting a peephole."

With great relief, I crossed the room to step into my father's arms, and Corina smiled. "I think that's a fine idea."

And that was the last I heard from Maurice.

A tap on the car window broke me out of my thoughts, and I grinned like a loon when I saw who it was. "Hey, you!"

Cherrie yanked open my door. "Get out here and hug me!"

"You're letting out all the air!"

She stuck her head in. "Ooh, you're right." She closed my door and jogged to the driver's side, sighing when she hit the cool seat. "This is the life."

"Enjoy it while you can. I'm sure someone will be blowing up your phone soon."

"At least we have room for all the freshmen, thank God. I couldn't take a repeat of last year." She turned in the seat to face me. "So what are you doing?"

"Thinking about how much has changed since the last time I was in that park."

"Yeah." She reached for the volume knob on the radio. "But not everything."

I prepared to flick her with my fingers. "Don't be turning down Reba."

She looked around. "No stash of Peanut Chews for this trip, huh?"

"Nah." I pulled two packs of Kandy Kakes out of my snack bag. "But those are overrated."

"I guess they were. You seemed to move on from

them pretty quickly."

"Are you judging me?"

"Not at all." She grabbed a napkin from the glove compartment. "Just saying maybe you didn't love Peanut Chews as much as you thought."

I met her gaze. "I guess not."

We ate our snack in silence as Reba sang in the background. When Cherrie finished hers, she chuckled. "I hope you have a crate of these back there."

"Why?"

"Because when Bernie finds them, she's gonna clean you out."

"Bernie's back?"

"She moves in tomorrow."

"How is she?"

"About what you'd expect." She folded her used napkin and stuck in her pocket. "Leaving Tone was tough, but her parents are sending her back for Thanksgiving Break. And…"

"And?"

"She's taking French this semester."

The idea alone made me laugh. "I might take it too, just to hear her butcher the accent."

"Bet! Let's broaden our horizons together." Cherrie ignored her ringing phone. "Oh, and the three of us are on the sixth floor."

"With the renovated kitchen? You are the best!"

"Don't I know it? And your dad is in there talking to Mordecai."

"What?" I sat up. "Why didn't you say that sooner?"

"Because Big Ade paid me big bucks not to. And

Mama needs Dining Dollars."

"You are the worst!"

"That was fast." She tilted her head to look at me. "Aww, look at you blushing and gushing!"

"You are not helping." I slipped my thumbnail between my teeth then remembered my manicure. "What should I do?"

"Come inside in fifteen minutes. That'll give them time to stop talking about you and land in safer conversational pastures."

"And if they don't?"

"Maybe Mordecai can pull the fire alarm again."

"He was joking about that."

"Are you sure?"

"Get out of my car."

As Cherrie giggled her way up the walk, I locked the doors to keep from storming the doors like some Nervous Nellie. Adrian talking to Mordecai wasn't the worst thing that could happen, but I'd wanted to see him first. The very thought of it made my cheeks warm, and I pressed my cool palms against my face to calm down.

Guess Cherrie was right about that blushing and gushing.

After Mordecai and I cleared much of the murky air during last semester's faux fire drill, we had serious work to do, namely the gift for his neighbor's wife's best friend. The weeks of weirdness shrank our timeline, and we spent the first two days of the Reading Period hole up in his room. We finished the book with a package of Oreos between us, the kiss and our potential future never mentioned. Once we finished that project, we moved on to studying for Dr. Maddox's final, easing to the point of sitting beside each other during the exam.

But when the test was over, so were our opportunities to redefine our relationship. Mr. Darcy and I returned to Philly, Mordecai went home to Maryland, and from the look of it, summer was slated to remain silent.

Until I came home from work one July afternoon and found a bouquet of sharpened No. 2 pencils in a kaleidoscope of colors beside a gigantic book of crossword puzzles on the dining room table. Corina swore she was innocent and advised me to read the card. When I saw Mordecai's note and the enclosed phone number at the bottom, I couldn't grab my cell phone fast enough.

"Thank you for leaving a card this time," I said in lieu of a proper greeting.

"It's your birthday. Figured I should act like I had some sense."

"It's about time." I looked closer at the pencils. "They're personalized! And with my full name."

"I wanted to add 'Hurler of Chocolate' but ran out of space."

"Well." I plucked a red pencil from the arrangement. "I hope you don't expect me to finish all these by myself."

"I wouldn't dream of it."

"Good." I sat down and flipped to the first puzzle. "What's a three-letter word for 'dance'?"

And thanks to an influx of cell phone minutes from my parents, Mordecai and I spent the rest of the summer on the phone: doing crosswords, comparing Top Ten countdowns on the radio, and brainstorming ideas for upcoming books. He received two requests from church members, I had one from my manager at Borders, and Corina wanted a commemorative gift for a beloved customer. And as neither of us had a clue what to do when we grew up, this lucrative little hobby was fast becoming a viable option.

But between the mergers and merriment, we found something I didn't expect so soon. Something precious and suddenly possible.

And that scared me.

I was afraid at first that our burgeoning bond was rooted mainly in my need to replace Maurice. But nothing could be further from the truth. For one thing, Mordecai let me talk about Maurice, asking questions as a friend and not a would-be suitor. And in talking about that, I realized Mordecai and I could talk about anything.

We talked about his relationship with his mother and her desire to reconnect with Melody. We talked about the B's we each received in Dr. Maddox's class—that wicked final exam would have made his wife proud—and how I was dealing with the loss of my precious 4.0.

Funny, it didn't hurt like I thought it would.

With each conversation, the miles between us faded, and by the time we talked last night, they all but disappeared.

"So," he said. "I'm going to see you tomorrow."

"Yes, you will."

"And, um, I'm going to need some help knowing how to be or not to be."

"Are you talking about Shakespeare?"

"Grammar." He cleared his throat. "Personal

pronouns."

"Singular, plural, or possessive?"

"You tell me, English major."

I glanced at the picture he took of me at the Bison Ball, smiling in its framed location on my nightstand. It would have been easy to deflect or extend the suspense. But not after he so bravely asked the question. And not when I was so eager to give my answer.

"You know what's better than personal pronouns?" I asked slowly.

"Enlighten me."

"Conjunctions. And I have one with your name on it."

"The second one?"

"The second one."

"Wow." An adorable smile warmed his voice. "Yeah, okay."

"So I'll see you tomorrow?"

"Yes, Ms. Nelson. You will see me tomorrow."

Tomorrow had become today, and it was time to stop hiding.

I turned off the van and stuffed the keys in my pocket, gathering courage as I walked up the ramp toward Meridian. For all the hustle and bustle in the lobby, I had but one face in mind.

And didn't see it anywhere.

"There you are." Adrian approached me. "Ready to get started?"

I studied the group behind the info desk and only found more disappointment. "Sure."

"If you're looking for Cherrie, she's helping someone use the new phone registration system and said she'll find you later."

"Okay." I stood in line with the others for my room assignment. "Anything else you need to tell me?"

"Nope. Anything else you want to ask me?"

"I guess not."

The line moved quickly, and once I received my key and Room Inspection Form, Adrian decided to return to the car.

"I'll unload, and you can meet me after your inspection."

"Sure."

"Oh, and Cherrie said she stashed a utility cart in your room." He glanced at the crowd by the two working elevators. "But if you want it before sundown, I'd take the stairs."

I took his advice but had to take my time in the humid stairwell, pausing on each floor to catch my breath. When I finally reached the sixth floor, I threw open the door and leaned against the wall to appreciate the cool, marginally-fresh air. The elevator dinged at the far end of the hall, and I hoped that one kept working for the rest of the day. Otherwise Adrian might be right about me moving in by moonlight.

Across from me, a sign advertised the first Meridian social event of the semester: a screening of *Café Latte* in the main lounge next Friday night. And I wondered if anyone ever claimed the DVD I snuck into the freebie bin at Borders last week. I had no use for the movie anymore but kept the CD, having fallen in love with a certain old-school hip-hop track.

And I would never be sorry about that.

Smiling again, I noted Cherrie's decorative touches

on the festive bulletin board beside the elevator and the welcome rug outside her door. I wrote a note on her dry-erase board, promising to host our first all-girls game night once Bernie moved in. Finding my new room across from Cherrie's, I opened the door and found a huge cart waiting for me.

With an even huger surprise beside it.

"Here you are!"

"Here I am." Mordecai came toward me with his hands behind his back. "I was starting to wonder if your dad played me."

"I'm so glad he didn't."

"Um, I have something for you."

"You spoil me."

"I try." He handed me a CD. "It's the playlist from last semester's Born in April Listening Party. I thought you might want a copy."

I turned it over to scan the track list. "How'd you know?"

"Lucky guess."

"You're full of those."

"I'm full of something."

I set the CD on the desk without looking away from him. "Your hair is lighter."

"It changes color in the summer."

"Never noticed that before." I ran the shoulder-length strands through my fingers. "It's beautiful."

"You're beautiful."

"You're biased. But I like it."

"How was the ride from Philly?"

"You really wanna know?"

"Yes." He slipped his hands around my waist. "So

would it be rude to say 'not right now'?"

"Not at all."

"Good." As I rested my hands on his shoulders, his voice deepened. "Is this the second 'but'?"

"Mmm-hmm. And it's ginormous."

He bent down, his gaze flicking briefly to my eyes, and brushed his lips against mine. My eyes fluttered shut, a pleasant shiver spreading through my body, and I pressed myself closer to savor him better. This kiss was worth waiting a whole summer for. It was worth enduring teasing from Cherrie and climbing six flights of stairs for.

And it was more than worth coming all the way to DC for.

Mordecai pulled back, and as I studied his glowing face, I couldn't help but think of how differently our last kiss ended. "Thank you for waiting for me."

"No problem." He kissed me again. "Thank you for trusting me."

"No problem."

"So …" He glanced around. "How much time do we have before your father comes looking for us?"

"I don't know. But Mordecai?"

"Yeah?"

I cupped his cheek. "I don't want to talk about my father right now."

Mordecai looked at me with a gentle smile, and we didn't talk at all for a good, long while.

About the Author

Denise is not naïve ... at least, not as much as yesterday. A born-and-raised Philly girl, this editor and essayist uses her English degree to bemoan text-speak and champion the rights of the Oxford Comma. Denise never met a stiletto she didn't like but will gladly switch to sneakers to chase her children through Vernon Park or harass her hubby for hugs. The faith-filled characters in her modern stories are real, and they're spectacular.

Additional Works

"love by any means necessary: Horace Lee Madre, Jr." Color Him Father: Stories of Love and Rediscovery of Black Men. Eds. Stephana I. Colbert & Valerie I. Harrison. Philadelphia: Kinship Press, 2006. 87-92.

"Diary of a Naïve Mom ... (or Everything I Didn't Know)." The Motherhood Diaries 2: Humorous and Heartwarming Musings and Motherhood. Ed. ReShonda Tate Billingsley. Houston: Brown Girls Publishing, 2014.   20-30.

Excerpts

From **"love by any means necessary"**

Horace recognizes the importance of being affectionate with all of his children, but he will discipline them when need be. He often uses their five-way dynamic to teach them how to deal with others. Nothing straightens his sons up faster than the thought that the way they think about girls is the same way some other young man might be thinking about their sister. As a result of his innovative yet evolving parenting style, Horace boasts five respectful and happy children who are a delight to be around.

From **"Diary of a Naïve Mom ..."**

Many words accurately describe me.

Creative.
Insightful.
Passionate.
Optimistic.

But the one I like least... and which most thoroughly applies, I'm afraid... is naïve.

In high school, I heard a story about Toni Braxton being "discovered" while pumping gas. As I also harbored deep-seated dreams of singing stardom, I believed such a thing would happen to me. Only in my early 20's did I discover—to my great shock and confusion—that this occurrence was not only highly improbable but also a poor substitute for a life plan.

Just before Thanksgiving during my freshman year at Howard University, I was hustled out of two hundred dollars by two gentlemen who didn't trust the American banking system and needed me to prove its accessibility with a quick ATM transaction. When I later discovered their treachery, I was dumbfounded. After all, one of them claimed to be a pastor and wore a gold cross around his neck!

But my *preciousness*—let's try that word for a while, shall we?—is nowhere clearer than in my expectations of   motherhood.

Discussion Questions

1. Denise Leora Madre describes *Another 4.0* as "a love letter to Howard University." How does that love come across in this story? Do you see the novel differently?

2. What is the significance of the title? Would you have titled the book differently?

3. Describe Daria's relationships with her mother and father. How do they influence her choices?

4. Describe Daria's relationships with Bernie and Cherrie. What does each girl bring into Daria's life? Is she closer to one girl than the other?

5. Did Maurice ever love Daria?

6. Should Daria have accepted Maurice's ring? Why or why not?

7. Dr. Treble's class debates the merits of PWIs and HBCUs. Which do you think is the better academic choice for African-American students and why?

8. Dr. Treble's class discusses Ebonics and Standard American English. Do you think Ebonics is something to be treasured or shunned? Why?

9. Dr. Maddox's class discusses the biggest issues facing black couples today. What are your thoughts on that subject?

10. Bernie and Tone try (and fail) to abstain from sex. Is chastity a valid, viable option for romantic relationships today?

11. When do you think Mordecai's feelings for Daria began? If not for the Bison Ball, do you think would he have confessed them?

12. Maurice claims he wasn't cheating on Daria during the first two years because they weren't officially a couple. Do you agree or disagree with his logic?

13. How do your feelings for the following characters change as the novel progresses? Adrian Nelson, Dr. Treble, The Chesty Cheetah, Suzika.

14. Who was your favorite character and why?

15. Which was your favorite scene/moment and how did it affect you?

16. Which scene/moment surprised you? What did you expect differently?

17. Where do you think the following characters will be in five years? Daria, Maurice, Mordecai, Bernie, Cherrie.

18. How did you experience this book? Did you speed through it or take your time? Did the story grab you right away or was it a slow progression?

19. If you could ask the author one question about the story, what would it be?

20. If you could change one thing about the story, what would it be?